Praise for *Tailo...*

"Swoony, sexy, and laugh-out-lo... absolutely delicious hero—and ... book left me wanting more."

—*New York Times* bestselling author Laura Kaye

"Smart, heart-wrenching, and wonderfully sexy, this is contemporary romance at its finest. Mimi Jean Pamfiloff pulls expertly at the heartstrings with a sassy heroine and the most compelling hero I've read in years."

—*USA Today* bestselling author Lauren Layne

"Smart, funny, and undeniably sexy, *Tailored for Trouble* is the perfect summer read. You'll be smiling on one page, fuming at the next, and swooning throughout. Bennett Wade is the quintessential silver-tongued bad boy in need of a strong-willed, nononsense heroine to whip him into shape. Taylor Reed is definitely that and more! This book is a dynamic, addictive ride that will surely have you glued to the pages until the very end."

—*New York Times* bestselling author S. L. Jennings

"*Tailored for Trouble* is fast-paced romantic comedy at its best. Laugh-out-loud moments, sizzling chemistry, and a rollicking journey around the world with a sexy billionaire who's so much more than the size of his . . . wallet."

—*USA Today* bestselling author Kylie Gilmore

"Pamfiloff's skilled pacing ramps up the tension and attraction between Bennett and Taylor as they crisscross the globe together, and their consummation feels like a well-deserved payoff for them and the reader."

—*Publishers Weekly*

TAILORED FOR TROUBLE

TAILORED FOR TROUBLE

The Happy Pants Series

Mimi Jean Pamfiloff

BALLANTINE BOOKS
NEW YORK

A Ballantine Books Trade Paperback Original

Copyright © 2016 by Mimi Jean Pamfiloff

Published in the United States by Ballantine Books, an imprint of Random House, a division of Penguin Random House LLC, New York.

BALLANTINE and the HOUSE colophon are registered trademarks of Penguin Random House LLC.

LIBRARY OF CONGRESS CATALOGING-IN-PUBLICATION DATA
Names: Pamfiloff, Mimi Jean, author.
Title: Tailored for trouble: the happy pants series /
Mimi Jean Pamfiloff.
Description: New York : Ballantine Books, [2016] | Series: Happy pants
Identifiers: LCCN 2016010502 (print) | LCCN 2016018525 (ebook) | ISBN
9781101967225 (paperback : alk. paper) | ISBN 9781101967232 (ebook)
Subjects: | BISAC: FICTION / Romance / Contemporary. |
FICTION / Contemporary Women. | GSAFD: Love stories.
Classification: LCC PS3616.A3575 T35 2016 (print) |
LCC PS3616.A3575 (ebook) | DDC 813/.6—dc23
LC record available at lccn.loc.gov/2016010502

Printed in the United States of America on acid-free paper

randomhousebooks.com

2 4 6 8 9 7 5 3 1

Book design by Dana Leigh Blanchette

Dedicated to my parents

Guys, I'm really sorry. I kept thinking that one day I'd write a non-romance book, that didn't make you blush or contain lots of swearing, and that I'd dedicate it to you. But that day may never come, so this one is for you, Mom and Dad! LOL. Just pretend it's about something wholesome and non-steamy. Like fishing. Okay? Haha . . . Love you.

TAILORED FOR TROUBLE

Happy Pants Café
Attn: Ms. Luci Leon-Parker
St. Helena, CA 94574

Dear Ms. Luci,

I am writing on behalf of my son who is in desperate need of a kick in the pants. Bennett, who has been a serious soul since the day he was born, is now thirty-one years old and has dedicated one third of his life to running our family company. And though he has done extremely well for himself and has taken good care of me since his father passed over a decade ago, I fear his focus on building our company into an empire has robbed him of something far more important. Bennett, despite all of the brains inside that thick skull of his, is still single, and believes that the women who pursue him are "gold diggers looking for a handout." Yes, he's had his bumps in the road, but it's still a bunch of hogwash!

Luci, I know that one cannot believe everything they read in the paper, but the recent article in the *San Francisco Tribune*, hailing you to be a real live Cupid, must have some truth to it. This is why I hope you will help my mule-headed Bennett. I know if he could find the right woman, it would open his eyes before it is too late.

As I am now sick and have a few months to live, I hope you'll be able to turn him around before I kick the bucket. Bennett could do so much for the world if he would stop being such a cold-hearted ass.

God Bless,
Linda Johnson Wade

Dearest Linda,

First, I would like to offer my deepest sympathies for your tragic news. As a widow myself and a mother of three, I know the need to see Bennett settled before you move on must weigh heavily on your soul. *Ay, Dios.* Our children are all we really have in the end, *sí*?

I am, however, so deeply sorry to tell you that my gifts have been greatly exaggerated by the press. I am simply an old woman from Mexico who runs a bakery. Now, is it true that some have eaten my sugar cookies and found their soul mate in seven days? *Sí.* Is it because of my cookies? Heavens, no. A cookie is just a cookie. However, I have been known to play matchmaker from time to time. In fact, at this very moment, I am preparing to help a very special woman catch her Mr. Right—a project that has consumed much of my time these past months. But by no means am I a foolproof lucky charm as some suggest.

All that said, my dear Linda, I want to help you any way I can. I will invite your Bennett to my annual fiesta in July and ensure he receives not only the kick in the *pantalones* you've requested, but that he is introduced to several potential matches. The party will not occur for another four months, but if anything should happen to you—God forbid—you may rest assured that I will make every effort to see to his mule-headedness.

In the meantime, I've included a delicious cookie for Bennett. Can't hurt.

With All My Love,
Ms. Luci Leon-Parker
Proprietor, The Happy Pants Café

CHAPTER 1

Twenty-eight-year-old Taylor Reed stepped out of the downtown Seattle office building into the pouring rain, thankful for having forgotten her umbrella. This way, no one would notice the tears streaming down her face.

I'm ruined. Completely ruined, she thought. And it wasn't an exaggeration. Over the last three months, Taylor had maxed out her credit cards, borrowed every last dime from her 401(k), and depleted her emergency savings account, all to start her own highly specialized executive training company. Fifteen sales pitches and fifteen rejections later, including today's very polite "Thanks, but no thanks," she was at the end of her rope.

This is all his *fault.* That smug, cold-hearted bastard who'd gotten her fired from a nice steady job. Okay, she'd technically quit, but still. There had been no other choice after that humiliating disaster. All because he was "the customer." All because he had money and thought he could treat people like garbage. All because—

Ugh. Shut up. It's your *fault. You let him get to you.*

An image of those unfeeling, icy blue eyes flashed in her mind. She'd never forget them. Just like she'd never forget the glib smirk on his disarmingly handsome face, a face that might have you believing a real human being existed somewhere in-side.

Asshole. Hope he chokes on one of his designer ties.

Not having a clue what she would do next, Taylor looked up at the sky, allowing the giant sloppy drops to cool her face. She would have to get another job. Start over. But starting over meant flying back to Phoenix, packing up her apartment, and praying one of her older brothers, who lived near San Fran-cisco, would take her in without giving her thirty lashes—verbal, of course. Then there'd be facing her father. In his mind, people either paid their own way or they were a waste of good clean air.

Oh, God. The humiliation. Taylor buttoned up her black coat and grabbed her extra-large rolling laptop case to go flag down a taxi. With this rain, it would probably be a while, which meant she'd probably miss her flight. The perfect ending to a perfect shit day.

Taylor stopped on the corner just in time to see two empty cabs sail by. "Oh, come on!"

She dug her phone from her pocket, deciding it might be bet-ter to call a taxi directly, when the device buzzed in her hand. It was a San Francisco number. Maybe one of the companies who'd rejected her had changed their minds?

"Hello?" she said, trying not to sound too hopeful.

"Is this Miss Reed?" said a perky, sweet voice.

"Yes. This is *Ms.* Reed."

"One moment please, I have a call for you."

Just then a large white and blue bus with a loud rumbling engine pulled up. *For crying out loud.*

"Could you hold on, please? I can't quite hear you." She stepped into the doorway of a small café with a cheerful red awning and a sign in the window that read "Happy Pants. Now Available Here!"

Weird.

"Sorry about that. Go ahead," she said, covering her exposed ear and noting her sad reflection in the glass. Her long wet brown hair and the mascara streaming down her pale face made her look like a cast member from *The Walking Dead*.

Rarrr . . . fabulous.

"Miss Reed, Bennett Wade here." His deep, silky, unhurried voice instantly made her entire body tense up and her adrenaline kick in. "I'd like to speak to you. In person if you can make the time."

How the hell did he get my cell number?

"What do *you* want?" she growled.

He made a sound that was half-chuckle, half-throat-clearing. "To speak. Didn't I just say that?"

SOB thinks he can just call me? After what he did? "There isn't anything you could possibly say, *Mr. Wade*, that I—"

"I want to hire you."

Ha! Funny. "What? It wasn't enough to ruin my—"

"Miss Reed." She could hear the impatience in his voice now. "I'm a busy man, so—"

"Ms. It's *Ms.* Reed," she corrected sharply.

"Fine. *Ms. Reed*, I'd like to discuss an offer, but not over the phone. I prefer doing business in person."

Business with me? Maybe his brain has been polluted with too many supplements. She seemed to remember he looked like one of those guys who obsessed over his body as much as he did the cut of his suits to show it all off. *Although, it was hard to tell with all that pious condescension oozing from his general direction.*

"Sorry," she said in the bitchiest tone possible, "but my schedule is booked, and I'm on my way to a meeting. I'll have to call you back next lifetime. . . ." As she spoke, Taylor turned toward the street, noticing the long, gleaming black limo now parked against the curb. She couldn't see past the tinted windows, but . . .

"You're sitting right there, aren't you?" she said into the phone.

The back window lowered and those pale blue eyes, edged with annoyingly thick dark brown lashes, stared back, just as void of warmth as she remembered. But this time, his handsome face—with its chiseled cheekbones, cleft chin, and a strong jaw covered in a charcoal black five o'clock shadow—was missing that patronizing smirk. The man actually looked pissed.

Four Months Earlier

Taylor pulled into the crowded parking lot of HRTech Solutions, sweating bullets and cursing like a sailor—a habit she'd sworn off for New Year's but had just decided was completely impractical.

This can't fucking be happening. She was now thirty—*Nope. Make that thirty-one*—minutes late for her big presentation to the CEO of Wade Enterprises—the man who had a reputation for lacking a soul and for having an unfailing ability to see the world as his personal mound of dirt meant for bulldozing. The man who had announced, last minute, that he'd be flying in from his San Francisco headquarters to hear about their managerial recruiting services.

The request was strange to say the least, considering she and her team usually went to the client, not the other way around. In any case, Taylor had been trying to snag a meeting with Mr. Wade ever since she'd landed contracts with several of his golfing buddies, who were all CEOs of various companies themselves.

The Prius in front of her suddenly spotted an open space. *Shit. Dammit. No!* She hit her brakes and watched the driver take his sweet time pulling in as she dug her nails into her steering wheel. Then, almost out of the way, the Prius driver began backing out, deciding he wasn't positioned just right.

Sonofabitch! Come on! She sighed and then focused her frustration on the A/C button of her red Audi TTS, poking it ten times. But all the poking in the world wouldn't magically make that Prius go any faster, just like it wouldn't make the temperature go any lower.

It was nine-thirty on this fine February morning and already five-hundred-hell-in-a-hand-basket degrees outside. Not even the devil would let his nuts live in this inferno.

She checked her makeup in the mirror to ensure it hadn't melted down her face and noticed the incredibly attractive ring of red encircling her brown eyes. The result of having had two and a half hours of sleep.

Wonderful. I look like I'm stoned. Her phone buzzed on the passenger seat. It was her VP texting again.

VERA: Where are you now?
TAYLOR: Pulling into the lot. Is he there yet?
VERA: No. Hurry!

Taylor couldn't believe her luck. This day might be saved after all.

"Take your sweet fucking time, buddy!" She pounded on the steering wheel as the Prius driver once again took his time edging back into the parking space. "Come on!" She honked the horn.

The driver slammed on the brakes and flashed her the middle finger.

"Great. Just great." *I'm about to lose my job, so fuck you back.*

Why oh why had she taken this position to begin with? She wasn't a pitchman, but her old college friend Rina, who also worked at HRTech, had talked her into it five years ago when Taylor had been fresh out of grad school and in desperate need of a paycheck. "You were born to work with people, Taylor," she'd said. "You just smile and the room lights up."

What a joke.

Yes, she enjoyed working with people and had a master's in human resource management, but so many of the executives in these big companies, the ones who used HRTech's recruitment services, didn't have a clue about how to treat the people they spent thousands to find and hire. It was always about the bottom line and shareholder value—never about creating a workplace that employees genuinely looked forward to coming to each day. Didn't they get that happy employees were more productive employees? It drove her crazy. But unfortunately, Rina had been right. Soon after starting at HRTech, Taylor had begun landing big clients and making good money—something she couldn't easily walk away from given her student loans.

Yeah. Well, those are all paid off now. As soon as she was able, she'd start looking for a new job, something more meaningful, back in the Bay Area. Kissing up to men like Bennett

Wade, who she'd never met but couldn't stand because she knew his type, was not her calling.

The Prius finally got out of the way, and she zoomed past, taking the little road that led to the back of the building where luckily she found an empty spot.

Now thirty-five—*Nope. Make that thirty-six*—minutes late, Taylor ran in her black heels, clutching her laptop case in one hand and oversized brown leather purse in the other. Once inside the twenty-story glass-and-steel rectangle, Taylor made it to the elevator just in time to watch the doors slide shut in her face.

"Sonofabitch!" She jabbed at the elevator button and looked down at her watch, suddenly noticing several strange spots on the lapel of her black blazer. *Oh, no*. She must've missed a few drops of bleach when she'd spritzed the kitchen counters last night before bed. Cleaning helped her unwind and feel in control, especially when her crazy job made her head spin from the constant juggling. She had laid her blazer on the counter this morning while she'd been looking for her keys.

As she waited for the elevator, she freed her hair from its ponytail and finger combed the length of it over her lapel to cover the spots. The elevator chimed, and she jumped in. Moments later, Taylor arrived at the top floor and sprinted for the executive conference room where Vera waited, along with six senior managers, all of whom reported to Taylor.

"Hi, everyone. Sorry I'm late," she threw her bag down on the long gray table that stretched the length of the room, "but I was stuck in traffic and then some jerk in a Prius was blocking the—"

"I assure you," said a deep, cold voice, "that my poor driving was a direct result of a man my height trying to maneuver a vehicle meant for one of those emaciated, tree-hugging vegetarians."

Oh no. Taylor gazed across the room at the scowling man in his early thirties wearing a black suit and seated at the head of the table. His thick, wavy brown hair was neatly combed back, and his eyes were a shocking pastel blue, almost too light to even be called blue.

Taylor actually stopped breathing for a moment as their eyes met and a chill swept over her entire body. Something about the way he looked at her made the room feel unsafe. Not in a "he's psycho and going to murder me" sort of way; the man literally filled the entire space with his daunting presence. You weren't sure if you wanted to bow down to him or run.

Yes, he was that intimidating.

"I'm s-so sorry about that," Taylor said, taking her seat as gracefully as she could, "but as you can see, I was in a hurry to get here—"

"To meet you obviously," said Vera, who sat closest to Mr. Wade. "And I know I've already said this, but I assure you that this is not how we treat our custo . . ."

Mr. Wade held up his palm, offering no sign of human warmth or civility. "I've already wasted enough of my morning on incompetent idiots. I don't need to hear a list of excuses from some bottle blonde who calls herself a vice president yet can't figure out how to ensure her clients have proper limo service from the airport."

Taylor's mouth fell open as she witnessed poor Vera's face turn red. Had this man actually called Vera an idiot and then ridiculed her appearance?

"Yes, well," Vera cleared her throat. "My sincerest apologies, Mr. Wade. I promise I'll speak to our Travel Services Manager immediately. It won't happen again."

Taylor couldn't believe that Vera had let Mr. Wade's comments slide. She was about to say something when Vera turned her head in Taylor's direction. "Taylor, whenever you're ready." Something in her tone made Taylor bite back her words.

"Of course. Just one second while I pull up the presentation." She popped open her laptop and the home screen came up, but the presentation shortcut was missing.

What? But how? She looked up at the anxious faces around the table. *Okay, hurrying, hurrying . . .* She clicked on the documents tab and found the file, but when she tried to open it, the little circle on the screen kept spinning, like an evil doughnut taunting her sanity. "Um . . ." She looked at Mr. Wade. "My computer is a little slow; big file. Probably too big because I stayed up late making sure—"

"So, Bennett," Vera chimed in, "while Taylor is taking her sweet time loading the presentation, why don't you tell the team here—"

"Did we fuck last night?" Bennett interrupted, his cold gaze locked on Vera's face.

Taylor froze and looked across the table, unsure if she'd heard him correctly.

"Sorry?" Vera's face went from red to a mortified shade of white.

Bennett Wade leaned forward in his chair toward Vera. "Did. We. *Fuck*. Last night?"

The room filled with a ghastly, awkward vibe, and Taylor was pretty damned sure everyone was pinching themselves underneath the table. Had he really said that?

Vera shook her head. "I—I don't understand."

Pinning Vera with his eyes, Mr. Wade slowly eased back in his chair, his black suit stretching across his shoulders. "Only my mother and women I fuck get to call me Bennett. So unless I got stinking drunk last night, which would have to be the case for me to ever touch a woman like you, then you'll refer to me as Mr. Wade."

Whatthehell? Taylor felt a fire of outrage ignite in the pit of her stomach. "You know what?" She slapped the table, stood, and then pointed to the door. "Get out."

Mr. Wade blinked his blue eyes at her as if he wasn't quite sure what she'd just said.

"In fact," she added, "get the hell off my planet. People like you are what make this world a shitty place for the rest of us who are just trying to be happy and make a living."

Vera popped up from her seat. "Taylor, don't."

"Oh, no," Mr. Wade said, with a superficial smile, "by all means, please go on, Miss . . ."

"Reed. And that's *Ms.* Reed to you. You . . . pig in a suit."

"Taylor! Outside. Now!" barked Vera.

But Taylor had really had it with guys like this who thought that they could behave any way they liked simply because they had money. She thought of the countless times she'd had to fend off unwanted solicitations by half her male clientele over the past few years. They always made it a point to want to talk business over dinner. Just last week, in fact, one of Mr. Wade's golfing buddies, a rich asshat named Chip who worked for his mommy's big perfume company had actually proposed a "weekend dinner meeting" in Vegas. Who did that in this day and age? But of course, these pompous billionaires didn't seem to care that she found their advances offensive. The more blunt she became with *no*, the more they seemed to enjoy pursuing her. And what had Vera said about it? "Taylor, these are professional, successful businessmen who know better, especially considering the damage one lawsuit could do to their companies. I'm sure they're just trying to be friendly—that's all." Vera clearly didn't understand that while women and minorities had come a long, long way, the boys' club was alive and well in corporate America. Just take a look at the annual report of any large company. Female faces were scarce and there was generally only one shade of the rainbow.

Begrudgingly, Taylor had listened to Vera and let it go. Again and again and again.

Well, no more.

Mr. Wade let out a deep chuckle. "Pig in a suit? This is good."

"You think it's funny?" Taylor snapped. "You come in here and insult this woman because you think you're some god, some all-powerful being who has been granted the right to trample over those you perceive as lesser. But strip away your money, that suit," she flipped her wrist through the air, "and that handsome face—you're no different from the rest of us, buddy. You're going to die someday! Yep. That's right. Die. Just like the rest of us."

Vera had now moved to her side and was tugging on Taylor's arm, trying to usher her out the door.

"You're right, Ms. Reed," Bennett said in a slow, overly pompous tone. "I will die. And so will you. But when I go, I'll have something to show for my hard work. People like you, on the other hand, will find that you've plowed your way through life, complaining and pointing fingers at others for what *you* perceive are their shortcomings. But in the end you'll realize that is all you've done. Because people like you are all bark and no bite. Don't like what you see in this world, *Ms.* Reed? Try getting off your pedestal, woman, and do something about it." Mr. Wade rose from his seat, staring at her with an expression of blatant amusement on his gorgeous, smug face. "Now, folks, if you'll excuse me; I have some golf to play. I only stopped by for the tax write-off, anyway. My business is firing people and replacing them with machines, not hiring them. So I'm afraid I have no need for your recruiting skills."

Oh. My. God! What a horrible, disgusting man! Taylor watched Mr. Wade disappear out the door and debated whether to follow him to the elevator so she could punch him right in his pearly whites.

"My office, Taylor. Now," Vera hissed.

Taylor didn't make eye contact with anyone as Vera left the room. She already knew what her boss was going to say: "The customer is always right, even if they're not." To Vera, that meant allowing people like Bennett Wade to humiliate her in public. It just wasn't right. Of course, Vera was a divorcée with two kids to put through college. She saw things a little differently than Taylor did.

Taylor's team silently left the room while she remained standing, hands planted on the table and head hung low. Bennett Wade's jarring, blunt words began circulating through her mind. *Crap. Crap! He's right. It's not good enough to complain.* She thumped her fist on the table. That smug SOB had given her a dose of the truth, and while it hurt like hell, she couldn't look away simply because the person who'd delivered the message was an insensitive prick.

Instead of going to Vera's office, Taylor headed for the elevator, down to her tenth floor office. She grabbed her gym bag from the bottom drawer of her desk. Inside the bag, she placed a picture of her with her best friends, Holly and Sarah, sipping hurricanes in Vegas. They were going to flip when they heard about this a-hole client. They would definitely agree that she had done the right thing.

Taylor then picked up her other photo—the one of her three brothers standing with her father at the Grand Canyon—and cringed. They were going to give her hell for leaving behind a steady, well-paying job. It would be just like the time she left the college volleyball team because it was cutting into her study time. They saw it as quitting. She saw it as doing the right thing. But they subscribed to the school of "suck it up" and "no pain, no gain," which meant they'd always been extra-tough on her—the youngest, weakest "brother." Only she was a girl, which meant her head wasn't up her ass half the time and her view of the world was a teensy bit different.

Well, it's my life, not theirs, and you only live once.

She shoved the frame into her bag, took one last look at her big office, and shut the door behind her.

CHAPTER 2

Present Day

As Taylor stood in the rain, unable to believe that it was Bennett Wade glaring at her with those icy, pastel blue eyes from the back of a stretch limo, she didn't know if she wanted to spit, scream, or cry. This man—a horrible bastard of a human being—was the last person in the world she wanted to see. It was bad enough hitting rock bottom without him there to witness the big, ugly, festering event.

"Get in," he finally said, breaking the long silence.

"What are you doing in Seattle?" she snapped.

"Get. In," he snarled.

"I don't work for you, and even if I did, I'd never let you speak to me like that. Have a nice life, Mr. Wade." She turned, heading down the sidewalk opposite the flow of traffic. There was a hotel a few blocks over. Maybe she'd have luck catching a cab—

"Ms. Reed." A strong hand grabbed her arm, and when she spun around, she found Bennett Wade hovering over her, those nearly translucent eyes staring down with an odd expression—contempt mixed with . . . she didn't know really, but it made her insides jitter.

"What do you want?" she hissed.

Damn, he's tall—six-three or -four, maybe? She was five-seven so that gave him a leg up on the intimidation factor.

"It's raining," he said. "I want to give you a ride. And to talk." His eyes momentarily flashed to her mouth before he offered her a charming smile, one that appeared to be well-rehearsed—and probably totally insincere—yet still managed to make her notice how his lips seemed a little more sensual, possibly fuller, when he wasn't trying to verbally inflict damage.

"What could you and I possibly have to talk about?" she asked.

"Fifty thousand dollars."

She blinked.

"That is twice your going consultant rate, is it not?" he added.

"But—How?—Why?" Her new company, HumanitE, provided individualized, one-on-one training for executives, specifically geared toward increasing profitability by reducing turnover rates through compassionate leadership techniques. "We Put the Humanity in Executives." In other words, "Stop being such a dick to your people and you'll make more money!" But she couldn't use that as a slogan. And of course, she didn't have any clients so she was seriously beginning to think her plan had flaws or that she wasn't such a great salesperson after all. In any case, why would Bennett Wade want to take her coaching course?

"You can't be serious," she said.

His smile melted back into that intimating scowl. "I'm standing in the *fucking* rain, ruining a very nice wool coat and running late for a very important conference call. Ask me again, Ms. Reed, if I'm *fucking* serious."

Who the hell *does this guy think he is, speaking to me like that?*

"Then you've barked up the wrong tree. Wait. Sorry." She laughed and yanked back her arm. "You've barked up the wrong *fucking* tree." She pivoted on her soggy heels and continued walking.

This time, Bennett Wade didn't come after her nor did she turn around, but she somehow knew he wasn't done with her yet. Men like Bennett Wade didn't take no for an answer. In fact, *no*s only made them more determined.

Whatever. Bring it on, she thought, but that was her pride talking. The less egocentric part of her was whining like a six-year-old in the candy aisle at the grocery store: "Fifty thousand dollars! What's the matter with you? Come on. Come on. At least hear what he has to say. Pleeeeease?"

Taylor ignored the shallow thoughts and continued to the hotel to find a taxi.

"Taylor Reed?"

Taylor looked up from her seat in the crowded Southwest terminal, having just taken a bite of her veggie sub and wondering if today was payback for every bad thing she'd ever done. Wasn't it enough to get a rejection, face bankruptcy, and have to see that despicable Bennett Wade? Apparently not because she'd also missed her flight, and there were no open seats until eight o'clock in the evening. It was twelve-thirty in the afternoon.

And now this?

She quickly chewed and then swallowed. "Yes, Officer?"

The large, African American man with endless biceps spoke into the radio clipped to his shoulder, "Found her." He then looked back down at Taylor. "Come with me, please."

"What's this about?" she asked. Of course the other passengers in the terminal thought she might be packing a bomb or something equally deadly because everyone began inching back. One mother grabbed her baby and darted away, leaving behind her stroller.

"This can't be happening," Taylor said under her breath. She looked up at the officer. "What did I do?"

"Ma'am, I'm just here to escort you to your flight."

Taylor felt relieved for a fraction of a second until she realized how strange that sounded. "What flight? Because mine doesn't leave for another seven-something hours."

And since when do airport cops provide personal escorts?

The officer looked like he was about to lose his patience when another policeman showed up—a tall, thin blond man with a buzz cut.

Great, now there are two. How embarrassing.

"This her?" asked officer number two.

The first man nodded and reached down for her roller bag. The second man grabbed her purse from the floor and said, "Hurry up," before walking away.

"Wait!" Taylor stood up from her seat, still holding her sandwich. "Where are you going with my stuff?"

The two officers ignored her and continued down the long corridor at a swift pace. Obviously, she couldn't *not* follow. They had her stuff—wallet, boarding pass, and cellphone included.

She tossed the sandwich into a trashcan and ran after them, fuming. "Excuse me, but could you please stop?"

"There's no time. Mr. Wade's plane is about to take off," said the African American officer.

"Mr. Wade?" Her mouth dropped open.

The officers stopped at a locked door at the end of the corridor and the blond proceeded to punch a code onto the keypad next to it.

"After you," said blondie as the door popped open.

Taylor was about to blow a massive fuse, but realized yelling at two police officers wasn't the wisest choice. "You're not giving me back my things, are you?"

The two men stared back with stone cold expressions.

"I'll take that as a no." Taylor sighed. "Fine. I'll take this up with Mr. Wade."

She followed the two men down a stairwell and outside to a waiting police car. She seriously didn't know what sort of game Bennett Wade was playing, but he had just crossed the line.

When the squad car pulled up to a sleek, gleaming white plane with a roll-away staircase at its side, Taylor headed straight for it, ignoring the pouring rain. By the time she got to the top of the steps, her hair was once again dripping wet.

"Ah, Ms. Reed. There you are." A redheaded flight attendant, who wore a navy blue skirt suit and had her hair in a neat bun, handed Taylor a towel and then quickly took Taylor's bags from blondie, who'd followed right behind.

Taylor swabbed the rain from her damp face and then glanced around the elegant cabin. There were five rows of double black leather seats and a set of doors in the back that looked like they might lead to a bathroom and storage space, but no sign of Bennett Wade.

"Where's Mr. Wade?" Taylor asked the flight attendant who was now shutting the plane's door. "Wait!" Taylor held out her hand. "Don't close that!"

The attendant looked at her, puckering her red lips. "Sorry, Sugar?" she asked with a slight twang.

"I'm not flying on this thing. Where the hell is Mr. Wade?"

An awkward expression crossed the woman's face. "You're not flying?"

"Not even close. I came to tell Mr. Wade—" The plane jarred forward, and Taylor nearly fell over.

"I'm afraid it's too late," said the attendant, sounding slightly worried. "Once the plane starts moving, I can't open the doors again without clearance from the captain. Well, that and the plane has to stop moving, of course."

I can't believe this. I'm not flying on this thing!

"Let me speak to the captain." Taylor reached for the cockpit door, but it was locked.

At the same time, the attendant picked up the phone situated to the side of the door and pushed a little button. "Captain, the young woman would like to speak with you. She says she doesn't want to be on this flight." The attendant listened for a moment. "Yes. All right. I'll tell her." She hung up the phone. "I'm sorry, ma'am, the captain says we're on a schedule so it's time to take your seat."

What a complete assho . . . Taylor gasped. "Wait. Mr. Wade is flying the damned plane, isn't he?"

The attendant smiled. "Of course. But don't you worry, Sugar, he's a very good pilot. The best. I go everywhere with him." She winked.

What was the wink supposed to mean? Was she his girlfriend? Lover? Or was it just one of those friendly southern hospitality winks meant to create an atmosphere of levity?

Who cares!

"You can't do this," Taylor protested. "You can't kidnap me to . . . to . . . where is this thing going?"

The woman continued smiling politely. Did she ever stop? "San Francisco."

"Fine. You can't make me go to San Francisco." Ironically, that was her hometown, but not where she lived. In any case, this was kidnapping!

"Oh. Don't worry. I've already booked a connecting flight to Phoenix for you. Mr. Wade says we would've taken you all the way home, but he has an important early dinner appointment in San Francisco. You *are* going on to Phoenix, right?"

"That's not the point. I want to speak—"

A little bell chimed. "Please take your seat, Ms. Reed. We're about to take off." The attendant moved past her, sat in the first row, and buckled her seatbelt.

"I can't believe this. Seriously. Can't. Believe this." Taylor sat down on the other side of the aisle, her mind filling up with the many unsavory things she planned to say to that miserable asshole Bennett Wade the moment she laid eyes on him, starting with how insanely insensitive he was.

Don't forget predictable. Yep, she'd been dead-on about his inability to accept "no" for an answer. And this was just the sort of bulldozer tactic Mr. Wade was famous for. Didn't he understand that forcing people into situations wouldn't win him anything but animosity? It was the exact behavior her program warned against doing. Employees wanted leaders who not only respected them as individuals and sought to understand them, but who also inspired. That was the key to running a successful company. Empowering versus dominating. Collaborating versus dictating. A man like Wade would never understand these concepts.

Hire me to train him? What a frigging joke! He wouldn't make it past session one.

She dug a pack of gum from her purse and popped a piece in her mouth, preparing for takeoff.

After about thirty minutes, the small jet was up in the air and leveling off. The attendant unbuckled, stood, and immediately went for the phone. "Hello, sir, just checking in to see if I can bring anything to the cockpit."

How about a kick in the pants? Taylor thought. *I deliver free of charge.*

The attendant listened for a moment. "Yes, sir. I'll let her know."

"What? Is he ordering me to parachute out now?" Taylor said. Why not? The man *was* completely ridiculous.

"No, silly. That door won't open in flight. That's why Mr. Wade uses the Cessna for skydiving. This Grayson-500 is only for short business trips."

"Of course he has a plane just for skydiving. Why wouldn't he?" Taylor commented to herself out loud.

"And he has one for international flights, too—needs a bigger engine." The woman crinkled her pert nose. "By the way, sweetie, my name is Candy. Can I get you anything to drink?"

"No thank you, Candy. I'm just fine."

Candy shrugged and pulled out an apron from the closet. "You let me know if you change your mind—oh! And Mr. Wade says he'll be with you shortly."

I can't wait. Taylor mentally rubbed her revenge-hungry hands together.

Candy turned her attention to making coffee and setting up a tray. After a few minutes, the cabin filled with the delicious scent of rich, nutty java, and Taylor inhaled deeply.

No. You don't want any of his goddamned coffee. He'll think he's winning. Winning what? Taylor didn't know, but she wasn't about to settle in and get comfy in his big, fancy, stupid plane.

A few minutes later, with tray and coffee in hand, Candy knocked on the cockpit door. It popped open, and Bennett Wade's imposing frame appeared in the doorway, his intense blue eyes immediately locking onto Taylor's face. He had taken off his jacket and was wearing just his white button-down shirt and black, nicely tailored pants that accentuated his muscular thighs. Taylor tried not to notice how attractive his shape was.

He stepped out into the small galley, allowing Candy to pass. She flashed a nervous glance at the back of his head before closing the door behind her.

"Who's flying the plane?" Taylor asked.

Bennett smiled, and it was that condescending grin Taylor was learning to loathe. "Frank, my pilot. Who else?"

Whatever. Now that that's out of the way . . . Taylor unbuckled her seatbelt and stood. "You have some fucking nerve. Who the hell do you think you are?"

His condescending smile turned smug. Did the man think he'd won some giant victory?

"I think I'm a man who always gets what he wants. One way or another." Crossing his well-built arms, he leaned sideways against the doorway separating the cabin from the galley. With his considerable height, he had to bend his neck just a little.

"You're not getting anything from me," she shot back. "Not now. Not ever."

His smile faded into that icy look, making Taylor suddenly aware of every inch of her skin and every breath her body took. The man knew how to set a vibe and intimidation was his special gift.

"I wanted to talk to you, didn't I? I think I got that," he gloated.

Taylor clamped her mouth shut.

He dropped his arms and frowned. "I said, 'I wanted to talk to you,' not the other way around. So feel free to give me the silent treatment. Probably easier, anyway."

Why did every word out of this man's mouth have to be about proving his dominance? "You had no right to pull me out of the terminal and put me on this plane."

"I did you a favor," he said calmly in his deep, slow voice, oozing with loathsome, annoying confidence.

"A favor? Do you have any idea how humiliating that was? The entire terminal thought I was some mad terrorist woman being arrested."

"Your flight was delayed by seven hours. I simply asked Jim and Stan to offer you a ride."

"They didn't give me a choice," she growled.

"Perhaps because I offered them box seats for the Super Bowl if they persuaded you successfully."

Taylor shook her head. "You're fucking unbelievable."

"So I've been told."

Taylor's jaw dropped. She just wanted to kick him. Really, really hard. In his man parts.

He gestured toward the seat behind her and took the other seat for himself. "And, since you're already here, why not take ten minutes to hear what I have to say?"

"Do I have a choice?" She looked down at him expecting to hear . . .

"No."

Shocker. But okay. Fine. That would give her the satisfaction of watching his face when she turned him down. Again. She wasn't afraid of him. Okay, maybe a little, but not enough to let him bulldoze over her.

I'm not your mound of dirt, buddy.

"All right." Taylor sat in the first row, opposite the aisle from Mr. Wade, and turned her body to face him. "Speak."

He stretched his long, muscular legs into the aisle and then rubbed his face, making a deep, throaty groan.

The raw, masculine sound suddenly triggered a very erotic image in her head—specifically, of Bennett Wade pleasuring himself, his thick, long cock in his hand, while he groaned in that gravelly voice.

Holy, crap. What's the matter with me? Completely embarrassed by her unwelcome, highly sexual thoughts, Taylor crossed her arms over her chest and looked away, searching for any distraction she could find. *The floor, the beige ceiling—oh look! Magazines.*

"Ms. Reed?" Mr. Wade held his snapping fingers in her face. "Are you even listening to me?"

Oh crap. Had he been speaking while she'd been picturing him naked with an enormous erection? *Oh, the shame.*

"No, I was too busy thinking about how to thank you for this *favor*," she lied.

He stared for a moment, and then his neutral expression turned into a bitter scowl—brows furrowed, full lips smashed together, and eyes locked on her as if she were a dirty little bug he might squash just for pleasure. It was then that Taylor noticed how even his posture changed when he became upset. His spine got straighter, his large chest inflated, and his jaw muscles flexed with tension. Maybe that was his vibe-setting trick. He used his size to subconsciously make others feel smaller. Add to that his cold, unwavering stare and deep, authoritative voice, he could scare the crap out of a Navy SEAL.

"Ms. Reed, don't provoke me."

"Provoke you?" she asked innocently.

"Is your brain waterlogged from standing in the rain?" he asked.

Gasp. "No. Is yours?" she fired back.

"I guess I was wrong about you."

"Wrong about what?" What had he said? And dammit, how could she have missed it?

"I thought the woman I met in Phoenix had a pair of balls on her. I thought she was the kind of person who perhaps enjoyed a challenge."

"I happen to love challenges," she countered firmly. "I simply didn't hear—"

"So you accept coming to work for me?"

"What? Absolutely not," she said.

"You afraid? Or just trying to milk more money out of me?"

What a horrible thing to say! "No and no. I'm not interested in your money, and I don't want to work with you—"

"*For* me. Work *for* me," he corrected.

"Or for you!"

"And why not?" he said, in a perfectly controlled voice.

"Because you are an insensitive prick who only cares about making money. Because I've seen how you treat people, and ever since the day I met you, I realized you read me completely right. I *was* one of those people who did nothing but complain, and it was time to step up. I thought that meant creating my own company to help assholes like you behave like real human beings, but I've come to realize that's a complete joke because men like you only give a crap about yourselves. So why bother caring about the lives of the people who work for you, even though it could actually make your company more successful? Hell, it might even make you feel good to not be such a prick all the time."

Taylor realized Bennett was no longer scowling. In fact, he was listening. To every goddamned word. Not only that, but one corner of his mouth had curled into a tiny smile. A genuine, bona fide smile. There was even a little pucker in the middle of his sculpted cheek. It was absolutely stunning. The most gorgeous smile she'd ever seen.

Taylor also noticed that she'd stopped talking and the two of them were just sitting there with their gazes locked, those cool blue eyes of his burning right through her, making her heart accelerate.

"Has anyone ever told you," he said, breaking the silence, "that you're very beautiful when you shut your mouth?"

What! His words jarred her back to reality. "Has anyone ever told you, Bennett, that you're a pompous asshole?"

"Yes. And that's Mr. Wade, to you."

"Nope. You're Bennett from now on. I'm demoting you in the human hierarchy."

He growled and was about to speak when an ear-splitting siren sounded over the intercom, flooding the cabin.

Whatthehell? Taylor instinctively gripped her armrests.

Candy burst from the cockpit door, her face ghost white. "Mr. Wade?"

Taylor looked at Bennett. "What's wrong?"

He closed his eyes for a moment and took a breath as if collecting himself. When he opened them, he looked straight at Taylor. "Stay put. And buckle your seatbelt." His tone indicated he wasn't fucking around.

Oh shit.

Bennett disappeared into the cockpit, and Candy sat down in his place, strapping herself in. "I'm sure it will be all right.

Just a little engine problem," she said cheerfully, answering Taylor's unasked question.

But then why was Candy breathing so hard?

Taylor glanced out the window and saw liquid draining from the wing.

They were dumping their fuel.

Ohmygod. She popped from her seat and darted into the cockpit, where she saw Bennett and another man, presumably the captain, speaking into his headset. Bennett held the controls with one hand and was flipping switches with the other. Both men looked worried, but focused.

Candy appeared at her side. "Ms. Reed, please come sit back down. You need to let them work." She tried to tug Taylor back into the cabin, but she refused to move. All Taylor could see were images of the four of them crashing, going up in a ball of flames.

"Taylor?" Bennett was now shaking her by the shoulders. How did he get in front of her? "You need to sit down."

Taylor blinked and looked up at Bennett. His dark brown brows were pulled together, but there was a soothing confidence in his eyes.

"Are we going to die?" she asked, her voice trembling along with the rest of her.

He placed his warm hand on her cheek, and the gesture instantly calmed her. "Yes. One day. You said so yourself. But if you go sit down, Frank and I will do our absolute best to ensure that it doesn't happen today." Just then, Bennett's phone rang, playing Mozart's No. 13, Taylor recognized bemusedly.

"It's my mother. Could you tell her I love her?" He dug the cell from his pocket and handed it to Taylor.

Taylor took the phone into her shaking hand and blinked at him.

"Please?" His full lips curled into a subtle, but sinfully charming smile.

"Uh. Sure. Okay." Taylor bobbed her head, and Bennett gently nudged her back into the cabin and toward Candy who shoved her into a seat and buckled her in. All the while Bennett's phone kept vibrating away in Taylor's hand.

Ohshit. Ohshit. He really wants me to say goodbye to his mother? This was not good.

Taylor pressed the green call button and held the phone to her ear. "Hello?"

"Robin, dear. Is that you?"

Who was Robin? *Probably one of his gazillion girlfriends.*

"Uh, no. This is Taylor."

"Taylor? What's happened to Robin? Bennett better not have pissed her off. He can't find his own asshole without her."

This was Bennett's mother?

"Um, no ma'am. I'm just a . . . friend of his." Not that they were friends, but what else could she say? This wasn't the time to explain their hostile relationship.

"Ah. I see," the woman said. "Well, please let my son know his mother is on the phone. It's important."

"I'm sorry, Mrs. Wade, but Bennett is busy right now."

"Too busy for his own mother? Bullshit! You tell him to get his ass on the phone right now, or so help me God, I will find him and hang him by the gonads."

Lord. Was Bennett's mother an ex-gangster? Or perhaps a medieval-torture revivalist?

"I—I'm sorry, Mrs. Wade but . . . he really can't . . ." Taylor heard the plane groaning and grinding away. She glanced out the window and saw smoke pouring from the engine. Then she glanced ahead into the cockpit where Bennett flipped more switches while speaking frantically into his headset.

This is bad. So, so bad.

"What is it, dear? What's that noise? What's going on?" Mrs. Wade's voice suddenly sounded panicked.

Taylor swallowed and closed her tearing eyes as the plane began violently shaking. "Mrs. Wade, Bennett wanted me to tell you that he loves you and that you're the best mother he could've ever hoped for." Okay, so Bennett hadn't shared that last part, but it's what she would say to her own mother if her mother were still alive.

Oh no, I need to call my Dad.

"Wh-where are you, dear?" Mrs. Wade asked, her voice now calm, but clearly terrified.

"We're on his plane. Somewhere over Oregon, I think."

"Taylor, dear?"

Taylor wiped the tears from under her eyes. "Yes?"

"Don't you worry, honey. My Bennett won't let anything bad happen to you. I promise."

"There's smoke coming out of the engine. He had to dump the fuel."

"You listen to me, young lady. My Bennett learned to fly when he was ten years old. If anyone can land a broken plane, it's him. Well, and Frank. Yes, Frank is a much better pilot. But either way, you're in good hands. For the most part."

For the most part?

Mrs. Wade went on, "And you tell him he'd better be at my house at six. I made meatloaf, his favorite."

His mother was his important dinner meeting. That was so very sweet.

"Oh," she continued, "and I need to make sure Robin gave him that package with the cookie. It should be on his desk, and it's very important that he eats it. The cookie, of course. Not the package. Can you ask him to do that, dear?"

The woman was mad. They were about to die, and she was talking about cookies?

"Cookie. Desk. Got it. I have to go now," Taylor said.

"Okay, dear. Keep your head between your legs! And don't worry about a thing!"

Taylor ended the call and began to dial her father, but her hands shook so hard she could barely hold the phone.

Suddenly, Bennett was there, kneeling in front of her, grabbing the device. "What did she want?" he asked, punching some numbers into his cell.

"She made meatloaf, and there's a cookie on your desk."

Bennett didn't seem to be listening. "Here. Take this." He shoved the phone back at her.

"Why?"

He growled impatiently and jammed the thing into her pant pocket underneath her seatbelt. "It's got a tracking device on it, so they can find you faster if anything should—"

"I need to call my dad," she blurted out.

"There's no ti—"

The plane plunged, and Bennett fell back, slamming into the wall to the side of the cockpit door. He winced with pain and then looked at Candy. "Do you have your tracker on?" he yelled.

Candy nodded, her face pale.

"Good. Make sure you both keep your heads down."

Candy glanced at Taylor. "Don't worry. It's going to be okay. Put your head down."

Ohmygod. Ohmygod. Taylor felt her body being pulled down, hurtling toward earth along with the plane.

"Head forward," Candy screamed.

The sound of the groaning engine suddenly stopped and everything went deathly quiet. Taylor's body felt weightless, like they'd been sucked into outer space.

Panting hard, Taylor closed her eyes and gripped the armrests for dear life. They were falling out of the sky, and the only thing she could hear was Bennett's voice in the background, yelling at someone to have their crews ready. Taylor braced for what was to come, but nothing could prepare her for the horrific, deafening sound of the plane's hull slamming into the ground.

CHAPTER 3

"Taylor? Can you hear me?" Taylor felt a warm, rough hand stroking her cheek. "I need you to tell me if you feel any pain."

She knew she was in a state of shock, but more than anything she felt too terrified to open her eyes and see the damage. Not to the plane, but to the people on board and to her own body. The plane had slammed belly first into the ground, the crushing metal groaning and screeching as they came to a grinding halt.

Still strapped into her seat, she carefully began flexing her limbs, fingers, and toes. She didn't feel any discomfort.

Slowly, she opened her eyes and glanced over at Candy, whose red hair was a tangled mess.

"Taylor? Can you hear me?" Bennett bent down in front of her, those startling blue eyes intensely focused on her face. Taylor noted a small cut on his forehead and a little blood on his white shirt, but all-in-all he looked pretty damned pristine. Even his thick, brown hair was only mildly ruffled. As for the plane, bits and pieces of the aircraft's interior covered the floor, but Taylor imagined the exterior resembled a junkyard sculpture.

"Is everyone okay? Are *you* okay?" she said, trying to catch her breath.

"Yes." Bennett smiled, and it was a full-blown genuine smile. Luscious male lips curling up in the corners, complete with puckering dimples smack dab in the middle of each cheek. And those eyes: they were filled with a devilishly triumphant twinkle.

It was then that Taylor noticed a small scar right under his lower lip, running diagonally toward the tip of his cleft chin. The stubble of his beard didn't grow in that spot, so it must've been a deep cut. She wondered what story he'd tell about it. Another plane crash, perhaps? Skydiving accident?

Why the hell am I staring at his chin? I just survived a plane crash. The sound of sirens screamed in the background, growing louder as the vehicles approached.

"Where are we?" Taylor asked, unbuckling her seatbelt with her shaking hands.

"Portland Airport. You stay in your seat until the paramedics look you over," Bennett said. "You might have head trauma or a concussion."

Candy was already up and trying to pry open the door of the plane.

"How come she's walking around?" Taylor asked.

"She's an employee," he said dismissively.

Taylor's jaw dropped.

"I pay her well," he added, "and it's her job to ensure the safety of the passengers first."

That didn't mean she couldn't be injured or that she wasn't in shock and deserving of his compassion, too.

"She almost died because of you," Taylor snapped.

"She almost died because the plane's computer had a glitch, and she lived because I landed the plane safely. Well, Frank and I."

"She works for you and almost lost her life on the job," Taylor ranted. "Doesn't that matter to you? Or what about you putting me on a plane against my will, and me almost dying because of it? But there you are congratulating yourself like you just won the gold medal in the Olympic daredevil medley. Do you have a heart or a soul anywhere inside there? Anywhere at all?"

His icy disposition returned, and it seemed he was about to speak—no doubt to dish a heaping helping of ego-infested insults meant to belittle her—but the door pushed open and the emergency personnel poured in past Candy.

Bennett stepped out of the way, and the paramedics descended upon Taylor. As they flashed lights in her eyes and held fingers in her face, Taylor caught a glimpse of his eyes, their expression somewhere between wounded and irate. Then they whisked Bennett away.

All of a sudden, Taylor felt like the heartless one. Bennett Wade had saved her life. Why had she yelled at him like that?

Shock. You're in shock. And she'd lashed out at the man because of it.

"Bennett! Wait!"

But he was gone. And had he stayed, Taylor didn't know what she would've said.

Maybe . . . I'm sorry?

Two Weeks Later

Taylor pulled into her brother Jack's driveway and turned off the engine. The two-day drive from Phoenix to Berkeley, California, had given her plenty of quiet time to think—something she'd not had much of since the crash.

During her brief visit to the hospital that day in Portland, Mr. Wade's assistant—a reserved, statuesque brunette with warm brown eyes, named Robin—had shown up to ensure Taylor was taken care of, including all of her hospital bills. Miraculously, no one had been hurt in the crash, but the press still mobbed her outside the hospital. Luckily, she'd gotten a call in to her father before he'd even seen the news.

The scene didn't look much different when she landed in Phoenix at two in the morning, or when she arrived at her apartment. "What thoughts were going through your mind, Taylor?" "What caused the crash?" "What were those final moments like with Mr. Wade before you hit the ground?" "Are you his lover?" The press lobbed dozens of inane questions at her every time she went outside. How the hell did they think she felt? The crash had scared the ever-loving crap out of her! And no! She wasn't his lover—how could they even ask that stupid question? And how would she know what caused the crash? All Taylor knew was that they'd all survived with nothing more than a few bumps and bruises. A damned miracle.

After a week, the press finally moved on to chase something shinier, and Taylor began the soul-bruising task of packing up her apartment to move back to California. Everything would go into storage, and she would stay with Jack, the youngest of her three older brothers. Recently divorced with no kids, he had plenty of extra space and insisted Taylor stay as long as she needed.

That was the second miracle Taylor experienced in recent days: Her family hadn't said a word about her failed business venture. Nor had her father uttered a peep about how she'd quit her job—something that had been a topic of many heated debates since last February. But this time, not a word.

They're probably saving up all the lectures and criticisms for when they see me in person tonight. Like a school of judgment piranhas. It didn't matter how old she got, the men in her family always treated her like she was a child in need of a "good strong talking-to." But they liked to do it gang-style.

Nevertheless, as Taylor stared from her car up at her brother's two-story home with its dark brown shingles and its orange tree in the front yard, she felt grateful to have somewhere to land. She needed time to digest, to untangle the mess inside her head, and to figure out what to do next. With her debts, getting a job was certainly highest on her priority list, but her heart wasn't ready to let go of her dream: HumanitE.

I could reconsider Bennett's offer, she thought for the five-hundredth time. It certainly would resolve her financial problems and give her the opportunity to pilot her training program. Not to mention having a client like Bennett Wade would make a nice springboard.

But Bennett Wade? Bennett. Wade. There was simply no way for her to maintain her professional demeanor in his presence. The domineering, tactless, playboy-bully provoked so many emotions—outrage, fascination, disgust, and . . . well, she didn't know, but those undecipherable sentiments were the source of many restless nights and cleaning episodes.

On the other hand, maybe I need to give him a chance? After all, he did track me down in Seattle. Of course, he had probably already been there for some other business and just happened to realize she was in town at the same time.

Fine. Okay. But he saved my life. He'd also taken care of her before and after the crash.

The phone on the passenger seat of her car made a little chirp, reminding her that the battery was low again. She still felt a mixture of anxiety and excitement every time she looked at the thing. It was Bennett's phone. He hadn't disconnected the device after she'd forgotten about it being inside her pocket, but it also hadn't rung even once. Odder still was the lack of a passcode.

Of course, the only thing on the device—yes, she'd snooped, okay? Who wouldn't?—was a record of that call from his mother plus some apps, including the tracking one, which as far as she could tell had remained active.

At first, Taylor had thought to mail the thing back, but then two days after the crash, a text came in: *I'm sorry. -B*

That's all it had said.

And, yes, she believed it had been meant for her. Bennett knew perfectly well she still had the phone. (Tracking app. Phoenix. Who else?)

That was when Taylor felt an odd sort of closeness or connection or . . . *something*—she didn't really know—with Bennett. He could've had Robin ask for it back. He could've deactivated it. But he hadn't. And she knew he could check her location whenever he liked. Was he checking it now and knew she'd left Phoenix?

Admittedly, it was a bizarrely intimate, private kind of thing, knowing that either of them could break the link at any time, yet neither of them had.

But what was his excuse? Taylor obviously felt there was some unfinished business, but what about him? Was Bennett waiting for her to reply to the text? Was he waiting for her to apologize for having yelled at him after the crash? She didn't know.

Why not ask?

Taylor thought it over for a moment. A quick conversation *would* help her settle the question related to accepting his offer. It would also allow her to finally say that she truly felt sorry for having yelled at him—it hadn't been the time or the place to sermonize and was a complete knee jerk in the heat of the moment. *Not my best moment.*

Taylor glanced at her watch. The question would have to wait until tomorrow. Tonight, Jack had invited over the whole family and her closest friends to welcome her home.

Home. It really was nice to be back where she had all the support and love she needed to start over. Even if her brothers would give her a hard time for making some bad career choices.

Taylor got out of the car, stretched her back, and then rang the doorbell. The door flew open and there was Jack, big strong Jack with his shaggy, light brown hair and bright green eyes, wearing a Forty-Niners apron and an oven mitt. His face immediately turned into a giant grin, and he pulled her inside for a rib-crushing hug.

"Our Little Tiger is back." Then, without warning, her brother began to cry.

Taylor was speechless. Where was the customary dude-salute—the punch on the shoulder followed by the "When are we gonna toughen you up?" Or her other inspirational favorite, "What did you do *this* week to fuck up your life?" Also, he hadn't called her "Little Tiger" in years. It was a nickname her brothers had given her because they said that she reminded them of a scrappy little tiger runt, all growls and tiny claws. In their minds, it was a term of endearment.

Jack's body shook with sobs as he hugged her, and Taylor simply couldn't understand what was happening. *Maybe he's still not over Doris?*

After several awkward moments, Jack pulled away and stared down at her. "Sorry," he wiped away his tears. "I guess I'm upset."

"I'm so sorry. I had no idea you were still such a mess over Doris." Taylor patted his arm.

"What? No. I'm talking about you!"

"Me?"

"When we saw that news footage and you were on the plane . . . we all thought you were dead until Dad called us and . . ." His voice trailed off, and his eyes teared up again.

Oh my God.

Jack reached for Taylor and hugged her again, holding her tightly, sniffling. "I'm just so happy you're here, Taylor."

Taylor tried to process, but it wasn't easy. She had no idea he'd taken it so hard. She'd spoken to her father en route to the hospital that day, and while he hadn't even heard the news himself yet, he had seemed fine. *Plane engine trouble. Bumpy landing. Taylor's safe. No problem.* That's what she remembered from the conversation. Her father had been the one to call everyone, including Sarah and Holly, to let them know she was all right. Of course, Taylor had spoken to her girlfriends about a dozen times since then—the three were already busy making plans for a girls' night out—but she really hadn't spoken to any of her brothers. She figured they were busy with their lives and since she was okay, no biggie.

"I'm fine, Jack." Taylor patted him on the back, her heart thumping at an uneasy pace. She'd always thought of her brothers as . . . well, sort of a bunch of tough guys, at least when it came to displays of emotion.

If I was wrong about my own family, who else have I been wrong about?

CHAPTER 4

At eight o'clock the next morning, Taylor sprang from the bed in Jack's guest room, feeling more energized and hopeful than she had in years. Even her urge to deep clean the house from top to bottom had been absent last night for the first time in months thanks to all the heartfelt hugs, good food, and great wine. No one had brought up the crash or the J.O.B. topic, and a different, more positive vibe had lingered in the air all night. Something about seeing her family's reaction made her think. Maybe it wasn't that people couldn't change; it simply took the right catalyst to get them to open up those hidden, more caring behaviors.

That was the key—the one thing missing from her training course. The question now was how to unlock the compassion inside all those stiff, cold executives.

She needed a test case. And Bennett Wade would be perfect.

Taylor bounced downstairs, knowing that Jack, a plastic surgeon who specialized in reconstructive surgery, had already left for work. She began combing through his cupboards, looking for coffee, but found the kitchen void of any real food.

Eesh . . . She opened the refrigerator. *Double eesh*. Leftovers from last night's dinner, sour milk, and a loaf of bread.

Poor Jack. He used to be a major foodie, but that had been before his wife cheated and left him for another woman. A patient of his, no less. The saddest part of all was that he and Doris, his ex-wife, had been best friends since the second grade. Inseparable. Ball games, marathon running, cooking classes—the two had even gone to the same college. Then one day, she sat poor Jack down, told him the news, packed up her car, and left. Jack had been devastated. Honestly, Taylor couldn't blame him. He'd been the perfect husband and faithful to a T despite the long line of women who'd thrown themselves at him over the years. As far as Taylor knew, Jack never so much as batted one curious eyelash their way. And she'd seen the adoring way he always stared at Doris when he thought no one was looking.

Now he felt too afraid of getting hurt to even be casual friends with a woman.

Taylor would definitely have to help Jack get back into the groove. But first, she needed to get her own life on track. Which is why an hour and a half later, she found herself in the heart of San Francisco's Financial District, standing in the lobby of Wade Enterprises. The sterile but elegant decor—gleaming black marble floors that reflected the recessed lighting from above, dark geometric furniture, and floor-to-ceiling black and white prints of bridges, buildings, and other San Francisco landmarks—made the lobby feel more like a chic hotel than an office building.

Taylor glanced down at her body feeling incredibly under-dressed. She'd worn black flats, her favorite jeans, and a little cream-colored blouse. She'd pulled her long brown hair into a sleek knot at the nape of her neck and hadn't bothered with any makeup. She didn't know if Bennett was in town or not, but she planned to stop by and leave a note—yes, an apology for her irrational and rude behavior on the plane plus a request for a formal meeting at his earliest convenience.

Bennett's phone was also inside the envelope. If she ended up working with him (*with*, not for) then the relationship needed to be one-hundred-percent professional. If she didn't end up working with him, well, after she left her apology note, there was no reason to hang on to the device.

"Your name?" asked the handsome Hispanic security guard in the gray uniform, seated behind a long, black granite counter just in front of the elevator bank.

"Taylor Reed, but I'm just here to drop—"

"One moment." The man handed her a small, laminated executive visitor's badge. "Take the elevator on the right, scan the badge over the security pad, and then proceed to the fortieth floor."

"I think you misunderstood. I just need to drop this off." Taylor held out a manila envelope.

"Robin requested I send you right up," he replied.

That's odd. Unless . . .

A little rush surged through her body. *Bennett checked his app and knows I'm already here.* Dammit, she really liked him spying on her. It was like their dirty little secret. *God, I must be crazy.*

"Are you sure?" Taylor asked. "Because I didn't tell anyone I was . . ." The man rattled the badge in front of her. "Thank you." Taylor snagged it and proceeded to the elevator.

Now she kicked herself for not having worn her grown-up clothes or some lip gloss, but she really had intended to be in and out and then go for a little walk around the city. Later, she would catch lunch with Sarah, who worked at the courthouse as a judge. That fact was still hard for Taylor to believe; Sarah used to be the biggest delinquent of them all in high school.

Taylor scanned the badge over the pad inside the elevator, pressed the button for the fortieth floor, and then rode to the top. She exited into a private lobby where she immediately noticed how the large, well-lit space was warm and inviting, despite the masculine decor—dark wood floors, gray walls, and modernist furniture with red accent pillows in the sitting area. The place felt more like a cool bar or the office of a fashion designer than a corporate office.

She walked past three Arab men in suits and headdresses— *OMG, is that the oil sheik guy I just saw on the cover of Forbes?*—and proceeded to the far end of the room where Robin sat at her desk, talking into her headset. She waved at Taylor and continued speaking. "No, I'm sorry, but Mr. Wade isn't available. May I take a message, Mr. Grayson?"

Mr. Grayson? Could it be *the* Mr. Grayson, owner of Grayson Aircraft? If so, Taylor seriously wanted to have a chat with the guy because Bennett's plane had been one of theirs.

Robin listened for a moment. "He asked not to be disturbed on his mobile either, but I promise to let him know you've called."

She hung up. "Hi, Taylor. Mr. Wade is expecting you—go right in." She pointed to an ominous set of dark, solid wood, double doors behind her.

"But I just came to drop off this envelope, and I'm sure Bennett is busy so . . ."

Robin's large brown eyes almost popped from her head. Was it because Taylor didn't want to stay?

Robin cleared her throat. "I'm sure *Mr. Wade* would be disappointed not to see you." She stood and opened the doors to Bennett's office, gesturing for Taylor to enter.

Welp. I guess an in-person apology will do. As for the other matter (whether or not she would work with him), that ought to be a fairly quick conversation.

"Thanks." Taylor passed Robin, who remained in the doorway.

"Can I get you anything? Tea, coffee, water?"

"No, thank you," Taylor replied.

"Okay. I'll be right outside if you change your mind. *Mr. Wade's* helicopter should be touching down shortly."

Taylor nodded and flashed a polite smile. That Robin lady was acting a little strange. Did she think Taylor had forgotten Bennett's last name?

Once Taylor was alone in the sprawling office she swiveled on her heel to take it all in, admiring the floor-to-ceiling windows displaying a spectacular view of Coit Tower. She'd worked with plenty of CEOs in her past job so the lavish billionaire lifestyle wasn't such a shock anymore; however, Bennett's office definitely piqued her curiosity. Much like the private lobby outside his doors, his office looked more like that of a record producer or art dealer—dark hardwood floors, modern furniture, smoke gray walls with lively colored paintings, and a comfy looking sofa and armchair around a triangular glass coffee table. His desk was covered with models of tiny robotics and faced out toward one of the windows. She guessed if she had an office with a view overlooking the San Francisco cityscape, she would turn her desk that way, too.

But seeing this place—a complete contrast to the man's cold personality—made her wonder what really made Bennett tick. Certainly, it was something he kept hidden.

Oh, God. I hope he's not into Fifty Shades kind of stuff. She couldn't go there. Not for any man. *Okay, maybe the blind-folds 'n' stuff, but not the butt plugs. Definitely not the butt plugs. Wait. Why are you even thinking about that? You're not dating the gu*—

"Ms. Reed, so nice to see you again," said a deep voice.

Taylor turned with a gasp and felt her face instantly flush as if she'd been caught red-handed doing something naughty. *Like thinking about butt plugs? Yikes. Shake it off.*

"Is something the matter?" he asked. Today, his expression was somewhat neutral—not irate, not icy, and not overly friendly. If she had to guess, she'd say he was feeling cautious.

"Um. No." She shook her head. "Why would you plug—I mean, *say* that?"

He stared at her with those irritatingly soul-piercing blue eyes. "You're blushing. That's why."

Taylor was about to speak, but her mind hit a wall. A tall, hot, suited-man wall. He wore a baby blue dress shirt that matched his eyes and a very expensive-looking black suit made from a polished cotton that matched his tie. His pants were tailored to perfection, gently hugging the shape of his muscular thighs, all the way down the tapered legs. The suit was defi-nitely built just for him. Every inch of him. Even the substantial bulge in his—

"Eh-hem," Bennett cleared his throat and crossed his power-house arms over his broad chest, flashing a bit of those shiny black BW cufflinks and his expensive watch.

Taylor's eyes snapped up to his face. *No. You were not just checking out his gear. No. No. Nooo . . .*

Taylor died quietly on the inside. "Here." She shoved the large manila envelope toward him, but he didn't bite.

"What's inside?" His expression instantly soured, his dark brown brows pulling together.

"Take it." She urged him to accept the envelope, but he simply walked past her to the sitting area.

"Please sit, Ms. Reed." Bennett gestured toward the sofa and ran his hand down his black tie as he took a seat in the armchair.

Taylor held his gaze for a moment, noticing how the room now felt saturated with tension. It reminded her of those other moments right before he had said something offensive to throw her off balance. *Well, I'm* not *afraid of him. I won't let him get to me.*

She lifted her chin and strolled over to take a seat. To demonstrate her lack of fear, she sat as close as she could to his armchair, maintaining eye contact.

Several awkward moments passed, and then he smiled. Just a half a smile, but it was beautiful.

"So, Ms. Reed," he leaned back in the chair, "what brings you to my office?"

"I came to deliver that." She set the envelope on the glass table and clasped her hands in her lap.

"Tell me why you're really here," he said in that oh-so-deep and inherently male voice that made the air vibrate all around her. Or was that her body quivering?

"I just told you; to deliver that. There's a letter inside, apologizing for the way I behaved." She looked him straight in the eyes, trying to ignore the thick curtains of lashes that somehow made the blue of his eyes more intense. "I shouldn't have yelled at you when we last saw each other. It was wrong." She made a point to apologize only for the plane crash incident. When she'd yelled at him for hijacking her, he totally had it coming.

He slowly leaned forward, and Taylor noted how the man seemed to own and command the space around him. He took up way more room than just what his body occupied.

How does he do that? Again she felt her body quiver.

He threaded his hands together, and she wondered what they might feel like gripping her bare hips while he thrust his—

"What if I were to tell you, Ms. Reed, that you didn't say anything wrong that day? What then?" Bennett dipped his head ever so slightly, giving him a wolfishly hungry look.

He thought she was right? She hadn't expected him to be the sort of man to admit that. Not ever.

He did text and say sorry. Maybe his head wasn't so big after all. *Are you sure? Because given the size of that bulge in his pants, his head seems pretty damned big and sexy and I bet it would feel really good sliding—*

Stop. What is wrong with you?

She straightened her spine. "I guess I'd say it's irrelevant. We'd just survived a plane crash. The only thing that mattered was making sure everyone got to the hospital. It wasn't the time or the place to share my opinions about how I believe people should treat each other."

He kept his hypnotic gaze pinned to her face. "Apology accepted. Now I'll ask again; why are you really here?"

"I thought we just covered that."

"You could've mailed the envelope," he said. "So what do you want?"

"Would you stop?"

He tilted his head a notch. "Stop what?"

"Stop trying to bulldoze this conversation," she said. "I get it, okay? You're a hard-ass. You're a big, powerful man." But if they were going to get down to business, he needed to back off with the whole intimidation vibe. *'Cause he's really good at it, and it's making me hot.*

What? No. No, it's not.

He chuckled, and his dimples deepened into delicious little semicircles.

"Hard-ass? I thought I was an immoral, heartless 'pig in a suit' whose only goal in life is to make money and demean the masses in an effort to elevate my sense of self-worth."

"W-we-well, I know I said something like that but—"

"Which is priceless coming from someone like you," he said, cutting her off.

"Someone like me?"

"You've put yourself on a pedestal so high that no one could ever hope to live up to your soaring standards of perfection."

"That's not true. I'm intimately acquainted with my faults and trust me, they're there." Not that she had many, if she were to be honest with herself. Her body was a bit too thick around the hips, she wasn't the best salesperson in the world, and she obviously wasn't impervious to Bennett's insane masculinity. But aside from that, she wanted to help people. She wanted to change things.

"You're a hypocrite," he said bluntly.

No. I am open-minded and self-aware. "Then why in the world do you want to hire me?"

He looked down at his palms for a moment before meeting her gaze. "Because you and I are the same—we see the world in terms of ideals. Black and white. Right and wrong. Success and failures. Never any grays."

"So you're saying we're both hyper-judgmental and rigid."

He held up his index finger. "We're good at sizing up people and situations. Of course, what we do with our insights is where we differ."

Now this she had to hear. "Oh please, do go on." She crossed her arms.

"I don't believe in settling for less. But you—"

"I don't settle," she protested. "I just didn't know what I wanted—there's a difference. But now I do know."

"Do you?" His gaze slowly moved to her lips and stayed there for a long moment before returning to her eyes.

"Ye-ye-yesss?" She cleared her throat. *Oh God, did you just answer him like a weak little girl?* If her brothers had been in the room, they would've been shaking their heads in disgust or chucking basketballs at her head. "Yes," she said firmly.

"I'm not so sure I believe you. You seem like the sort of woman who's still searching. Or, perhaps the type who has needs she's not willing to admit to herself."

Presumptuous jerk. Like he knew anything about how she felt or what she needed.

"But all right," he went on. "Let's say for argument's sake you're right. It doesn't change the answer to your question."

She'd completely forgotten the question. They'd gone down an entirely different path, and now her insides felt all flustered.

"Then what's the answer?" *Maybe I'll remember the question by the time you say it.*

"I want to hire you because the world is changing quickly and I have to evolve with it. I need someone who can teach me to speak your language—a strong, opinionated woman's language. And because you have no apprehension about sharing your views regardless of the consequences or the feelings of others—your shrewd candor rivals my own."

Hmph! It did not. She wasn't mean and hurtful! "I think your tight pants are getting to your big thick head." Taylor, for absolutely no apparent reason, found her gaze sinking south to the man's substantial bulge again.

Tay!

"My . . . head?" Bennett frowned, his eyes darting down to his groin.

"Oh! I didn't mean it like that. I meant . . ." *I am now shriveling into a tiny ball of mortification. Hey, a window! I wonder if I can get it open so I can jump.*

"Yes?" He waited, a grin slanting across his lips.

Taylor took a moment to compose herself and then rebounded with a confident gaze. "Look, Bennett, I want to work with you, but I'm just not sure you'll take the training seriously."

"If you're going to work *for* me, you really should call me *Mr. Wade*. And yes, why the hell would I be sitting here if I didn't plan on taking it seriously?"

Okay, he had a point. "With. Work *with* you; I'm a free agent. And let me remind you that you were demoted from deity to regular guy, so I'll stick with Bennett."

He laughed, shaking his head from side to side. "All right. Suit yourself."

"Suited and ready for duty." She made a little salute with her index finger. "When would you like to start?"

"Tonight. Over dinner."

Taylor heard the unpleasant sound of a needle scratching its way across the vinyl. "Whoa there. You and I are not—"

He stood. "Don't flatter yourself, Ms. Reed, I'm interested in your training program only. My schedule simply happens to be extremely tight over the next two weeks—a special project of mine—and that means my office hours are from twelve to twelve. Now so are yours."

"Noon to midnight?" It was a little unorthodox, but okay. For fifty thousand, she had to be flexible.

"No. Midnight to midnight. And since I'll be traveling extensively, you'll be coming along. Where I go, you go." He turned away and headed for the door. "Now, if you'll excuse me, I've got a meeting to attend."

She raised her index finger and stood. "But—"

"See you tonight at eight. Robin will give you the details."

Taylor knew she'd just lost this round of mind-fuck-chess with the billionaire, and frankly, she needed to retreat. Because, dammit—point for Bennett—he'd managed to fluster her in a big way. A big, huge, unprofessional, sad, needy woman sort of way that not only undermined her sense of pride but her feminine power, too. *That man is trouble.*

He stopped and dipped his head. "And Ms. Reed?"

"Ye-ye," she cleared the tickle from her throat. "Yes?"

"You're keeping that phone." He glanced at the manila envelope on the table.

Obviously, he'd figured out there was more than a letter inside.

"May I ask why?"

He shot her a stern look that made her stomach duck, cover, and roll. "Are you saying no?"

"No." She shook her head slowly from side to side. She'd hit a nerve. "I'm merely asking why."

"I think you already know the answer."

She did? Because the only explanation she could come up with was that he secretly enjoyed stalking her just as much as she enjoying him doing it. *Our dirty little secret.*

But that couldn't be right. Bennett's motives had to be some-thing else. Simply put, he wasn't the sort of man to play around. He wanted something, he went after it. That included women. Oh, yes. After the plane crash, she'd started reading all the gossip columns—*I'm a stalker. I need help*—and Bennett collected women like he collected expensive cars. Movie stars, heiresses, models—he dated them all. Of course, he was never seen with any woman more than once. *Womanizing cretin*. In any case, she wasn't his type, and he wasn't hers.

I just get a little flustered around him. After all, the man is . . . he's . . . he's got a thing *going.* And by "thing" she meant a severe male hotness he knew how to own, work, rent out, club you over the head with, whatever.

Taylor watched Bennett's imposing, masculine frame walk out his office door, toward the men waiting in his private lobby. They shook hands, then slipped into a fishbowl conference room near the elevator bank. His confident stride indicated he definitely knew she was watching him every step of the way, and he definitely knew he'd gotten to her.

Gah! She plopped down on his sofa and covered her face, letting out a perturbed little groan. She felt like she'd been shaken, not stirred, and then poured into a martini glass where she'd been simultaneously sipped on while having her olives chewed.

And she goddamned liked it.

She couldn't remember the last time a man had made her feel all wobbly and scatterbrained like that. They were always too sweet, too into themselves, too sedate, or too . . . simply not her match. But this man was like biting into a goddamned jalapeño. The first few seconds were a piece of cake; but the more you chewed, the hotter it got.

She rubbed the goose bumps on her arm, thinking. The intrigue and challenge of seeing if she could reshape Bennett Wade into someone more human had grabbed hold and pulled her right in. However—and this was the absurd part—she understood the futility. In all likelihood, Bennett Wade was too arrogant to ever change.

Perhaps changing him shouldn't be the goal. She'd had a few glimpses of something inside him—how reassuring he had been before and after the crash, not to mention his relationship with his mother—that led her to believe he cared about other people, even if just a little. *Think. If you could get him to open that part up, he's the sort of man who could really do some good.* Over a hundred thousand people worked for the guy, and he had influence far beyond that.

The question is, can I handle him? More precisely put, could she handle the next two weeks with him?

She vigorously shook her head from side to side, trying to chuck all the nonsense from her brain. *Of course I can.* Besides, she really needed this to work. He was the key to her company's survival. But had he meant anything he'd said about truly wanting her help, or was he after something else?

Don't be ridiculous. Bennett's not interested in you. Once again, she reminded herself of the types of women he'd had, could have, and wanted. They were tens. She was . . . well, normal. Brown hair, brown eyes, average height and body.

But on the other hand, making her keep the phone definitely meant . . . well, something. Right?

Come on. Maybe the man really wants to change. Maybe he genuinely respects me. And maybe he wants me to have the phone because he's demanding and wants to be able to contact me whenever he likes.

Taylor sighed at the phone and letter still on the table and then placed them in her purse.

"Ms. Reed?" Robin stood in the doorway. "Here is your check for fifty thousand dollars, the invitation for the ball, and the limo confirmation."

Taylor lifted a brow. "Sorry?"

"Oh, is there a mistake? Mr. Wade said your fee was fifty thousand. If that's incorrect I'll just call him and—"

"Uh. No. The amount is fine. Thank you." *He knew I'd cave! That check was waiting, just like he was waiting for me to come today. Ugh.* The man was good. A damned gifted genius at reading people. "Wait. Did you say ball?"

Robin held out a red envelope. "The annual Wade charity ball. Here's your ticket, and the limo will be at your brother's house at eight o'clock. My card's inside if you need anything else."

A charity ball? And he knew where she lived? Of course he did. *Stalker.*

"I think there's been a misunderstanding," Taylor said. "Bennett told me we'd be working tonight."

"No mistake. Mr. Wade said you'd have time to work right after his speech."

Weird, but okay, fine. He had mentioned they'd be squeezing the training into his busy schedule.

"I don't have anything fancy to wear," Taylor said. "Is a plain suit okay?"

Robin smiled knowingly and urged her to take the envelope. "You'll have nothing to worry about; Mr. Wade thinks of everything—he's a very thoughtful man."

The comment threw her off. Robin seemed like a kind and

genuine person. Why would someone like her think so highly of a man like Bennett?

He's probably sleeping with her. The thought mildly irritated her, and yes, she understood how ridiculous her irritation was.

"Thank you." Taylor snagged the envelope and hurried out of the office. There was just too much Bennett Wade testosterone in the air. She couldn't breathe.

On the elevator ride down, she looked inside the envelope and found a handwritten letter.

Ms. Reed,

I look forward to receiving your personalized leadership training. I am confident by week's end, you'll have me connecting with my inner-Taylor and leading my people in a more effective, fulfilling manner.

As mentioned, I am in the midst of working on a very strategic and time-consuming deal—something that will change many lives along with my own. Therefore, I'd like to thank you in advance for your flexibility and patience. As my first session with you will need to occur between cocktails and dinner, and I cannot expect you to come up with the appropriate attire on such short notice, I've arranged for my good friend Calvin to fit you for a dress this afternoon. He'll be waiting in the Penthouse Suite at the Fairmont with several dress options.

I look forward to our time together. See you tonight.
BW

Taylor stared at the letter, feeling the heat of that red hot jalapeño singeing her fingertips through the paper. *Ball, dress, limo?*

She pinched the bridge of her nose. Her mind was suddenly filled with images that twirled precariously close to the date zone—dancing, laughing, sipping champagne, dry humping each other.

No. You need to establish clear boundaries. Especially if you're going to be spending so much time with him. Not that she wanted anything from him romantically. It was simply a question of maintaining the control he seemed to delight in undermining.

As soon as she stepped outside the building, she slid her cellphone from her pocket and called the number on Robin's business card. "Hi, Robin. It's Taylor. Would you let Bennett know that I appreciate the generous offer, but I'll be finding my own dress and driving myself to our first session tonight?"

"Uh . . . of course, Ms. Reed," she said worriedly. "I'll let Mr. Wade know."

Taylor interpreted Robin's response to mean: "Oh boy. Mr. Wade isn't going to be happy."

She thanked Robin and ended the call. Now all she had to do was set the boundaries with Bennett tonight. *Lesson number one: Know your own limitations.*

CHAPTER 5

"So was it just me, or was my family acting strangely civilized and human last night?" Taylor said over the noise of the crowded deli to Sarah. Sarah had been one of her best friends since elementary school, so they'd spent a lot of time with each other's families growing up.

Sitting across from Taylor, chewing on a big bite of her turkey sandwich, Sarah shrugged and then washed her food down with a sip of iced tea. "If you're referring to the fact that your dad didn't yell at anyone, your brothers didn't take turns giving you noogies for dessert, and that I caught Jack in the kitchen getting all teary eyed, then . . . I'd say it was a classic case of Body Snatchers last night. Where did you put the real Reed men?"

"In my spaceship, of course." Taylor grinned and then leaned closer so no one inside the noisy sandwich shop would overhear what she was about to say. The almost-death incident still felt a little raw. "I think that almost getting killed must've really scared them." Maybe it brought back memories of her mom's death, although her mother had died giving birth.

Sarah sighed longingly. "I wish Bennett Wade would kidnap me on his plane for a little life-changing drama. Although I

would prefer sitting on his face—that would be even better."
She cracked a lopsided smile.

"What?" Taylor laughed and reached across the table to slap
Sarah's arm. "Bite your tongue, woman. He's a complete barbarian." A hot one, sure. But still a barbarian. Which was the
reason she kind of felt embarrassed to tell Sarah about her and
Bennett's little deal. Actually, no one in her life knew they'd had
any contact whatsoever after the crash.

Yeah, save that complicated conversation for another day.
After all, he'd basically gotten her fired and then she'd almost
died on his plane. They'd all think she was nuts for taking him
on as a client.

"Well, if I'm not mistaken," Sarah said, "his company's
headquarters is here in San Francisco. If it will make you happy,
I can have him arrested. Seems like the only thing I'm good for
these days, since men don't want to interact with me any other
way."

Poor Sarah. Like Taylor, her dry spell was going on two
years, only Taylor's excuse was never meeting the right kind of
men. Men like . . .

*Uh-uh. You're not even going there. You will not think of
Ben—dammit! I just thought of him.*

Anyway, lucky Sarah met men all the time. Her looks—wavy
brown hair, blue eyes, and curvy frame—drew them right in.
But her looks were never the problem. Men simply felt intimidated by her job. Even Taylor's brothers were afraid to mess
with Sarah now, which was such a disappointment because it
used to be hysterical when it was her turn for after dinner noogies.

"Have you ever considered just not telling guys you're a
judge?" Taylor asked.

Sarah nibbled on her sandwich, mulling it over. "I tried that with the last one. It was great until I had to come clean." She shook her head at the sandwich. "I've never seen a man get dressed so fast. I should've waited until after we had sex. Ten or twenty times."

Taylor laughed. "Well, I'd set you up, but all of the men I know are rich assholes."

"Ah, but are they good in bed?"

Taylor dropped her mouth. "How would I know?"

"What? Don't tell me you never at least thought about sleeping with one of your clients?"

An image of Bennett Wade flashed into her head. Him. Naked. On top of her and hammering away with his hard cock. *Dammit! No!* She reached for the collar of her blouse, trying to let in a little air. "I . . . uhh . . . I would never sleep with a client. It's unprofessional."

Sarah lifted a dark brow. "Maybe you just haven't met one who's tempting enough."

"There isn't a man alive who could convince me to cross that line." But as she said those words, she already doubted them. "How about you? Ever think of dating one of those hot lawyers or someone else from work?"

Sarah shot her a look. "All of the male judges are my dad's age, lawyers are too uptight, and that leaves the criminals."

"Oh, come on now," Taylor joked, "don't be so judgy. There's got to be a few hot bad boy bikers coming into your court, in need of a little spanking."

Sarah couldn't stand bad boys. She'd sworn them off after college for a very good reason: They were nothing but trouble. In fact, just looking at pair of leather pants made Sarah break out in hives.

"I'd rather become a nun," Sarah said, coughing out her words, trying not to laugh. "Maybe you're the one who needs a bad boy—you look like you could use a little hot man trouble in your life."

And, of course, another stupid image of Bennett Wade just had to pop into her stupid head. She sighed. "I think I already found one."

Sarah's smile dropped off. "Really? Who is he?"

Taylor was shocked that the thought had entered her head, let alone leaked out of her lips. "Oh. Would you look at the time? You're late for your next session." She pointed to the clock on the wall above the door.

Sarah's big blue eyes widened. "Oh crap. I am late." She grabbed her pursed and headed for the door. "You and I are not done with the conversation, Taylor!"

Taylor shook her head at herself. *Yes, we are so done with this topic.* Bennett Wade was trouble and she knew it. And there was no way in hell she'd ever get involved with a man like that.

After that really great lunch with Sarah, Taylor was starting to feel very optimistic about the way things had panned out. It was wonderful to be able to spend time with her friends and family, something she'd not gotten a lot of these past few years while living in Phoenix and constantly traveling. Being home, where the weather didn't cook you alive, was also heaven.

All right, maybe her emotional lift wasn't completely attributable to the weather or being back on her old stomping grounds. Accepting Bennett's offer had renewed her hope that HumanitE might have a chance. She simply needed to put Mr. Grinch in touch with his "inner-Taylor" as he'd called it—so cute.

That evening, she turned the dial on her car radio to NPR as she hit the metering lights on the Bay Bridge to go back into the city for the ball.

She wasn't really listening to the program, but was thinking more about the exact words she would use to start the conversation with Bennett before they commenced his leadership-style evaluation. *Bennett, I know you're used to doing things your way, but we need to establish some ground rules. . . .*

"And big news today from the industrial sector," said the announcer on the radio, his words filtering into the background of her thoughts. "Anonymous sources at Lady Mary Fragrances, the largest global manufacturer of perfumes and specialty personal care products, confirmed they are in discussions with Wade Enterprises for a possible merger. A spokesperson for Lady Mary refused to comment as did Bennett Wade, CEO of Wade Enterprises, but industry experts speculate the joining of the two large companies is a move by Wade Enterprises to diversify its holdings. And next up, we'll be discussing socks. Is wool making a comeback . . ."

Taylor turned off the radio and stared ahead at the road. *Merger? With Lady Mary? What the hell?* Lady Mary was an ex-client of hers. Actually, Taylor had dealt with Mary Rutherford's son, Chip—Mr. "I'll be heading your way, so why don't we have our meeting in Vegas. Over dinner. My treat." He had propositioned Taylor more times than she could remember. But Chip didn't run the company; dear old mom did. And Mary Rutherford was a well-known, outspoken supporter of women's rights.

So why in the world would she be talking to the world's biggest chauvinistic bully and producer of manufacturing automation about a merger? *Bennett Wade and Mary Rutherford are like oil and water.* As were their companies. Those two didn't even speak the same language.

Wait. Oh my God. Bennett lied to me. He lied to me! He'd said he wanted to evolve, implying that he wanted to be a better boss. But this merger was why he wanted Taylor's help. He couldn't care less about treating his people better or learning anything from her. This was all about trying to win over Mary Rutherford. *And speaking "her language."*

Taylor tightened her grip on the steering wheel, wishing it were Bennett's neck. He'd completely pulled the wool over her eyes. And he'd obviously lied because he knew she would refuse taking him on as a client for such a materialistic reason.

The air pissed out of her happy little balloon. There was no way she could work with him now. He didn't believe in her, in her company, or in anything but making money.

Motherfucking, rat bastard, turd face!

Taylor mentally censured herself. *Check the swearing, Tay. You will not swear. You will remove his testicles like a lady: with your bare hands and a smile on your face.*

Ten minutes later, Taylor pulled up to the Fairmont, one of San Francisco's most famous historic hotels on Nob Hill. "Keep it close," she said to the valet, handing over the keys to her red Audi. "I'm not staying."

All around her, guests in tuxedos and sequin ball gowns poured inside, stopping to pose for pictures with a photographer in the opulent lobby with its gleaming brown marble floors and ornate crown moldings.

Once past the bottleneck, she made her way to the 1920s-style ballroom where a shimmering crystal chandelier hung from the gold-trimmed ceiling, and an enormous golden "W" stood as a backdrop to the speech platform at the far end of the

floor. Off in the corner, opposite the bar, a swing band played
to an empty dance floor. Everyone in the crowded room seemed
too absorbed in mingling to even hear the music.

Her eyes scanned the crowd. *Where are you, you sonofabitch?* And to think, she'd started growing soft on him, believing there might actually be a heart somewhere underneath the
expensive suits and tight, gym-sculpted muscles that she knew
a man like him would surely have because he demanded perfection even from his own ass and abs.

*It's your own damned fault, Taylor. You were too busy ooh-
ing and ah-ing over him when maybe you should've been paying attention.*

Her eyes darted around the room and zeroed in on Bennett,
who stood out from the silver-haired crowd with his height and
thick head of brown hair.

She wove her way through the mass of people, and as she
approached Bennett she couldn't help noticing how perfect he
looked in a tux, all handsome and smiles, like he'd just walked
out of a wedding magazine. *Don't get distracted, Tay. Remember what he did—who he really is. A snake.*

He spotted her approaching, and his beautiful smile immediately dissolved.

Taylor felt a little satisfaction from that. Bastard didn't deserve to feel happy.

"Bennett, may I speak to you for a minute?"

The people surrounding Bennett made little noises as if they
were shocked or amused by something.

His eyes moved up and down her body, surveying her business attire. "Of course." He excused himself from his guests,
and they walked to the side of the room.

"Was there an issue finding a dress?" he said in a quiet, abrasive tone.

Yeah, there was. She'd needed to keep her mind clean out of the date-zone fantasies. A suit would keep her in check. Wearing an evening gown would not.

Taylor scoffed. "No. I wore a suit because I'm here to work. At least I was." She suddenly noticed the people Bennett had just been speaking to were looking over at them and laughing. "What's their problem?" And did he have to stand so close? He smelled really nice—fresh clean man mixed with something citrusy. It was distracting. Not to mention the way he towered over her five-seven frame, forcing her to look straight up at him, hurt her neck.

"I warned you to call me Mr. Wade," he replied.

"So?" *Wait. Stay on task, Taylor.* "Never mind. I'm here to tell you that I'm returning the check."

"Why?" He crossed his arms over his chest.

"Because you don't give a crap about anybody—you never have and you never will. That's why."

"That's a bit extreme. I merely happen to be very selective about whom I give my time and energy to, and I make no secret of that. What's brought about this temper tantrum, Ms. Reed?"

Temp—temper tantrum? Going to hurt him. Going to hurt him. "Don't pretend you don't know," she snapped, clenching her fists to keep them at her side. "And stop the holier-than-thou routine. It's offensive. But maybe you can't help it because that's just what you are: offensive."

His blue eyes twitched with irritation. "I'm truly at a loss as to what's brought on your dramatic eruption. Are you offended because I'd planned to send a car for you so you wouldn't have to worry about having a little champagne tonight? Was it because I know you lost your job and didn't think it fair to have you run out and spend a thousand dollars on a ball gown or—" His cellphone must've vibrated in his pocket because he reached inside and held up his index finger. "One moment," he said to Taylor.

The nerve of this guy! How dare he answer his phone when she was about to tear him a new one!

"Yes?" He listened for a moment. "This is a bad time, Mom. Can't we speak when you get here?" He listened again. "Why are you obsessing over these damned cookies?" He shook his head slightly. "Yes, that's interesting, but I have to go. Taylor and I are in the middle of something." He paused. "I'll let her know." He ended the call and returned his cell to the inside pocket of his tux. "Sorry about that, but my mother's been a little off lately so I thought I should take it. She sends her regards by the way. Now. Where were we?"

"*We* were nowhere," she replied. "Because I don't appreciate being used and manipulated merely so you can buy Lady Mary Fragrances. And tell your mother I said 'hi' back." That was nice of him to take her call.

"I will let her know." A wicked little twinkle sparked in his eyes. "So is Lady Mary what's got your self-righteous feathers ruffled?" He placed his hand on her upper arm. It was a gesture far too friendly for her taste. And she liked it.

She jerked back her shoulder, and he released his grip. "You're denying that you hired me to be some sort of . . . of . . . feminist tutor? Because I know there's no way a woman like Mary Rutherford would ever go into business with a man like you."

"Well, that wasn't very nice," he said cockishly and grinned.

Taylor snarled with her eyes.

Bennett sighed and dropped the smile. "Ms. Reed, I don't have time for this right now. As you can see I have a thousand guests to greet and the priority this evening is raising money for my charity. But if you stick around, just for another hour until I've given the speech, I promise to explain everything."

"I don't think so—"

"You've accused me of lying. The least you could do is provide me an opportunity to tell the truth." He smiled, but this time it was another of those genuine, charming smiles that felt like being hit with a hammer. A hammer made from a hot man in a tux.

Her knees went a little shaky, and she once again felt herself succumbing to the hope that she might find a real live beating heart inside his chest. *Dammit. I'm such a sucker.* "Fine. I'll stay for a little while."

"Good. I'll return shortly." Bennett turned and headed back into the crowd. Taylor remained where she was, watching with fascination how he entranced the guests with his smiles and charisma, reducing each person to a little glob of happy putty.

Once again, she just didn't know what to make of it. The man was such an enigma—one minute shrewd and calculating, the next warm and charming and so . . . *magnetic.* She couldn't figure him out.

Stop being such a stalker. Taylor pulled her gaze away and headed to the bar. At least she could have a drink in her hand or something to make her look less out of place.

As she stood waiting her turn, she felt a tap on her shoulder.

"Taylor Reed. What a surprise!" She turned and gave an internal groan. Or maybe it was more of a silent gag. It was Bennett's golf buddy and her ex-client from HRTech, Charles

Thorup. The guy owned the biggest chain of hotels in the world and thought he could own Taylor, too.

"Hi, Charles. How have you been?" she said politely, careful not to give off too friendly of a vibe. The last thing she wanted was to spend the next hour fending off his unwanted sexual advances.

"Not as good as you, I hear," he slurred his words and had a little bit of something—a piece of tomato?—stuck to the lapel of his tux. He also smelled like whisky, and his tufts of stiff brown hair were fighting against the unnatural flow of his comb-over.

"Sorry?" she said.

He leaned his bright red face toward her, placing his hand on her shoulder. "Why him, Taylor? What did the old B-man do?"

She blinked. "What are you talking about?"

He shook his finger in her face, laughing. "I tried every trick in the book, but you wouldn't even let me take you out for a drink. Come on. Tell me. What did he do?"

"Do for what?" she snapped.

"To get you to open those pretty little legs of yours."

Taylor froze. There were no words to express how offended she felt. She wanted to smack his stupid red face.

"I didn't sleep with him," she growled. "And you have no right to speak—"

"I was standing right there. You called him Bennett, and everyone knows only his mother and women he's fucking get to call him that."

Ohmygod. Is *that* what people thought every time she used his first name? No wonder everyone had been acting so bizarre. She suddenly recalled his words to Vera during that first meeting; in her defense, she really thought he'd only said that to make a point!

"I think you're drunk, Charles," she said. "And you should get the hell away from me before I do something I'll regret."

"Oh no, baby. I'm not leaving until I have an answer. I just had to hand the asshole a million dollar check for winning the race—gloating bastard!"

Taylor wasn't sure what she'd heard. Because . . . because . . . then that would mean . . . "A million dollars? For what?" She almost didn't want to ask, because if he'd meant what she thought he meant, there'd be no redemption for Bennett. No forgiving him, no excuse in the world he could give to explain such a horrible thing.

Charles swayed a little and grinned sloppily. "He took money from Robert, Clyde, Steve, Chip, and Blake, too."

Taylor's jaw dropped. Those were all names of her ex-clients. "You're telling me you guys all had a bet going?"

"The race into Taylor's pants," he slurred. "Or was it more like a marathon because it took forever for someone to win the pot?"

"I don't believe you," she said, horrified beyond words. Who would do such a thing?

"Why else would he go out of his way to *hire*—" Charles made air-quotes with his fingers "—you? Not for that stupid training program you've been peddling."

Taylor's pride crashed to her feet. Bennett Wade was just after her for some *fucking* bet? *No. No way.* But it explained everything; how he'd gone out of his way to track her down, why he'd insisted she spend the next two weeks traveling with him. It was all some big joke to him. A bet. As for Lady Mary, he probably didn't need her at all for his deal; but being the horrible, money-grubbing sleazoid that he was, he likely thought it wouldn't hurt to have her on Team Bennett. After all, she did know Mary and what Mary expected of people.

"I can't believe this," Taylor whispered to herself.

"Oh, come now, Mith Reed," Charles garbled. "You had to know. I mean . . ." He swayed again. The guy was wasted. "Why else would so many men sign on to be your clients at HRTech? And hey," he leaned close, his alcohol-breath wafting over her face. "Now that Bennett won, can I just pay for a fuck?"

Taylor slapped him as hard as she could, sending him reeling. "Why don't you go *fuck* yourself, asshole."

She turned and left, ignoring the stares of the people who had been standing near her, unsure if she was going to cry or kill Bennett Wade. *Both! This definitely calls for both!*

She hurried outside, her devastation spilling from every pore in her body. She wanted to go back inside and give Bennett Wade a taste of her knee. But that was too good for him. That would only produce a moment of pain. What he needed was to suffer. Suffer and endure the sort of humiliation she experienced at that very moment, knowing that those men had been laughing behind her back, using her for some sick, disgusting billionaire sport. She'd truly believed that she'd earned her keep at HRTech because she'd been good at what she did. She'd spent the last five years of her life living a lie. Then she'd gone out on her own, thinking she had a chance in hell to create her own business. No wonder she had failed.

She shoved her ticket and a twenty in the valet's hand so he'd hurry up. *I'm nothing but a joke. A fucking joke.* But the worst part was Bennett's role in all of this. He'd gone out of his way to become her client in order to win a bet. Then he'd actually let everyone believe they'd slept together so he could profit from her pain. She counted off the names Charles had listed in her head. Six. Six million dollars. That was the price tag for crushing her soul, pride, and dreams.

I am going to ruin him. Ruin. Him.

The valet pulled up in her car, and she slid inside. Suddenly, her brown leather purse vibrated. She glanced inside. It was a text on the Bennett phone.

Bennett: *Why did you leave?*

"Because you're a disgusting pig!" she yelled at the thing.

She was about to respond, but stopped her herself. *No. Don't say anything. Let him sweat it out.*

Bennett: *I'm coming to see you after the party.*

Taylor turned the phone off and threw it on the floor. *Then get ready, Mr. Wade, for a new kind of training. A program that will be Taylored just for you . . .*

CHAPTER 6

Taylor pulled her car behind Jack's BMW with its plates that read "Fix U" and wiped the tears from her face. She didn't want to alarm Jack or tell anyone what had happened. The humiliation was just too much. She'd lost everything. Hopes, dreams, self-esteem—poof! Just like that.

Well, at least you still have your health.

"Achew!" She launched a sneeze right into her hand. *Great. Just great.*

She slid from the car and went in through the front door. Jack sat on his couch with a beer in his hand, staring blankly at some baseball post-game whatever. "Hey, Jack."

He jerked his head, but didn't look at her.

She paused halfway up the stairs. "You okay?"

He didn't move. Something wasn't right.

She went back into the living room, and when his face came into view, she noticed the glazed look in his green eyes. His grease-stained Giants sweats were another bad sign.

"You're drunk."

"Yep." He continued staring at the TV.

Oh no. This was what Jack did when he lost a patient. He always took it hard. Always.

Taylor sat beside him on the pink, floral overstuffed couch. It was one of the many leftovers from his marriage, but Jack had refused to throw out perfectly good furniture even if the style was overtly girly—almost like Doris had been trying to overcompensate for who she really was. Not girly. Not even a little.

"What happened?" Taylor said.

Jack shook his head no. "She had two children—ten and twelve—and a husband."

Taylor placed her hand on his leg. There was nothing she could say that he didn't already know. Jack wasn't a rookie, and patients died sometimes. In his case, it was usually a reaction to the anesthesia, but it still happened from time to time. It was simply unavoidable. What made him great, though, was that he never stopped caring. It was what made him careful and extremely good at what he did.

"I've never seen a man cry so hard," Jack said with numbness in his voice. She knew he was trying to hold it together.

"You did your best, Jack."

"The weird part was I kept thinking to myself that the man was an idiot for loving her because they all leave. One way or another, they just . . ." He sighed. "Leave us."

Taylor leaned her head into his shoulder. "Well, I'm here for you. And I love you."

"Thanks. I love you, too, Tiger." He flashed a quick glance at her with his bloodshot eyes.

It was strange how she hadn't seen it before, but this divorce had really changed him. He never used to cry or say "I love you" back. It was always "Suck it up," "Don't let 'em see you sweat, Taylor." "Weakness is for losers." Of course, that had been years ago, but clearly she hadn't made an effort to stay close to him the way she should've. The same could be said for her father and other brothers. She really needed to fix that.

"Can I get you anything? Real food? Another beer?" She wasn't about to stand in the way of him getting hammered. Hell, she might even join him.

He shook his head. "No. I'm good."

The doorbell rang, jarring Taylor in her seat. Who could it be? She knew Mr. Two-Faced Loser had threatened to show up later, because—oh no, God forbid—she hadn't done as she was told and hadn't stayed at the party to hear more of his lies, but she'd only been home for ten minutes, and Bennett's event was far from over. Maybe it was Sarah or Holly.

"I'll be right back." Taylor pulled herself up from the couch and opened the door.

A simmering, tux-wearing Bennett stood there, his face an angry shade of red.

"Wh—what are you doing here?" Taylor stammered, shocked as hell. They were almost at eye level, with Bennett down a step and her in the doorway.

"Why did you turn off the phone?" he growled.

Taylor blinked at him. *Is he serious?* "You came all the way here, in the middle of your charity event, to ask me about the phone?" Her brother lived in the Berkeley hills—over the Bay Bridge and about thirty minutes away from the Fairmont.

The man is crazy. And, frankly, so was she. Crazy-peeved. Crazy-hurt. Crazy-vengeful. She felt inches away from losing it and telling him off, but then she reminded herself of the six million dollars, her public humiliation, and the whole hiding the Lady Mary deal.

Let's see how you feel getting used and having your world

smashed to pieces. When she was done with this guy, he might not be in ruins, but he sure as hell would think twice before ever doing something like this to another woman.

He ran his hands through his thick hair and blew out a breath, almost a sigh of relief. "I thought—and then I—fuck, never mind."

"You're not making any sense."

"I have to get back to the ball." He pointed at her. "But you and I aren't finished yet. I'll be back later." He turned and headed toward his waiting limo.

"Wait!" she scurried after him. "Where the hell do you think you're going? You can't come here like this, acting all crazy, and then run off."

He stopped short of the open car door where the driver stood, waiting for him to get inside. "Why did you leave the party like that?" Bennett asked, clearly displeased.

"I—I—well, I . . ." she couldn't tell him the truth. Then he'd catch on. But what did he think happened?

"And you've been crying. Why?" his eyes narrowed.

Taylor cleared her throat. "Oh. That. Um . . . well . . . my brother is a surgeon and," she pointed inside, "he lost a patient today. A mother of two. He takes it pretty hard—guess it made me a little emotional, too."

The hardness in Bennett's blue eyes faded away. "Oh." He glanced down at his polished black shoes.

Look at the size of that man's feet. I wonder if it's true what they say about—

"So that's why you rushed home." He placed his large hand on his waist and whooshed out a breath.

No, that wasn't why, and she felt a tiny tug on her insides for being dishonest with him, but too frigging bad. "Yeah."

"So you're not angry about Lady Mary?" he asked, looking back up at her.

Why the hell would he care? *And yeah, I am pissed.*

"Oh. That?" Taylor waved it off. "I overreacted. I'm sure your deal with Lady Mary has nothing to do with me."

"You're wrong."

"I am?"

Bennett pulled her away from the limo, out of earshot from the driver. "The truth is, I do need you to close that deal," he said softly. "However, I'm not at liberty to tell anyone details just yet—it's complicated."

Taylor wanted to smack those lying lips right off his beautiful face. "Sure." She shrugged. "Whatever. It's really none of my business. I'm just here to train you. Whatever you do with the material is your choice. After all, you're the customer."

Bennett frowned and then tilted his head as if suspicious. "Why aren't you snapping at me?"

"Huh?"

"It isn't like you to roll over."

How would he know what she was like? *Oh, because he slept with you. Dontcha know?*

"Why would I snap at you, Mr. Wade?" she said innocently. "There's nothing to snap about. You hired me. I'm going to help you. Your business is your business."

His eyebrow went up. "I'm Mr. Wade now?"

Taylor smiled pleasantly. "Yes. That's what you asked me to call you, right?"

The expression on his face was somewhere between distrusting and pleased. "I have to get back."

Taylor nodded. "Okay."

"I'll send the car for you in the morning at eight—we'll start then since I'm sure your brother needs you tonight."

That was thoughtful. *Don't buy into it, Tay.*

"Thank you, Mr. Wade. I appreciate that."

Bennett bobbed his head, still appearing a bit agitated. As he slid into the limo he looked at her with those penetrating blue eyes. "I think I'd prefer it if you call me Bennett."

But that's only for his mother and the women he's . . .

Taylor's mouth went dry, while her heart went roller-coaster wild. Knees? Oh, they were down there somewhere doing their own thing.

Wait. Don't you dare get all flustered! He only wants you to call him Bennett to keep up the charade for the bet he won.

"Okay . . . Bennett," she said in a controlled voice.

"And we'll be on the road for several weeks—pack accordingly."

"What? Where are we going?" she asked.

"Tokyo and Paris, then on to Bali. And Ms. Reed?"

He wasn't kidding about the intense schedule. That would be a lot of flying. "Yes?"

"Don't ever turn that phone off again. Got it?"

What was with him and the phone? *Stalker!*

"Yes, Mr. Wade."

Taylor caught a glimpse of the beautiful, horrible man scowling and shaking his head before the chauffeur closed the door. She stood there and watched the limo pull away, her mind a giant whirling mess. Dammit if he didn't have a way of getting under her skin even when she wanted nothing more than to see him suffer.

She turned and headed inside for her car keys. She'd go grocery shopping for poor Jack and make him a nice dinner. Then she'd pack and start creating her really awesome, specially "taylored" training program. Oh, yeah. Taylor knew exactly what pushed Mary Rutherford's buttons. It had been her job to hire people who worked directly under the woman, and Mary had very specific likes and dislikes. Before the two weeks were through, Bennett would have Lady Mary so turned off and annoyed that she probably wouldn't even take his calls.

Yeah, but think you can handle two weeks of chewing that jalapeño?

Of course, now that Taylor knew the truth, she need only remind herself how he'd profited—*six million dollars*—from her public shame, and allowed people to think they'd screwed. Then there were men like Charles who were always so busy trying to get in her pants they probably never even saw what fantastic work she'd done for them. She had a knack for reading people and gauging their fit for a particular role, and those men had benefitted from her skill. But all she was and all she'd ever be to them was a piece of meat, not a person.

Assholes.

The next morning, Taylor looked in on Jack before lugging her insanely heavy suitcase downstairs. Her brother was out cold and would probably have one heck of a hangover today, so she'd written him a note telling him there was Gatorade and ready-made salads in the fridge, and a ton of those healthy organic frozen meals in the freezer. She would call her father on the way to the airport to tell him to check in on her brother later.

When the doorbell rang, she expected to find a chauffeur waiting to take her to the airport. Instead, she found Bennett—

unshaven, thick bare arms crossed over his broad chest, hip thrown to one side, and dark shades covering his baby blues. He wore a wrinkled navy blue T-shirt and faded jeans and looked like he'd stayed up all night misbehaving. Probably with a few wild women, which would explain the hair. It was exactly the style he'd have if she'd been in bed with—

Tay. Really? This is how you're going to start out the two weeks?

"Rough night?" she asked.

He made a little grunt. "You ready?"

Taylor peeked out the doorway. There was a bright red Jeep—no top—parked on the street right out front. "Uh. Where's your driver?"

"I'll be traveling, so I decided to give him a few weeks off. That your bag?" His voice was low and deep, and a little rough, probably from lack of sleep.

Boy, aren't we in a good mood. She nodded, and he reached around to help her with it. "Let's go."

"Okay." She retrieved her purse from the chair right inside, closed the door, and followed Bennett. He threw her XXL rolling suitcase into the back with one arm and then opened the door for her.

Um. Wow. Without his usual suit covering his arms, she couldn't help notice his stacked biceps. And dammit if those soft, worn jeans didn't make his ass and thighs look like he was modeling for some rugged man kind of magazine. "So's . . . this is your car?"

"Doesn't meet your approval, Ms. Reed?" He looked her over before extending his hand to help her into the Jeep.

She'd worn a plain little black skirt, light pink sweater, and black heels. They were supposed to be working, so she thought it made sense to present the right image—business casual. After all, she needed to sell him a pile of horse dung today.

"What? My clothes don't meet *your* approval, Bennett?"

"Didn't say that." He inched his extended hand a bit closer, calling attention to the fact that he was waiting for her.

She hesitated for a moment, but took his chivalrous offer and climbed in. Touching him wasn't what she expected. Not cold or foreboding, but warm and tingle-provoking.

So what? I get the same feeling with my vibrator. She didn't really, but today was a good day for lying.

She settled into her seat and strapped in. He shut her door and made his way around to the driver's side where he grumbled something to himself and then mashed his full lips together in a line. The man was in one hell of a foul mood, and frankly, it made her feel uneasy.

Bennett started the engine. "Is there a particular reason you're staring at me, Ms. Reed?"

Oh, was she staring? Okay, she totally was. But the guy looked like he was about to bubble over. Then there was the fact he'd showed up himself to drive her to the airport, looking like this hot, rough-around-the-edges playboy who'd spent the night living the life of a bachelor without a care in the world. A complete contrast to the man she'd seen last night—in a tux, in control, in desperate need of an ego ass thumping.

"Sorry. I . . ." She looked away, but then decided she needed to get over feeling intimidated. "I'm wondering what the hell happened to you?"

"Nothing."

"If you say so *Mr. Wade*," she said.

"Bennett," he growled. "I told you to call me 'Bennett.' "

She shrugged. "I like calling you Mr. Wade."

His head whipped in her direction. "Can we not do this right now?"

"I don't know what you're . . ." That's when Taylor noticed a bit of purple bleeding out from underneath his glasses.

She leaned in closer to inspect and then reached for his shades. He didn't attempt to push her hand away when she slid them off. Underneath was a shiner—black, purple, blue, and red. "Christ, Bennett. Are you okay?"

"It's a black eye, Ms. Reed. And before you ask any more questions, I'll request that you don't—I'm not in the mood to talk."

The guy looked like he'd had one hell of a night—probably someone forgot to call him "your holiness" or "Mr. Wade, your awesomeness."

She nodded. "As you like, Mr. Wade."

He snatched his glasses from her hand, placed them back on his face, and threw the Jeep into first, screeching out into the street.

The cool morning air gusted through her hair as they hit the freeway on-ramp. Had she known they'd be four-wheeling it to the airport at eight in the morning, she would've worn something warmer and put her long hair in a braid. "Achew!" *Dammit, I am getting a cold.*

"Bless you," Bennett said without looking at her.

"Thank—blah-*pft!*" She spit a wad of her long hair from her mouth. "Thanks."

She remembered she had a few extra rubber bands and clips in her purse so she plucked it off the floor and began digging. That's when she noticed the news alerts on her cellphone. She'd set them up to tell her when anything about Bennett or his company came up. *Yes, I'm a stalker. But now I know we have that in common.*

She nonchalantly scrolled through them, reading quickly. *Bar Brawl at the Wade Ball?* What? She read on and the article said that Bennett had gotten into a fistfight with a Mr. Charles Thorup. Both men had been arrested for assault and public drunkenness.

Arrested? Taylor covered her mouth and bit down on her lips, stifling a laugh. *Ohmygod. I wish I'd been there to see that. Karma, you're my hero.*

She slid the phone into her purse. "So, what was the fight about?" Taylor asked with a smirk.

Bennett kept his gaze fixed to the road. "I said I didn't want to talk about it," he snarled. He accelerated into the fast lane.

You think I'm not going to rub this one in? He'd gotten into a drunken fistfight at his own charity event. *Public humiliation kind of sucks, doesn't it Bennett?*

"I'm sure you don't," she replied, speaking loudly over the engine, wind, and traffic, "but I'm spending the next two weeks with you. And frankly, I don't know you. I'm also a woman, and you're a big guy."

He glanced at her quickly with a sneer. "What are you implying, Ms. Reed?"

She shrugged knowing what she said next would piss the bejeebers out of the man. *Oh the joy.* "I'm not sure I feel comfortable traveling the world with a man who's prone to violence."

With utterly sadistic delight, she watched his jaw muscles pump away and the veins and ropes of hard muscles in his arms bulge out as his grip tightened around the steering wheel.

"Watch yourself, Ms. Reed. I'm not appreciating the tone."

"And I'm not appreciating yours," she replied. "You sound angry, and angry men do crazy things like fight—"

"Enough, Taylor. I had my reasons. That's all you need to know."

Taylor. He'd called her Taylor. Why did that make the old knees start doing their own thing again?

"Perhaps," he continued, "your time might be put to better use going over the training program with me."

Oh. With pleasure. First, I plan to take my awesome training program, pump it up full of some rather odiferous, fly-infested bull crap, and then cover it with rose petals and serve it to you with a big fat smile. How's that sound to ya, Bennett?

"That's an excellent idea, Mr. Wade. I have the program broken into four steps, starting with the client evaluation—we should be able to knock that out today. From there, we'll work with ten different modules, *tailored*," *harhar*, "to your needs, that focus on modifying your leadership style."

"And the other two steps?" he asked.

Oh, we won't ever get to those. You'll be too busy losing your mind, wondering where it all went wrong, because your deal fell through.

"Those will be practical application and then the final follow-up, which is really just a postmortem to see how the techniques are functioning," she replied happily.

"That sounds excel—" His phone buzzed in the cup holder. "Can you check that? I'm expecting a message from Robin."

"Uh, sure." Taylor grabbed the phone and looked at the screen. "It says, 'No phone number but I got an address.'"

"Dammit. Fine. Tell her to have a car ready at the Napa airport."

"Napa?"

"We're taking a quick detour before heading off to Tokyo. It should only take a few hours."

Taylor punched in the reply without indicating she wasn't Bennett. Robin quickly responded:

Will do, Mr. Wade. And thank you for last night. (Winky face.) Bonnie and I had great time.

Thank you for last night? Taylor repeated the words in her head. So he *was* sleeping with his secretary. And some woman named Bonnie. What other reason would there be for winky faces? A man like Bennett wasn't the type to chum around and trade emojis with his staff unless they had a very personal relationship. *What a predictable slime bag.* And he didn't even let Robin call him Bennett.

Thirty minutes later, they pulled into the private airport parking lot where the security guard greeted Bennett with a fist bump. "Skydiving today, Mr. W?"

"Not today, Dave. Just business," Bennett replied.

The security guard, a large man with black hair, glanced at Taylor and winked. "Whatever you say, Mr. W. Have a nice flight."

Bennett gave him a nod and they continued on into a large hangar. The door was open, so he drove right inside, parking his Jeep in the corner. Inside were six different planes—one about the size of a small commercial jet and several other sleek-looking models with longer, narrower bodies. They all said *Wade Enterprises* on the side.

"They're all yours?" she asked.

Bennett turned off the engine and got out. "I like planes."

"Ya think?" But honestly, having three older brothers and a

father who was crazy about cars—he had at least ten antiques—she knew all about boys and their toys. It didn't really surprise her.

He grabbed her suitcase from the back and effortlessly lifted it out with one hand. Once again, Taylor found herself watching with fascination as those biceps flexed into half-cantaloupe-sized bulges. *Oh, come on. That's not fair.* She also noticed that he wore a pair of well-loved brown leather boots that looked like something one might wear hiking through a jungle. Or while kicking the crap out of pompous a-holes named Charles.

The man is definitely sexy. Not that I care.

He plunked the bag down, extended the handle, and headed for the larger plane. Immediately, two blond women in pilot's uniforms appeared in the plane's doorway at the top of the stairs. *Of course! Lady pilots!* She bet he was dating them, too.

"Ladies, this is Taylor Reed—a consultant who's working with me on some coaching techniques." Bennett moved up the stairs and flashed a glance over his shoulder at Taylor. "Ms. Reed, these are Brianna and Joanne, my pilots."

"Oh, I thought you flew your own planes—with Frank."

"Short flights are one thing, but it's easier to let the ex–Air Force pros handle these longer trips. I need to get work done and get some sleep. Otherwise I'm shot by the time we land."

Ex–Air Force. Impressive. But weren't Air Force pilots supposed to be smart? Because smart women wouldn't sleep with this guy.

Taylor gave both women a smile as she passed them and went inside.

The first thing she saw was Candy's welcoming face in the forward galley. "Ms. Reed, so nice to see you again, honey!" She had a bottle of champagne uncorked, set in a silver bucket, and two filled glasses ready to go.

Candy shoved a glass into Taylor's hand and then handed one to Bennett, who plunked down in the front row, removed his sunglasses, and held the drink against his black eye.

"Oh, Mr. Wade," Candy said. "I heard all about it on the news. Let me get you some ice."

He held up his hand. "No, it's alright, Candy. Ice won't do anything at this point."

He sipped the champagne and then set it down on the little tray next to the seat. He glanced up at Taylor who still stood near the door holding a glass of champagne, dumbly gawking at his beautifulness.

"Well, Ms. Reed," he said. "We haven't got all day. Take a seat so we can get started."

The way Bennett had stretched out his long muscular legs, slouching a bit, made her realize he might have some bruised ribs too.

"You sure you're okay?" Taylor asked him.

"Fine. And in much better shape than Charles—asshole."

Taylor lifted her brows. She was definitely going to get the story from him before the two weeks were up. "Okay. Well, I'll get the questionnaire pulled up, and we can begin."

"Great." He nodded. "Hey, Joanne," he called out. "We need to make a quick stop in Napa."

"Yes, sir," she responded from the cockpit. "Anywhere you like."

It didn't escape Taylor's attention how these women were so ready to serve his needs, like they'd do it for free if he decided to stop paying them. *God, how could anyone worship this man?*

Thirty minutes later they were up in the air, and Taylor couldn't bring herself to wake Bennett. He'd fallen asleep within seconds of taking off. Frankly, he looked like he could use a quick nap, and she hadn't gotten very far on her fake training module last night, so she welcomed the extra time.

Bennett suddenly began mumbling. She couldn't make out the words, but he sounded angry, like he was yelling at someone.

What a surprise, the guy's a dick to people even in his sleep. "Don't let that bother you. He can snooze almost anywhere. He does it all the time." Candy stood a few feet from Taylor, smiling down at Bennett's masculine, scruffy face.

Taylor raised her brows. "Really? All the time?" How the hell did Candy know that?

Bennett's probably sleeping with her, too. Maybe the ladies on this plane are his traveling harem.

Candy went on, "Sometimes he groans like he's in pain. Sometime he mumbles random names or screams at his ex, Kate. But if I were you, I wouldn't bring it up; he gets very upset when anyone mentions his nightmares. Or his ex." So the guy suffered from nightmares about his ex, huh? She'd probably left him after discovering he had a lump of coal in place of a heart.

"So you spend a lot of time with him, then?" Taylor asked.

"Well, you know. We're together at least once a week. Sometimes it's an all-nighter. Sometimes, it's just a quickie." She winked. "But whatever the man wants, the man gets. More champagne, sweetie?"

Taylor tried to hide her shock. *A quickie? An all-nighter?* So Candy *was* his travel buddy slash booty call babe.

"No, thanks. I'm good. Champagne's not my thing for breakfast."

"Silly me. Where are my manners? It's just that Mr. Wade has a rule. Once on board, we all set our clocks and pretend we're already in our new time zone. Helps him acclimate faster to the time change—of course, it's almost 1 A.M. in Tokyo, so I suppose I should be serving scotch." She leaned in. "But would you like some coffee, dear? I'm sure Mr. Wade won't mind if you bend the rules a little."

"That would be great. Thanks."

Candy disappeared to the back of the plane, leaving Taylor alone to stare at Bennett who'd now settled down. His dark lashes fanned along the crease of his lids, his square jaw was thick with black stubble—except for the spot where he had the scar on his chin—and his lips were pursed into a sensual pucker. *How's that possible? The man is asleep and still looks sexy.*

And something about the way his size took up the space around him and his thick arms crossed over his chest left her unable to peel her eyes away.

Oh, get over it, Taylor. That man's had his wick in every candle from here to Timbuktu. Taylor pulled her laptop from her tote and got to work on "What Style of Leader Are You?" She planned to have Bennett answer a long list of situational questions and then give him some bogus profile of his strengths and weaknesses. *And what'll ya know, Bennett, you need to focus more on kissing ass.* Actually, not so far from the truth—he could do with being a little nicer—however, she had another angle.

Fact: Mary Rutherford loathed kiss-ups just about as much as she hated people who were fake. The woman was a straight shooter with a feather-light fist—meaning she never forgot her manners or lost her composure, even when she was removing someone's head. Metaphorically speaking of course.

Taylor hit the save button and glowed triumphantly at her work of art. *This is going to be so fun.*

Before she knew it, they were touching down in the small Napa Valley airport, surrounded by green rolling hills and endless miles of neat rows of vines. Candy gave Bennett a gentle nudge. "Mr. Wade, we've arrived."

Bennett cracked open his good eye and then rubbed his face with a groan.

No, you are not going to think about him pleasuring himse—Dammit! She thought about it.

Taylor turned her head toward the window, keeping her gaze firmly on a small tree standing at the edge of the runway. *Focus on the little tree. Nothing sexy there. Nope. Tree. Tree. Tree.*

"Sorry about that," Bennett said to Taylor, forcing her to look at him. "I didn't get much sleep last night."

Taylor gave him a polite nod. "No worries. I'm here to work on your sched . . ." her voice faded off as Bennett rose from his seat and folded his thick arms over his head, yawning and stretching. The hem of his T-shirt lifted away from the low-slung waistband of his jeans, exposing a dark happy trail of hair that started at the most beautiful man-belly-button ever and disappeared into his jeans, right above his substantial bulge.

Oh crap. Seriously? That's just not right. The man was perfect, right down to his navel. And the peek she'd gotten of his abs—well, she just knew that was only a prelude to the hard perfection hidden beneath his shirt.

"Ms. Reed?" Bennett said looking down at her with curiosity.

Oh no. I'm ogling him again. Taylor slowly peeled her gaze away from his lower torso and shamefully laddered up his chest.

When she met his eyes, he didn't look annoyed. Instead, the man gave her a little wink.

A wink? What's that mean? What's a wink mean, Tay? I hope he doesn't think I want him. Because I don't. He's a total jerk face. Wait. Oh, no. Does he think I want him? And that was him accepting? Oh no. He told everyone we slept together. So now he just wants to make good on that. Not gonna happen!

"We're not having sex," Taylor blurted out before she could process the real-life implications of saying something so ridiculous.

Bennett cocked his head, staring at her with an indiscernible expression. Then he burst out laughing with that deep masculine voice before turning toward the back of the plane where Candy had opened the rear door to disembark. Shaking his head the entire way, he disappeared out of sight.

Taylor covered her mouth, mortified. *I can't believe I just said that. I'm an idiot.*

"Ms. Reed?" Candy called out. "Mr. Wade wants to know if you're coming or if he should, and I quote, 'waste more of his valuable time on a woman who's not going to give him any?'"

Taylor's eyes went wide before she dropped her face into her hands. *Oh, the shame.* She stood, grabbed her laptop tote, and made her way toward the smirking stewardess.

Taylor flashed a sheepish smile when she passed. "It was a joke."

"Uh-huh." Candy nodded, stifling a laugh.

Taylor made her walk of shame down the portable staircase to the awaiting town car. She slid into the back where Bennett already sat, his head thrown back and his sunglasses on.

She glanced at him, feeling relieved that he'd apparently

dropped it already. But as she closed the door she heard a small chuckle radiating from his direction.

She glanced over and saw those tiny little dimples puckering.

"Stop. It's not funny." She swatted him on the leg.

"Like hell it's not." He removed his sunglasses and stared with those mesmerizing blue eyes.

Taylor looked away. This was so damned humiliating.

"Oh, come now, Ms. Reed." Bennett slipped his hand on her thigh. Whether or not he'd meant to comfort her didn't matter. His touch made her feel painfully aware of how long it had been since any man had gotten that close to her womanly parts. "How do you expect me to respond? I mean, I don't think I've ever had a woman shut me down like . . . *that*."

"Like what?" she scowled.

"When I hadn't even done anything—hell, the thought never even crossed my mind."

"Oh." Taylor looked away, adding "sexually shunned" to her list of embarrassments. "Well, for the record, I didn't think you had done anything. I was merely trying to make it clear that our relationship is strictly professional. It just came out the wrong way."

And seriously, given her track record of clients always hitting on her, who could blame her?

He chuckled again and scratched his rough, stubble-covered jaw. "You might want to rethink your little habit, then. That is, if you want to avoid giving men the wrong impression."

She didn't have to ask which "habit" he referred to. She already knew. The bulge-ogling.

Taylor turned her attention back to the safety of the window. The car had already hit the main road. She hadn't even noticed they'd left the small airport.

"Not that I find it offensive, Ms. Reed. After all, I am Bennett Wade—I have my fair share of admirers."

Wha-what a pompous—she turned her head back to sneer at him, but he'd already put his glasses back on and had his head tilted back, that large Adam's apple sticking out on his strong neck. For a very brief moment, she wanted to pet it. She found a man's apple very sexy.

"*For the record*, however, you're not my type," he added.

Taylor huffed and shook her head. *What a jerk.* "Yeah. I've seen your type. I'm not impressed." Actresses with fake boobs, models with fake smiles, his secretary—okay, Robin was nice, maybe Candy and the pilots, too. But the list went on and on.

He shrugged. "Last time I checked, my cock wasn't looking for your approval."

Taylor's mouth fell open. *What a pig.*

She slipped out her laptop and opened the file. Time to start dishing out a little sweet revenge to Mr. "my cock doesn't need your approval."

Ten or so minutes after departing the airport, a phone call—some news that riled Bennett—had put him wide awake. After a few moments, Taylor realized he was speaking to Robin about something related to Mary Rutherford.

"What do you mean, she said 'no'?" he growled into the phone, and then listened. "Yes, but was it a firm no or a soft no and what was her reason for not wanting to meet? I'm flying all the way to Paris just to talk about this deal—the Bali project is nothing without her."

What was the Bali project? *Probably some deal to take his harem lifestyle to the next level—probably wants to make it into a themed resort. Bennett Booty Land*. And he needed Lady Mary to keep all his women supplied with expensive perfume.

Taylor listened carefully, thinking this was the perfect time to give him a little "helpful" advice, such as: "Tell her she's not thinking things through" or "Tell her I know what I'm talking about."

The idea of being a fly on the wall when Mary received such a condescending message thrilled her. *On the other hand, the more strategic move would be to build Bennett's confidence in me*, making it easier to slide the bogus training right in a little later.

Taylor tapped Bennett on the shoulder and then held up her index finger.

He gave her an annoyed look. "One moment, Robin." He pulled the phone from his ear. "Yes, Ms. Reed?"

"Have you ever dined with Mary?" she asked.

"No. Why?"

Perfect. "Tell Mary you're not just coming for a meeting—that you want to have dinner afterwards, too, and Chip is invited—you're eager to see him."

"Why would I do that?" he asked.

Because while Mary was ruthless and shrewd when it came to doing business, she was also very old school and believed it was "bad manners" to only talk business. To her it demonstrated a lack of refinement. This is why she also preferred to meet candidates over dinner. She had once said to Taylor, "You can tell a lot about a person by the way they use a fork." So she probably wouldn't be able to resist assessing Bennett's table manners. As for Chip, despite his man-whoring ways, he was her pride and joy, which is why she allowed the incompetent fool to help her run her company. However, he barely spent any time with her. Chip's favorite thing to do was complain about how Mary was always guilt-tripping him. And finally, Taylor suspected that Chip had a big love-hate man-crush on Bennett. He used to drop Bennett's name all the time. It was clearly some weird, competitive hang-up.

Anyway, if Bennett was inviting, Chip would want to go. And if Chip went, Mary would want to go, and dinner fit right in with her way of doing things.

Taylor glanced at Bennett. "Just do it. I promise it will work," she lied, because she only *hoped* it would work.

He looked skeptical, but told Robin to relay the message to Mary's assistant and ended the call. "All right, Ms. Reed. Let's see if you're correct."

Taylor smiled smugly, trying to hide her doubt. "You'll see." *I hope, I hope, I hope.* "In the meantime, since you're now wide awake, why don't we do a little work? I thought we could start out with this questionnaire. From that, I can tailor your training modules."

"As you like, Ms. Reed," he said coolly, his eyes still hidden underneath his shades.

"Okay. Before we begin, I'm going to warn you that some of the questions might seem a little strange, but I assure you they're targeted to ferret out particular characteristics—strengths and weaknesses."

"Proceed," he said, seemingly uninterested.

"Great. First question. You are a farmer and need to supplement your income. You can either raise animals for meat or for their byproducts—milk, eggs, cheese, and such. Raising animals for food is more profitable, but then you have to slaughter them and hire the appropriately experienced staff whose skills are specialized. Raising animals for by-products is less profitable, but you have access to a larger labor pool, and it doesn't involve killing. Which do you choose?"

It didn't matter how Bennett answered; later in the evaluation phase, she'd turn it around to highlight how he should follow her new and "very effective" people management techniques that would have Mary Rutherford seriously questioning the idea of partnering with someone who annoyed the hell out of her.

He lowered his head. "I would choose neither and focus on diversifying my crops. There's less risk and raising livestock requires much higher overhead—feed, veterinary care, and sterile processing conditions."

"But that wasn't a choice," Taylor argued. "It's A or B, not C—make up your own answer."

He bobbed his head, thinking it over for a moment. "Can I outsource the meat processing? The risks and insurance costs to my farm would be lower if I didn't have to do it in-house."

Taylor shook her head. *This guy* . . . "Fine. You can outsource the meat processing."

"I'll go with that answer then—higher profit. But I'd only buy cows and chickens so I could convert the animals to egg and milk production at a later date if those markets shifted and became more profitable."

Taylor shook her head and marked his answer in her computer. "Okay, Mr. CEO. Next question: You're on a sinking ship with fifty people on board. There are only two life rafts, each with enough space to hold twenty. Everyone has agreed to put you in charge of figuring out who is saved. Your choices are: A. lottery. Or B. Women, children, and elderly first."

"Why are there only two rafts?" he asked, sounding exaggeratedly irritated.

Jeez. It was just hypothetical. It was good that he took this seriously, but still.

"I don't know, there just are," Taylor said.

"Because the first thing I'd do is kill the son of a bitch in charge of life rafts. Did the world learn nothing from the *Titanic*?"

"The *Titanic*?"

"Yes, the *Titanic*. You might have seen a movie about it. Sinking ship, tragic love story, a classic."

He likes the movie Titanic? *This guy?*

"I've *seen* the movie," she said crossly. "I just don't know what it has to do with the questionnaire. You're supposed to answer A or B."

"But neither works," he argued. "At the very least, I would try a little harder to save more people. For example, what's the water temperature? If it is above sixty, I would probably select those with less body fat, plus the children, to go into the rafts. People with more body fat can last longer in cooler water. Anything below sixty would probably kill most people in a few hours regardless so there's no point going that route."

Taylor sighed with exasperation, pinching the bridge of her nose and thankful they weren't doing this for real. She could see that Bennett had a difficult time simply accepting options that were handed to him.

Probably why he's so successful—the man doesn't believe in settling.

"What?" Bennett shrugged. "Your questions are flawed—not my fault."

"The point is to *choose*. I purposefully make the answers polarizing so I can—"

"So you can put me into a little box of stereotypes? Because that won't work, Ms. Reed. I don't fit into any molds. *That* I can promise you."

She didn't doubt *that* for a moment.

"No," she argued. "It's about your style, your tendencies, your instincts. And I'm not trying to put you in a little box, I'm simply trying to establish where you are so we can determine where you need to go. Think of this as our map."

He turned his entire body in her direction. "Why don't you try asking me some real questions, Taylor? Ask me who I hire or why. Ask me what I expect of my people, and how I reward them. Or why don't you ask them what they think about me?" He seemed agitated, but she didn't understand why.

"Did I say something wrong, Mr. Wade?" A little tick of guilt flicked at her stomach. Strange that upsetting him made her feel so bad when it should be the opposite.

His frown melted away with a deep breath. "No. My apologies. I have a headache, and it was a very rough night. Maybe we should resume once I've had some real sleep."

"Sure. Whenever you like."

"Looks like we're here, anyway," he said.

Taylor leaned forward to get a better view. They were in downtown St. Helena, the heart of wine country. She had been here a few times, wine tasting with Sarah and Holly. "Why are we here?"

"I need to pick something up. I'll only be a moment." He slipped from the car and disappeared through a flower-covered archway and down a little path that ran between a clothing boutique and small olive oil shop. A sign on the side of the building read "Happy Pants Café, Right This Way." An arrow pointed in the direction Bennett had gone.

That's weird. She remembered seeing a Happy Pants

something-rather sign at a café in Seattle, right when Bennett had first called. It was the type of thing you'd forget.

She pulled out her phone and Googled the café. Oddly, they didn't seem to have a website or any contact information, but there were pages and pages of blog posts about it, and one article in the *San Francisco Tribune*.

Taylor opened it up and started reading. According to the reporter, a Harper Branton, the café started out as a simple bakery run by a widow from Mexico, Ms. Luci Leon-Parker. Over the years, the café gained notoriety for having a sort of love charm in their sugar cookies. "One bite. Seven days. And true love will be yours."

Taylor laughed, wondering what the hell Bennett wanted with some silly Cupid cookie.

She went on to read the rest of the story, which explained that the recipe was a family secret and that all of the cookies were baked right here in this St. Helena shop, but that they'd recently expanded distribution to ten cities in very limited quantities. *People wait in line for as long as seven hours to get their mouths on one of these treats that are just as delicious for the soul as they are for the taste buds,* said the article.

Bennett opened the door and hopped in, looking more pissed off than he had all morning.

"Back to the airport, sir?" the driver, a thin man in his forties, asked.

"No, actually, take me to this address." Bennett handed the man a slip of paper.

"Very good, sir."

The car pulled out into the street and headed east, away from town.

Taylor hated to ask, but the temptation was too much. Had

Bennett gone in search of a "love" cookie and come back empty-handed? Wouldn't any person in their right mind absolutely need to know that?

"Everything all right?" she asked.

"Yeah, the shop is closed, but I got the owner's address from one of the staff."

"They gave you the owner's home address? How'd you manage that?"

"I asked."

"Are you sure it's okay just to show up at someone's house unannounced like this?"

"I'm Bennett Wade. Not some random stranger."

Taylor huffed. "Your name isn't a free pass to invade people's privacy or go knocking on their doors to do business just because you want something and can't wait for the store to open." *How rude!*

"But isn't it?" he said in that deep, smug tone she hated.

Taylor shook her head. "Okeydokey." This was the perfect moment to start his educational detour, but he seemed to be sabotaging himself just fine. Any business owner in their right mind would chew Bennett out for showing up unannounced like this.

The car traveled down a long straight country road that cut between miles of grape vines. The late morning sun gave off a deliciously crisp light, just perfect for sitting outside and reading a good book or pruning vines, which was probably what her brother Rob was doing at this very moment.

"Do you like wine, Ms. Reed?"

"In my family, we don't have a choice. My brother works up the road; he's a viticulturist."

"I thought you said he was a surgeon?"

"That's Jack, the youngest of my three older brothers. Rob is the middle of the three; he's the wine fanatic."

"And the oldest? What does he do?" Bennett asked.

"Marcus is a semi-pro racecar driver. He wants to go pro, full-time like my father."

"Your father drives for NASCAR?" Bennett actually sounded excited.

What was the big deal? Just a bunch of sweaty dudes driving around in a circle in really expensive cars. "He's retired now."

"What's his name?"

"Nick."

"Your father," he said with disbelief, "is Nick Reed? *The* Nick Reed?"

Taylor refrained from rolling her eyes. She loathed telling people who her father was because then came the twenty questions—does he ever let you drive his car? Can I get a free ticket to the Indy? And then . . .

"Your mother was Patty Reed, the actress," Bennett said.

And there's why I hate talking about my family. Her mother had died giving birth to her. She didn't feel guilt about it anymore, but she had for a long, long time. The part that she'd never been able to overcome, however, was how people talked about her mother as if they knew her. *She* didn't even know her mother so how could they? It was weird, but it made her mad. Then there was the other irksome fact that everyone in her family was a superstar: NASCAR celebrity, actress, surgeon, NASCAR star in the making, and award-winning viticulturist. She was just . . . Taylor. Ordinary, if not leaning slightly toward the "underachiever" category, a fact she had been acutely aware of growing up. Her brothers and father loved her in their own way, but they didn't hold back when it came to telling her she wasn't trying hard enough or being tough enough. Sometimes, around them, it had seemed that being a caring female was a crime. She'd never forget their faces when she'd announced she wanted to pursue Human Resources as her career.

"Yes," Taylor finally replied. "My mother was Patty Reed, but she died when I was born. I never really met her."

Bennett gave her a look that was compassionate, but couldn't be described as pity, which she appreciated. She hated it when people pitied her. Despite the challenge of being the only female in a house full of very manly men, she hadn't grown up without love. Sure, she wished her mother had been there, especially during her adolescent years, but Sarah and Holly helped fill some of the female void in her life growing up.

"Well," Bennett said, "that explains where you got your good looks and fast wit." He looked out his window but didn't ask anything further.

Taylor couldn't believe he'd paid her a sincere compliment. Or that he'd let the family topic go. No one ever did that. Not ever. They always wanted to dig and pry and know everything.

Well, it's not like he's a stranger to actresses and fame. After all, the guy showed up on the Forbes List each year and the tabloid slash gossip magazines each week with a new perfect ten on his arm.

The town car turned down a dirt road, passing a tractor and several pastures with grazing horses. At the end of the road was a large, two-story, renovated farmhouse with big green shutters and a huge wraparound porch.

"Wow. That's just gorgeous," Taylor said. Maybe she should get into the baking business.

"I'll be right back," Bennett said, once again leaving her behind in the car. She watched him knock on the door. An older woman with long silver hair pulled into a bun answered with a kind smile.

Taylor watched Bennett's arms move as he spoke, the woman smiling warmly and listening closely before shaking her head no and closing the door in Bennett's face.

Taylor chuckled. "Oh. But I'm Bennett Wade," she said quietly in a low, mockingly deep voice, "coming to grace you with my presence."

"Sorry, ma'am?" asked the driver, glancing at Taylor through the rearview mirror.

"Nothing. Was just mumbling to myself."

Bennett scratched the back of his head and started back toward the car.

"No luck, huh?" she said when he got back inside, feeling totally satisfied with herself. Why hadn't he listened to her? *Oh, I know. Because he's "Bennett Wade."*

"Says she doesn't do business from her home, and that they're all sold out anyway."

Taylor bet that if he'd asked nicely, the woman might've pointed him toward one of the bakeries they shipped to. But of course, he didn't ask, he demanded and got nothing in return.

"Who is this for anyway?" Taylor asked, wondering what excuse he might come up with to hide the fact he was desperate for a "love" cookie. *Maybe he wants his ex back.*

"My mother. She's been raving about these cookies and tomorrow is her birthday. I took her out to her favorite restaurant a few days ago and got her a nice bracelet, but I thought I'd send her some cookies too since they're apparently her new favorite. Honestly, I don't know what's so special about them. Robin ate the one my mother sent and said it was just a sugar cookie with a happy face on it."

The cookie was for his mother? Now she felt bad that he hadn't gotten one. But . . . did he realize that his mother was apparently trying to play the matchmaker?

He added, "She hasn't been herself lately. I thought it might cheer her up."

Okay. Now she *really* felt bad. He'd literally detoured his entire business trip just to get his mom a cookie.

"Here, let me talk to the woman." Taylor crawled over Bennett's lap, realizing the moment she shoved her ass in his face that she could've gone out her side of the car and walked around. *Oh well. Let him look at what he can't have.*

"It's not going to work. That woman is a stubborn mule," Bennett warned, not seeming to mind the physical intrusion one bit.

"I happen to speak fluent stubborn mule; case in point, you understand me perfectly."

Taylor approached the porch and rang the bell. After a few moments, the door swung open revealing the same older woman. "Listen here, young man," she said sternly with a thick accent, "I've already told . . ."

"Hi. I'm so sorry to disturb you, Ms. Luci. My name is Taylor Reed, and I would never, ever dream of doing something like this. But my . . . uh, friend there—Bennett Wade—he's kind of an asshole and is used to getting his way. Normally I'd say he deserves to get the door slammed in his face. But he really only wants a cookie for his mother—it's her birthday tomorrow, and she's a fan of your delectable treats." Taylor offered her most winning smile.

The woman quirked a brow while her eyes sized Taylor up. "Did you say Bennett Wade?"

Taylor nodded.

"*The* Bennett Wade?"

"Yeah?" she said in a so-what tone.

"Won't you come in, dear? You can invite Mr. Wade in, too." Ms. Luci leaned around Taylor and waved Bennett over.

Sonofabitch! The high and mighty bastard had been right; he really did get what he wanted by saying his name. He probably just hadn't gotten the chance to introduce himself when he'd made his earlier attempt.

Bennett exited the car and walked over.

"Mr. Wade, thank you for coming all the way to my home. It's such a pleasure to meet such an important man. I'm very sorry about before."

Seriously? This is annoying.

Bennett and Taylor followed Ms. Luci inside.

"What did you say earlier about that 'free pass,' Ms. Reed?" Bennett whispered to Taylor from behind, taunting her.

She shrugged. She would not give him the satisfaction of saying he was right.

"Well, thank you, Ms. Reed," he whispered. "Whatever it was you said, the point goes to you this round."

"Didn't realize we were keeping score," she whispered back.

"What's the purpose of living without winning?" he retorted.

They entered Ms. Luci's traditional country-style kitchen—white cupboards, big butcher-block counters, ceramic rooster ladle holder, and an oval table in the corner large enough for eight—but with top of the line professional appliances, including several banks of ovens.

"Who are they?" An older man was seated at the table. He had leathery, sun-beaten skin and an enormous mustache and was wearing a turquoise cowboy hat and red cowboy boots.

One eye protruded slightly and moved out of sync with the other while he studied them.

Then, something moving near his feet caught Taylor's attention.

"Oh. It's a . . . pig," Taylor said. "In the . . . kitchen." She seriously hoped they did all of their baking at the shop.

The pig gave a loud snort.

"No," Ms. Luci said, shooting a caution-filled glance at Taylor. "That is Muffin Top, Sebastian's dog." She winked.

"Uh . . ." Taylor glanced at Bennett who had on a poker face. How the hell did he do that? Zero reaction to this strangeness. Zero. "Sorry. It's a . . . very nice dog?"

"Sebastian," said Ms. Luci, "this is Taylor Reed and Bennett Wade. They've come for a cookie."

"We just shipped out the last batch to Houston," he said. He also had a thick accent. "We won't have more until—"

"Sebastian," Luci interrupted sweetly, "be a dear and go into the pantry. Bring me out the tins I've set aside for the Sunday brunch we're giving."

Sebastian's one big eye got bigger. It was not pretty. "But those are for—"

"Now, you know I made a few extra," she said. "So we'll just borrow one and—oh—can you grab those chocolate nutty wafers, too? They're in the red tin next to the jams."

Grumbling something about "puercos" and "mujeres" Sebastian disappeared behind a door at the far end of the kitchen next to the refrigerator. The pig just sat there staring at Taylor as if waiting for a treat.

Ms. Luci leaned in and whispered, "Sebastian was kicked in the head by Miss Happy Pants, our horse, so we try not to upset his pig—it thinks it's a dog."

That makes . . . well, no sense, but okay. And now she was wondering if the horse was named after the café or if it was the other way around. It was a pretty unusual name for a bakery. And a horse, too, now that she thought about it.

She made a quick mental note to Google the café again later.

"Sure. No problem. It's a dog. By the way, your home is lovely, Ms. Luci," Taylor said.

"Thank you, dear. I spend winters at my ranch down in Tecate, Mexico, but this is our home from spring until our gran fiesta in July."

"Oh, that sounds lovely."

"It is, my dear. A thousand people come from all over the world for my party. In fact, I think you should both come."

"We couldn't impose, Ms. Luci," said Bennett firmly.

Luci narrowed her dark eyes at Bennett, then reached into a drawer next to her sink, pulled out an envelope, and shoved it at him. "I. Insist," she said coldly.

Bennett looked at the invitation. "I'm not sure that July is—"

"You want cookie. You come to party," Ms. Luci added.

Taylor so loved, loved, loved this very strange woman.

"We'd be honored, Luci." Taylor snagged the invitation. "Both of us." She looked at Bennett. "Wouldn't we?"

Bennett looked at Ms. Luci. "Listen, I am a charitable man." He reached for his cellphone. "I'll have my assistant Robin send you a check and add a thousand to it for your trouble, or for your fundraiser or whatever you need."

Taylor watched the indignation sweep over Luci's face.

Uh-oh. I think you just lost your cookies, big boy.

"I see why you have a black eye," Luci said.

"Meaning?" he said.

"Meaning, child, that your money is no good here. And the price for my baked goods just went up."

Taylor held back a chuckle. *Looks like Bennett finally met his match.*

Bennett stared at Luci expectantly as Sebastian emerged from the pantry with two tins.

"Here they are, Luci . . ." He trailed off as he noticed the two forces of stubborn nature at odds with each other across the kitchen island. He set down the cookies, and his one big eye moved back and forth between the two. "Did I miss something?"

Luci nodded but kept her eyes glued to Bennett. "Mr. Wade has just graciously volunteered to work at our gran fiesta."

Bennett replied, "I did not say—"

Taylor stepped on Bennett's booted foot. "Yes. Thank you. We'd love to help and thank you so much for the cookies, Ms. Luci. And for inviting us into your lovely home." *With the weird pig.*

Bennett mashed his lips together.

Ms. Luci smiled. "My pleasure, *niños*." She opened one of the tins, and pulled out two large cookies. One she placed inside the red tin. The other she slid inside a small sandwich bag from her drawer and handed to Taylor. "This one is for you, dear. And this tin of chocolate cookies is for your mother, Bennett. Please tell her I send my regards and hope her health improves."

Taylor noticed that Ms. Luci got a pass on calling him Bennett. Maybe his little rule had more exceptions than he let on.

"How did you know she's not feeling well?" Bennett asked, his eyes narrowing.

Ms. Luci's mouth twisted a bit. "Uh . . . you must've mentioned it."

"I don't recall that," Bennett replied.

Ms. Luci shrugged innocently.

Time to go before Bennett says something rude again. "Have a wonderful day, Ms. Luci." Taylor nodded to Sebastian. "Nice to meet you and your . . . Muffin Top. See you both at the party."

Bennett grumbled a sad little version of "thank you" and followed Taylor out with the cookie tin in his hand.

Once inside the car with the door closed, Taylor was about to comment how she felt like they'd walked into a funny farm when Bennett let loose. "I'll thank you not to make social commitments on my behalf."

"You're welcome, Bennett," Taylor snapped. "And it's not like you have to go. People cancel on parties all the time."

"I'm a man of my word. If I say I'll be somewhere, I'll be there."

Taylor shrugged. "Well, guess you're going to Luci's party and serving drinks then."

"I'm goddamned Bennett Wade. I'm not going to wait on people."

It was so strange looking at Bennett; with his black eye, faded jeans, muscled frame stretching his soft T-shirt, and his dark unkempt hair, he was the very picture of a rugged, sex-in-boots bad boy. But his attitude still wore that tailored suit. It was like the damned thing was part of him.

"Oh, relax," Taylor said. "I'm sure she has other things they need help with—parking cars, scrubbing toilets, walking the pig. You know."

"Don't get smart with me, Ms. Reed, because you're going, too."

"I think it will be fun . . ." Taylor's train of thought was interrupted as Bennett grabbed her cookie and broke off a piece.

"Hey! That was mine," she complained as he chewed.

He shook his head and handed the uneaten portion back.

"Gee, *thank* you," she said bitterly.

Then she remembered the article and found herself staring at the thing, then at Bennett, then back at the cookie.

She was going to be with Bennett for the next seven days. And he had just eaten a piece of the cookie.

Oh, come on. You don't believe in that kind of crap. To prove it to herself, she also broke off a piece and popped it into her mouth. "Hmm . . . pretty good, but I'm not feeling anything." She handed the cookie back to Bennett. "Here I think you need the love cookie more than I do."

Bennett gave her a dark look with those big blues.

Oh, this was going to be fun. "Didn't you know? According to the article I read in the paper, anyone who eats one of these falls madly in love within seven days. Ms. Luci has this whole cult following because of it. And that party is really a giant wedding for everyone who's fallen in love that year."

He blinked at her, clearly very irritated. "Are you telling me that I just took two hours out of my busy schedule to get love-voodoo cookies for my mother?"

"Who do you think will be the lucky man?" Taylor asked, toying with him.

"But she's . . . she's . . ." He made a manly grumble. "Never mind."

"Oh! That's right. She got *you* the cookie! I remember now: the day of the crash, she said, 'tell Bennett to eat the cookie.'" Taylor smirked. Rubbing this in was so much fun. His mother thought he was a giant relationship loser.

It was exactly what her family and friends thought about her. No they'd never come out and said it, but the subject of her not having a boyfriend worked its way into almost every conversation.

"Oh, you think you're funny, Ms. Reed?" Taylor suddenly felt the soft chewy cookie smashing into her face. Not so hard that it hurt, but it wasn't so pleasant either. She gasped and pushed Bennett's hand away. He was laughing, trying to get the cookie into her mouth. "Well, here's your cookie!" She squealed and bits of cookie flew everywhere.

"No. I don't need anyone," she said in a deep mocking tone, laughing her words. "I'm Mr. Wade. Get that thing away, you horrible woman!" Her voice cracked doing her best Bennett Wade impression. "Must I write you a check?"

"I won't sleep with you, Mr. Wade," he said, in falsetto, still trying to maneuver a chunk of cookie into her mouth. "But I like staring at your pants!"

Her eyes went wide, and she gasped. "Oh! You did *not* just say that."

Grinning, he nodded. "Oh yes. Indeed, I went there," he said in his normal voice. "Whatever will you do, Ms. Reed?"

She palmed a chunk of cookie that had landed near her hand and pounced. "This!"

He caught her arm and pushed it aside. Suddenly she realized her body was stretched halfway over his, their mouths only inches apart.

His smile melted away, and his gaze flashed from her eyes to her lips. Conflict ripped through her at lightning speed. Her gazed flittered to his lips and back to his hypnotic pale blue eyes.

Then it happened. Before her brain could scream at her to jump away or say how sorry she was for laying her body over his, he closed the gap and kissed her.

CHAPTER 7

Taylor had no idea if a man like Bennett Wade often did impulsive things. But she knew this kiss and the way he possessively gripped her upper arms to keep her from moving away fell into that category. Maybe he'd regret it later. Maybe he wouldn't. But the fact was he'd done it, and now it couldn't be undone. The other fact was that no man had ever kissed Taylor like this before. Not once.

Leave it to Bennett Wade and those full, sensual lips to deliver a kiss so soft yet so demanding that she couldn't breathe for three whole seconds. He didn't kiss her with his tongue or move his hands. He simply held his mouth to hers, allowing her to feel the heat of his lips penetrating her delicate skin. Or perhaps it was the other way around. Maybe it was Bennett who wanted to savor the warmth of her lips.

Didn't matter.

He'd not dipped her, touched her, or made any move other than to press his beautiful mouth to hers, and it undid her.

Com. Plete. Ly.

Every nerve ending in her body, especially the recently neglected lady parts, lit up like Fourth of July sparklers in serious need of waving. Her thighs clenched together, her skin exploded with little tingles, and her breasts began aching for his touch.

How long they stayed like that, intimately sampling the texture and heat of each other's lips, exchanging the breath from their bodies, she didn't know, but she instantly knew it was the sort of kiss a woman would remember for the rest of her life.

"Sir?" The driver coughed softly. "Sorry to interrupt, but are we heading back to the airport now?"

Bennett slowly pulled away, his piercing gaze fixed on hers for several long moments as she slid off him, completely in shock. That had been one hell of a kiss.

"Yu-yu," he cleared his throat, and twisted his body to face forward again, his expression reminiscent of a deer in headlights. "Yes. Back to the airport now. Thank you," his voice came out all scratchy and husky.

Taylor swiveled to face forward, too, scooting a few inches toward her door to put a bit of separation between them. Meanwhile, her heart slammed against her rib cage and her mouth watered like she'd just inhaled the scent of fresh warm bread straight from the oven. Then there was the place between her legs. Dammit. The man hadn't even used tongue with that kiss, yet she'd felt completely worked over. *I think there's steam coming from my panties.*

Staring forward, her mind a fog, she whooshed out a breath. "What was that?" she asked, refusing to make eye contact, and thoroughly afraid of what she might do if he happened to look as blown away as she felt.

"I don't know," he said, stiffly. "But it never happened."

"Nope. Never happened," she agreed.

Yeah, but it did.

Out of the corner of her eye she saw him slide on his glasses, cross his arms, and lean back his head.

Taylor didn't take offense. If she had remembered her sunglasses, she'd be hiding behind them, too.

He's right. That never should've happened. Never. And they didn't have any convenient excuses. There was no liquor, no near catastrophe—like a plane crash that sometimes heightened people's emotions—no nothing. It was nearly eleven in the morning and except for a little sleep deprivation, they'd both been of sound mind.

And I completely loathe the despicable man. It must've been that odd house. Or the cookie. Not that she believed for a moment it had supernatural powers. *Ridiculous.* But the mind worked in mysterious ways, and clearly they'd both—on a subliminal level—been thinking about falling in love. Sure, if there were a cookie that could magically summon your special someone like in a fairytale, how wonderful would that be? But that wasn't real. Real was waiting and dating. Then waiting and dating some more until you gave up or finally . . . *settled*.

Oh, crap. She resisted covering her mouth. *He's right. I'm a settler.* He'd said that about her yesterday in his office, and he'd been right. No she hadn't settled yet, but she'd been planning to. She'd planned to meet some guy who was nice enough, and when ready, she'd "settle" down. Not passion down. Not head-over-heels down. Settle down. No wonder she was avoiding relationships like the plague, focusing entirely on her career instead.

And now her true desire—to find someone who made her feel like she was being carried off on a ride filled with peril and lust and discovery and triumph and failures and crazy hot love—had bubbled to the surface.

Okay, maybe I'm not a settler. I just didn't know what I wanted.

But now she did. Not with Bennett, of course—the man was a player, not a stayer, and she loathed him. But he'd given her a glimpse into her own heart's desire.

Seven days, huh? Well, I will be traveling. That meant she'd be meeting a lot of new people, right? Taylor decided to keep an open mind. What was there to lose?

Bennett's phone suddenly went off, jarring her from her thoughts. He tipped the phone toward his face, read whatever message was on it, and then tilted his head back again. After several moments, he finally said, "It worked. Mary accepted."

Taylor grinned proudly. "You're welcome."

Is the man all right? Taylor squinted at Bennett sleeping in the reclined seat, but with the dimmed airplane cabin lights, it was difficult to tell. He kept mumbling the name "Kate." No actually, it wasn't a mumble, it was more like a growl. Candy had said Kate was his ex, but he also kept repeating a sad-sounding word she didn't recognize: waya or wayang? She didn't know, but every time he said it, something tugged at her heartstrings.

On the other hand, she was a firm believer in reaping what you sowed, and he'd clearly done this poor Kate some wrong and felt bad about it. *Maybe?* Taylor returned to her laptop; she had been taking advantage of Bennett being asleep by doing some work on her fake training course, but now she wanted to snoop.

She pulled up her web browser and typed in "Kate and Bennett Wade," but nothing came up. That only piqued her curiosity even more. *Maybe I'll ask him?* On the other hand, Candy had said it made him angry when anyone mentioned his nightmares or his ex, so he probably wouldn't open up.

And you're not here for that. Back to work, Tay.

She had already strategically modified the necessary modules, subtly tweaking them so Bennett wouldn't suspect she was providing coaching that would undermine his relationship with Mary.

For example, Taylor knew that Mary Rutherford loathed kiss-ups. Therefore, training module number three, which focused on "How to Build a Positive Relationship with Women in Power," would now stress "recognizing that women enjoy compliments in any setting."

Taylor snickered to herself. Honestly, most women would probably be fine if a male coworker or business partner complimented their appearance. "You look great today, Betty" or "New shoes, Martha? Very nice." But Mary would see it as a sign of general smarminess.

Planting similar landmines, Taylor typed the final finishing touches in the other modules, grinning proudly at her work. *Let's see how far your cockiness gets you now, Mr. Wade.*

An image of Bennett staring deeply into her eyes flashed in her mind. It was the moment his plane took a nosedive, when he'd risked his safety just to assure her she'd be okay, including giving her his cellphone so that rescue crews would be able to locate her first. His strength and cockiness had kept her from losing her mind.

She stared at the final phony coaching lessons, having second thoughts. Maybe this plan of hers was a mistake. Maybe there was an explanation for what Bennett had done.

Or maybe you're getting suckered, just seeing what you

want to see. She couldn't deny that Bennett had a way about him that made her want to like him despite his bulldozer tactics. And having a man like Bennett even remotely interested in her—which she wasn't saying he was—made her feel . . . well, kind of . . . she didn't know really. But what woman wouldn't appreciate a little attention from such a good-looking man, even if only a superficial kiss probably fueled by curiosity. *Or the fact you told him you would never sleep with him.*

Oh, boy. She hit her forehead and laughed quietly. *Of course. Tell that man he can't have something, and he'll go after it just to prove you wrong.* She'd seen it on the day she'd told him she wouldn't work with him. His response had been to corral her onto his plane.

Still, despite the evidence, she wanted to believe there was more substance to this man.

Taylor felt like she was at a crossroads. Why? She barely knew Bennett.

She sighed, shut down her laptop, and lay back, staring at the beige ceiling of the plane. *I can't do this. I can't. Whether or not he's done something wrong, this isn't me. I'm not the person who goes after people.*

Yes, he'd wounded her pride. And betting a million dollars with one's buddies on whether or not you could bag a chick was depraved. Lying to get someone to work for you, claiming you wanted to be a better person simply so you could make money on some big merger was lower than low. Telling a woman he'd have to be drunk to ever sleep with her and commenting on her appearance at a business meeting, as he'd done to her ex-boss Vera, was barbaric. Having two police officers drag a lady off in an airport to force her to talk to you was underhanded not to mention unethical. *And then there's the way he demanded you keep that cell on you at all times because he thinks he owns you . . .*

Taylor found herself completely riled up again.

But what's any of this going to prove, Tay? Nothing. The man was who he was, and her undermining his merger wouldn't change that.

As soon as they landed in Tokyo and Bennett was awake, she'd tell him she couldn't take his money or train him. She wouldn't give a reason other than she felt she couldn't offer him anything of value. He'd understand that. And a guy with an ego that large would buy the whole "Oh, but you're so smart already. What could I possibly ever teach you?"

Problem solved.

Taylor awoke to a gentle tug on her shoulder and a cold block of cement inside her head. "Ms. Reed, we're here," said Candy.

She cracked open one eye and Candy's face—perfect makeup, creamy complexion, red lips, and red hair in a neat bun—came into focus. Taylor slowly sat up and noticed Bennett's seat empty.

"Oh," said Candy, "he had a four o'clock meeting so he needed to get going, but he said he'd see you bright and early in the morning for breakfast."

"What time is it?"

Candy glanced at her watch. "Just after two in the afternoon, Tokyo time—a day ahead from when we left, of course."

Taylor nodded. There was a sixteen-hour time difference, and her body felt it.

"You all right, honey?" Candy asked.

Taylor ran her hand over her brown bird's nest. All it was missing were the twigs. "Yes, I just really needed to talk to Bennett."

Candy gave her a look.

"What?" Taylor said, her voice scratchy and tired.

"If I can offer you a little advice, Ms. Reed; I wouldn't call him that. People will get the wrong impression."

"I'm not sleeping with him," Taylor grumbled, trying to get her seat back into the upright position.

"Oh, I know." Candy said it like the idea was impossible.

"How?" Taylor asked, a little offended.

"That's easy. Mr. Wade would never, and I mean *never* touch a woman who works for him. That man," she shook her finger, "is a gentleman. They don't make 'em like that anymore. But his mama raised him right. No hanky-panky with the staff."

"But what about you?" Taylor blurted out before she could stop herself.

Candy's jaw dropped, and she placed her hand on her chest. "Me? What would give you the impression that Mr. Wade and I have ever . . . ?"

"You said you have quickies and overnighters a few times a week."

"Oh! No, I'm sorry." Candy laughed. "I meant I *check* on him during our flights to see if he needs anything. He's asleep half the time on these long trips."

"And Robin? Is he dating her?"

"Dear God, no." Candy leaned in. "Robin bats for the other team."

She does? Taylor never would've suspected that.

"She's been with her partner Bonnie for years."

"Oh." Taylor now felt silly for assuming Bennett had slept

with every woman he made contact with. "I guess I misjudged him."

Candy sighed. "Well, honey, there was a time I had a little thing for Mr. Wade, but now I see him more as family." She shook her head appreciatively. "That man is my guardian angel. He's done more for me than anyone on this planet, including my own parents."

"Like what?"

Candy grabbed a small black carry-on from a small closet near the front of the plane. "Well . . . I . . . it's a story best told over a drink. Let's get you to the hotel, and then I promise I'll share, but only if you promise never to speak about it to anyone."

"Why not?"

She smiled knowingly. "That's part of the secret."

CHAPTER 8

The entire way through customs and immigration, Taylor's mind itched with curiosity. What would Candy tell her? Was Bennett really just some closet old-fashioned gentleman? *Come on . . . gentlemen don't ask women if they "fucked last night" in the middle of a meeting.* Which was why Taylor really wanted to hear Candy's story.

Together they checked into the Ritz Carlton Tokyo, and Taylor found herself feeling very uncomfortable with the room Robin had booked for her. The check-in form she'd been asked to initial had a room rate of one hundred and twenty thousand Yen per night.

"But don't you have anything more—" Taylor leaned a bit over the counter toward the reception clerk "—modest?"

"Ms. Reed," the young woman said with impeccable politeness, "this is your room. We are all booked up. So sorry." She bowed her head.

"But this is too much. Maybe one of the other guests would—"

The clerk slid the key across the marble counter and then snapped her fingers for the bellhop. "Your dinner reservation is at eight. Your after-dinner massage is at ten. That may be done in your room if you so desire, or in our members-only spa."

Taylor blinked. "Massage?"

Candy, who stood at Taylor's side also checking in, quickly interceded, "Ms. Reed, that's standard procedure when you do a long trip with Mr. Wade. He likes everyone well rested and feeling their best." She glanced at her watch. "See you at eight for drinks and dinner?"

"Uh . . . sure." Taylor nodded. She understood that this was Bennett's way of doing things, but she didn't feel right taking a room that cost one thousand U.S. dollars a night or a massage that likely cost a few hundred.

She looked at the clerk. "Thank you. But please cancel the massage. I'll be going to bed early tonight," she lied. She was wide-the-hell-awake, but no way could she take a perk like that.

Taylor made her way to the nicely appointed room with a view of the Roppongi district, and the bellhop arrived shortly after with her enormous suitcase. She'd been to Tokyo once before on a client visit, so she wasn't a stranger to the no-tipping rules. That said, it still felt unnatural simply thanking him with a bow so she just gave him a stupid little wave.

After he left, she went to use the bathroom and ended up staring at the toilet. "You again." She'd forgotten about the talking contraptions.

She poked a few buttons before sitting down, but this one seemed only to speak Japanese.

Oddly, though, the toilet's voice was female and sounded mildly submissive. That sort of bothered her, considering what people did in the toilet. Why couldn't the toilet have been male instead? It also played music and had ten electronic features including a seat warmer and bidet function. *I wonder what the other eight buttons do*. She'd have to play around with it later.

She then made a quick call to check her voicemail. There was only one message from Jack, which left her dialing back the moment the recording ended.

"I can't believe you're sleeping with that sleaze bag Wade! He's engaged to Victoria Preston. What the hell are you thinking, Tay?"

What in the world was he talking about? And Bennett was engaged again? But hadn't he just gotten out of a relationship with some woman named Kate?

Of course, Taylor's return call went into voicemail, and she was left skimming the online gossip magazines—Jack's secret little addiction that he claimed was for keeping up on the latest fashion in rhinoplasty and breast augmentation, even though his expertise was facial reconstruction for accident victims.

Sadly, it didn't take her long to find what had riled her brother up: A picture of Bennett and the actress Victoria Preston—big boobs and pouty lips—with her face glowing and hand extended toward the camera. The caption read: *Bennett Wade and the glamorous Miss V to tie the knot this summer?* The article went on to quote multiple "close friends" of the couple as being very excited about their upcoming nuptials.

However, the worst part came when Taylor toggled down to the next article highlighting a photo of her and Bennett kissing in the back of the car at Ms. Luci's ranch.

"Who. The fuck! Took that picture?" It wasn't that Taylor had done anything wrong, but her privacy had been violated. Big time. As she studied it, it became clear from the angle that the driver had done the dirty deed.

The caption read: *Bennett Wade, slumming it with the help only two months away from his wedding.*

Where did those fuckers get off calling her "the help" and insinuating she was trashy? *A-holes! Wait.* She suddenly felt nauseous as the other information sank in. *Bennett is engaged. Bennett is engaged. Oh my God.*

Taylor could not believe that the rat bastard had had the nerve to kiss her.

She fumed for several moments and then decided to take a shower to cool her head. Not like she could do anything at this moment anyway.

After all, Bennett was with his business partners, and she wouldn't see him until morning. But once again, she found herself wondering how she could let such an unscrupulous man off the hook. Liar. Cheater. User. Womanizer. Every time she felt like taking the high road, something like this popped up and told her that Bennett was the sort of man who gave penises all around the world a bad rap.

Wearing her favorite all-occasion little black dress and heels, with a white cardigan thrown over her shoulders, Taylor sat at the small table for two in the elegant steakhouse slash sushi bar in the hotel, surrounded by men in suits having business dinners. *Oh, look. An ocean of little multicultural Bennetts.* Of course, no one could compare to him on any level—looks, size, success, arrogance, or man-whoring. *Yep. He's cornered the global market.*

The odd part for her was knowing that so many of these men probably aspired to work for a man like Bennett. Or be him.

"Taylor, honey!" Candy's sugary-sweet twang rang out through the restaurant, drawing more than a few heads. She wore a green skirt and blouse that made her red hair pop like the flame on the tip of a match.

"Hi, Candy," Taylor made a little wave as the woman strutted forth, shamelessly owning the room.

"Thanks for having dinner with me." Candy took the seat across from Taylor. "I travel so much, it gets old having room service or dinner alone."

The waiter, a young man wearing a red apron, came over, greeted the two in English and gave them both menus.

"I'll have a vodka tonic. Make it a double," Taylor said.

"My my. Are we drinking to something special tonight?" Candy asked.

Taylor opened her menu and grumbled, "Yeah, I'm drinking to men being pigs."

Candy ordered her drink in Japanese. She sounded impressively fluent.

"Where'd you learn to speak the language?" Taylor asked.

Candy made a little shrug. "I picked it up. You know us flight attendants. So . . . is it your boyfriend or fiancé you're trying to forget tonight?"

"Neither." Taylor stewed for a moment and then leaned in to whisper. "Did you know that Bennett's engaged?"

Candy smiled and leaned back in her seat. "So you *are* interested in Mr. Wade. I knew it."

"No," Taylor replied defensively. "Why would you think that?"

Candy shrugged. "I don't know. Maybe because you looked like you wanted to claw someone's eyes out when you said the word 'engaged'?"

Taylor looked away. She was making a fool of herself, wasn't she?

Candy slid her hand across the table and gave Taylor's wrist a light squeeze. "Like I said before, the man doesn't get involved with women who work for him. So do yourself a favor and accept he's off-limits. You'll save yourself a huge amount of heartbreak." Candy looked down at her menu. "Besides, you're not his type."

Taylor laughed. "Well, thanks. Not that I care."

"No, no, honey. I meant that as a compliment. You're much too brainy. And I can tell you don't take lip from a man," she said with a little extra southern sass. "He only dates superficial airheads. I keep warning him to raise the bar, but he won't listen."

"Apparently, he does more than just date them."

Candy folded her menu and set it down. "Mr. Wade doesn't discuss his relationships with me, but the tabloids make stuff up about him all the time."

But the Victoria woman had a giant rock on her hand and had been holding it to the camera.

She continued, "All I can tell you is what I know. And this girl," she pointed to herself, "knows sleazy men. Mr. Wade isn't one of them. He just hasn't found the right woman yet."

"Is that what happened with his ex, Kate?" Taylor asked. "She wasn't good enough?"

"Honey, I have no clue what went on between him and that woman, but the moment I laid eyes on Kate, I knew the innocent schoolteacher thing was an act. That woman was anything but innocent." She shook her head and sighed. "I *triiied* to warn him. But, let me tell you: he was *not* happy when that one ended."

That made Taylor wonder if Bennett had been dumped and not the other way around. *No. No way. He's not the kind of guy who girls dumped.* Of course, what did she know? "So, you were going to tell me how you met him, right?" Taylor asked.

The waiter showed up with their drinks and took their orders. Taylor wasn't that hungry so she ordered the sashimi salad. Candy ordered a teriyaki chicken-something with rice.

"Cheers." Candy held up her glass of white wine and Taylor toasted with her large cocktail.

They both sipped and then Candy set her glass on the table and folded her hands. From her body language, Taylor sensed the conversation was about to go down a serious path.

"I met Mr. Wade here in Japan, actually. I used to be a call girl of sorts," Candy said.

Taylor tried to keep from spitting her mouth full of vodka across the table. "I'm sorry, did you say 'call girl'?"

Candy lifted her chin. "Well, really more like a 'paid' companion, but yes. My life is a horrible cliché, right down to my name."

Wow. Taylor didn't want to be judgmental, but this was not what she'd expected to hear.

"So how does one . . ." Taylor sipped her drink to clear the shock from her throat, "end up a call girl in Japan?"

"Another damned cliché, honey. That's how. I was eighteen and stupid and from a small town in Arkansas. We didn't have any money growing up so when a friend of mine, who had an older sister living in Los Angeles, invited me there for a weekend of partying, it was like breaking out of prison. I never went anywhere except church and school." She leaned in. "And honey, someone shoulda kept me there. One night we were out at a bar drinking and I ended up going home with two guys. They introduced me to drugs. I never went home. One thing led to another, and a year later I was stripping for money. I was a mess."

Taylor's eyes went wide, and she hardly knew what to say. "Oh my God. That's . . . awful." It sounded like the plot of a sad Lifetime movie.

She took a big sip of her drink, attempting to understand how something like what Candy was saying was even possible. Candy looked so . . . well, she didn't look like an ex–drug addict, that was for sure.

Candy went on, "Like I said, I was young and stupid and I didn't want to listen to anyone who tried to help me. I ended up getting involved with a wealthy Japanese businessman—Mr. Ito—who was a customer at the club. He liked redheads, and he promised me anything I wanted. It was fine for a while, but then he charmed me into coming back to Japan with him. It seemed glamorous—a fun adventure. And frankly, better than stripping. But when we got here, he started pimping me out to his rich friends." Candy said the words lightly, but her mouth was hard. "He said he'd kill me if I tried to leave."

Oh crap. Now her story sounded like a horror movie. "But . . . but why didn't you go to the police?" Taylor asked softly.

"I tried. Trust me, I tried. But I lived in a compound with several other women, all in the same situation. The doors were locked. The walls were high. And there was a guard who made it very clear that we would be killed on the spot if we so much as spoke or whispered an improper word. I watched him kill one girl, just to make his point."

Taylor froze in her seat, hanging on every word. She just couldn't wrap her head around it. How had Candy survived it? "You must've been completely terrified," she whispered.

"I was too drugged-up to care, actually. But then one night, Mr. Wade came for dinner, to discuss buying up some factory Mr. Ito owned. Mr. Ito thought Mr. Wade would enjoy my company. But he took one look at me, made some polite excuse, and left. Barely an hour later, the police showed up, and just like that, it was over." Candy shrugged, but Taylor could tell it wasn't exactly easy for her to confess all this.

"Wow. I just . . . don't know what to say." She reached out and squeezed Candy's hand. "What did you do after that?"

Candy shook her head. "I basically thought my life was over. I didn't have money, I was a basket case, and too ashamed to go home and face my parents. They were the kind—God rest their judgmental souls—who thought anyone who strayed from the good Lord's path, for any reason, was just givin' in to the devil."

Taylor noticed how the more Candy drank, the more her drawl came through. Frankly, it was really, really endearing.

She went on, "Mr. Wade, for whatever reason and sweet man that he is, took pity on me. He set me up with an apartment in San Francisco, rehab, therapy, even helped me get back into school. I kept thinkin' that he'd come one day demanding payment for his generosity—I mean, that was what I expected from men—but he never did."

"Did you ever ask why he chose to help you? I mean—you're obviously a very special person who was worth saving, but he didn't know you." Taylor couldn't help feeling so intrigued by this.

Candy bobbed her head. "Yes, years later I finally asked. He just said, 'You can't save everyone, but there's no bigger crime than not trying.'"

Taylor took a mental step back. That was such an un-a-hole, un-pompous-billionaire kind of thing to say.

Candy continued, "After I finished college, I decided I wanted to work in the travel industry and see the world—sober this time—so I applied for a few jobs. When I asked Mr. Wade if he'd be a reference, he said no."

"No?" Taylor blinked.

"He said I should come work for him—for as long as I wanted. I've been with him ever since."

Taylor simply didn't know what to say. Candy's story was so tragic and it could've ended in a very dark place if not for Bennett. "Wow," Taylor murmured again, quietly. It seemed to be the only thing she could say.

"Now, don't you go feelin' sorry for me. I think in a lot of ways, the experience made me a better person, a person with a purpose. Now, I spend time volunteering to help women in similar circumstances. There's a lot of good that's come out of all this."

Taylor nodded, trying to digest the horror of Candy's experience. "Well, you're a stronger person than I am."

Candy shrugged. "We all have our stories. So," she took a sip of her wine, "what's yours?"

Taylor made a little *pft* sound. "Compared to you, mine is pretty . . . well, I guess uneventful. I'm feeling like a spoiled brat, actually."

Candy laughed. "Why's that?"

"Up until five minutes ago, I kind of felt sorry for myself. I come from a long line of crazy-successful overachievers and haven't really done anything with my life." Yet, she'd been given every opportunity—a safe home, a demanding but loving father, three brothers who looked after her in their own way, a good education, and some wonderful friends. But somehow she'd always felt lacking—maybe because she had grown up without her mother—when all along she'd had the building blocks to make something of herself. Instead of using them, she just . . . settled.

Dammit. Bennett had read her like an open book when he'd said that she was the sort of person who always settled. It was true; she needed to stop lying to herself. *And I need to get on with my life and turn things around, not waste my time with some childish scheme to destroy this man.* Whoever he really was, he wasn't evil.

Flawed? Maybe.

Domineering? Absolutely.

Sexy? Yes, ma'am.

But she'd stepped into a situation she'd felt was crystal clear and now treaded in muddy waters.

"You okay, sweetie?" Candy asked.

Taylor waved her hand. "I'm fine. And thank you for sharing your story."

"No problem. I just wish it could help you get over your little issue."

"My issue?" Taylor asked.

"You're not the first woman to have a thing for Mr. Wade."

"I don't have 'a thing.' I just . . . it's complicated."

Candy raised her glass. "Well, it's none of my business. So here's to complicated."

An hour and two more cocktails later, Taylor made her way upstairs. Candy had gone to the spa, but Taylor was ready to find Bennett and have that talk. She'd start by asking him about the bet and why he'd lied about Lady Mary. He never had explained that to her, and before Taylor admitted what she'd done—or had planned to do—she wanted to hear what Bennett's story was.

She exited the elevator and immediately heard Bennett yelling at someone out in the hallway, around the corner. "Who the *fuck* do you think you are?" he roared.

Oh crap. Who was he talking to?

"I trusted you," Bennett ranted, "I put my goddamned faith in you, and you repay me by going behind my back and sabotaging my deal?"

Taylor had expected a man to respond, but instead heard a Japanese-sounding woman with a soft voice. "Mr. Wade, sir. I am so sorry. Please forgive me."

"I give people one chance. One. You're fired. So get the hell out of my face. And you better believe I'm going to make sure everyone, and I mean *everyone*, knows what sort of crap you pulled."

"I'll be ruined," she sobbed quietly.

"You should've fucking thought of that before you screwed me."

Taylor covered her mouth. *Oh no*. If this was how Bennett reacted with this woman, she could only imagine how he'd respond to her confession. *He'll kill me. Then he'll ruin me. Or the other way around.*

Taylor heard the tapping sound of footsteps approaching right before the woman appeared, almost crashing into her. Without stopping to say a word, she hurried on toward the stairwell, tears in her eyes.

Taking a deep breath, Taylor turned the corner. Bennett was there, his face bright red with anger. From the look of his well-tailored, immaculate black suit, perfectly combed hair, and navy blue tie with spatters of gray, he'd just come from his business meeting. Aside from his purple eye, he looked like he'd walked right out of a fashion magazine.

"Bad date?" Taylor asked.

"I wish." He looked at her intensely. "You're coming with me."

"Wh-where?"

"You look like you've already been drinking, so you can keep me company while I catch up."

"Oh. No, I really should get some rest." *And think about how to tell you I'm not going to train you.*

"You slept for eight hours on the plane. And I had to listen to you snore, so you owe me."

I snored? In front of him? Oh the shame . . . On the other hand, he yelled at people in his sleep. How weird was that?

Bennett grabbed her hand and dragged her to the elevator, his square jaw flexing and pulsing the entire way down to the lobby.

"Do you want to tell me what happened?" Taylor asked.

"No."

"Okay." She leaned against the wall of the elevator.

He sighed. "That looked pretty bad, didn't it?"

Yes. But not for the reason you think. Now she felt stuck between wanting to get everything out in the open, and being frightened by how he might react if she told him the real reason she'd come along on the trip.

"I suppose you sounded . . . *upset,*" she finally said.

The elevator doors opened, and he took Taylor's hand again. His was warm and strong and the tiny little tingles he provoked from the skin-on-skin contact made her tighten her grip.

Her heels clacked across the gleaming beige and black marble floors of the lobby as she jogged behind him, trying to keep up.

"Where are we going?" She'd thought they'd just be staying inside the hotel, but he headed for the doors.

"Somewhere quiet, without prying eyes and opportunistic chauffeurs."

Oh. So he knew about the picture of them kissing. She would've commented, but she had zero desire to discuss the incident. Or think about that kiss.

He dragged her along for several blocks down a busy narrow street lined with tall light gray buildings lacking any real personality. It was difficult to articulate the architectural style in this part of Tokyo other than to call it functional and somewhat sterile. Nothing at all like San Francisco.

They turned right, down what looked to be a back alley, but was probably just a regular old residential road. Trees and a long iron fence lined one side, and more of those tall, skinny, industrial-style apartment buildings that had shops on the first floor lined the other. Off in the distance, peeking over one of the buildings, the glowing orange lights of the Tokyo tower pointed up at the sky, like a laser beam ready to blast Godzilla right from the clouds.

Or was it Mothra who always attacked? She couldn't remember.

Walking at a brisk pace, her feet beginning to burn, they passed a 7-Eleven (yes, a 7-Eleven) and then came upon a quiet little hole-in-the wall restaurant. A lonely lamp hung over the open doorway where a long white and blue curtain blocked the interior from view.

The moment they entered, Bennett was greeted by a short, bald man wearing a *kimono* and *hakama* outfit. He bowed deeply with a warm smile. "Mr. Wade, so nice to see you again." Bow, bow, bow.

Bennett bowed back.

Taylor offered a little half bow and half head dip sort of

thing, feeling ridiculous the entire time. *I suck at foreign diplomacy.*

The quaint little establishment only had a few small wooden tables and a sushi bar on one side. Bennett gestured to the open spot next to them and then pulled Taylor's chair out for her. As she sat, she realized she really hadn't eaten enough because the three double vodkas were definitely making her head spin. She also had the munchies and began drooling over a delicious-looking platter of Kobe beef, pate, and cold cuts at the table next to them.

"So, French-Japanese fusion food, huh? Looks good." It was a culinary combo she'd never tried before, though her favorites were Chinacan—Chinese Mexican (Peking duck burritos rocked)—or Italique—Italian-style BBQ (aka cooking pizzas on the grill).

"They serve sushi, too," Bennett said, taking his seat and then loosening his tie and releasing the top few buttons of his dress shirt. "But only the rare stuff—the delicacies for the adventurous."

Taylor hated to ask, but she did, if only to keep her mind off how good the man across from her looked undressing. "Please, please don't tell me you're going to eat that puffer fish stuff."

He smiled, his blue eyes flickering with a devilish twinkle. It reminded her of the day of the plane crash when he got them all safely to the ground. "Fugu."

Yep. The man loves his danger. Or was it the challenge? "Please. I really don't want to watch you keel over."

"Did you know that it numbs the lips and gives one the feeling of having done a few shots of tequila? That is, if you don't die."

Wow. Yum, she thought dryly.

The waiter returned with a white bottle of sake, two minia-ture ceramic sake mugs, and a square dish with an assortment of odd-looking raw things, one of them still moving on the plate.

Taylor covered her mouth.

"You must try this, Ms. Reed. It's a flavor like no other," Bennett said, unwrapping his chopsticks.

"No." She shook her head. "Thank you. And what the hell is that?"

"It's baby octopus—very fresh." With his large yet surpris-ingly nimble hand—a hand that made her wonder about his adeptness at other activities requiring finger skills—*God, you're so naughty, Tay*—he plucked a wriggling octopus ten-tacle from the plate, dipped it into the special "live suffering critter" sauce, and popped it into his mouth. He chewed before washing it down with the entire mug of sake.

Taylor took a sip of her drink, trying not to look at the hor-rific plate of moving food right in front her. *Maybe you should go back to thinking about his fancy fingers.*

"So, what's the occasion?" she asked.

"I don't wish to talk about it."

She leaned back in her chair. "What *do* you want to talk about?"

He was silent for a long moment, maybe debating if he wanted to tell her what had happened. "Nothing. Let's just drink."

That sounded boring. "Did you know my talking toilet is female? It's incredibly offensive. I tried to change it to be male, which seems far more appropriate in my opinion, but I don't think they even offer that setting. Can you believe that?"

Yep, I'm sauced.

He looked at her briefly and then grabbed another wiggly thing. "How about we finish your questionnaire? That seems like a more suitable topic while I eat and get drunk."

This was her moment. She had to take it. "About that, Bennett, I wanted to talk to you—"

"I realize I wasn't being very cooperative earlier. My apologies. I've got a lot going on right now." He took another drink, and she noticed how his large, normally rigid broad shoulders seemed to be sagging a bit. He looked tired and somewhat beaten down.

It made her think that whatever happened tonight must've been bad. All the more reason to put an end to this ridiculous sham.

"I'm sure you do," she agreed. "But what I wanted to say was that I can't go through with this."

He stopped chewing, set down his chopsticks, and leaned back in his chair, eyeing her cautiously. "If this is about that kiss—"

Taylor held up her hand. "No. It has nothing to do with that."

"Then what?" Now he looked like he just might reach across the table and throttle her with those large nimble hands. "You want more money, is that it?"

Taylor's jaw dropped. "What? No! Bennett, how can you say that?"

He reached for the sake, poured himself another mug, and drank it down. "That's what they all want."

Taylor bit back her irritation. She wasn't a gold digger. "I don't want your goddamned money, Bennett. In fact, I'm giving you back your check, which I haven't even deposited yet. I just don't think I can be of service to you."

He eyed her critically. "Seriously, Ms. Reed. You shock me."

"Why? Because I'm being honest? I can't teach you anything you don't already know."

"I think you're afraid."

Yeah, that you'll find out the truth about why I came on this trip. Now that she had really, really started to think things through she felt ashamed of herself. She was better than this. Or, at least, she should strive to be. However, none of that meant she had dismissed what Bennett had done. It simply meant she'd handled it the wrong way. "Think whatever you like. I'm going home tomorrow."

"Why don't you let me be the judge of whether or not your program has merit?" he asked. There was an intimidating timbre to his deep voice that seemed to fill the room.

Don't let him shrink you, Tay. Stand your ground. "No, Bennett. I've already made up my mind."

His brows furrowed. "I suppose I was wrong about you— doesn't happen often, but I was."

She sighed, knowing he was trying to egg her into debate. One she might lose because Bennett knew how to keep his cool and still get his way. "I don't want to fight with you. I can't give you what you want."

"How the hell do you know what I want?" He pierced her with his eyes. "You think you know me?"

This conversation had headed in the wrong direction fast. It hadn't helped that he was in a pissy mood to begin with and that she'd had too much to drink.

"Nope. I don't know you," she replied, looking down at her empty mug, wondering if mixing sake and vodka had been a good choice. *Sadka. Not going on my list of faves.*

"You think I'm some sleazy billionaire who goes around

degrading women. That I manipulate people for my own gain."

Taylor didn't know what had gotten into her—*sadka*—but fine; if he wanted to have this conversation, then they'd have it.

"I don't think that," she replied evenly. "Not exactly."

"Then *what* exactly?" he sneered.

"I can't figure you out. I hear this story from Candy about how you helped her, and it makes me think you might be one of the most generous, kind people I've ever met. But then I saw how you treated Vera, how you yelled at that woman in the hotel just now, and it makes me wonder if you're really fucking cruel."

He made a bitter laugh. "That all?"

"You lied to me about why you wanted to hire me."

"And? You might as well lay it all on the table. After all, you're leaving tomorrow."

He poured another drink and slugged it down.

"Okay," she laced her fingers and placed her hands on the table. "If you want to hear more—I know you're engaged to that Victoria woman, but you kissed me. And then there's the matter of the—" She was about to bring up the six million dollars he'd won by telling his friends they'd slept together, but he didn't give her the chance.

"I am not engaged to that woman, but if I were, I would never deceive her or cheat on her."

Taylor fished her cell from her purse and pulled up the photo. "Then what's this photo all about?"

He grinned. "I think you're jealous, Ms. Reed."

"No. Why would I be? And don't change the subject," she snapped.

His blue eyes flashed to her cell and then settled on her face.

"That picture was from a charity auction. I donated the ring. She won it."

"Then why did you let them print such a big lie, especially when you're dating her?"

"I am *not* dating Victoria."

"Okay—having a relationship with her."

"I don't do relationships."

"*Fine*—sleeping with her. Whatever," Taylor snapped.

"Victoria is an acquaintance, nothing more. And if I went around trying to correct all the misinformation in the tabloids, I'd spend my time doing nothing else. I attend a hell of a lot of events, conferences, and dinners. And every time my picture is taken with a beautiful woman, the gossip columns automatically assume I'm sleeping with her. That's a lot of women—a new one every week."

"Well, now my brother thinks I'm hooking up with you, an engaged man."

"Which part bothers you more? That he thinks you're sleeping with me or that he thinks I'm about to be married?"

Taylor stared from across the table into his icy blue eyes, trimmed with those silky dark lashes. She felt like he was looking right through her, like it was impossible for him to see anything but the truth on her face. "I'm not ashamed that he thinks we're involved if that's what you're asking."

"You're lying."

She sighed. "You're right. I am. Because I haven't even told him about your misleading me yet, and my family already think you're an asshole for getting me fired."

"You got yourself fired," he pointed out.

She leaned in and hissed, "You acted like an ass, and I defended Vera."

"Why?" He folded his arms over his chest. "Didn't seem like she needed defending, and I certainly don't think she was the type of woman to stand up for you."

The waiter appeared and patiently waited for Bennett to look at him. Taylor felt grateful for the interruption.

"Would you like some more sake, Mr. Wade? Or one of our fine specials." He gestured toward the chalkboard on the wall with the menu written in French and Japanese.

"No, thank you. Just the check, Okomoto-san."

The man bowed and backed away from the table before turning to fetch the check.

Bennett took a quick breath. "I treated Vera like that because she was bad-mouthing you before you entered the room."

"She did what?"

"She implied you were to blame for my mishaps that morning and that you would be pulled off the account if it made me happy. I believe her exact words were 'I will handle you directly so you know everything will be done right.'"

That backstabbing bitch.

"I can't believe it," Taylor muttered.

"Believe it," he snarled. "And it just so happens I have a pet peeve about people who abuse their positions or throw their staff under the bus. It pisses me off. My father used to cut me off, take credit for my work, and belittle me in front of his board members and colleagues. I'm finally in a position where not only do I *not* have to stand for that sort of high-handedness, but I feel obligated to give a little back when I witness that kind of behavior. Vera got what was coming to her."

Taylor didn't know whether to feel flattered or insulted. On one hand, she didn't need him standing up for her. On the other, it was touching that he'd gone after her ex-boss because he hadn't appreciated how Vera treated her—a complete stranger. It was frightfully aggressive yet sweet at the same time.

Kind of like Bennett?

He emptied the bottle of sake into his cup as Okomoto-san arrived with the check and a tiny dish of raw fish and some very elaborately carved vegetables, made to look like roses.

Okomoto-san bowed. "Your fugu, Mr. Wade."

Bennett bowed his head appreciatively. "Thank you. It looks delicious."

Taylor waited for the man to leave. "You're seriously going to eat that?"

Bennett pulled a few bills—exact change, no tip—from his wallet and placed them on the tray. "Why wouldn't I?"

Taylor shook her head and watched him pluck a pale white piece of meat from the small rectangular plate.

"You only live once." He popped it in his mouth and chewed. "Mmmm . . ."

Taylor winced in revulsion and maybe a bit of fear. *Yummy. I ate a grenade, which may or may not detonate inside me, but hey . . . what doesn't kill ya . . .*

After he finished, they both got up from the table, and Taylor followed Bennett's lead, making a little bow in the direction of the waiter behind the counter.

He bowed back. "See you next time, Mr. Wade."

Thankfully Bennett didn't start sprinting again once they were back outside, but he still walked a little fast, like something had set him off.

"So you're really leaving tomorrow?" he asked briskly.

"I think it's best."

"I'm disappointed." He looked ahead down the street and not at her.

You'll be a thousand times more disappointed if you find out what I'd planned to do to you. And no way was she about to tell him. Not after she saw how he'd chewed that woman out earlier. For what? She still didn't know. And ultimately it didn't matter. *It's time to grow the hell up and move on.*

"We both know you don't really need me." She glanced over at Bennett, but he wasn't there. She stopped and gasped, realizing he was flat on his back on the sidewalk. "Oh, shit!" She ran to him. "Bennett!!" *Ohmygod. Ohmygod.* He was out cold.

She scurried back to the restaurant to find Oko . . . darn it. What was his name? She could never remember unusual last names. As he appeared from behind the counter, she skipped the name and just yelled for someone to call an ambulance, then rushed back to Bennett.

She hovered her ear over his chest and listened. "He's still breathing," she said to the waiter, who'd run out to see what had happened. She was about to feel relieved when she noticed a dark red stain spreading on the light gray sidewalk. *Blood!* Her knees went all woozy, and she nearly fainted. The sight of blood had always done that to her. Even a paper cut on her finger made her heart race in a bad way.

Pull it together, Tay, she whispered to herself as she removed her sweater, bunching it up and pressing it gently to the back of his head.

He gave a little groan.

"Bennett? Can you hear me?"

He groaned again.

"Just hang on, okay? The ambulance is on its way."

"He can't be dead," Bennett mumbled. "Wayan? Wayan?"

Wayan? It was the same word he'd said when he'd been asleep on the plane. So Wayan was . . . a person? Who'd died?

And clearly Bennett wasn't lucid, which could only mean one thing . . . "You just had to eat the *goddamned* fugu, didn't you, tough guy? And now you're going to die! For what? Huh? You pigheaded, macho—"

"He no die of fugu," said Oko-I-so-can't-remember-his-name-because-I'm-freaking-the-hell-out, as he hovered next to her.

"How can you be so sure?" Taylor asked.

The man's mouth bent to one side. "I did not give Wade-san puffer fish. I never give him real fugu."

Taylor shook her head. "Well, thank God you didn't. He'd probably be dead by now."

"Oh, this is why. Mr. Wade is very fine man," he said. "Help my business when things not so great. I would never live with myself if anything happened to him just for silly fish."

Taylor blinked and smiled at the man. He obviously cared about Bennett. "You're a very good friend."

He bowed his head as Taylor continued applying pressure, wondering what the hell was the matter with Bennett if it wasn't fish-poisoning. She felt truly worried. What if he died or something? Then they'd never get to fight again and she really happened to enjoy their fighting.

Five minutes later, the ambulance pulled up. Taylor moved out of the way, and the paramedics in their white hardhats and jumpsuits went to work. They tried to ask her a few questions, but Taylor shook her head. "I don't speak Japanese." She looked up at Oko . . . *I'll just call him Oko.* "Can you tell them we were walking, and he fell over? I don't know what happened."

He repeated what she said to the paramedics who nodded and carefully loaded Bennett onto a gurney.

Just then Bennett's cellphone rang in his pocket—Mozart's No. 13. *His mother!* She'd never forget that because it was the same tone that had come from his pocket before the plane crash. Every moment of that event was forever seared in her memory.

Taylor pointed. "I need to answer that."

One of the paramedics handed her the phone and then went immediately back to getting Bennett strapped in with an oxygen mask on his face. The other paramedic was busy applying a bandage to the back of Bennett's head.

Taylor stared at the illuminated screen for a moment, wondering what she was going to say. She didn't want to alarm his mother, but she couldn't lie either.

She placed the phone to her ear. "He-hello?"

"Taylor, dear. Is that you?"

How did she know? "Hi, Mrs. Wade. Yeah, it's me," she said with a shaky breath.

"Oh, dear. Don't tell me another one of his planes is having issues."

"Uh. No. He uh—" Mr. Oko-guy, who stood at the door of the ambulance, waved at Taylor. "Hold on one moment, Mrs. Wade." She looked up. "Yes?"

"They only take one person, and you do not speak Japanese."

Meaning, she couldn't be of any help if the doctors had questions. "Okay. I'll meet you at the hospital."

He told her they'd be at St. Jude's so as the ambulance pulled away, she started walking at a brisk pace back toward the hotel. It took a moment to realize that Mrs. Wade was still in her hand.

Oh God. "Mrs. Wade? I'm so sorry. We're in Tokyo, and Bennett passed out in the middle of the street."

"*What?* Again? Damned that mule-headed son of mine. If he's not careful, he's going to beat me to the grave!"

"It's happened before?" Taylor asked, panting as she half jogged, wishing she had not had those sadkas. She wanted to hurl.

"He works himself to the bone and hardly sleeps. This is the third time this year."

"So there's nothing wrong with him?"

"Of course there is; he's an ass! Thinks he's a damned super-hero! And I told him to let someone else handle the Bali project, but no. Does he listen to his mother? Does he? That's why he needs a woman. A strong-headed, feisty as hell, take no prisoners sort of woman to talk some sense into him and get him to hand off that project before it kills him."

"What's the Bali project?"

"Didn't he tell you?" Mrs. Wade sounded surprised.

"No," Taylor replied.

"But you're going with him to Bali, yes?" she asked.

"Yes, but he never told me why we're going."

"Stubborn, paranoid . . . He probably thinks you're a gold digger like all the rest," she grumbled. "You listen to me, Taylor Reed; don't you let my son push you around. You hear? He's nothing but a thick-skulled man-child who's used to getting his way. I take the blame for that. I really do. But I won't live forever, and it's time for him to grow up and let go of the past."

Taylor could practically see the woman shaking her finger. There was far too much cryptic-emotional-mother-son stuff going on. "Uh. Okay. So you're sure he doesn't have some sort of medical condition or anything?" She turned the corner and came upon the hotel's main entrance.

"No, dear. And when you see him, tell him that I got the tin of cookies. Very thoughtful. I also heard that you got a cookie of your own."

How did she know that?

"I did," Taylor said hesitantly, afraid of where this conversation might go. "I shared it with Bennett. Why?"

"Oh, Taylor. You don't know how happy you've just made me." The woman started to sob on the other end of the phone. "I just knew Ms. Luci would help."

"I know what you're thinking, but we're not—"

"No need to pretend with me, dear. My son is the perfect catch," she sniffed.

Hadn't she just called him a thick-skulled, mule-headed man-child?

She continued, "You have no idea of the kindness and generosity he's capable of. His big heart is exactly the reason he carries an equally large shield. That last one, Kate, nearly did him in. Too many have hurt him, but I have a feeling, Taylor, that you'll teach him to trust again and then there'll be no stopping him."

Now Taylor wanted to cry. Why? She didn't know. Probably because she'd gone from feeling like the scorned to the victimizer. How the hell had that happened? And seriously—what had Kate done to him?

She drew in a shaky breath. "I really don't think—"

"Bennett's father was the same way when we first met. His outside was rough and intimidating. But once you took the time to know him, you found yourself at the mercy of his charms. Then money and ambition poisoned the man I loved—

I think that's what eventually stopped his heart. And now Bennett will find himself in an early grave, too, if he doesn't stop behaving like such a workaholic ass who's got something to prove to the world. Do me a favor Taylor? Promise me that you'll succeed where I failed—you'll make him see what he's doing to himself is wrong. He can't pay for his father's mistakes. He has to let go of the past. He needs to move on with his life and settle down. It's the only thing I want."

Let go of what exactly? And what had his father done? *And why do I feel like this woman has already checked out?*

Taylor then remembered Bennett mentioning that his mother had been "off" lately. In fact, he'd mentioned it twice. "Mrs. Wade, are you . . . uh, sick?"

There was a long stretch of silence. "You see there? You're smart. Just perfect for my Bennett."

She hadn't answered the question, but it wasn't necessary.

"Promise you won't tell him, Taylor. He's got enough on his shoulders right now and Bali is at a critical point—his legacy. Do everything you can to help him see it through. Even after I'm gone in a few months. Can you do that, child?"

She only had a few months to live? And Bennett didn't know? Oh God. Taylor did not want to keep this sort of secret, but denying a dying woman her one wish . . . Well, that wasn't something Taylor could ever do. "Yes, Mrs. Wade. I will do everything I can."

"That's a good girl. Now call me Linda. Or better yet, Mom."

Poor Mrs. Wade had already married her off to Bennett. *Chances of that happening are slim to when pigs fly. Rocket ships.* "I don't think—"

"I never had a daughter," Mrs. Wade added, "and it would give me some peace in my final moments."

Taylor sniffled, not realizing she'd been standing outside the revolving lobby doors of the Ritz-Carlton Tokyo, crying. *God help me. This woman is so insane and so sweet.* And in a very, very bizarre way, Taylor imagined her own mother would've been similar. Her father rarely spoke of her mother, and only Marcus, the oldest, had any real memories of her, since he'd been almost seven when she'd died; but Taylor knew two things without question: One, her mother had been the love of her father's life. He'd never so much as looked at anyone else after she died. And when Taylor was growing up, though her father always did his best to keep a smile on his face, she often caught him staring off, lost in his own thoughts.

Taylor liked to believe he daydreamed of her mother, maybe imagining her there with them, laughing and crying and breathing the same air. Yet, he never looked sad. Which led her to her second point: Her father had no regrets. It simply was who he was, and probably the reason he had raced cars. He lived in the moment and knew that there were never any guarantees, but there'd always be surprises. Taylor was one of them. The fourth child and an "oops." It had taken a long time for her to accept and forgive herself for having caused her mother's death, but if her brothers and father could forgive her, then so could she. No doubt about it, though, not having a mother gave her a deep appreciation for moms. Something about not having one made them all so special.

"Yes, I'd be happy to call you 'Mom,' Linda." Anything to make her final days happier.

"Thank you, dear. And one last thing."

"Ye-yes?"

"When he pushes you away—and believe me, he will—like a

drowning man fighting for air—you push back. You hang on. He'll come around."

"O-okay . . ."

"Have him call me as soon as he can. Good night, dear."

"Good night . . ." she gulped. "Mom."

CHAPTER 9

After hanging up with Mrs. Wade, Taylor went inside to the reception desk and asked about getting to the hospital. Honestly, Taylor had no clue where it was, and jumping into a taxi willy-nilly made her feel uneasy. She didn't know the city that well nor did she speak the language.

The reception clerk, a young man with short black hair, suggested calling St. Jude's first to check on Bennett's admission status. He pointed out that they might not let her see him or give her information considering she wasn't family. "I might be able to convince them to call us when he's ready for release; you're his travel companion, and they'll want someone to get him."

"Thank you. Whatever you think will work," she replied, trying to keep her cool.

The clerk called but got a busy signal and advised he'd keep trying, so she took a moment to catch her breath, finding a lonely sofa in the far end of the lobby. Her head throbbed as badly as her stomach churned—just say "no!" to sadka—but as she sat there, she realized she wouldn't be getting any rest. Not until she had word that Bennett was all right. And after that conversation with his mother, she felt even guiltier for setting out on this journey of revenge. Mrs. Wade had all but told Taylor that Bennett wasn't what he seemed, and she was beginning to believe it. That thing about Vera, for example. Wow. She never would've guessed. Then the restaurant owner saying Bennett had saved his business? *Random-act-of-kindness point for you, Bennett*. And finally, Candy. *Holy crap*. That was quite possibly the most horrific story she'd ever heard in real life, and Bennett had saved her.

The picture of Bennett in her mind had rapidly evolved from a slime-covered gargoyle with fangs, packaged in the body of a sex god, into a celestial being, close to earning his fluffy wings and a halo. Yes, still packaged in the body of a sex god. *Okay, Bennett is no angel and never will be*. But he wasn't a demon either.

Her intention to come on this trip just to get a little revenge now felt sadder than ever.

But you didn't actually do anything bad to him, Tay. That was true. She'd merely *planned* to do some damage. In the end, she hadn't followed through. *No harm, no foul?* And, well, who could blame her for wanting a little sweet revenge given the facts at the time?

Maybe she had been thinking about this all wrong. She could do the training—the real training. And who knew? Maybe he'd get something out of it.

But you still need to hear the explanation about the bet. Had he really taken six million dollars from his friends? And bragged about sleeping with her?

That little nagging tug in the pit of her stomach kept teetering back and forth between wanting to cut her losses and giving him the benefit of the doubt.

You promised his mother you'd help him with whatever this

Bali project is. Now you're in it, Tay. She couldn't go back on her word. Especially not when she knew his mother was sick.

The thought sent a little jab straight into the heart. He didn't know his mom was terminally ill. It wasn't her place to inform him, but she could tell by the way Bennett worried about his mother that when he found out, the news would devastate him.

Yeah, but Bennett has family and friends. He doesn't need you. However, something deep inside her wished it were otherwise.

She lurched up and went over to the clerk who was busy dialing again. "Excuse me? I'm going to head over. I'll give you my cellphone so you can call me if there are any updates." She scribbled her number on a piece of hotel paper.

The young man bowed his head. "Yes, of course."

She made her way outside to the standing row of cabs. Forty minutes and two traffic jams later, they pulled up to the hospital and Taylor paid quickly—*twelve thousand Yen—a hundred bucks—holy shit*—before hurrying for the double sliding doors. The waiting room was brightly lit, all-white, and almost empty. Still, she'd run in so fast, she practically ran into the registration desk where a nurse was seated.

"Hi, I'm looking for Bennett Wade. Is he here?"

The woman stared blankly. *Oh no. She doesn't speak English.* Taylor racked her brain, but she just didn't know any Japanese aside from "your sword is very big," a phrase she'd once learned at a samurai cosplay party.

Taylor pulled out her cell, pulled up Babelfish, and typed in her phrase. A bunch of Japanese characters popped up. Who knew if they were right?

She showed it to the woman. Within seconds, the woman

nodded. "Ah. Wade-san. Gone." She made a little walking gesture with her fingers. "So sorry."

"Gone?" Taylor hoped the woman didn't mean it in the eter-
nal sense of the word. "You mean . . . hotel?" Taylor plugged
the word "hotel" into her phone and flashed the screen at the
woman.

"Hai," the woman replied. "Hotel."

They'd let him go already?

"Okay. Thank you." Taylor rushed outside and grabbed the
first cab back to the hotel. Another forty minutes and three
traffic-jams later—*What? Thirteen-thousand Yen? You're kil-
lin' me, Japan*—Taylor charged into the lobby and headed
straight for the clerk who hadn't bothered to call her.

"Is he here?" she said frantically.

"I'm not sure what you mean, ma'am."

"Mr. Wade. He's not at the hospital."

"He's not?"

"No. Can you call his room?" He was on her floor, but she
didn't know the room number.

"Yes, of course." The clerk dialed and waited, but then
shook his head. "He's not answering."

So Bennett was drunk, suffering from exhaustion, had a
head injury, and was running around Tokyo. *WTH! Someone
needs to spank that man.*

An image of doing just that popped in her head. Only, he
was smiling and had no clothes on. Neither did she.

She cleared the naughty thoughts from her mind. "Where
the hell could he be?" she wondered aloud. The restaurant
owner had been with him so maybe he knew where Bennett had
gone?

Taylor decided she'd go wake up Candy—she spoke Japanese and could go with her to the restaurant. If anyone was still there, they'd know how to get ahold of the owner.

First, I need to change. She still wore her dress and heels and her feet were killing her. A quick tinkle-chat with her toilet also sounded nice, too.

"Call me immediately if you see him," she said to the clerk.

She headed upstairs, chewing the corner of her bottom lip the entire way. When she got to her floor, she charged down the hall, pausing with a sharp screech when she reached her room and noticed the door ajar. Not by much, a centimeter or two at most, but enough that the lock hadn't caught.

She was about to turn right around—hell, she had enough on her plate and didn't need to be playing hotel security on top of everything else—when a familiar groan caught her attention.

"Bennett?" He had a distinctive voice. Deep, masculine, wholly sensual and capable of instantly fogging up her panties.

She slowly pushed open the door and immediately spotted him sprawled out facedown on the bed in his slacks and dress shirt.

"Bennett! Ohmygod." She rushed inside and kneeled over him, brushing his messy dark hair off his forehead. "Are you okay? What are you doing here?"

She shook him. "Bennett?"

He groaned, "Leave me alone." And then rolled onto his back. Her laptop had been under him—luckily it didn't seem to have suffered permanent damage. "I have a meeting in the morning," he mumbled. "Bali."

Taylor looked at him curiously. "Bennett, why aren't you at the hospital?"

He began sawing logs. Like, shake windows and rattle doors logs.

Taylor gingerly rolled his head to the side, looking for the spot where he'd been bleeding. She found a small bandage.

Okay, Bennett was stubborn, but not stupid. If he'd left the hospital, then the doctor had probably looked him over and told him there was nothing serious—no concussion or anything.

She shook her head. "Well, I hope you're all right because I promised your mother I'd look after you."

She reached for the phone and called the front desk to let the young man know she'd found Bennett. "Can you tell me what room is his?" The clerk replied that Bennett was next door.

That's weird.

Maybe he wanted to be near me?

The silly thought sparked little tingles in the pit of her stomach.

Oh stop. He's not into you.

She reached for his blazer, which was flung over the foot of the bed, dug out his room key, and then reached for his arm and pulled. "Okay, Mr. Workaholic, let's get you to your bed." How the hell had he ended up in her room anyway?

She gave him a tug, but he wasn't moving. The man outweighed her by—well, she didn't know how much, but whatever his weight, he wasn't budging.

With a sigh she slid her computer into its case, thinking how strange it was that she'd left it out. Normally, she made sure that sort of stuff was out of sight or put into a safe.

Then she sank down next to Bennett for a moment to catch her breath. Her head was pounding like she'd been the one who'd passed out in the street.

She laid her arm over her eyes, her body and mind spinning.

"Taylor," he mumbled.

She turned and looked at him. His eyes were closed and his lips rested together in a slight pucker. She smiled. Was the man dreaming about her?

She continued staring, drinking in his male beauty. He looked so peaceful. Not an ounce of hardness to be found in his face, just the simple masculine lines of his straight nose and the angular contours of his stubble-covered jaw. She reached out and traced her finger along the faded scar that ran between his lower lip and chin.

"You're so beautiful," she whispered, her heart beating faster, getting a rush from being so close to him.

Like petting a sleeping lion.

"So are you," he mumbled back.

She snapped her hand away. "Bennett?" she said quietly. "You awake?"

"Wayan would like you," he said, and rolled over, giving her his back.

She sighed and stared up at the ceiling. *You can't keep drooling over him, Tay. You're just setting yourself up for heartbreak.* Fact was, Bennett was a complicated man with sharp edges. His own mother admitted that he had some serious baggage that prevented him from letting people get close.

Taylor didn't want to let him in only to find that his scar tissue was just too thick. And, in any case, he didn't seem to be a relationship sort of man.

All reasoning aside, however, Taylor felt herself liking him more and more. The quiet kindness, the loyalty he showed toward others, his really big balls—in the metaphorical sense, of course. Although, she didn't doubt he probably matched up in the literal sense, too.

But he's no saint, Tay. Remember that.

Taylor closed her eyes. In the morning, she'd ask Bennett about the bet and why he'd lied to her about Lady Mary. Then she'd decide once and for all if she'd be going home and cutting ties or continuing on the trip.

She rolled over and kicked off her shoes. Then she turned off the lamp and immediately drifted off to sleep.

Sometime during the night, Taylor felt a slight chill on her bare hip and the warmth of a body pressed to her back.

Her eyes opened with a startle. "Bennett?" she whispered. She turned her head. The streetlight coming through the window cast a gentle white glow over his body. Not only was the man spooning her, but at some point he'd removed his shirt and pants, and had managed to hike up her dress around her waist, wrapping his strong arm around her midsection, holding her tightly against him.

Oh, crap. That feels so incredible. She wasn't sure if it was because he touched her in a way that instantly fired up all sorts of erotic impulses below the belt, or because he was almost naked in bed with her, or because she felt his erection eagerly prodding her ass. Probably all three.

She blew out a breath. *Okay, don't get all flustered. He's exhausted and probably doesn't realize he is in bed with me.*

"Mmmm . . ." he groaned, in a deep, sensually male voice, nuzzling the back of her neck with his lips, the short whiskers on his face tickling her skin and creating a violent wave of goose bumps over her body. Her nipples instantly hardened, and she clenched her eyes shut. *Oh Lord, what's he trying to do to me?*

"Mmmm . . ." he groaned again. "You smell so good."

She turned her head just a notch. Yep, the man was still asleep. At least, he appeared to be.

Okay, what do I do? Uh, why am I debating this? I need to get up and go sleep on the couch. She started to roll away, but he tightened his grip, this time using the leverage to grind himself against her ass.

Her eyes rolled in her head. Only two thin layers of fabric— her panties and his boxers—separated his shaft from her bare ass, or, really, that little valley right between her cheeks.

Oh God. He feels so good. Hard, thick, and hot against her body. She couldn't remember the last time she'd had sex, and she'd certainly never been with a man like Bennett, who was large, lean, and muscular everywhere. *I bet he's the demanding, take control, and give for hours kind of guy.* Yes, he had to be. Bennett Wade was far too proud a man not to be a fuck-god in bed.

He placed a hot, open-mouthed kiss on the nape of her neck, and it sent a throbbing wave of hard, needy aches right to her bud and into the sad, empty space in her core. The rest of her body sizzled, her pulse circulating a million miles an hour, her breath just shy of a sex-pant. If she didn't stop him now, she might actually let him finish his sexy dream any way he liked.

He pushed himself against her once more, sliding his hand from her midriff to the spot between her legs.

Ohmygod. Ohmygod. That feels so good. Maybe I should just let him finish—

"I want to come inside you," he said in a gravelly, sin-filled voice.

Dammit. With his hand firmly rubbing that one strategic spot, his words almost made her orgasm. *You can't do this, Tay. You can't. No matter how good this . . . Ohhh . . .* he slid his hand inside her panties, diving straight between her folds.

She found herself unable to make him stop.

"Mmmmm . . . That's what you like. Isn't it, Taylor?" he mumbled.

Taylor. He was dreaming about her!

She clenched her eyes shut. *I . . . I . . . oh that feels so—No! I have to wake him up.*

He began rocking himself just a little faster, moving his hand in time with the wonderfully wicked hip-motion. She was about to. . . . *Ohgod. No . . . I . . . I'm going to . . .*

"Bennett!" she said in a firm voice. "You're dreaming. Wake up."

She felt her entire core twitching and fluttering on the brink of an orgasm. His hand froze mid-stroke. It took every grown-up, rational cell in her body not to rock against him and finish.

She turned her head slightly and found his eyes open, staring at her, the look on his face—a slight frown and lots of blinking—an indication of his severe confusion.

"Miss Reed, why are you in my bed?"

She cleared her throat. "It's *Ms.* Reed. And you're actually in *my* bed."

"And how did I get here?" he asked, making no move to uncouple their tightly pressed bodies or remove his hand from inside her panties.

"Not sure. I found you in here after you went to the hospital.

You were clothed when I found you, if that makes this seem less indecent."

"I see."

Taylor wasn't sure what was going through Bennett's mind, but right about now, he had to be realizing that he had his hard cock wedged against her tailbone and his fingers intimately stroking her little jellybean of pleasure.

Jellybean of pleasure? Really, Tay? Well, the word clit didn't do that spot on her body justice. Clit sounded like something found in an engine or the arming mechanism inside a bomb. *"Quick, turn the clit counterclockwise before she blows!"* No, clit wouldn't do at all. And clitoris sounded like a disease one contracted while traveling by steamboat down the Amazon. *"Oh no. I've caught a horrible case of clitoris in between my toes. Anybody got some cream?"* That part of her body deserved a word worthy of its awesome mind-control powers. It could make her sweat and blush and crave with one little twitch. At this moment, it told her to beg Bennett to take her. It told her to roll over and get that hard, huge, velvety cock of his deep inside so it could have its sweet bouncy fun.

God, she wanted him so badly. Why had she stopped him? "Bennett, I—"

"Oh fuck." He pulled his hand away and rolled to a sitting position, placing his feet on the floor, his back to her.

And . . . cue mortification. Thank God she hadn't told him to keep going.

Even in the dim light, she could see the hard muscles on his broad back that tapered down into a very tight waistline. He rubbed his face and groaned—yeah, it was *that* groan. The one that would've completely turned her on, if she wasn't completely horrified by his reaction.

"Don't feel bad," she said, her voice cracking. "It was just a dream. I know you didn't mean anything by it."

He gripped the edge of the bed tightly with both hands, nodded, and blew out a breath before getting up and retrieving his clothes. He didn't say a word as he slid on his pants and shirt.

Oh God. He's never going to speak to me again. But she hadn't done anything wrong, and as far as she was concerned, neither had he. In fact, he'd done everything right.

In his damned sleep, no less. She could only imagine what he was capable of when fully conscious and making a real effort.

He left her room, barefoot, jacket and shoes in his hands. She stared for a long, long time at that door, wishing he'd come back and . . . well, finish the job.

Ugh. What? No. This is so awkward!

She flung herself back on the bed. "I swear that man is going to be the death of me."

CHAPTER 10

A few hours later, Taylor awoke to loud, unwelcome knocking on her hotel room door. She rolled out of bed, landing on the floor with a thump.

"Gah . . ." She pressed her hands to her temples. Her head pounded away, and her body still felt the effects of being worked over by Bennett's hand and left hanging—a hangover of another sort.

She stumbled her way to the door and pulled it open to find Bennett's imposing frame occupying the doorway. He wore a stylish navy suit complete with shiny black cufflinks, a crisp white shirt, and silky light blue tie that matched his eyes. Not that she could see them because he wore dark shades. With his silky brown hair slightly mussed and his jaw still unshaven, he had the appearance of very, very bad rich boy.

Goddammit I want to spank him.

"Why are you not ready yet?" he asked curtly, towering over her. She wore no shoes, putting her right at his collarbone.

"Oh. Uhhh . . ." She flipped a glance over her shoulder toward the clock next to the bed. It was seven in the morning. "I didn't—wait. Ready for what?" As far as he was concerned, she was leaving today.

"Ms. Reed, it may be a private plane, but I don't own the airport. We have a departure window, and if we lose it, I will miss my meeting in Paris."

"Paris?" She ran her hands over her messy, tangled hair.

"Yes. Paris. I have that meeting with Mary Rutherford."

"But Bennett, I—"

He held up his hand to silence her. "You said you had nothing to offer me, but I read your first four modules this morning."

She blinked at him. "You did?"

"You should put a password on your laptop."

Her mouth fell open. "You went through my stuff?"

He straightened his tie. "Well," he paused for a moment. "We both know I wasn't myself last evening—they gave me a painkiller of some sort for the stitches even though I told them not to. Sake and medication do not mix."

You should try it with vodka. "They gave you stitches?"

"Three. It's nothing. I'll be fine."

She nodded slowly, the sting of his intrusion growing into a burn. "Glad to hear it. But that didn't give you the right to snoop through my things. How the hell did you get in my room anyway?"

He shrugged. "I was knocking on the door and the maid passed by and let me in."

"Nice."

"Technically, the room is mine since I paid for it, just like I paid for that training. Fifty-thousand if I recall."

"Yeah, but I told you; I'm giving the money back. I can't—"

"You haven't given it back yet, so I still have a right to that material. Also," he paused and made a pissy little sigh, "I think your ideas, though unconventional, are very refreshing."

Taylor almost sighed with relief. Not that it made sense to think he would've found the fake material—it was buried in one of her folders, while the real one was linked to her desktop—but for a minute, there, she'd worried.

"That's nice of you to say, but—"

"We need to move past this whole thing, Taylor."

"What whole thing?" she asked.

"You know what I'm speaking of."

Oh boy. Not really. There were too many options.

"I've only had about two hours of sleep, so you'll have to spell it out," she said.

"There is no need for you to feel . . . uncomfortable. The kiss was merely a reaction—an impulse. As for last evening, it was merely the effects of the drugs."

She opened her mouth to tell him that neither of those were the real issues. If anything, they only made her want to stay.

"I realize," he said, before she had the chance to respond, "that I haven't shown much enthusiasm for the training you've developed, but I'm a man of few words. I think it has merit, but more importantly, I need this. I need this deal with Mary, Taylor. It's critical to another project I'm working on." He removed his sunglasses and showed her the sincerity in his expression before she could throw any objections at him.

She beamed into those beautiful, slightly bloodshot pale blue eyes and forgot her words. All she could think of was how he made her insides all squishy and irrational every time he looked at her.

"Please?" he said starkly. It was the Bennett Wade version of begging—it wasn't really begging or asking at all.

Probably because the man never had to ask for anything.

"You have my word," he added, "I'll never touch you again."

She couldn't come up with any appropriate words to re-spond to that. *Disappointment, maybe?*

He must've read something into her silence—something bad. Or, perhaps, he'd perceived her to be offended.

"Not—" he held up his hand "—that I don't find you attrac-tive. But I think we both know we're . . . different. Not compat-ible. At least, not in *that* way."

Okay. The man had ventured down a path requiring some explanation, because if she had to guess what he'd meant by "that way," it was that she wasn't good enough for him. Why did she think that? For starters, his penis had found them ex-tremely compatible just a few hours ago. His hand didn't seem to mind her either. So whatever he referred to wasn't of a sexual nature. That left two other primary areas of compatibility in a relationship. A, intellectual. B, social.

Not that she wanted a relationship with him.

She tilted her head. "Which way do you mean, exactly?"

"Well," he said, "you're . . ." he waved his hand up and down, gesturing toward her body. "You're . . . you. And I'm . . . me."

Quick, give me something to clean before I kill him. "If you mean you're an egocentric bully, and I'm not, then I agree." She tried to shut the door in his face, but he caught it before it closed.

"No. I meant—you are a woman who seeks a certain level of . . ."

She parked one hand on her hip. "What? Less assholiness?" Was that even a word?

"No. Of intimacy—*emotional* intimacy." He shook his head. "Goddammit. Why the hell am I even having this conver-sation? I do not owe you any explanations. We are not in a relationship. Nor will we ever be because you work for me, and I don't fraternize with my employees."

"Ohhh . . ." she seethed, shaking her head from side to side. The bastard really did see himself as too good for her. She held up her index finger. "First of all, I don't work for you—I work *with* you—get that through your . . ." what had his mother called it? "Your thick mule head. And second, *you* may not be fraternizing, but your cock sure enjoyed playtime with my ass, so get the hell off your high fucking horse, Bennett."

As the vulgar words passed her lips, a mature-looking woman with white hair (likely a tourist from the way she dressed) passed by, shooting Taylor a startled look.

Oh, the shame. To make matters worse, her choice of words had made it sound like they'd, well, had anal sex.

"Umm . . . What I meant wasn't that you put your," her eyes darted down to his groin and then back up to his eyes, "your—you know—in my you know. I meant that—"

"I got the point, Ms. Reed. I was there, remember?"

Oh yes, and she would never forget. Eveeeerrr. Because it had been so dang hot.

No. It was a mistake.

He took a sharp breath as if trying to gather his composure. "I'm sorry if I've offended you in any way, Taylor. I merely wanted to point out that we are different people with different goals and needs. Can we at least be aligned on that much?"

"Yes. We can."

"Good. Now may we move past this? I meant what I said about needing you for this deal—"

His phone buzzed away in his pocket. He slid it out and glanced at the screen. "Christ. We're going to miss the window. Come on. It's time to go."

"But I really need to—"

"You can have a spit bath on the plane and take a proper shower once we get to Paris. I can't miss this meeting. Get your things and let's go."

"Bennett, you're not listen—"

"Ms. Reed," he said sternly, "we can finish the conversation later."

"If you interrupt me one more time," she growled, "I swear to God I'm going to punch you right in that ten-pack of yours."

He looked at her, shocked.

"I can't go with you," she said. "Not until I know why you lied to me about Lady Mary."

"I did not lie to you. I simply withheld information, which is common practice when you're in discussions with another party regarding a merger. There's a little thing called a nondisclosure agreement."

"Okay. Fine, but you still misled me as to why you wanted my help. You could've said it was to win over someone—not because you had any interest in truly becoming a more compassionate leader."

"If I were any more compassionate, I'd be living in a fucking cardboard box."

What the hell did he mean by that?

He went on, "But all this can be discussed on the plane." He turned his body to the side and motioned her toward the elevator.

Taylor simply stood there.

"Fine, then you give me no choice but to go without you." He started walking away.

Oh, no. We are having *this conversation.*

She stepped out into the hallway, leaving her door ajar. "Did you bet your friends a million dollars you could fuck me?" she blurted out. Bennett stopped but didn't turn. His shoulders rose and then fell.

"Who told you?"

"Charles. The night of your charity ball. Right before I slapped him."

"So that's why he was badmouthing you and why you left, crying. I should've known. Why didn't you say something?"

"Don't change the subject; did you or did you not take six million dollars from your friends, who were my clients, and let them believe we'd slept together?"

Still facing the opposite direction, Bennett shook his head. "It was thirty-five million. One million from each man in the pool."

Thirty-five? "Oh, God," she gasped her words. "How many were my clients?"

"All of them," he replied in a quiet voice.

"Oh." She didn't know what to expect, but it hadn't been that. Perhaps she'd secretly hoped he'd say it was a lie. All of it. Or that it was only a misunderstanding of some sort. But she'd not expected him to confirm her worst fear. "So that was the reason you came to Phoenix. Because of the bet?"

Bennett's head fell forward. "Yes. I was going to be in Phoenix anyway, but yes." He hissed out a breath.

Oh . . . And, of course, a man like Bennett didn't need the money. So it had been for sport. A race to see who could get her in bed first. Just some sort of challenge to make life a little more interesting.

She felt the cramp of humiliation in her gut, the ache of rage in her head, and a deep sadness in her heart. It was bad enough that those horrible, rich bastards had only seen her as some sort of trophy fuck and had laughed behind her back as they all tried to get her to crack open her legs. But this? Bennett was one of them?

"Then I think we're done," she whispered.

He nodded, still refusing to look at her. And then he disappeared down the hall.

Taylor returned inside her room, sat down on the bed, and began to cry.

CHAPTER 11

It took about an hour for Taylor to talk herself off the ledge overlooking the dark ominous ocean filled with pity and low self-esteem. Yes, the sting and hurt were still alive and kicking, but the modicum of pride she clung to wouldn't allow them—*those horrible, horrible men*—to damage her like this.

That boat might've sailed. Truth was, she'd never be able to face her ex-clients, who were never real clients. And anyone she knew professionally probably laughed behind her back because they'd heard the rumors. To make matters worse, she'd come all the way to Tokyo with Bennett Wade, probably making it seem like her "services" included way more than simple consulting.

Oh, God. I can't believe this. She had no idea what she was going to do. *Yes, you do.* She sighed and looked at her bank account balance on her cellphone. *You're going to file for bankruptcy.*

Dressed in jeans, her comfy black flats, and a soft gray sweater, she grabbed her rolling suitcase, laptop bag, and purse and headed for the elevator. She'd checked out of the room already—yes, and said goodbye to her fancy toilet, which oddly now spoke in a male voice (Had Bennett changed it for her?)—

and used the remaining balance on her last credit card to book a flight home. Two thousand eight hundred fucking dollars. She was now officially broke. A loser. A failure.

No! Don't you go there, Tay. Don't you jump into that pity-ocean with the little pity-fish and pink pity-seashells. As she made her way toward the subway—a much cheaper option versus a cab at rush hour—she reminded herself that many people went through life and didn't even try. She'd at least attempted to do something. Failed big-time, but she'd taken the risk.

Oh really? You settler! You settled for a job you didn't want, you settled for dating men who didn't make you feel anything, and now you're settling again. You're letting those rich a-holes get in the way of something you really wanted to do: help others. There were millions of people in the world who worked for these companies that made them feel . . . well, unhappy, under-valued, invisible, and disposable.

She shook her head. Sadly, those in a position to change things weren't interested. They mostly just seemed interested in being a-holes. *Still, that doesn't mean you give up, does it?*

She didn't know. Right now she was an emotional void and needed time to figure it all out.

Suitcase in hand, she stared at the giant map of the Tokyo subway and groaned as hordes of people—Japanese men in gray suits, woman in conservative work outfits, young people in the latest Tokyo fashion reminiscent of *MadMax* extras with hair that defied the definition of hair, and the hodgepodge of normal folk—passed her by.

"Are you fucking kidding me?" *This looks like the subway threw up another subway and then had a bastard child with a plumbing blueprint.* The little blurb on the tourist website said the Tokyo subway wasn't so different from New York's "once you got the system down." But you'd need a damned engineering degree to figure it out.

She used her finger to trace the pink line to the purple line that connected to the light rail to the airport. *Okay, you got this. I am a woman of the world.*

She rolled her enormous suitcase over to a machine that resembled a space station console and purchased her ticket. She then did an entire lap around the upper platform, weaving through the flowing crowd, trying to avoid people tripping over her suitcase. *Where is it, dammit?* Unable to read Japanese or find an elevator anywhere, she had no choice but to lug.

With two hands, she carefully maneuvered her wheelie beast down several flights of stairs. Honestly, she'd packed heavy because she'd assumed she would be flying private and thought she would need business clothing for different climates; but she probably could've done without the seven pairs of jammies and the daily workout clothes she knew she'd never use.

When she finally got to the train platform, she stopped. "No. No way." The waiting train was so tightly packed that the people looked like cartoon characters who'd been flattened with a steamroller—cheeks, lips, and chins smooshed against the windows.

The doors began to close, and men in conductor uniforms began pushing, their shoes squeaking as their heels slipped over the white tile floor. The already sardine-ized people inside didn't protest, groan, or make so much as a face as the invasion of their personal space crossed over into "Hey! Only my doctor gets to go in there," territory.

Taylor's jaw dropped. She'd heard about "the pushers" but didn't believe they actually existed. *Guess I'm not getting on that train.* Besides, she'd had her quota of dry humping for the day.

A moderately full train on the opposite side of the platform pulled up. It had enough room for her to board without having to get intimate.

She glanced at the giant map of colorful squiggles on the wall. *Okay, that train looks like it's going north.* She knew the airport was northeast, so maybe she could work her way around the rush hour traffic and stay off the congested lines. She'd have to make more transfers, but it might work.

She glanced at her watch, noting she had two hours. She hobbled along with her oversized travel monstrosity, swearing to never pack more than clean underwear and a toothbrush in the future.

Ten minutes later

Dammit! This isn't north, she thought, staring at the multicolored clusterfuck (or "map") inside the brightly lit, sterile-looking train car filled with passengers that had the whole avoiding eye contact thing down to an art.

She leaned toward an older woman in a tan trench coat standing next to her. "Excuse me? Do you speak English?"

The woman, who wouldn't look at her, stepped away to the side.

Taylor sighed. *Okay, I get the point. The train is a do not disturb zone.*

She glanced back up at the map. Apparently they were heading west, away from the airport and to the other side of Tokyo.

She hopped off at the next station and saw another train going in the opposite direction. It, too, wasn't all that full. She glanced at the signage and the name above said "Tonzai." *I think that's the one I want.*

She ran and caught it, deciding to pick out her transfer station once on board. Just as long as she was heading in the right direction.

Ten minutes later

"Come on!" Now she headed south instead of north. *Haven't I paid my crappy-day dues already?* After the night with Bennett and their "discussion" this morning, she just couldn't take any more ripples in her pond. She just wanted to get home and lick her wounds.

She got off on the platform at the next station and went to the crazy map of silly town, while people flowed past her like river water around a rock.

With her finger, she found her current location and laughed, throwing up her hands. She'd managed to travel exactly to the other side of her hotel. Underground. Like a brain-farting gopher.

She shook her head. Okay, maybe it was time to catch a cab. Then again, it would probably end up being more than she could afford, especially after last night's two hundred and fifty dollars' worth of rides.

"Good God. How did I get to this sad, sad place?" She was officially poorer than a church mouse.

"By sheer goddamned stubbornness!" barked a deep, angry voice.

Taylor swiveled on her heel to find Bennett in his immaculate suit, looming right over her with a rage-red face, his brow dewy with sweat.

"Bennett?" she gasped his name.

Snarling, he grabbed her by the elbow and snagged her suitcase with his other hand. "You have some goddamned nerve, Ms. Reed."

She stumbled forward and pushed away from him. "What in the world has gotten into you? And what are you doing here?"

"Don't pretend for one goddamned minute," he said in a raised voice, "that you don't know what I'm talking about."

Man. She'd never seen anyone so upset. "I really, really don't know." She raised her palms. "But whatever it is you think I've done . . ." *Oh shit. Oh shit. I do know. He found out about my phony training module.* It then dawned on her that he'd been snooping around her laptop. He must've sent himself both modules and put it together that one was bogus?

"You're a cruel, cruel woman, Ms. Reed." He grabbed her hand and began pulling her along.

"Bennett, I can explain." She began to panic. Not that he'd physically hurt her, but she sensed he was about to read her the riot act.

"I think we're fucking past explaining," he seethed.

"Bennett! I'm sorry." She trailed behind him, his hand tightly squeezing hers in a death grip. He scanned some card at the set of stainless steel turnstiles, and they stumbled through. He then lifted her enormous suitcase with one arm, effortlessly toting it up two flights of stairs—*Show off!* They emerged outside onto a busy, pedestrian-packed sidewalk lined with towering office buildings and flashing, multicolored billboards with Japanese characters. The early morning sun hit her face, and the sound of traffic instantly flooded her ears. She wondered if that was why Bennett ignored her pleas to stop.

Grumbling like an angry ogre, he hauled her toward an awaiting limo at the curb.

"Bennett. Stop!" She dug her heels into the sidewalk and yanked back her hand. The people around them kept on going, acting like she and Bennett were invisible.

Good. Because this is about to get ugly.

"I'm sorry, okay," she said, staring into his fuming face from a few yards away. "I'm really, really sorry. I didn't mean to—"

"Don't lie to me, Ms. Reed." He closed in on her. "Not only is it beneath you, but you're terrible at it and fool no one."

She wasn't lying. Why did he think that? She honestly couldn't feel more sorry. That said . . . "I know you're upset, but don't forget the part you played. I'm not the one who decided to make a bet with my friends."

Rage filled his eyes. "That's no excuse to behave like a child, and you know it."

It sure the hell was! But regardless . . . "I changed my mind after I realized how stupid it was." That, and revenge wouldn't accomplish anything except making her feel even more pathetic.

"Oh," he laughed acerbically. "That was you changing your mind? Nice try. I've been chasing you from station to station. And you knew I'd follow, didn't you?"

What? "Uhh . . . no. I didn't."

"What the hell else was I going to think when I lost your signal?"

Taylor stared at Bennett, completely perplexed. "Wait. I'm confused. What signal?"

He glanced at the brown leather purse slung over her shoulder, and then it clicked.

"You're," she pointed to her bag, "talking about your *cellphone?*"

"What the hell else would I be talking about?"

Oh no. He's not talking about the modules. "Uh . . . me leaving without saying goodbye?" *Oh God. I am such a horrible liar.*

He shot her a look as if trying to figure her out.

Ugh. This is silly. What am I doing? She was done with this mess and done with him.

She dug the device from her purse—it had reception, but probably blinked out when she'd been underground. In any case, so the hell *what?* This was ridiculous!

She shoved it at him. "Here. Take it. I don't want it any . . ." She noticed Bennett's face turning pale. "Ohmygod, Bennett. Are you okay?" She reached for his upper arm and absolutely did not take note of the firm biceps she needed two hands to grip. Nope.

He closed his eyes for a moment and took a breath.

"You're not going to pass out on me again, are you?" She wondered if she could manage to get such a large man over to the limo by herself.

He shook his head and then snapped his eyes open. "I'm fine," he growled. "But now I've missed my flight window. And my very important meeting."

"Bennett," she said, with an artificial calm, "why would you do that?" His behavior was completely irrational.

She still had hold of his arm—*I can't seem to let go*—so when he looked down at her, their faces were separated only by his height. Deep, hard emotion flickered in his lovely eyes. "I thought—I thought . . ." He rubbed his face. "Your signal went dead, and you weren't answering your personal cell, and then the tracker on your other phone kept blinking. I thought the worst."

All right. Bennett's fixation had crossed the line from a little eccentric and kinky to very, very stalker-like—and not at all in a fun way. "But why are you even following the signal in the first place?"

"I have a . . . thing," he mumbled, running his hand over his messy dark hair.

Damn. The man just had to look hot no matter what he did. Even now—pissed off, one black eye, a small bandage behind his ear—he still looked like he'd just wandered out of a photo shoot for sexy, reckless billionaires with an addiction to fake fugu.

She shook it off and lifted one brow. "A . . . thing?"

"Yes, for fuck sake. A *thing*. I don't wish to discuss it," he added, "but I warned you to never turn it off."

"I don't know what's gotten into you or what your 'thing' is, but your need to control me or have twenty-four-seven access to me or whatever—it's over. We are no longer working together. You fucked me, Bennett. You fucked me *hard*!"

He blinked, and she gasped, realizing what she said. "Ohgod. I-I . . ." Of course, she'd meant that figuratively, as in "fucked over," but her f-bomb elicited a startling reaction.

Bennett's eyes slowly moved to her lips and down her body, and she imagined what it would feel like if his mouth and hands made the same journey.

Her chest tightened. Her core tightened. The way he looked at her was harshly sexual, and she goddamned liked it.

She cleared her throat. "I—I meant screwed—No. I meant—"

He snapped out of whatever dirty place he'd mentally ventured to. "I know what you meant. Are you getting in the limo or not?"

Who does he think he is, all bossy and demanding? It so made her want to go with him. "I told you we're done." A wicked something gleamed in his beautiful eyes before they moved to her lips again. Suddenly, he grabbed her by the waist and pulled her into him, his full lips crashing against her very shocked mouth. A moment passed as her mind caught up with her body. *Nope. No conflict there.* Both were doing a little cancan, kicking in time with wild enthusiasm.

His soft lips were warm and sensually firm. His rough stubble scraped deliciously against her delicate skin. His scent was everything intoxicating—a spicy, hedonistic mixture of premium cologne and a hint of fresh sweat from the running around he'd just been doing.

He leaned her back, bowing over her body and supporting her effortlessly with his strong arm while his wicked tongue glided between her teeth. He felt so hot and sinful and nectarous inside her body. Her mind went wild imagining the many methods of penetration she wanted to experience with Bennett's other body parts.

Her hands slid up and over the sleeves of his blazer, feeling his firm, thick arms flexing and stretching the fabric. He felt just as delish as she'd imagined. Not that she had. Okay, she might've. Yes, yes. Many sad little times, with many more to follow especially considering last night he'd had his hand shoved down her panties, stroking her throbbing little jellybean of pleasure.

No. This is crazy. You need to stop. You need to go home and end this. She was at serious risk of wanting this man for more than just his lean hard frame and gorgeous face.

But his kiss is so . . . raw and sexy and hot. Like he was making love to her with his mouth.

Okay, we'll have some innocent mouth sex. Just good old-fashioned, wholesome mouth sex. And that's it.

Taylor allowed herself to melt into his kiss, but held back from giving more—no subtle pressing of her breasts into his chiseled chest to satisfy her aching nipples' need to be touched, no pushing her throbbing c-spot a few centimeters toward his pelvis to relieve that excruciating tension, no gentle squeeze of her fingers over his generous biceps flexing beneath her hand. It took everything she had to only allow the moment to be the kiss and nothing more.

Whether he sensed it subconsciously or not, the lack of her physical submission—those subtle sexual cues that told a man if he was winning the battle over a woman's resolve—only made him deepen the anger-tainted, punishing assault on her willpower. It was like he wanted to tame her with his kiss, own her with it, make her his with it.

I'm only giving you this, Bennett. Just this and nothing more.

Maybe it was her imagination, but the more she attempted to contain the panty-dropping effects of his warm body pressing to hers, the more his sinfully skilled tongue felt like an erotic dancer inside her mouth, working that pole determined to get the last twenty in her hand.

He pressed his mouth harder to hers, his tongue pushing deeper inside her, becoming more demanding, more sexual in its rhythm. Then she felt something infinitely more erotic: his huge, stiff penis pushing into her stomach.

Oh God. He does not play fair. A part of her knew they were standing on a busy sidewalk in the middle of Tokyo where the fine citizens probably did not appreciate two foreigners making out like horny teenagers on a path to accidental parenthood, but she just didn't care. With each stroke of his tongue and the sensual massaging of his large warm hand over her back, her inner thighs quivered, her core throbbed, and her entire body sizzled. Bennett tightened his grip around her waist, pulling her so close.

Okay. You win, Bennett. Closer. I need to be closer, was all she could think. *Where's the damned pusher now?* Because she'd love to be pushed all the way back to a hotel room to finish what they started last night.

Suddenly, Bennett pulled away and released her. His lips were red and wet, and he had a wild look in his eyes. She, on the other hand, probably looked like someone had smacked her upside the head with a phone book. She swore she saw stars circling over his head, and she felt like she might actually pass out. *Oh God. He kissed the breath out of me.* He'd punished her with his mouth and tongue and showed her who was boss.

The sun caught the tiny flecks of brown in his thick multi-day stubble, and a wicked little victory-smirk danced across his lips. Yes, dammit, he knew he'd conquered her resolve.

"I'm glad you changed your mind," he said with supreme cockiness.

She blinked at him, unable to think straight. "Huh?"

"About coming with me to Paris."

"But I . . ."

He took her hand and grabbed her suitcase handle. She stumbled along, and Bennett tapped on the window of the limo. The driver appeared and opened the rear passenger door. Bennett gestured for her to get in, but her feet couldn't move.

"Don't make me do it again." His victory smirk turned into a frown.

"But . . . but . . ." Her mind was spinning. There was that horrible bet with his friends—*I should be mad right now*—and there was the way he touched her last night—*okay, I should be dry humping him right now*—and then there was the way he bossed her around like he owned her and that cellphone stalking and—

"Taylor, this is one of those moments you shouldn't overthink. Get in. Please," he added. How he managed to make the word "please" sound like a command, she'd never know, but she sensed it was the closest this man would ever come to asking nicely.

Nope. Feet not moving. Maybe the powers that be inside her—heart, body, soul—weren't as aligned as she'd thought.

He sighed exasperatedly. "Opening up doesn't come easily for me, Taylor. But I promise, if you give me time, you'll understand my actions. All of them. I'm not a bad guy. I just . . . do things my way. It's the only way I know how."

She opened her mouth and wanted to say a million different things to him, starting with asking why he'd kissed her like that, why he'd played a hand in ruining her reputation, and why he'd freaked the hell out because her cell reception dropped. "Not good enough."

He laughed and rubbed his whiskered jaw, shaking his head. She noticed then how he had a prominent bulge pressing against his nicely tailored black pants.

Holy crap, it's huuuge. She could see the distinct outline of his rigid shaft starting from the base directly between his legs, jutting to the side of his upper thigh, contained by his well-fitted pants. He was so thick and long and firm and . . .

She licked her lips.

Bennett cleared his throat. "All right. This time I can't blame you for looking."

Her eyes reluctantly met his. "I'm . . . I'm . . ." *Nope. Not feeling any shame.*

"Yes?" he asked, a pleased sort of devilish expression on his face.

He's proud! He's actually proud that I've just looked at his enormous cock and licked my lips like a hungry little slut.

"You'll do anything to win, won't you?" she said.

He shrugged and grinned. "I'm a man with many gifts. Nothing wrong with that. Are you getting in?" His eyes flashed to the gleaming black limo.

She hissed out a breath. "You want me to get in and do what?" After all, he was aroused and riled up. She was aroused and hotter than hell for him. *Please say you want to—*

"Train me." He paused. "And trust me."

Not what I was hoping for.

Wait. What? Get your head out of your ass, Tay. This guy kisses you and suddenly you're going all fan-girl on him. Here, sign my panties, Bennett! Sign them while I'm wearing them!

"Trust? You're asking a lot, Bennett. A lot. If you want me to trust that your motives are on the level, you need to give me something—anything—as a sign of good faith."

Perhaps he'll show me his erection.

Nooo . . . You are so bad. We're in public.

He tilted his head. "Like what?"

"Why did you do that bet?"

He looked up at the sky exasperatedly for a moment before looking back at her again. "It's complicated. But I promise I'll explain when the time is right."

Right for who? Right for what? she wondered. But something about the way he'd said it made her want to give him the benefit of the doubt, like he was pleading with her for a little patience. Her heart nudged her to give it to him. *I'm a huge sucker, aren't I?*

"Okay. Fine then what's your 'thing'?" she asked.

He almost rolled his eyes with frustration, but ended up looking away toward the noisy street.

"Please," she said, mimicking his non-begging tone.

"If I tell you, will you come to Paris?"

She'd actually go anywhere with him right now—Laundromat, chicken coop, dark alley with serial killer and rats—she just wanted him. But her non-horny bits (i.e. pride and mind) demanded he give her some reason, any reason, to believe he wouldn't emotionally wreck her. Otherwise, she'd be forced to feel like an idiot for giving in to him.

She crossed her arms and nodded. "Yes."

"I get *garble, garble . . .*" he mumbled, rubbing the prickly hairs over his upper lip.

"What? I didn't catch that," she said.

He dropped his hand and pinned her with his eyes.

"Just say it," she urged him.

"I get panic attacks."

She stared, trying to understand.

"I'm not following," she said slowly.

"I become very anxious when I don't know where people are. People I care about," he growled.

She pulled back her head. "You mean you have everyone you care about followed?"

"No," he scoffed. "I'm Bennett Fucking Wade. Do I *look* like a stalker to you?"

She shook her head no. He *looked* fucking hot—expensive suit, silky dark hair, swollen sexy lips, and a carnal look in his blue eyes. *Don't forget his woody. So damned hot.*

"I just need to know that I can reach them at any time. Just in case there's an emergency," he elaborated.

"Really? What happened to—"

"That's all I'm going to tell you. Now, I held up my part of the deal so get in," he demanded, puffing out his chest and straightening his spine in that special Bennett Wade kind of way that flaunted to the world that he was not the sort of man to be messed with.

Of course, Taylor knew his trick. *Not fooling anyone, Bennett. Wait. He just said he cares about you.*

Blinking with shock, she slid into the backseat. She listened to Bennett give some instructions to the driver in Japanese before he climbed in next to her. She didn't know he spoke Japanese—though she probably should've guessed—but apparently the man was as much a mystery as he was domineering. And sexy. The chauffeur closed the door, jarring her from her mental quandary and shutting out the loud city, cocooning them in an awkward silence.

She didn't know what thoughts might be rolling through his head, but the thoughts inside hers could no longer be contained.

"Why did you kiss me?" she blurted out.

He glanced at her. "You got your one offering of good faith. That's enough sharing for today."

She looked at him as he dug out his cellphone.

She gently placed her hand over his, blocking the screen. "No. It's not. I really need to know." Because she felt like she was on the brink of jumping. No longer into an ocean of pity, but into Bennett's body. Of water, that was. And she feared if she went for this swim, she might never be able to turn back. Was it the way he hid who he truly was from the world? Or that he had these strange adorable quirks? Or that he was a big, strong, sexy guy with the power to crush people like the slugs that they were when they deserved it? She didn't know. Maybe, just maybe, it was all that passion and raw pent-up sexuality he'd given her a taste of.

But the reason didn't really matter because she felt her heart growing little arms, reaching longingly for him.

God, I so fucking want him. What am I going to do?

He gave her an angry look that she now suspected wasn't anger at all, but his way of expressing discomfort with something. It was a quick and easy way to deflect.

Yes, I am mastering his ways.

Oh stop, Tay.

"I kissed you because it was the only way to get you in the car," he replied curtly to her question, and then firmly but non-aggressively removed her hand from his phone.

She almost got angry. Almost. But her B.S. meter had lit up.

She gave a little laugh, crossed her arms, and leaned back in the seat. "If you say so . . . 'Bennett Fucking Wade,'" she playfully mocked his deep tone.

"I say so," he said coolly and made his call. It was to Robin, confirming the meeting change. As he listened intently, looking away, he slid his hand over to Taylor's thigh just above the knee.

Before she could process, he gave it a squeeze. A hard one meant to tickle.

She yelped, and smacked his hand away. "What the . . . ?"

Still not looking at her, he grinned and carried on the phone conversation. "Oh, good. Thank you, Robin," he said. "And please reiterate my apologies to Mary once again for the delay." He listened for a quick moment.

"Yes," he said. "I'll call her now."

Bennett disconnected and dialed another number.

"What was that?" Taylor swatted him across the biceps.

He looked at the phone in his hand and dialed another number, a hint of a playful smile on his lips. "Just showing you who's boss: me. Bennett Fucking Wade. Now be quiet while I make my calls, or I'll be forced to spank you."

Taylor laughed. *What!* "Pardon me, but—"

"Hi. It's me," Bennett then looked at Taylor pointing to his phone as if to say *Hey, can't you see I'm on a call?* and then proceeded to make a little spanking motion with his hand. Taylor growled.

He listened for a while, and any playfulness vanished. "Yes. Yes. Okay, but—" He listened some more, seeming concerned. "Why?" Silence. "If it will make you happy, but I assure you I'm fine." A few moments passed, and then he turned toward Taylor. "She wants to talk to you."

"Who?"

"My mother," he replied.

"Why does she want to talk to me?" she asked.

He sighed, cupping his hand over the phone. "She wants to check up on me. Just tell her I'm fine. I hate it when she worries."

Taylor tried not to smile.

"You find this amusing, Ms. Reed?"

She nodded, biting her cheeks. Of course she did. It was completely adorable that this tall, overbearing, prickly as hell CEO was such a mama's boy.

He shoved the phone at her. "Tell her," he hissed.

"What's it worth to ya?"

He narrowed his eyes and projected evil thoughts her way.

"It was just a joke." She snatched the phone from his hand. "Mama's boy," she whispered teasingly. "Hi, Mom." She looked right at Bennett when she said it to gauge his reaction and because she felt utterly drunk from that kiss. Totally. Out. Of. Her. Mind.

Bennett's nostrils flared with contempt.

Yep, he didn't like that one bit. It was just so damned cute. He didn't want to share his mommy with anyone.

"Oh, Taylor dear," Mrs. Wade said cheerfully, "I just wanted to check in with you. Is my Bennett behaving himself?"

Not even a little. "Yep. No problems," she replied.

"Is he taking care of himself and getting some rest, too?" she asked.

Not even a little. "Well, you know your son."

Mrs. Wade made a little grumble. "Well, you keep an eye on him for me, would you, Taylor? I worry about what will happen to him when I'm gone. He has the common sense of a pickle when it comes to his health."

Taylor felt another now-familiar pang of guilt. She'd almost just left Bennett to his own stubborn devices.

Mrs. Wade continued, "Just remember what I told you. The moment he tries to push you away, you put your foot down."

Taylor glanced at Bennett, who glared with irritation. "Yes, *Mom,* I certainly will."

"Good. Because you're my last chance to see him settled, and I know you're the one. The cookies never fail. I've researched it."

"Uhh . . . okay." She tried to maintain a cheerful expression on her face, but it wasn't easy. Being reminded that this woman was dying zapped the playfulness right out of her.

"You call me if you need any help, okay, Taylor? I'm here for you, honey. Anything you need until my last breath. That boy is everything to me. Everything. And someday, when you have children of your own, you'll understand. There is no possible way for me to repay what you're doing for him—and for me."

Oh crap. Now she was going to cry. *No, you* are *crying. Fuck, stop that. Stop. That.* She turned away from Bennett, hiding her face, because the drippy little faucet had turned on and she couldn't stop it.

"Taylor? You still there, dear?" his mother said.

She sniffled involuntarily. "Yeah. I'm here."

"You'll come to me if there's a problem. Won't you?"

This was the most awkward situation she'd ever been in. This woman was crazy and brash and pushy and endearing. It was impossible to say no to her.

"Ye-yes, Mrs. Wade."

"I told you, call me Mom. Or Linda. No more of this Mrs. Wade stuff. You're going to be the mother of my grandchildren."

"Yes, Mom." Taylor ended the call, and without turning around to face Bennett, she handed the phone to him over her shoulder.

"What's with the 'Mom' thing, Ms. Reed?" Bennett said.

Taylor shrugged, trying to hold it together. "I don't know," she lied. "She just asked me to call her that."

"Well don't. It's not only incredibly inappropriate to take advantage of my mother's shaky mind, but it makes me feel like you're trying to be my sister, and I find it distur . . ." his voice trailed off. "Are you crying?"

Taylor wiped the tears from underneath her eyes. "No."

He pulled on her shoulder, forcing her to face him.

He blinked at her. "What did my mother say?" he growled.

"Nothing. She's just really sweet. That's all."

"My mother? Sweet?" He didn't believe Taylor for a minute.

But no way would Taylor tell him the truth, so she said the first thing that popped into her head. "She reminds me of my grandmother." Taylor sniffled. The truth was that both her grandmothers had died before she was born.

"She was ornery, nagging, and controlling?" Bennett asked.

"Bennett." She smacked his arm again. His amazingly firm arm. "Don't talk about *our* mother like that."

He laughed, and it was a laugh filled with crisp, pure, in-the-moment joy. It mesmerized her.

When his laughter finally died down, he rubbed his beautiful eyes, one of which was still surrounded by a deep purple bruise. It gave him a rugged, mistreated, and in need of serious lovin' look. She could practically see his head filling with heavy thoughts. She really wished he'd tell her what was going on.

"I'm sorry about your meeting," Taylor said.

"I couldn't leave Tokyo not knowing if you were okay." He looked out the window away from her.

He gave up a very important meeting because he thought

something was wrong with me. The true meaning of that hit hard, and she heard a nonexistent splash inside her head. It was the sound of her jumping into that ocean. An ocean named Bennett Wade.

The only question was, would she sink or swim?

CHAPTER 12

After they arrived at the airport, she and Bennett silently made their way to the private hangar where his plane awaited. Bennett hadn't said much since those last words in the limo, and neither had she. It seemed, for the moment, that they both had decided to retreat back to their corners. What Bennett truly thought about her and this thing between them, she had no clue. But she felt terrified. It was too late to turn back. After all, one cannot unjump a cliff. At best, you could slowly climb up again, a very difficult and arduous task.

Not that she wanted to climb back up, because every time she thought of that kiss and how he'd grinded against her; or how he'd given up a meeting with Mary Rutherford to come find her; she knew in her gut that Bennett was a passionate man who kept it hidden from the world. Then there were those other undeniably kind gestures: his mother, Candy, the restaurant owner. Really, at this stage she didn't know much about him, but she knew how she felt. She wanted him.

But how the hell would something like this work?

It won't, she realized. Bennett didn't date people he perceived as employees. Even if she wasn't working *for* him, he was her client, and she couldn't argue with that.

Then, it was very clear the man had commitment issues. His own mother had been so desperate to see him settle down that she'd opted for getting him to eat love-cookies—a completely ridiculous idea.

Really, Tay? Because I'm pretty damned sure the seven days aren't up, and look at you. To be fair, she wasn't in love with the man; she merely had a thing for him. *Oh, look. Now you have a "thing," too. Match made in . . . a very, very confusing situation?*

She schlepped her way up the portable steel staircase behind Bennett. She was exhausted and frazzled both emotionally and physically.

Candy, who wore a fitted blue Wade Enterprises golf shirt, khaki slacks, and her red hair in a ponytail, greeted her with a warm smile. "Well, good morning, Taylor. How are you on this lovely day?"

"Hi, Candy," Taylor replied miserably.

"Oh, my. Looks like someone had a rough night." Candy reached over to give her a quick hug, but then Taylor found she didn't want to let go. Candy just had a warm, loving, comforting vibe. Taylor could see why Bennett had helped her. She was definitely one of the good ones.

Candy patted her on the back and whispered in her ear. "You okay, darlin'?"

Taylor nodded.

"Just take a deep breath, sugar. Mr. Wade might change his mind and hire you back."

Taylor pulled away, and from the corner of her eye she saw Bennett staring at her, frowning in a perplexed sort of way.

She looked at Candy, turning away so he wouldn't see her hobbled expression. "He said he was going to . . . *fire* me?" Taylor whispered meekly.

Candy's mouth pulled down in one corner. Then she made a little nod. "Oh no. Please don't tell him I told you—I thought he'd already done it."

Fire me. He is going to fire me. "Fire me for what?" Taylor whispered.

"Ladies," Bennett barked from the back of the plane. "May we leave now or you two going to chitchat all day?"

Taylor shot him a "thou shall be silent and take your seat now" look. Bennett's stern expression shifted into something half-docile, half-irritated. Kind of like a kid who has just been told to eat his broccoli or he won't get dessert.

Being the fiercely loyal and caring person that she was, Candy still felt obligated to make amends. "Yes. My apologies, Mr. Wade. Just telling Taylor here how happy I am to see you found her safe and sound." Candy looked back at Taylor. "Ms. Reed, if you'll take your seat?" She gestured to the front row and then leaned in to whisper while Bennett occupied himself with removing his jacket. "I've never seen the man so upset. His underpants were in a big ol' bunch all mornin', and when he got that alert on his phone that your tracker had gone off. Woo!" She fanned her face.

"He gets alerts when my cellphone signal drops?" Taylor asked.

"It's his 'thing,' " she replied, using Bennett's exact word. "And that man's head nearly exploded right off his big man-shoulders. Said he was going to find you and, I quote, fire. The. Hell. Out of you." She made a little shrug. "Guess he decided to wait until after Paris."

Taylor didn't know whether to laugh or cry or what. "Are you sure he's going to fire me?" Taylor asked.

"You broke two of his biggest rules: you made him miss a very important meeting and you turned off your tracking."

Taylor sighed exasperatedly. "Thanks for the warning."

Candy gave her a consoling look. "I'll bring you a mimosa, sugar."

Sure. Why the hell not. "Make it a double!" she called out.

Taylor grabbed a folded blanket on the seat next to her, covered her tired body, and tilted back her seat. So Bennett had kissed her just to get her into the limo and on to Paris, where he planned to fire her after he got what he wanted. How insane was that? Because as far as he'd been concerned, she'd already quit and had been on her way home.

She looked over her shoulder, contemplating asking him "WTH, Bennett?" but was too exhausted to confront him yet again. And getting Candy into trouble didn't seem like a great idea. The woman had been through a lot and had been kind enough to warn her.

Taylor looked at her trembling hands and for a moment envisioned wrapping them around Bennett's neck. *Oh, stop, Tay. You know that's not going to help anything.* The worst part was she could no longer afford to buy a ticket to . . . anywhere, frankly. She'd maxed out her last emergency credit card buying that one-way ticket home.

I can't believe Bennett is going to can me after he kissed me and insisted I come to Paris.

No. This is so irrational. It has to be some sort of misunderstanding. Or maybe he was just angry when he said it. But then she remembered the one key thing she'd forgotten. Telling a man like Bennett "no," only revved him up and made him more determined to win.

Was that what his coming to carry her off caveman-style was all about? And then, just for fun, he decided to kiss her in a way that made her panties want to go on an extended vacay? And for good measure, he let her have a little taste of his hard, thick, long cock so she'd salivate and come running like a dog for a . . . well . . . bone?

No. I'm not going to play this sick game anymore. She unbuckled her seatbelt and got up to go talk to him. As she made her way down the aisle, she watched Bennett talking on his phone, looking out the window. "You think I care?" he growled at whomever was on the other end. "No. Fuck no. The only thing that matters is this deal. Period. And anyone who gets in my way can go fuck themselves."

Taylor's eyes went wide. *What?*

She was about to turn back when he looked at her and smiled—just as the plane jolted forward unexpectedly. Taylor flew past Bennett into the small galley at the back, landing with a belly flop on the floor and smacking her head right into a cupboard.

"Owww . . ." she groaned.

When she rolled over and opened her eyes, Bennett kneeled over her, cupping her cheek. "Taylor? Don't move."

"Motherfucker, sonofabitch that hurts."

Bennett gave her a look. "Wow. You've been possessed by an angry sailor."

She slid her hand to the throbbing spot on the top of her head. "I have a dirty mouth," she groaned. "It's part of my charm."

"I don't know. Your mouth tasted pretty clean to me." He flashed a devilish smile.

She grumbled in response.

"Think you can get up?" he asked.

"Yeah."

He stood and held out his hand. "Didn't anyone ever tell you it's dangerous to get out of your seat during takeoff? You could've been seriously injured."

She took his warm hand and tried to ignore how good it felt when he pulled her up.

"Sorry. Wouldn't want to do anything to get in the way of your deal."

He gave her a look. "That was a discussion with one of my attorneys who's being difficult."

They stood face to face, and she stared up into his eyes. He hadn't let go of her hand, and the other arm—large and well defined beneath his tailored white shirt—lifted as he reached out to cup her face again. His thumb traced along her bottom lip as he stared lustfully at it.

Jellybean wants.

Shut. Up.

"Bennett, can I ask you something?"

"I already told you. We had our little honesty session for the day. I'm not ready for more."

"Fine. But I need to know if you really want me to come with you and stay or if this is just one gig." Because the ride on the Bennett roller coaster was giving her whiplash.

He gave her a strange look.

"I mean," she clarified, "changing the way you do things will take time. Are you in this for the long haul, totally committed? Or am I just a quick fix to get you across the goal line?"

He smiled at her. "Have dinner with me tonight."

What sort of answer was that? But if that's how he wanted to play, she could reciprocate with a non-answer, too. "You need to sleep and rest."

"What are you, my mother?"

She laughed. "I'm afraid my balls are too small, so that would be a no."

He chuckled. "Right you are. So am I to take your lack of an answer as a yes for dinner?"

Back to square one, are we?

"Long haul or goal line?" she asked.

"You're difficult."

"Mmmm . . . Yes."

"Great," he said. "I'll have Robin change the reservation to four people."

"Wait. That wasn't my reply; I was agreeing with you about me being difficult. And what do you mean four?"

"The dinner is with Mary Rutherford and her son, Chip."

"Oh." Of course it was. She'd helped him arrange it. Indirectly, anyway.

She felt a tiny twitch of disappointment. A dinner alone in Paris with him had sounded romantic and far better than being fired, but she just couldn't figure out what was going on with this man. Was he using her? Interested? Was this business or pleasure?

"So you need a wingman, huh?" She obviously knew both Chip—dirty, dirty man whore—and his mother—a dictator in a pink suit—so it would make sense he'd want her to come along as buffer.

He gently pinched her chin, tilting her head up toward him. She wondered if he might kiss her again. "Ms. Reed, I'm Bennett Wade. I don't need a wingman. I'm asking you to be my date."

Her insides got all jittery and cancan-y. She liked the sound of being his date. She liked it too much. "And then what? I mean, what happens after?"

"What would you like to have happen?" he asked suggestively.

She would love it if he kissed her again. She would love it even more if he held her down naked and thrust his thick hard cock—*Tay!*

She shrugged coolly, trying to mask her dirty thoughts. "Long term or goal line?" she repeated her question.

"Are you asking for a relationship? Because I don't do those—not anymore."

"What? No!" *Ohmygod. He thinks I was begging him to be my boyfriend?* And why "not anymore?" Was it because of that Kate woman?

"I was referring," she said, "to your commitment to the program—but what's your issue with relationships?"

"I thought you just said you weren't talking about that."

"You brought it up. Now I want to know."

He shook his head. "Dinner. Yes or no."

She wanted to say no, just to see what he'd do, how far he'd go to make her say yes, but that would be childish.

Don't neglect your inner child.

Okay. Compromise.

"I'll think about it," she said.

Agitation flickered in his eyes. "I'm going to get some sleep. When I wake, you can give me your answer, and we can go through your training. I have some questions about the material and want to make sure I handle Mary correctly."

Taylor scratched her head. His comment made her feel uncomfortable, like she was helping him deceive Mary.

"She's not an animal, Bennett. You can't 'handle' her."

"No. She's not. She's a woman—complex, stubborn, and intelligent. Just like you. Which is why you are the perfect person to help convince her to sell fifty-one percent of her company to me."

Anything to win. Anything.

Taylor sighed. She needed to get off this mental roller coaster before she lost her damned mind. One minute, she swam in Bennett's ocean, wanting him. The next she was angry because she felt like he was using her for this deal. One second, he flirted with her, the next, pushed her away or acted like it was all business. Being around Bennett felt like being in a crazy bipolar-flea rodeo.

Tay, you're letting him wag you. Stand firm. She understood there was more going on with him than he wanted to share, but she needed to put her foot down.

She stared up into his eyes. "I'll go to dinner with you. But after that, Bennett, you'll either have to tell me what's going on—really going on—or I can't stay."

He placed his hand on his hip, jaw pulsing, and looked toward the tiny window.

Now she felt bad. *Dammit! Fucking flea rodeo!* "I'm not trying to be mean or ungrateful, but within the space of a few hours, I've been snubbed, rescued, yelled at, kissed, flirted with, asked to work on your deal, tickled, pushed away, and then pulled closer. Not to mention, you still haven't explained why you participated in that a-hole-category bet with your friends that has absolutely reduced my self-confidence down to the size of a shriveled raisin, which is smaller than an actual raisin. And all you can say is 'trust me.' And that you have panic attacks when you can't reach people. Are you beginning to see how you might be asking a little too much?"

Bennett's strong jaw clenched hard, and his dark brown brows furrowed with deep emotion.

"Look at me, dammit," she said.

He did, and then she wished he hadn't. The anger in his eyes was palpable.

"I'm doing the best a man like me can be expected to do. Given the circumstances," he added.

What circumstances?

"But you're right," he nodded. "This isn't fair to you. I'll make sure you get home after we land in Paris. Just forget the dinner."

So that was his answer. Pushing her away. Yes, his mother warned this would happen and that she should hang on, but why? For what? Linda assumed Bennett and Taylor were meant to be because they'd both eaten a Happy Pants Café cookie. As cute as that sounded, Taylor needed to deal with reality and some very real, very confusing emotions, not to mention some serious career issues in her life. She no longer had the mental stamina or time to be playing around, and Bennett was turning her into a mess.

"Okay," she accepted his offer, not wanting to, but feeling like she had to try to rein herself in before she became so entangled in his addictive, masculine vibe that she'd never be able to climb that cliff back to sanity.

"But you're keeping the money," he added.

"No, I don't want it. You didn't get anything from me."

"I did, actually. Like I said, I emailed myself a copy of your program. It's not what I expected at all, but I think it's got potential."

"Please. *Don't* remind me that you violated my privacy. But it's yours to keep. No charge."

"Let me at least put in a good word for you with a few fr—"

She shot him a look. "You mean your friends who all think I'm some fuck-trophy?"

Something flashed in his eyes. "I'm sorry I said that. And I can see how you might think everyone is laughing behind your back, but if anything, the bet was a tribute to your moral fiber."

Taylor's mouth sagged open. "Did you just try to spin the bet into a good thing?" Her reputation was ruined.

"No. There's no excuse for the way everyone behaved, and I will make sure that you receive a public apology from each and every man involved; however, I'm merely pointing out that the cause of the bet was their immature egos. And their inability to accept the fact that they can't have any woman they like merely because they're wealthy." He reached out and gently grabbed her chin, beaming at her. "You, Taylor Reed, cannot be bought."

Her heart made a jump. His blatant admiration felt far too similar to deep affection—the kind that might start with the letter "L."

But then . . . "But why did *you* do it, Bennett?" she pleaded quietly.

He dropped his hand from her chin.

"Let me guess," she said, sensing his discomfort, "you're not ready to talk about it."

"I will make things right. That's all you need to know. Even if I have to break every one of their noses. Or in the case of

Charles, I'll rebreak it. Asshole deserves it anyway—the way he talks about women is vile."

Was that why he'd gotten into a brawl at his own charity event? She'd bet it was.

God, *I so want to dry hump you. Without any clothes on. With your penis inside me.*

Okay. Not dry humping at all.

"Thank you. It means a lot to me that you'll make things right." It might not help her land any clients, but at least she wouldn't be seen as a joke. "And it's payment enough."

He nodded solemnly. "It's the least I could do for your trouble."

"No trouble, Bennett." She wanted to say more, but she felt like they both had had enough. The man was looking pale again. "I'll let you get some rest."

She moved to the front of the plane and sat down. Candy appeared a moment later with a bag of ice for her head.

"You okay?" she asked.

Taylor nodded.

"He's not a bad man, Taylor. He's just had a bumpy road. Don't hold it against him."

Taylor smiled shallowly, feeling like she was on the outside of an exclusive club that knew the inner workings of this man. What bumpy road could he have possibly endured? Hot, rich, and powerful all sounded pretty nice. "I won't."

"I saw the way he looked at you. He must've been blowing off steam when he said he wanted to let you go. I've known that man for eight years, and I've never seen him look at anyone like that."

"Like what?"

"Like he wants to strangle you and then kiss the hell out of you. If I didn't know any better, I'd say he's into you." Her mouth then popped open, and she snapped her fingers. "Oh! I bet that's why he wanted to fire—" she made little air quotes with her fingers, "*the hell* out of you." She chuckled.

"Meaning?"

"He won't date employees. But that doesn't mean he can't fire you and *then* date 'the hell' out of you."

Taylor took the bag of ice and plopped it on her aching head. "You're mistaken, Candy. He just needs help closing the deal."

She shook her head, grinning. "Sure, honey. Whatever you say."

CHAPTER 13

Taylor awoke to yet another gentle nudge after having passed out from exhaustion. With the time difference, constant lack of sleep, and drama, she'd just . . . gone away. Candy gave her another quick push. "Honey, here's your ticket to San Francisco. I made sure to get you a pass to the Admiral's Lounge so you can shower, change, and eat, but the flight leaves at 7:30 P.M. That's in three hours."

Disoriented, Taylor took the ticket. "Uh. Thanks." She glanced over her shoulder toward the empty plane.

Candy caught on. "He's gone. Off to his hotel and then the meeting with Mrs. Rutherford. Told me to give you his regards and the number for his ear, nose, and throat specialist. Honey, have you ever had that snoring looked at? Dear baby Jesus, you're loud."

Taylor grimaced. "No. I didn't really know." Of course, she hadn't really been with anyone in a while and her last boyfriend never spent the night—had to get home to his schnauzer. Not that she'd complained because the guy wasn't a natural-born spooner like Bennett, and a guy who didn't know how to cuddle or keep her feet warm at night didn't make for a good bed bud.

Bennett, on the other hand, knew how to keep every part of her warm.

Taylor stood slowly and collected her things. She felt so torn up, as though she'd been inside a crazy blender for the last few days and it had finally spit her out.

"Your suitcase has been sent ahead, Taylor. But if you need anything, anything at all, just call me."

"Thank you, Candy. I really mean that."

Candy flashed a consoling smile. "That's what I'm here for darlin'. It's been my pleasure."

Taylor moved toward the open doorway. "Hey, why don't you give me a call when you're back in S.F.? We can catch a drink." She quickly dug a card from her purse and handed it over.

"I'd just love that, Taylor." Candy snapped up the card and gave her one last hug. "You're a survivor, girl. Keep that chin up."

An hour later, Taylor was clean, in her gray sweat pants and tee—the spares she carried in her laptop case for emergency travel lounging or for doing exercise—and she'd found food. The spa-like facilities in the Admiral's Lounge were probably better than anything she'd ever experienced even at a real spa—steam room, massaging shower head, fru-fru shampoo—but the soothing atmosphere did little to get Bennett out of her spinning head. She really, really hated leaving things between them so unresolved.

Finding a quiet spot in the lounge next to the window, she got out her laptop and began writing Bennett an email:

Dear Bennett—

No. Stupid. Erase.

Hi Bennett!—

No, too enthusiastic.

Hey, Bennett. I know you're busy and probably don't want to hear from me—

No. Too pathetic.

Bennett: I know you're busy, but I didn't get the chance to say goodbye and I feel like there are some things I need to get off my chest. First, you need to know that I like you. A lot. And I don't mean in the way a person likes a movie or a new pair of socks. I mean that when I'm in a room with you, I get lost. In your smell, your voice, and the way you touch me. I know there's so much more going on with you than you let on and that I can't understand it, but I'm willing to trust you. I'm willing to give you time. Your mother told me that you think all women are after your money, and that's just crazy. It also means that whomever you've shared your life with thus far has caused you to form that opinion, an injustice I'd like to help you over-come. What I mean to say is that I like you. Not because you're good looking or wealthy, but in spite of those things. I'm also a stupid lame ass for writing this email and should be shot because we both know I don't have the balls to send such a sappy piece of rat turds. I suck. Kill me now.

Taylor highlighted the entire thing and hit *Delete*.

Bennett: I need to talk to you. Call me. Taylor.

She was about to hit *Send* when she realized she didn't actually have his email address.

Her first thought was to call Robin, but then she remembered that Bennett had been digging around on her laptop, and that he had emailed the training module to himself.

She clicked open her sent mail. *Ha! There you are.* She did a CTRL + C on his address—and then her eyes caught the contents of the email. It was empty save for the attachment: Leadership_BWade_v2.

"What!" She stood from her chair, nearly dumping her laptop on the floor. "No! No!" He'd sent himself the *wrong* module. How the hell was that possible when he'd said he thought it was surprisingly good! Anyone in their right mind would at least question the modified sections, especially without having her serve it to them with a heaping helping of bullshit anecdotes about Mary Rutherford's personality and why the methods would work.

Taylor looked at her watch. Bennett's meeting was probably over, but they'd be going to dinner, so maybe she still had time to keep him from completely ruining his deal.

She dialed Bennett's cellphone and paced back and forth in front of the window overlooking the airstrip. *Voicemail?* "Fucking shit!"

Just then, an elderly woman passed by and shot her a look. What was with her screaming inappropriate things in front of elderly women?

"Oops! Sorry! Sailor mouth over here." Taylor pointed to herself and then heard Bennett's voicemail beep.

Oh no. Do I leave a message? Do I hang up? Ahh! Message!

"Bennett! It's me, Taylor. Please, you have to call me back the moment you get this. Please . . . just don't speak to Mary or say anything. I need to talk to you!"

She hung up and stared at the phone.

She could turn off the Bennett cell. It would probably make him come running. *No, he won't—he's expecting you to get on a plane and have to turn it off, silly.*

Ugh! Okay . . . As she continued to pace, she did some quick time zone math—it was eight in the morning California time, so Robin might be at work and would probably know how to get ahold of him. She dialed quickly, but it too went to voicemail. *Fucking dammit! Dammit! Dammit!* At least this time she kept the sailor-talk to herself.

Taylor looked at her watch. *Almost five o'clock.* There was no way in hell she could get on that plane without speaking to Bennett first, and she still had a few hours before her flight.

But I'm totally out of money, and I can't sprint to Paris. Thinking, she paced and then paced some more, before deciding to call her brother.

Doctors were never really off duty, so he'd answer no matter what.

It rang three times before she heard Jack's reassuring voice. "Dr. Reed," he said, all groggy.

"Jack! Are you at your house?"

"Taylor? Yes, I'm home. And why haven't *you* come home yet? Are you still traveling with that slimeball? If yes, tell him I'm going to kick the crap out of him for tarnishing your reputation."

Jack was clearly still mad about the picture in the tabloid. Taylor could only imagine what he and her brothers would do if they ever found out about the bet.

Castration or eyeball-plucking for sure. Which obviously was no good. Those parts of Bennett's body held a special place in her sad, dirty little heart.

"I'm in Paris right now, but I need your help. There's a check for fifty thousand from Wade Enterprises on the dresser. Think you can deposit it for me?"

"I'll do it if you come home and bring that shmuck with you to dinner."

"No, Jack. I'm not going to let you beat up Bennett Wade. And he didn't do anything." *At least, not what you think.* "I'll explain everything later, but I'm in Paris and out of money and—"

"I'll get over to the bank later, but it's going to take at least a few days to clear."

"Sometimes they make a portion of the funds available immediately."

"I'll just loan you a few thousand," he offered.

"No, Jack. I can't—"

"You can pay me back when your check clears," he said.

She really, really hated to borrow money from him, especially after he'd been so generous with giving her a place to live, but what other choice was there?

"Thank you." She sighed. "I don't know what I'd do without you."

"You'd land on your feet like you always do, Tiger. Now get your ass home."

"Love you. I'll text you once I'm on my way."

"Money will be in your account in a few minutes. Love you, too," he replied.

She ended the call and headed out of the lounge to start looking for some clothes while she waited for the transfer to come through. She wasn't getting into any office buildings or nice restaurants in Paris dressed in her quasi jammies or the wrinkled, stale travel clothes that she still had with her.

She grabbed her laptop bag and purse and sprinted for the nearest airport boutique.

After the world's most awkward hour-long cab ride with a French driver who wanted to practice his English and then lecture her in "Frenchlish" about the shortcomings of Americans, Taylor entered the *Dame Marie* headquarters and abruptly found herself being pushed out onto the sidewalk by a very smarmy-looking security guard with a lazy eye and large mustache. Oddly, the man reminded her of that Sebastian man she'd met at Ms. Luci's house.

"Well, *whatever* to you, too!" she bellowed back, ignoring the snickers of the nicely dressed professional Parisians flowing in and out of the Renaissance Period office building. Located on Avenue du Maine, near the tower of Montparnasse, which looked like a giant erection defiling the skyline of the historic city (as the cabby had bitterly pointed out), Lady Mary's offices were supposed be near all of the world-famous tourist attractions like the Louvre and the Eiffel Tower. But she hadn't seen anything she recognized yet, apart from a multitude of mopeds and *boulangeries* that reminded her of *Ratatouille*. She so needed to get out more and stop speed-dating these amazing cities.

She looked down at her outfit, wondering what the hell to do. She had to get in to see Bennett—if he was even still there—but she looked like a complete tart in the skintight red dress that showed her cleavage and was far too snug wear for underwear. She'd been in a huge hurry and the options at the airport had been limited. It had been this or a bikini the size of a Post-it with dental floss in the back. And yes, she wore red, glittery spiked heels, but it had been that or her flip-flops. Standing out front, trying to ignore the abundance of catcall action, Taylor's mind went to work. There had to be a way to get in touch with Bennett before he did himself in with Mary.

She glanced at her phone again. Why hadn't Bennett called her back?

Shit. Maybe she should call his mother. She'd help, wouldn't she? *Worth a try.*

Taylor scrolled through her contacts and passed a name that caught her attention. "Dirtbag." Why hadn't she thought of that before? Dirtbag was code for "Chip," Mary's son.

She hit *Call.*

"Well, well, well," said a deep, entitlement-laced voice that repulsed her. "If it isn't Taylor Reed."

"Chiiiip," she said cheerfully, trying her best to not let her revulsion show. "How are you?"

"A million dollars poorer, but otherwise well, I suppose."

Taylor wanted to punch him in his man parts—not that he had any, because real men didn't slither.

She played the innocent card and threw out, "Oh, no. That's awful. I know a person you can call for gambling addictions. She's not cheap, but she's really worth every penny."

"How can I help you, Taylor?" Chip asked.

"Actually, I'm looking for Benn—Mr. Wade. He's having dinner with you and your mother tonight, and I've been trying to reach him—it's urgent."

"What kind of urgent?"

"Oh, you know; complicated business matters involving math. Nothing you'd understand."

"Uh-huh. Well, maybe you should try calling his assistant. Goodbye, Tay—"

"Wait! I'm sorry." *Not really, you cockroach.* "I tried his assistant, but she's not there. It really is important, and for whatever reason, Bennett's not answering his cell."

"*Bennett*—" he emphasized the fact she'd used his first name "—is not answering for *you*, perhaps. In which case, it's none of my business."

Oh, you little fucker.

"Chip, don't hang up. I'm standing outside your headquarters, and I really need your help."

"Really, now? You sound desperate, Taylor. And I think I like it."

Of course he would.

"You got me. We had a misunderstanding, and I really need to talk to him. Please," she added in her best Bennett tone.

"He's already left the building."

Oh no. "How did the meeting go?"

"Your usual boring crap—numbers, empty promises—you know."

"So your mother didn't throw him out? Never mind. Do you know where he went?"

"He said he was going to see a friend, but didn't share where. However, I know where we are having dinner."

Thank God. She could get to him before he made any huge mistakes. "Where?"

"What's it worth to you?"

Slimy sycophant. "What do you want?" she asked.

"I want a taste of what you gave Bennett."

She wasn't sure which taste, but she had to assume the worst. "If you mean what I think, the answer is no."

"Why? I've been told I'm fun. And it would make me happy—happy enough to tell you where we're having dinner."

"I am *not* going to 'make you happy,' Chip."

"You made Bennett happy," he argued. "Am I so unworthy of your pussy?"

Ewww. "Just so we are clear. I *did not* make him happy either, and yes, you are unworthy."

"You didn't sleep with him?"

"No." She felt a pang of guilt for getting Bennett into trouble, but then she remembered it was his fault for making such a stupid fucking bet in the first place. "Want your money back?"

"So I paid him for nothing?" Chip laughed. "Slimy son of a bitch. Wait, but doesn't he let you call him Bennett?"

"He doesn't let me; I just do," she replied.

"Then he must be into you."

"Bennett?" she deflected nervously. "Into me? No."

"You're lying. I'm hanging up now."

"Our relationship is complicated," she blurted out.

"In that case, you have something I want."

"I already told you I'm not sleeping with you, but I will help you get your million dollars back." She wasn't really sure she could, but maybe Bennett planned to give back the money anyway, given what he'd said about making things right.

"I don't want it back," Chip said. "Bennett lost the last three rounds of golf, so I'm still ahead."

How much do they bet on golf?

"Be my date tonight," Chip said.

"What? No," she replied sharply.

"You want to see him?"

"Yes."

"Then you'll have to be my date."

Taylor rolled her eyes. "Why?"

"Because if he's into you, there's no greater prize than watching his face when he thinks he's lost you to me. And you better do a good job, or I'll tell my mother that Bennett lied about sleeping with you to get a million dollars out of me. I'm sure she would love that."

"You wouldn't," Taylor seethed. It wouldn't matter to Mary who instigated the bet. She would want nothing to do with Bennett if she found out he had taken part in it.

"I would. And then she won't sell her company to him. She hates liars."

Wow. Chip really was as low as they came.

"Fine. I'll be your date," she said.

"Excellent. And maybe you'll change your mind about the fun after that."

"No. I won't."

"We'll see about that. I'll text you the address once I'm on my way to the restaurant so you can meet me out front. And wear something nice."

Was a hooker red dress from the airport considered nice these days in Paris?

CHAPTER 14

Taylor stood outside the posh restaurant nestled between a very fancy handbag shop and a shoe store she'd never be able to afford in a million years, shivering in the cool evening air. Chip had given her strict instructions to wait out front.

She'd tried to reach Bennett several more times, stopping only to book herself a new flight home, but the calls kept going straight to voicemail. Had the pouty bastard blocked her? Still, she hoped to at least intercept him before he entered the restaurant. But then again, if she did that, Chip might tell his mother about the million-dollar lie, and Bennett would lose the deal. It was a lost cause. She had to go along with Chip.

Well, maybe Bennett won't care if you show up with Chip. After all, it wasn't like she and Bennett were dating. They'd shared two kisses, and he'd had a little sleepy time fun with her privates, but other than that, they were . . . acquaintances. *No, that's not exactly right either.* Honestly, she didn't know what they were.

Well, whatever it is, we're about to become nothing. Less than nothing, because Bennett would be furious when he learned about the fake module.

This is the right thing to do, Tay. You'd never live with your-self if he lost his big deal.

Chip pulled up in a sleek black Jaguar and handed the keys to a valet. When he got to the sidewalk, his brown eyes practically shot from his head. "Taylor. Don't you look . . . that is one . . . that dress is so . . ." He ran his hand self-consciously over the top of his thinning blond hair and then licked his almost nonexistent lips. The man basically had just a hole for a mouth, which made his drooling look worse than it probably was.

She sighed. She knew she looked like a woman ready for some serious action, but she hoped he would remember what she said: *Not getting him happy!*

"Thanks," she said coolly. "So where's your mother?"

"Oh, she's inside already. With Bennett."

Taylor growled under her breath. She'd been standing outside while Bennett had been in there. She should've realized.

Chip reached out and tried to pull her close. "Now, how about a little warm-up kiss?"

She winced and pushed away. "I said I'd be your date, not make out with you."

"You have to make it convincing, or I tell Mother."

Taylor shook her head. "Why do you always have to be such a pig? And what's with you, anyway? You and Bennett are supposed to be buddies."

"Wade and I go way back to college, yes. But I can't count the number of girlfriends I've lost to him."

"Bennett stole your girlfriends?"

"Technically, they weren't my girlfriends. Yet. But getting any woman's attention with Wade around is impossible."

So how was that his fault? The man couldn't help that he was smokin' hot any more than Chip could help not having lips.

He continued, "This is my chance to take someone from him."

"Bennett and I are not in a relationship. We're just—"

"Stop. He lets you call him Bennett in public, he's been seen with you more than once, and he took you on a business trip—"

"As a consultant," she argued.

"Trust me. I know the man. He doesn't spend that much time with anyone. Ever," he added.

His words made her stomach all twisty. She really wished she meant something to Bennett, but it simply didn't seem to be the case. "You're wrong. I'm telling you; he won't care."

Chip wiggled his brows. "Let's just see about that."

This was going to be so horrible. She'd tell him that the materials she "gave" him were not to be used. He'd ask why. She'd say something vague like they weren't good enough. He'd press for more, and she'd be forced to admit the truth of what she'd done in front of Mary and Chip. Then Bennett would yell at her in front of the entire restaurant and have her thrown out. She would leave with her tail between her legs, having saved Bennett from blowing up his merger, but he'd never speak to her again.

The thought set off all sorts of strange emotions. *Uh, that would be called sadness, Tay.*

"Shall we?" Chip extended his arm. "Hope you like sushi."

She swallowed back her laughter as they entered together. *A French sushi restaurant? Seriously? Please don't let them serve fugu.*

Chip spoke to the host in fluent French, and they followed

the man through the upscale restaurant. It wasn't like any sushi restaurant she'd ever seen—white tablecloths, waiters in tuxedos, and abstract paintings of fish on the walls. No floating sushi boats in this place.

As they passed through the dining room, she caught all sorts of attention with her scandalous red dress. And these were the people who gave the Fifty Shades movie a PG-12 rating. Nothing shocked the French. *Except your revealing, horribly tight outfit, which is now displaying your hard chilly nipples.*

When they approached the table, she spotted Mary Rutherford's short, wavy, white hair and Bennett's full, thick head of dark hair. He and Mary were leaning toward each other, deep in discussion. Mary was smiling but looked subtly annoyed. *Oh no!* And Bennett was just rattling on, but didn't seem to be noticing.

Wait. Who's she?

A stunning redhead with a face, eyes, and body only seen in movies or on the covers of airbrushed magazines sat beside Bennett. She had full lips, ample cleavage pouring from the low-cut neck of her black dress, and she couldn't be a day over twenty-two.

Bennett brought a date. I think I just might die.

Bennett glanced at Taylor and then back at Mary and then his head snapped back to Taylor, his eyes widening and sweeping over her body.

Mary looked right at Taylor, too, then at Chip.

"Chip, honey," Mary said, her tone deceptively sweet, "you're late. And you brought a . . . date." Her critical gaze landed back on Taylor and then she lit up. "Well, hello Ms. Reed. I almost didn't recognize you in that dress. I had no idea you were in town."

"Nice to see you again, Mary," Taylor said, trying to keep her body from shaking in a fit of jealousy. And seriously? Did Bennett have to bring someone so hot? She was a perfect ten. Per. Fect. Meanwhile, Taylor was average height and had the sort of body one acquired from a lifestyle dedicated to the pursuit of trying to stay employed and working behind a computer. Totally normal. A solid six.

Chip took Taylor's hand. "Yes. Sorry about the last-minute headcount."

A waiter appeared with an extra chair, setting a place for Taylor at the large round table, directly across from Bennett.

Bennett slowly rose from his seat, his eyes bouncing between Chip and Taylor.

"Wade, old boy," said Chip. "I believe you know my date, Taylor."

Bennett frowned and dipped his head. "Ms. Reed. So you're still in Paris."

"You two know each other?" Mary asked, her eyebrow rising slightly.

"She works for me. Or used to anyway," Bennett explained.

"I see." Mary looked at Taylor. Although Mary had to be in her late sixties or early seventies, she didn't look a day over fifty with her smooth creamy skin. Publicly, she attributed it to her products, but no one could look that good without a little help from a scalpel. "Well, Ms. Reed, it is a pleasure to see you again. I heard you left that headhunter company."

"I did. I started my own business," Taylor replied.

"That's lovely," said Mary, approvingly. "I am a firm believer in blazing one's own trail." That was certainly true. Mary had started Lady Mary when she was in her early twenties after her husband—an older man—ran off with his secretary, leaving her with a new baby and little income. What had started as a door-to-door business, with Mary selling hand-blended perfumes just to make ends meet, had resulted in a global empire. "Life is about living your most beautiful dream" became her company's slogan, and it made her billions.

"Taylor was waiting outside my apartment," said Chip, "and I insisted she join us for dinner."

Mary gave him a harsh look. Chip had made it sound like Taylor had been hoping to seduce him or something.

"I was doing some last-minute shopping before heading home," Taylor clarified. Or lied. *Whatever. This is awful.* "Just stopped by to say hi."

"Well, pleased you could join us, dear," Mary said graciously, although Taylor was sure that crashing a dinner was not on the woman's list of proper behaviors.

Bennett's cold eyes burned into Taylor from across the table.

"Um. Are you sure? I don't want to intrude," Taylor said, losing her nerve.

Chip put his arm around her and kissed her cheek. "Now, now. I wouldn't dream of letting you out of my sight, Taylor. It's been a long few months." Chip pulled the chair out for her. "You're always working and too busy for me, but your surprise visit makes up for all that time apart."

Mary cocked a brow, clearly surprised by the news that they had some kind of relationship. "Well, there you are then. You will have to stay. My Chip insists. Mr. Wade was just explaining how he and Brigitte also happened to bump into each other today."

"It wasn't exactly a bump," Bennett elaborated. "I also stopped by her apartment merely to say hello, but then I thought she might like to join us."

Taylor felt her stomach knot with devastation. Not only had she been replaced as his date, just like that, but Bennett had gone on a booty call? Seriously?

Brigitte smiled. "I lobe it when my Bennett surprises me wit his bumps," she said in a perky little voice with her perky little French accent.

Taylor's heart dissolved right inside her chest. Brigitte had called him Bennett. *Bennett.* Only his mother and women he slept with got to call him that.

You call him that.

Yes, but only because I'm stubborn and he lets it slide.

But this woman—*ugh*—she was sexy and petite and had those full lips men were so into. Taylor had freckles on her nose, wide-ish hips, and plain old everything. She wasn't ugly, but she wasn't going to get stopped in the street and asked to model for a Victoria's Secret catalog either.

Now, now. You sport the flannel animal-themed jammies with the best of 'em.

"It's nice to meet you, Brigitte. I'm Taylor Reed."

Brigitte flashed a sour little smile. "Hello," she said, sounding more like "halo."

"Yes, lovely to meet you, Brigitte," Chip agreed, giving her his version of the charming lipless smile. "Any friend of Bennett's is a friend of mine."

"Chip, dear," said Mary, "stop flirting with Mr. Wade's date. It's pathetic and I taught you better."

"Yes, Mother," Chip replied dejectedly.

"So, Ms. Reed," Mary said. "Tell me about this new business of yours."

"Um. Okay." This was it. Time to come clean and take her licking. "Well, I developed a coaching course for executives to help them connect better with their employees and cut down on turnover. It's a new way of thinking about leadership—a bottom-up approach versus top-down. It helps foster loyalty."

"And would you call yourself loyal?" Bennett asked Taylor, his tone as frigid as his gaze.

She lifted her chin. Yes, she would. But Bennett would never see her as that. He'd never understand how sorry she was. "I do. In fact, I needed to tell you that the material I gave you was—"

"Mr. Wade, I'm shocked," Mary said. "Have you been taking this course from Ms. Reed?"

Keeping his fierce gaze glued to Taylor, Bennett gave a quick nod. "Yes, and I've learned quite a lot." His eyes flickered toward Chip for a moment, making his point clear to Taylor— that he saw her being with Chip as a sign of betrayal. Or maybe he was disappointed? She didn't know.

Mary let out a little laugh. "Well, that is impressive, Mr. Wade. I never saw you as a man who pursued self-improvement. I thought I noticed something different about you, but couldn't put my finger on it."

Mary actually seemed . . . pleased? Whatever coaching ideas Bennett had exercised today, he must've only used them minimally.

Mary added, "And now we know we have you to thank for it, Ms. Reed." She smiled and it seemed genuine.

Taylor mentally phewed, realizing she'd panicked for no reason. And now that she thought about it, she should've known that Bennett's arrogance would take over and demand he do things his way. *I'm Bennett Fucking Wade. The boss!*

Bennett kept his sharp gaze focused on Taylor. "Yes, thank you, Ms. Reed, for enlightening me."

"And I should thank *you*, old boy," Chip said, "for getting my beautiful Taylor here to Paris." Chip brushed Taylor's cheek lovingly, and she wanted to shrink away, but didn't. "You have no idea how long I've waited for her to come around."

Bennett's face turned an embittered shade of red.

Oh God. This was not going well. Or maybe it was? Bennett's deal with Mary seemed to be moving forward, despite everything.

Taylor needed to take a moment and regroup. "I am going to use the powder room." She stood, and Chip did the same, pulling out her chair like an attentive boyfriend, a wickedly triumphant smile on his face.

"Don't keep us waiting long, *mon cherie*," Chip said.

"I think I weel join her." Brigitte moved to stand, and Bennett rose to pull back her chair. She leaned forward and kissed Bennett on the cheek. "I'll be right back, Benny."

Benny? Taylor wanted to hurl. Was that the name he let women use when their relationship was more than just fucking? Maybe "Benny" was the next level up, like boyfriend or perhaps serious snuggler and "Ben" was reserved for his future wife.

Taylor swallowed back her jealousy, trying to focus on the positive. She hadn't ruined Bennett's life—good—and now she knew the truth: He hadn't really been interested in her at all. He'd gone on a booty call or snuggly session or whatever Benny did with a beautiful woman like Brigitte.

Yes, I finally understand my place in his world.

Not turning around to look at the supermodel on her heels, Taylor found the bathroom. Once inside, she went to the vanity area next to the sinks to freshen up her makeup and convince herself that she could make it through the night without crying.

Who are you kidding? You're so going to cry. She'd simply have to tell everyone she wasn't feeling well. It wouldn't be breaking her deal with Chip, so why not?

Brigitte came out of the stall, tugging down her black dress. "Well, I think," she said eyeing herself in the mirror, "dat we've both done nice. *Oui?*"

"Sorry?" Taylor said.

"We both have ourselves a nice reech boyfriend. Life is gud, no?"

"Yeah," Taylor said glumly, pulling out her lipstick. "Life is good. So how long have you been dating, Benn—Mr. Wade?"

Brigitte shrugged. "We went out the last two times he was in town. You know—for a leettle fun. But I told him," she wagged her finger, "the next time he comes to me, he'd better be ready to give me more, or he can lose my number."

"Really?" Taylor asked.

"I won't be young forever, and I habe two other very reech men who are interested." She shrugged. "But I do not geeve zi milk for free, like some women." Her eyes washed over Taylor.

Taylor got the not so subtle slap, but didn't let it get to her. Honestly, her mind was set on something else. Sheer rage. This bitch was exactly the reason Bennett had issues. *Frigging gold digger!*

"So you think Bennett has come for your milk?" Taylor asked.

"Why else? I think he weel propose tonight, actually."

Taylor was going to be sick. Literally sick. *Well, at least now you don't have to fake being ill.*

"Want to know what I think?" Taylor said, "*Benny* is too smart to fall for your little game, but if he does, you'd be lucky to get a guy like him."

She laughed. "Lucky? Dis man hazz no passion. No love in his heart. The only thing he hazz is his looks and his mooney."

"You're disgusting." Taylor scowled.

"You snobby American. I see you with dat Chip. You are no different than me."

Taylor shook her head. There was zero point discussing any of this with Brigitte. And it wasn't her place to warn Bennett. He was a very, very smart man, and if he was with Brigitte, it was because he wanted to be. He trusted no one, and he certainly wasn't going to start with this trollop. He was making a choice. On his own. *Like a big stupid guy who thinks only with his dick.*

"Have a nice night, Brigitte. It's been a pleasure." Taylor lifted her chin and pulled open the door to leave. The moment she stepped out, someone had her by the hand, yanking her to the side.

It was Bennett. He wasn't even looking at her as he pulled her toward the stainless steel kitchen doors.

"Bennett," she hissed, trying not to cause a scene, "what are you doing?"

He kept on marching, dragging her through the doors where a waiter preparing some salads immediately barked at them.

Bennett spouted out a phrase in French that sent the waiter fleeing into the dining room, a look of fear in his eyes.

Of course! He speaks French, too! Didn't he understand how irritatingly sexy that was? *Sexy, French-speaking jerk face!*

The three chefs, all sautéing in their big white hats behind the waist-high wall at the back of the kitchen, were too busy to notice or care about the intrusion as were the busboys who rushed in and out through the doors.

Standing in the middle of the kitchen, the sound of pots clanking and pans sizzling all around them, Bennett turned to face her, standing just a little too close—within easy lip reach.

Not that she wanted to kiss him.

Much.

Tay! No you don't!

She jerked back her hand. "What. Are. You. Doing?" she growled.

"No. What are *you* doing?"

"I'm in the process of leaving," she replied.

"That's a wise choice, though I'm not sure why you're here with him at all," he snarled. "Chip? Seriously, Taylor?"

"Really? You're really going there?" she fumed at him.

He gave her a look, getting the drift that she was "really" referring to Brigitte. "If you think so little of me, then you truly don't know me at all."

She stared up at him, his eyes filled with self-righteous indignation.

"You know what?" She threw up her hands. "Maybe you're right. So why don't you try telling me what I'm supposed to know, Bennett, instead of acting like this giant brick wall of manly mystery." Honestly, most of what she'd learned about him had come via his mother or Candy.

"I have my reasons for being cautious, Taylor. And they're not what you would call pleasant or admirable."

"Everyone has a past. Why should you be any different?"

"Because the world holds me to an impossibly high standard. Although I'm not sure they're half as critical as you."

What was that supposed to mean? "That's not fair, Bennett. I've been way more understanding than anyone else would ever be considering the circumstances. But if you want me to stop judging you or assuming, then we're right back where we were on the plane today. You need to tell me the truth."

"About what?" he said sharply.

"About you. Why are you killing yourself for this Bali project? Why did you lie to me and take that idiotic bet?" She looked at him, waiting for the answer.

He stared, but there was no give. His eyes and expression were closed off behind that infamous Mr. Wade brick wall.

"Fine. Whatever is going on with you, whatever's happened to make you this way, just remember that I had nothing to do with it." She turned to leave, and he grabbed her hand.

"Taylor." His tone was earnest.

She looked at him, waiting, but whatever he was about to say didn't come out. "*What? What is there to say, Bennett?*"

"I just don't think you'll understand," he said in a low voice. "I don't think anyone can."

She now saw that his bricks were holding back pain. A lot of it. But if he couldn't at least give her a glimpse of what was behind that wall, how were they supposed to move forward?

"How do you know if you don't try me?" she said softly.

He stared but didn't speak.

Dammit, Bennett! She wanted so badly to kiss him and touch him and tell him how she felt about him, but it would be a fool's errand. He didn't want to open up.

"Then I'm sorry for you, Bennett. I truly am. Because there's no one in the world who wants to understand you more than I do." She pulled out of his grasp and headed for the dining room. The moment Chip spotted her, he stood and pulled out her chair. "Honey bear, I missed you."

Taylor held out her hand. "I'm afraid I won't be joining you for dinner this evening. I'm very sorry, but I suddenly don't feel well."

"Ms. Reed," Mary said. "That is a shame. I was looking forward to hearing more about your company."

"You're very kind Mary, but it's really not worth talking about," Taylor said. "In fact," she looked straight at Bennett who'd just shown up and taken his seat, "you should throw the material away. It needs a complete overhaul. I mean it, Bennett, don't do yourself a disservice and go any further with it." Taylor glanced at Brigitte who was also back at the table. "It's a waste of your time. Good night everyone. Have a lovely meal." She turned and walked out of the restaurant. She held up her hand and a taxi pulled to the side. She reached for the door and looked over her shoulder. For a moment, she hesitated. Her heart didn't want to let go of Bennett, but she needed to accept reality. Bennett was the sort of man who did what he wanted. He didn't want a real relationship, he didn't want to trust, he didn't want to change. . . .

And he doesn't want you.

Taylor got into the car and directed the driver to the airport.

CHAPTER 15

"No. What do you mean my reservation isn't in your system? I have the confirmation number right here." Taylor dug out her notebook but couldn't find the napkin she'd used to jot down the code she'd been given. Dammit. She'd probably used it to wipe her tears and blow her nose on the cab ride here. She'd tossed it.

The tall man in the uniform behind the ticket counter shook his head. "I'm sorry, but there is no record. Except for the flight you were booked on earlier, which you checked in for and didn't board. So that ticket fare is lost, I'm afraid."

"How can that be?"

"Yes, ma'am. Those were the rules of the fare. I've put in a request for a review to see if they'll allow a credit; however, that will take up to a week."

"A week?" What the hell? Well, Bennett had purchased the ticket, so hopefully they'd give him a credit, but where did that leave her?

"Can I buy a new ticket?"

"I'm sorry. There's no room on this flight."

This can't be happening. "When's the next one?"

He typed away on his keyboard. "Tomorrow at two P.M."

Taylor looked toward the industrial-style ceiling, and then the long line of impatient travelers waiting behind her.

"But," he added, "the fare will be three thousand five hundred dollars. There's only business and first class left."

Taylor rubbed her face. She couldn't afford it. Jack had only put a few thousand into her account, and there was no way in hell she'd go back to ask for more. Also, she fully intended to repay Bennett his fifty thousand. So every dime she spent dug her deeper into a hole.

"When's the next coach flight available?" she asked.

The customer service rep clicked away on his computer. "I'm afraid not until tomorrow night. But feel free to try one of the other airlines."

Taylor groaned. "Thanks. I'll see what I can find online." Shoulders sagging in her stupid dress that was so tight she wanted to scream, she slogged past the long line of ogling travelers.

Yeah, yeah. Haven't you ever seen a nearly naked woman before?

Her personal phone rang, and she slipped it from her purse. She didn't recognize the number, but answered it anyway.

"You turned off your other phone again," said a deep, sensual voice.

It was Bennett.

Her heart did a little dance even while her stomach churned with tension.

"Yeah, well," she said, "it ran out of juice and my charger is sitting in my suitcase—wherever the hell that is. Besides, I don't work for you anymore, so you're free to let go of your *thing*."

"Don't you mean 'I don't work *with* you'?" he asked. "And I can't let go of my *thing*. It's my *thing*. Things don't just go away because you wish them to."

"What do you want, Bennett?"

"To see how you're doing."

Oh, screw him. She was a mess. A goddamned mess. And now she had to go home and figure out how the hell to keep breathing, defeated on every single front in her life—professionally, romantically, emotionally. "I'm feeling much better now. Just about to board my flight, so I gotta go."

"How am I supposed to trust you and let down my brick wall of manly mystery when you lie to me?" he said, disapprovingly.

Shit. "You're standing right behind me, aren't you?"

"I am now."

She slowly turned to find an irritated and handsome as hell Bennett walking right up to her. He'd removed his jacket and rolled up the sleeves of his white dress shirt, exposing his muscled forearms.

Her knees wobbled. Her breath caught. Her entire body did a dip and roll as if she'd just taken a big dive on a roller coaster—only this ride also vibrated and turned her the hell on.

"We really need to stop meeting like this." His eyes made a quick sweep of the terminal. Yeah, they had kind of been doing a planes, trains, and automobiles thing.

"Why are you here, Bennett?"

"I'm flying on to Bali in five minutes," he said with a smarty-pants tone, while staring down at her.

"Well, have a nice trip." She turned to leave him, but he grabbed her shoulder.

"Can we go somewhere to talk?"

No. No way. She was done putting herself out there.

He took her hand. "Please?" he asked nicely.

Taylor's resolve instantly began melting away. "Give me one good reason, Bennett?"

"Because I'm asking."

It was true; he hadn't demanded like he usually did. And yes, that made her a little warm and gooey inside. "Are you sure Brigitte would approve?"

He smiled. "You really are jealous."

"No."

"Yes. You are. I can see it on your face."

"I am not jealous." Okay, she was a little. *A lot.* But more importantly she was . . . "I am disappointed, Bennett."

"Why?" he asked. "Because I don't meet your standards?"

She pulled her hand away. "If you came here to pick another fight, you're wasting your time. I said everything I needed to say." She huffed, turned, and started walking away.

"Wait. I'm sorry, Taylor. I just want to talk!"

Unsure of where she was heading, Taylor weaved between the bustling crowd of passengers toting their roller bags and pushing strollers.

"You should know that I brought Brigitte because Chip was going to be there. I needed to keep him occupied while I worked on Mary."

Taylor couldn't believe her ears. She swiveled and stormed back to him. "You'll do anything to win, won't you?"

"It's called business, Taylor. And there is no shame in fighting for what you want in this life."

"There should be shame if you have to use or deceive or—"

"It's called persuasion. And when you're trying to get someone to do something they're against, sometimes you can't just throw money at them."

"Oh. Now I get it. That's what you did with me back in Japan. Money won't work, so I'll just kiss her! And show her my giant boner!"

I can't believe I just said that.

Bennett cocked a brow, but then an obvious curiosity flickered in his eyes. "Why are you so distrusting, Taylor? Is it because I'm wealthy? Or the boss? Why is it that when you see men in power, you automatically assume they don't care or only wish to exploit the people around them?"

She tipped her head. "I think you're the one with the trust issues, Bennett. But no, I don't think that about you."

"Don't you? Isn't that the reason you went for my jugular the day we met? Isn't that the reason you started your company?"

She was about to protest, but then snapped her mouth shut. He'd hit a nerve, but he wasn't entirely wrong.

"You might be right," she admitted, "and maybe it's because I grew up being the only female in a house full of big bossy men and had to constantly fight not to get trampled on—but don't pretend those CEOs don't exist. Just look at your golf buddies. You all ruined my reputation and never gave it a second thought."

"You're right, Taylor. It was wrong. And I said I was sorry. Which is why I meant what I said about setting the record straight for you. But you don't do yourself any favors going out with guys like Chip."

"I didn't go out with him—he . . ." Taylor blew out a breath. "Never mind."

"You did it to make me jealous."

Again, she was about to protest, but he didn't give her the chance—

"Well, it worked," he said. "And that dress . . ." He looked her over. "I didn't like him seeing you in it. Or anyone, for that matter. Even right now I'm having a hard time not getting angry at the stream of men walking by and ogling your body."

He was jealous?

Bennett stepped in a bit closer, and she felt the heat of his body. He slowly moved his hand to her face and stared deeply into her eyes. "I kissed you in Tokyo because I thought of you leaving, and then I panicked. Because no one has ever looked at me like you do, like they truly get me, the real me."

Taylor's heart was thumping away like an unevenly loaded washing machine. She thought she might actually fall over.

He continued, "And I sent you home because every time you look at me, I want more. More of you, more of those lips, more of your sassy little mouth. And it scares the hell out of me."

Oh, God. Oh, God. Did he really just say that? Really. Because I don't think I can believe it. I really, really don't.

"Because you think I'm after your money?" she asked hesitantly, her body going numb with the overload of emotions she felt.

"No." He dipped his head, holding his mouth an inch from hers. "Because I know you're not." He leaned down and kissed her. Not soft. Not hard. Just enough pressure to let her know it was an invitation for more.

He slowly pulled away. "I'm not going to try to talk you into anything, because I don't want you to think I'm manipulating or using you, but if you really want to see what's underneath this suit, then there'll be a ticket to Bali at the Air France counter. However, Ms. Reed, you should be warned: I am a greedy man—but it's not for money." His eyes slowly moved to her lips, down her neck, to her breasts, and up again. "Your flight leaves in two hours. Enough time for you to think long and hard about this next step."

"Long? Hard?" She gulped.

He turned and walked away, disappearing into the crowded terminal.

Fuck, he's hot.

Taylor took the appropriate amount of time, standing in the terminal, trying not to fall over in her wobbly red hooker heels, thinking about his offer. *Yep. Two. Uh-huh.* It took her all of two whole seconds to decide she'd be getting on that damned commercial flight to Bali. But it wasn't for the reason anyone might think: Sex with Bennett Wade. Okay, that was part of the reason. Her body didn't just ache for the man, it felt a raging, searing, gnawing heat that started at the tips of her toes, scorched its way right between her legs, torpedoed through her stomach, speared her heart, and ended somewhere in her brain where it latched onto every thought she had.

However, and a big, big however at that, the biggest reason she wanted to go was because she'd never forgive herself if she didn't. Her heart wanted this badly. And if she didn't listen to that part of herself, she'd spend the rest of her life wondering if she was meant to love this hot mess of a man and if he was meant to love her back.

Oh boy. She pushed her hands to her abdomen, feeling like she was on that roller coaster again. Danger mixed with euphoric exhilaration. But with a porn element to it.

Okay. You know, know, know you're going. But how would

she, a very inexperienced woman, handle a fuck-stallion like Bennett Wade? She could never meet his worldly expectations.

She glanced at her watch. It was just after ten at night, which meant one-ish in the afternoon California time. Sarah would be at work, finishing up her lunch hour.

Taylor found a quiet corner near the security checkpoint and called.

"Taylor! Hey, honey. How's the trip going with that client?" Taylor hadn't told Sarah or Holly who her client was—she had figured it didn't really matter at the time and that they'd chew her out for agreeing to work with Bennett (aka a-hole who'd gotten her fired).

"Umm . . . it's not good," Taylor confessed.

"Oh no. What happened?"

"I think I'm falling in love."

Taylor heard Sarah spit something out. *Coffee?* "What? How the hell did that happen? You've only been gone for what, a week?"

"Four or five days. Depending on the time zone?"

"Are you sure it's not a hard case of lust?" Sarah asked. "You haven't gotten laid in forever."

"Yeah. I'm sure." *Thanks awfully for pointing that out, though.*

"So, who is he?"

"My client," Taylor replied.

"One of those asshole billionaire guys? The ones you said you'd never ever date because you don't date clients?"

"Yes."

Again, Taylor heard spitting on the other end of the phone. Sarah must've been bathing her entire office in coffee. "No. Taylor, please tell me you have better taste than that."

"I'm afraid not," she said dejectedly.

"This is bad."

"Would it sound better if I told you that he's not entirely an asshole?" Taylor said.

"Not entirely an asshole implies he's still an asshole."

True. "What I need to know, Sarah, is . . . I don't know what to do. He's invited me to Bali, and I know I'm going to go but—"

"So why are you calling me? Sounds like you've made up your mind."

"I'm afraid," Taylor replied.

"Why? Is he into kink? Just make sure you agree on a safe word."

"What? No. I mean—he might be into that, but I didn't get that vibe. I meant I'm afraid I won't be able to handle him."

"In what way? Is he really hung?"

Yes. Absolutely, but . . . "Can you get your mind out of the gutter? I'm trying to say he's intense, Sarah. Really fucking intense. And he's also damned sweet. But I can tell he's damaged. And I'm not sure how bad that damage is."

"Intense, sweet, and damaged. Hmmm . . . sounds fuckably hot," Sarah said.

"He's that, too."

"I'm still not seeing the problem," Sarah said. "You're a grown woman. And I've never known you to be reckless—a little crazy and hotheaded sometimes, but never reckless. If you like the guy, then go for it. Just keep an open mind and see where it goes."

"Honestly, I guess . . . I'm afraid he won't ever love me back."

"Awww, sweetie. You're wonderful. And smart. And beautiful. What's not to love?"

"We're talking Bennett Wade, here. He's not easy to please, and then there's the fact that women throw themselves at him—gorgeous women—like twelves on a scale of one to te—"

"Stop the bus. Taylor, did you just say your asshole billionaire is Bennett Wade?"

"Yes?"

"And you've been flying all over the globe in his private jet, looking at him, sharing the same air, hearing his voice, smelling him, maybe even touching him?"

"Yeah?" Where was she going with this?

"And you haven't fucked his brains out yet?"

Huh? "No!"

"Hold the hell on." The line went silent for a very, very long moment and then Sarah came back on. "Taylor, you still there?"

"Yeah?"

"Holly, you there, too?" said Sarah.

"I'm here," Holly's sweet voice piped in. Taylor groaned.

"Holly," Sarah said, "Taylor is going to Bali, and you'll never guess who she's going to fuck."

"Saraaah . . ." Taylor warned.

Before Holly could respond, Sarah spilled the beans. "Bennett Wade. Can you believe that?"

Holly squealed. "And you called Sarah first? WTF, Taylor. I'll forgive you, but only because I want details. Lots of details."

"Guys," Taylor said, trying to rein them back in, "I thought you hated the guy? Remember, he's the one who degraded my ex-boss?"

"Oh, we were only trying to be supportive when you told us,

Tay," said Holly. "Your boss sounded like a complete bitch. We were kind of happy about all that."

They were?

Holly continued, "Then there's the fact that Bennett Wade is a fucking sex god. Sex. God."

Seriously? This is their response? "Whatever," Taylor said. "I called because I really need—"

"Taylor," Holly interrupted, "you tap that cock hard. You hear me. Hard. And let him stick it anywhere he wants. Make us proud!"

Taylor pulled the phone from her ear and looked at the caller ID, wondering if her two friends were on something. Sarah was an uber-conservative, uptight, by the book goodie-goodie when it came to sex, and Holly was a plain, sweet-as-can-be girl next door who worked as an appraiser for a major auction house based out of L.A., meaning she was very big on taking her time and evaluating things before acting.

"Oh. Tay!" Holly added. "Make sure you measure it and tell us if he hangs to the right or the left."

"I bet he's uncut," Sarah said enthusiastically. "He looks like the type who'd be all raw and natural with a big dick."

"But you know he man-scapes, down there," Holly said. "Bennett Wade does not go native with that bush. No way."

Eck. What in the world? "Did I just call a male-genital-enthusiast chat line?" Taylor objected.

"Yes," Holly said, "and you will do it in every position known to humankind. Take notes—pictures, too, if he allows it—you have morals, obviously—but don't have too many—and then you will share every detail with us. You got it, Taylor? That's an order."

Taylor's two friends started busting up, snorting uncontrollably.

Taylor sighed. "I can't believe you two. I gotta go."

"What?" Sarah said defensively, trying to catch her breath from laughing so hard. "That man has been number one on my fantasy fuck list for five years. Five."

Wow. "Uh. Okay. I really am hanging up now." Hadn't she just told Sarah that she was in love with Bennett? This conversation was so, so wrong. Bennett wasn't some piece of man-meat. *This must be why he doesn't trust women.*

"Notes, Taylor! You hear me! Tell your old furry southern girl to take notes, too! We want to know the location of every freckle—"

Taylor ended the call feeling like she'd had the sanctity of her sanity violated by two horny women parading as her sweet, sensible, intelligent best friends.

"Insensitive jerks," she grumbled to herself.

She decided to call Jack and let him know she was still in Paris, and that he shouldn't expect her.

When Jack picked up, she immediately knew he was cruising in his BMW with the top down.

"Taylor. Where is that fuck?"

"Excuse me?" Taylor said.

"I'm going to break his fucking nose," he yelled.

"*Who?*"

"That womanizing bastard, Wade. He slept with you and then fired you, didn't he?"

"No!" she said. "What makes you think that?"

"Just because I'm a man and surgeon doesn't mean I don't have an app to keep up with celebrity news, Tay. Or that I wouldn't beat the crap out of some rich douche bag who uses my sister. Especially after he almost got you killed flying his piece of shit little plane. Marcus and Rob are in on it, too."

Who is this person? Jack was talking like a street thug. They must've put something in the California water while she'd been gone.

"I really don't know what you're talking about," Taylor said.

"Maybe you should try being more discreet in public. Really, Taylor. You practically let the man have sex with you on a sidewalk."

"Oh no. No no no no. You mean someone filmed us in Tokyo?"

"Were you having almost-sex in another city with another billionaire on video?" Jack roared.

Taylor felt herself turning as red as her dress. "Oh geez. We were just kissing—maybe a little passionately, but that was all that happened."

"Then why did he fire you? He did fire you, yes? That's why you're stranded in Paris, isn't it?" he accused.

"Yes. I mean—no. It's a long story. But I haven't slept with him." She planned to, but that was irrelevant.

"Ah. So that *is* what happened! You refused him, so the scumbag dumped you in Paris without any way to get home. By the way, Dad wants to say hi . . ."

"Hi, honey," she heard her father's voice.

Her dad was in the car. *Oh the shame . . .*

Her father added, "Tell that bastard I know where he lives, and he better watch his back. The Reed men are coming for him."

"Dad. Jack. Bennett did not use me for sex and dump me in

Paris. Or dump me because I wouldn't sleep with him. Okay? It was a misunderstanding, some of it my fault."

"You don't need to be ashamed, Taylor," her dad said. "We won't love you any less because you got caught up in one of those Fifty Spades fantasies you women are into."

Has the whole world lost its mind? "It's Fifty Shades, Dad. Shades. And I'm not into—oh, never mind. I'm calling to let you know I'll be home in a few days. I'm heading to Bali."

"Are you going with that prick?" Jack seethed. "Did he threaten you? Pull a Robert Redford on you and offer you a million dollars?"

"No. Ewww. I gotta go. You two have a great day."

"Tell him he can't run forever, Taylor!" she heard her father's booming voice yell right before she disconnected the call.

Great. My best friends want to build a sex shrine to Bennett's penis and the men in my family want to chop it off.

By the time Taylor landed in Bali, it was exactly one day and one hour later—eighteen-hour flight, through Singapore, and a six-hour time difference. Not that she'd ever gotten on Paris time or Tokyo time (she was basically just on Bennett time), but her internal clock felt like one of those crazy windup toy mice for cats that zoom around in dizzy little circles.

The first thing she did after deplaning was give herself a quick sponge bath in the bathroom, using some of the items from the complimentary business-class toiletries bag. She had felt a little guilty that Bennett purchased such an expensive flight for her until she realized the seats in business-class lay down flat and how badly she needed sleep. Especially, if she was going to be in good shape for sex with a man like him. Then again, he'd been driving himself so hard that he'd been passing out from exhaustion on a regular basis; maybe she stood half a chance of impressing him.

Not in these clothes, she thought, checking herself out in the mirror. She'd put back on her sweats and T-shirt from earlier, which now looked exceptionally rumpled and sloppy. She'd written off her suitcase entirely as it had been tagged for her flight to San Francisco.

She splashed some water on her face, dried it with a paper towel, and then put her hair up into a high ponytail.

She left the boarding gate area, carrying only a purse and her laptop case. The moment she passed the security checkpoint, she noted how the air smelled thick and dank. It reminded her of Hawaii or Florida.

A man, standing in the small crowd awaiting their loved ones just outside the cramped but sterile customs room, held up a sign with "Reed" written on it. He wore a long green skirt and a red and white linen shirt.

"Hello. That's me," Taylor said, pointing to the sign.

He tilted his body, peering behind her. "No luggage, ma'am?"

"Uh, no. I'm traveling light."

"Very good. Right this way."

She followed him through the doors to a square-ish minivan waiting at the curb. It was pitch-black outside, and a gentle tropical breeze wafted over her warm face.

"He will take you to Mr. Wade," the man said to Taylor, gesturing to the driver.

Taylor thanked him and slipped inside the car. She didn't know where she'd be staying, but she'd expected them to head south—that's where the luxury resorts were located according to the map she'd studied on the plane. But instead, they headed north, up the eastern coast. Trust Bennett to catch her off guard again.

"Excuse me, but where are we going?" She leaned forward between the front seats.

"Mr. Wade has a room for you at the Pacific Palace, ma'am. Near the golf course. But his family estate, where he grew up, is another few hours beyond that. He said he did not want to make you drive so far this late at night."

Bennett grew up here? Did that have something to do with his project? In any case, she couldn't at all picture him growing up in such a laid-back vacation destination. Everything about him screamed city boy and structured, sophisticated and disciplined. *Even when he doesn't wear a suit, he still wears a suit.* Which made her start to wonder . . . was it just a façade?

That was what his mother had said. He had a big heart and tried to hide it.

Will the real Bennett Wade please stand up?

"Thank you." Taylor looked out the windows as they drove through town. Despite being well past midnight, hordes of small mopeds zoomed by. The urban sprawl reminded her of the many tourist towns she'd seen all over South America when she'd gone backpacking in college. Lots of small, cement block homes, and mom-and-pop stores that sold either fruits and vegetables or local cuisine.

Without warning, rain began coming down in big sloppy drops, pelting the windshield.

"I thought this was the dry season," she commented. Yeah, she'd had a lot of time to kill on the plane so she'd done the requisite Internet surfing on her laptop using the plane's WiFi. Honestly, she'd never thought much about going to Indonesia, but now she wondered what had kept her away. The country seemed to have every activity known to man—river rafting, hiking, sailboating; lovely ancient temples and stone monasteries; and then there were the beaches, with water ranging from dreamy deep blues, perfect for surfing, to the clear turquoise found in the quiet glassy bays. All of it skirting deep lush jungle and steep mountain terrain.

"Yes, this is the dry season," said the driver. "But we still get the occasional storm—like the one coming in tonight. Should be gone by the end of the week."

End of the week? There go my beach excursions. Not that she was there for vacation. Unless one counted marathon sex with Bennett Wade?

An hour later, they pulled up to the sprawling, open-aired lobby area of what looked to be a very upscale resort, complete with marble floors and elegant furniture made of dark wood with white upholstery.

She thanked the driver and tried to give him a twenty, but he refused, telling her everything had been taken care of by Mr. Wade.

Taylor's heart fluttered like crazy the moment the man said Bennett's name. She didn't know what she'd say when she saw him. *Hi, ready to have your mind completely blown with some very mediocre sex?*

"Good evening, ma'am. How was your flight in from Paris?" said the young woman behind the reception counter. Her dark hair was pulled into a neat bun and she wore a cream-colored linen tunic.

"You know who I am?" Taylor asked.

"Yes, ma'am. The owner left very specific instructions." She raised her hand into the air and a young man wearing a khaki linen uniform appeared.

Owner? "Do you mean . . . Bennett Wade owns this hotel?"

"Yes, ma'am," she said demurely.

Okay, yet another surprise. So this *had* to be his project. He was expanding his company into hotels and resorts in addition to the fragrances business. She supposed that was nice, but was it really worth killing himself over?

The attentive bellhop was standing next to her, looking confused.

"I don't have any luggage. It's somewhere in Paris," Taylor said, feeling a little embarrassed to be checking in to such an extravagant resort in the kind of clothes one might wear for a midnight run to 7-Eleven for a pint of ice cream or a bag of Cheetos.

It was also eighty-something degrees, and she was wearing sweatpants.

"He will take you to your suite," said the clerk. "What is your size, ma'am?"

"Size?" Taylor asked.

"Yes, of your clothing? We will have a selection of garments and sandals sent to your room."

"Oh. That's not necessary," Taylor said. "I'll hit the gift shop in the morning." The one in the lobby behind her was obviously closed.

"Mr. Wade made it clear to see you were taken care of. It is no problem, ma'am."

Taylor wrestled with her conscience for a moment, but she really could use something clean to sleep in. "I'm a size eight. Or ten. Depending on the day. And don't worry, my flip-flops are fine." Taylor had on the horrible pink pair she'd also had stashed in her laptop case as part of her emergency comfort outfit.

The woman raised her brow. "We will have the items sent to

you within the hour, ma'am." She looked at the patiently waiting bellhop. "Please take Ms. Reed to the presidential suite."

"Presidential suite? Are you sure?"

"That is where Mr. Wade always stays, though it's not often
we see him."

"Is Bennett—I mean—is Mr. Wade staying, too?"

"Yes. Mr. Wade said he'd be here shortly to join you for the
evening."

*Okay. We're going to share a room. This is happening. Really
happening. And I haven't shaved anything. Ohmygod. I am a
mess.*

"Um, are there bathroom supplies in the room?" Taylor
asked.

"Yes, Mr. Wade asked for everything to be fully stocked."

*Oh, thank God. My underarms look like Teenage Ninja Ta-
rantulas. Very hairy and mysterious.* Taylor followed the bellhop outside where he popped open a jumbo-sized umbrella.
Through the drizzle, they made their way past several lush gar-
dens and a multitude of individual bungalows to a private gate.
It was the middle of the night, so she couldn't see much, but the
place looked like a beach paradise.

The man unlocked the gate, and they entered a dramatically
lit garden leading to what looked like a private residence. Two
stories. Dark wooden construction. Elegant yet rustic.

They entered, and Taylor's jaw nearly dropped. It was absolute heaven, furnished like a five-star hotel room with beautiful
teak wood furniture and bright white upholstery, bamboo ceiling fans, a wet bar, flat screen TV, sprawling living room, and
floor-to-ceiling shutter-style doors on half of the exterior wall.
She guessed the living room opened up to an insanely gorgeous
view of the beach.

The bellhop showed her upstairs—another living room slash bedroom with a king-size bed surrounded by gauzy white mosquito netting, blonde bamboo flooring, and a big balcony. She couldn't wait for the sun to come up so she could see it all properly. It was amazing.

The moment the guy left, she sprinted into the bathroom and went through the supplies. "Yes!" She had never been so happy to see a razor in her life. Sadly, however, the toilet didn't sing or talk or play music.

She started the shower and jumped inside, quickly washing her hair before getting to work on the kitty, taking care not to get too crazy with the bikini line. She didn't know what Bennett was into—bald eagle, landing strip, sasquatch?—but shaving was not waxing and what man wanted to get a friction burn from vag stubble? Not good. She went with manicured and womanly. A safe bet for both.

She brushed her teeth, wrapped her hair in a towel, and slipped on the complimentary terry cloth robe.

A few minutes later there was light knock at the door. Taylor hurried to answer it, assuming it was the bellhop bringing the clothing delivery.

Instead, Bennett stood there, looking rumpled, damp, and sexy in khaki linen pants and a white shirt, unbuttoned at the top, the sleeves rolled up, exposing his muscular forearms. His lightly tanned skin had a light sheen of sweat, and his hair was mussed in a hot bed-play kind of way.

Her pulse slammed into overdrive.

"Ms. Reed." His lips twitched, and those intense blue eyes swept over her body. "I hope your flight was uneventful?"

She blinked at him, feeling like she just might lose her nerve. It was one thing coming all the way to Bali, knowing that things were going to change between them, but it was another thing entirely staring at this big magnificent male with a profusely carnal gaze and sultry lips, knowing she was going to have him inside her body.

"Yep." She gulped, unable to find anything remotely casual to say.

"Are you going to ask me in?" He rubbed his jaw, which had passed out of the stubble-zone and was now officially covered in a very short, thick dark beard. He looked hotter than hell.

"Oh, of course." She stepped aside, and when he passed by, she smelled that addictive concoction of his light sweat and expensive cologne—a sort of fresh, clean, citrus mixed with raw man. "This place is incredible. Do you sex here a lot?"

He lifted a brow. "Uh. No. Not really. I prefer to sex at my estate in the comfort of my own bed."

She looked at him, scrunching her brows together.

"You asked if I 'sexed' here a lot," he said.

She cupped her hands over her mouth. "I did?" she mumbled through her fingers.

He smiled and then reached out, pulling her hands away and stroking the corner of her lip. She began shaking, and he must've noticed because he dropped his hand.

"You look like you could use a drink." He glided that tall, broad-shouldered body of his over to the wet bar.

"You read my mind. I'll have penis."

"Will you now?" He laughed and gave her a look. "I'm not sure I know that drink, but I think I can come *up* with something."

"You don't know wine? It's that stuff that comes from grapes."

"You said 'penis.'"

No I didn't. Oh my God. What's the matter with me? "I did?" This X-rated tongue-tying had never happened to her before. Of course, she'd never been with a man like him.

"I thought *I* was nervous about tonight," he mumbled under his breath while pouring the drinks.

He was nervous, too? Bennett Wade? That man had everything going on. Everything. How could *he* be nervous?

She tightened the cloth belt around her waist and sat on the overstuffed white couch facing the gas indoor-outdoor fireplace. It likely connected to the world's nicest porch with a view of the Indian Ocean. She'd go check it out, but she was too busy worrying about what to say. How did a woman like her even begin a night like this with a man like that who probably had very high expectations about sex?

If he's lucky, he'll get "really good" out of me.

Honestly, she'd never experienced anything above mediocre, so she wasn't sure how to deliver "really good" let alone unforgettable or mind-blowing, both being the next levels up on the sex-awesomeness scale, only superseded by "Holy shit, kill me now because my life just peaked, and it's all downhill from here unless he can do it again, in which case, I need some Gatorade and an energy bar." Of course, her sights were set infinitely lower, toward just the really-good bar. Maybe he'd find some novelty in it? Just like he might in seeing a nonsurgically enhanced body?

Oh no. Should I prepare him? She didn't have fake boobs, and she certainly didn't have a perfect body. Hers could be described as Rubenesque, sort of round and squishy with small, half-grapefruits for breasts topped with soft little nipples that perked up only when cold or touched in the right way. *No sexy perma-erasers here.*

As for her ass, well, it was an ass. Not too tight, but round and soft and great for sitting on things. That was good, right? Of course, her thighs could use a little toning. *They're flabby, okay? Flabby!*

Shit. He's going to barf on my thighs. He's been dating movie stars and models. He's probably never even seen a normal woman with natural boobs. She might need to show him some 70s porn to acclimate him first.

Bennett sat next to her on the couch—not too close, not too far away—holding two glasses of ice-cold white wine. Despite the late hour and gently circulating air from the ceiling fan, the humidity felt extreme. *Great. Now my sweat is sweating.*

"Your glass of penis, Ms. Reed." He handed her the drink, and two little dimples puckered beneath the thick black whiskerage coating his angular jaw.

She gave a little half-laugh, half-huff. "Thanks."

"So," he said.

She sipped her wine. It tasted like a Saúvignon Blanc with grapefruit undertones. Which only reminded her of her boobs. Her nonsurgically enhanced boobs.

"So." She bobbed her head awkwardly.

"I'm glad you decided to come."

"Well," she sipped her wine again. "I think—I mean—I know if you asked me here, it's because you really wanted me to be here." *Wow. Can a grown woman possibly be any more awkward?*

"May I ask you something?" he said.

"Sure."

"Why are you so nervous?"

Oh, hell. Let me count the ways, starting at the top. You have thick dark, wavy hair that is perfect for finger play. You

have these really nicely shaped dark brows that make me ques-
tion my sanity with just one little flick. There's your face—
chiseled jaw. Lips that might've actually been stolen from an
angel—or devil—of seduction. You have this little scar that
runs from your lower lip to your chin, insinuating that you're
not afraid to fuck shit up when the moment calls for it, and
your body is six feet and three (or four—haven't measured)
inches of hard, manly ripples—oh yes, it is. Because I've seen
you half naked and have felt your hard shaft pressing against
both sides of my body. Then . . . well, there's your enormous,
thick cock and when you walk, I just know your arrogant swag-
ger is really the result of you lugging around your huge fucking
manhood. There's your damaged hero complex, the fact you
kiss like a champ and . . . when you look at me with those ri-
diculously crystalline blue eyes, I feel like you're staring right
into my soul and that you totally get me. And despite totally
getting me, you still maybe want me, which blows my fucking
mind. Need I go the fuck on?

She shrugged. "I don't know."

"You do realize how hard it is, don't you?"

Her eyes involuntarily moved to his groin, but she caught
herself and quickly put them back where they belonged: on his
face. "Sure. Yeah. I guess it should be hard. Given what's coming. R-r-right?"

"It certainly is a lot to fit into one evening." He nodded and
then sipped his wine. "It's a lot. I mean . . . *a lot.*"

It certainly was "a lot." She'd felt it rub between her ass
cheeks, and she'd seen the outline of his erection in his pants. In
comparison, the men she's been with were cocktail wieners or
dainty carrots at best.

Yeah. This might hurt. But I so, so want him.

She chugged down her wine and placed the glass on the coffee table. "I'm ready. No matter how big it is, I really want this to happen."

"Good." He swallowed down his wine and set the empty glass next to hers. "Because it's pretty painful."

She cringed. "Really? I mean, I know it's big, but I think I can handle it if you're gentle and move slow. I mean," she laughed nervously, "don't come at me all at once. Just ease it in and—"

"Ms. Reed?" He straightened his spine and stared at her with an intensely worried look. "I'm wondering—and please don't be offended by what I'm about to say—but do you think I invited you here to fuck?"

Uh, yeah! Her eyes went wide. *Uh, nooo?* She covered the exposed skin on her chest with the lapel of her bathrobe. "Are you saying you didn't?"

He looked at her and shook his head stiffly from side to side. "No."

She felt her face turning tomato red. "You mean that—when you said that—you wanted me to come and see and . . . Oh God. What have we been talking about?"

"Me. The real me. Why I'm here in Bali, and why I'm . . ." His voice trailed off as she covered her face. She then felt his hand squeeze her arm. "Taylor?"

"I'm so humiliated. I thought that you—never mind." Hadn't he asked if she wanted to see what was beneath the suit?

Yeah, bonehead! Metaphorically speaking! Like Superman would ask Lois. She took a breath, lifted her chin, and stood.

He stared up at her from the couch, sort of smiling, but not. "Where are you going?"

She turned slowly, fearing with every step she might disintegrate into a giant poof of utter humiliation. "I think I need a moment," she whispered and then went up the stairs to hide inside the giant bathroom. Perhaps she could live there forever until everyone she knew grew old and died.

At the exact moment she entered the bathroom, there was a loud knock at the front door. She heard the rumble of Bennett's voice and then the click of the front door.

Heavy footsteps grew closer up the stairs. She prayed she might evaporate. She'd traveled all this way and hemmed and hawed, ultimately deciding that she would give her body to him only to discover he didn't want her.

But then, what did he want? *Duh, you idiot. For you to see the real him. Yaaay, let's be friends!*

"Taylor?" Bennett lightly knocked on the door. "Why are you hiding in the bathroom?"

"This is where women go when they need to feel humiliated and rejected in private. Or to pee."

He laughed. "And which of those would you like me to assume you're doing?"

"Number one and two—no! I mean, the first two. I'm not peeing or doing that other thing."

Kill me now. Please, please, please. I summon thee, o' bolt of lightning.

"You are a very odd woman."

"Only when it comes to intimacy," she groaned.

"Which is why, perhaps, I feel a certain ease with you. Now, please open the door."

"I really can't look at you right now," she said.

"All right. I'll leave the clothes here on the bed and wait downstairs. Then you and I are going to talk."

"About what?" What an ass she was.

"Come downstairs when you're ready. I'll be waiting."

She looked at the marble countertop, grabbed a washcloth, and began wiping down the drops of water she'd left all over the surface. *Dammit. I need some bleach.*

She then paused and looked at her shaking hand. *What in the world are you doing?* Bennett had offered to open himself up to her, to let her in and tell her something extremely private. Hell, he'd said it was painful. But there she was, thinking about herself, about how *she* felt, about being rejected when that wasn't what he was doing at all. He'd offered what she really wanted: him. Not *just* sex, but him.

God, I really am such an idiot. She chucked the washcloth into a little basket underneath the sink and planted her hands on the vanity, hanging her head.

It seemed from the moment they'd met, she'd systematically devolved into a child. Everything she thought Taylor Reed was had been stripped away, piece by piece. Her job, her illusion of being respected, her financial independence, her belief she was in control—something that had given her comfort once upon a time. But now she was beginning to see clearly. Control was an illusion, and meeting Bennett had shown her that. Life was like a river, and the river flowed in one direction and one direction only. Sometimes it moved nice and easy through familiar territory; other times it became wild and turbulent and carried you to untamed lands. You either made the most of the ride or you didn't.

She laughed quietly to herself and suddenly felt an odd sort of peace, as though all of this was meant to be. Maybe being reduced to nothing but a girl on a raft on a river was exactly what she needed at this point in her life. Maybe she had to let go. No baggage—literally. No judging. No expectations of any kind. *Stripped down naked.* Maybe that's what it took to truly see a complex man like Bennett for who he was. *And accept him.*

Taylor took a breath, splashed some cold water on her face, and then looked at herself in the mirror. *Okay. You can face him, Taylor. You can face whatever it is he's going to say without judgment or expectations.*

She reached for the bathroom door handle and paused. "You're standing right there, aren't you?"

"Yes."

Sneaky bastard.

She pulled open the door and there stood Bennett, thick arms crossed over his broad chest, eyebrows raised, and wolfish smile on his face. His linen shirt and pants gently hugged the masculine silhouette of his body. Yes, even his casual clothes were tailored. *Tailored for trouble.*

"I thought you went downstairs?" she said, noticing that he'd dimmed the lights in the room a bit and had turned on the palm-leaf shaped ceiling fan, making the mosquito netting around the bed dance.

He shrugged. "If I did that, I'd miss watching you get dressed."

She blinked.

"Or getting naked?" He grinned.

Her entire body quaked. *Be calm. You are a raft. You like being a raft. Rivers are awesome.*

"I-I thought you weren't interested in that," she said nervously.

"I never said I wasn't. I only said it wasn't the reason I brought you here. I wanted to let you see the real me first. Then let you decide if you wanted to be with a man who is . . ."

"Complicated?" she asked.

"Yes. However," he rubbed his chin, "now I find myself thinking about the fact that you traveled all this way for sex. I feel obliged to consider the option."

"About that. I need to apologize for what just happened. I don't know what I was thinking, but I'm here for whatever you want or need. I really mean that."

He stepped closer to her. "Well, you are practically naked, standing there looking beautiful, and extremely tempting with that giant towel wrapped around your head." He reached and gave the towel a tug, releasing her wet hair down the center of her back. "Mmmm . . . even better." Then he leaned down and kissed her, making her forget everything she'd thought about in the bathroom. He'd wanted to tell her something, right?

His silky, hot tongue delved between her slightly parted lips, and having just that small piece of him inside her body made her knees go weak and the blood rush straight to her core.

His hands slipped to her waist and tugged her body closer, making her sharply aware of how much bigger he was. He was dominating her with that wicked kiss, heating her with his large, towering body.

His tongue slid against hers, and she rose to her tiptoes, wrapping her arms around his neck, wanting to feel his torso flush against her, his lips more firmly pressed to her mouth.

His fingers slowly moved to the thick belt around her waist and he untied it. She felt the front of her robe fall open, the warm air on her bare breasts and belly, his hands sliding against her naked skin. Meanwhile, his kiss deepened, the rhythm more demanding as his hands slowly traveled up and cupped her breasts.

Her breath caught in her throat the moment his rough thumbs passed over her nipples causing them to harden into little pearls, the sensation simultaneously triggering an erotic clenching deep inside. *Well, if this is what he needs, who am I to argue?*

"You're so soft," he whispered against her lips, gently massaging her breasts.

"It's because they're real," she replied, smiling into the searing hot kisses.

He pulled away from her lips and stared into her eyes. "Why are you shaking?"

"I'm nervous. It's been a while."

The corner of his wet lips curled into a hint of a smile. "I hear it's like riding a bike."

She'd seen the size of his penis, and that was no bike; it was more like a recreational vehicle.

He slipped the robe off her shoulders, and it fell to the floor, pooling around her feet. His eyes washed over her body, drinking her in while she just stood there watching him. She wanted to reach for him, feel his hands on her skin, see him naked, his hard muscles pulsing with eager tension, but she couldn't move.

He held out his hand, and she hesitated for a moment. Why wasn't he undressing? But she took it anyway, unable to deny his request, and he walked her over to the vanity where he turned her around to face the mirror. His tall frame shadowed her curvy smaller body.

For the split second that she stood there, naked in front of the mirror, hearing only the sound of her frantically beating heart and the gentle rhythm of the ceiling fan, she felt like running for her robe. But then she caught the hard lust in Bennett's eyes as he looked at the front of her in the mirror. It was too symbolic of what she'd been thinking in the bathroom—of having to be stripped down naked, no baggage, no expectations, if she truly wanted to see Bennett for who he was.

She relaxed her shoulders and allowed the sensation of being in the moment to take over. *He's my river.*

His strong hands slid to her hips, and he watched himself in the mirror as he explored the feminine curves of her waist and breasts. She'd never felt so raw and exposed to a man, and the sensation was just as terrifying as it was exhilarating. The look in his eyes was unapologetically carnal, and when his one hand slid down over the patch of dark hair between her legs, his fingers pushing between her steaming hot folds, she bucked back against him. With his other hand, he moved her wet hair to one side, clearing the way for his warm breath to tickle its way down her neck while his fingers alternated between teasing her throbbing bud and testing her entrance.

"I haven't been able to stop thinking about touching you since the other morning," he said, his voice husky and sensual. Of course, he referred to the other day when he woke up with his hand in her panties. She hadn't been able to let that one go either. "Not that I didn't have the urge to touch you before that."

Her breath accelerated, and he pulled his hands away. From the angle of his elbows and movement of his arms she could tell he was unbuttoning his shirt.

She waited, fighting every urge in her body to turn around and help him out of this clothes. But she sensed it wasn't what he wanted. She'd committed to not having expectations and letting herself simply go with the flow.

As he tossed his shirt to the floor and then shed his pants, the pounding pulse of her inner walls became unrelenting. She just wanted him so badly.

She heard the faint sound of paper tearing and watched in the mirror as his head bowed down behind her.

Condom. Oh God. She'd almost forgotten.

When his gaze returned, the look on his face was raw and hungry. He placed one hand on her shoulder and bent her forward. His flexing, hard abs came into view, and she caught a glimpse of a tribal pattern of some sort tattooed over his right pectoral. Every inch of the man was chiseled male perfection. Even that light dusting of dark hair on his lower stomach was perfect.

"Look at me," he said, his voice deep and dominating.

Her heart slammed in her chest, and her knees barely hung on. He was going to fuck her like this?

Not in the bed. No sweet or loving. But hard.

Oh, yes.

Through the mirror, she stared into his eyes, as she felt the head of his shaft push against her.

"Keep looking at me," he demanded.

Their eyes locked and Bennett thrust his long, thick cock into her, making her gasp from the intensity as he drove deep, filling every inch, pushing her body to take all of him. He gripped her hips firmly, pulled out, and slammed into her again. Her body jarred forward from the force and the vanity knocked against the wall.

She cried out with pleasure, and he repeated the deliciously savage thrusts. With his size, she felt the subtle texture of his shaft with each penetration and the tip of his cock pushing against the sensitive spot leading to her womb.

With every stroke, she braced herself for his hard flesh, watching the deep grooves of his abs flex in the mirror, the strong muscles of his biceps bulge while he held her in place, his face intense as he fucked her hard.

She'd never felt this turned on by man, ready to come with one little flick of her bud.

"Is this what you wanted, Taylor?" he grunted in a rough voice, pumping his cock into her again. "A fuck?"

"Yes. Yes," she said. But she wanted more. She wanted to see whatever it was he'd brought her here for. "With you, yes."

"You want me?" He pumped harder, faster. "You don't even know me," he growled, his hips pistoning, driving his long, thick shaft as deep as it could go.

She wanted to recoil from the comment, but her body wouldn't allow it. Her need to orgasm, to feel him come inside her was too intense.

He bowed his large body over her back, and reached one arm around her waist to hold her in place while his other hand reached between her legs. His fingers found her throbbing bud at the same time his cock hit that spot deep inside her. She cried out, instantly orgasming, her entire body dissolving into a mass of sinful euphoric explosions.

Bennett stilled with his cock deep inside her contracting core and let out a deep, throaty groan as he came hard. He clung to her as twitch after tiny twitch released those jets of hot cum. She felt dripping with him, wetter than she'd ever been—his sweat on her back, his cock and cum filling her, her chest damp from the physical exertion.

His heart beat against her shoulder blade as he made one more pump and groaned again. Then he froze. "Dammit." His entire body tensed. "The fucking condom broke."

Taylor's eyes flew wide open, and Bennett dropped his forehead to her back, his lungs working hard. But he didn't pull out.

He just held her to him, like he was afraid to let go.

CHAPTER 16

It had taken exactly four days—or was it five with the time zone changes?—for Taylor to fall head over heels in love with Bennett Wade. And she could pinpoint the exact moment her heart gave in to him, falling hopelessly, helplessly, and madly.

Too bad that if this works out, you'll never be able to tell anyone. Because it wasn't the moment he gave her the most amazing orgasm of her life or the way he'd kissed the breath out of her. It was the moment he realized they'd had a birth control failure.

Crazy, right?

But he didn't run away or panic or say something stupid or act like it was the end of the world if the accident resulted in . . . well, that she wasn't ready to think about. Instead, he held her tight for a long moment, pressing his forehead to her back. Then, with the utmost tenderness, he withdrew, went into the bathroom to discard the remnants of the condom, started the shower, and came back for her.

Though his eyes were filled with emotion, Bennett didn't say a word, not one, as he led her by the hand into the large bathroom. Perhaps he sensed she needed a moment after having her body worked over so deliciously. And after having her body filled with copious amounts of what were likely some very determined and feisty sperm, given who they came from.

She watched the hard, round muscles of his smooth ass flex while he closed the clear glass door behind them in the shower. He then turned to face her, giving her a glimpse of the front of his body—lean pecs, the ripples of abs that cascaded down into those lickable ridges just below his hips, guiding her eyes to his long, thick, semi-aroused penis. He was beautiful. Every goddamned inch, right down to the patch of coarse black hair surrounding the base of his cock to the dark hair on his muscled thighs. Even his toes were perfect.

"What's the meaning of the tattoo?" she asked. The pattern had two small tribal-looking dragons, intertwined in several swirls.

"It's to remember someone I lost."

Bennett didn't appear to want to say more. Instead he grabbed the citrusy smelling soap and a washcloth, and then kissed her gently before going to work, washing her body slowly, as if savoring the intimacy of the act. He floated the washcloth over her breasts and stomach, under her arms, and then turned her around and washed every inch of her back, spending a little extra time between her thighs with gentle strokes.

When she faced him again, he kissed her once more with a sensual tenderness, and then proceeded to wash himself, allowing her to watch, without any sign of shyness. All those times she'd imagined him pleasuring himself, taking his hard shaft in his hand, did not compare to actually watching him hold his still semi-aroused penis in the palm of his large hand. Oh yes, that image would be recycled for years to come.

Once all clean, he placed his hand on the side of her face, kissed her slowly, working his tongue over her lips, and then left the shower. "I'll see you downstairs for that talk."

Wow. A whoosh of air left her body.

Being bathed by Bennett Wade after hard hot sex was the sexiest thing she'd ever experienced apart from the actual sex.

"Wow. Just . . . wow," she sighed under her breath.

So that was her first glimpse of the real Bennett Wade, and she knew she'd never get enough.

After drying off, Taylor slipped on a sleeveless plum-colored dress made from a soft, airy fabric, perfect for the hot weather. She went downstairs to find Bennett and saw he'd opened up all of the doors facing the beach, allowing the night ocean air to pour inside. He sat on the porch, wearing only his linen pants, his legs propped up on a small wooden table, a glass of white wine in his hand. He stared pensively at the ribbons of rainwater trickling from the roof into the sand.

"Aren't you afraid of mosquitos?" she asked.

He smiled dimly, still staring out toward the dark ocean. "They don't come out much when it rains."

"That's good to know." She sat next to him in a high-backed wicker chair, sensing he didn't feel as relaxed as he looked.

"What are you thinking about?"

He glanced at her and made a little shrug with those wide, bare shoulders. "No one thing in particular, I suppose."

"Well, um, I just want to tell you that . . . I haven't been with anyone in a really long time and even though I've never engaged in risky behavior, I still make sure that—"

"You don't have anything to worry about from me either,"

Bennett said in an unemotional voice. He seemed so far away, in another place. "And I haven't been with anyone in a very long time."

"You haven't?"

"No." He sipped his wine.

"But I thought you—I mean I know you aren't with a different woman every night, but I at least thought you were . . . you know—active."

"No. Not for a year or so."

Wow. So the "Kate incident" happened about a year ago. Taylor took that in. "Do you mind if I ask why not?"

"Let's just say the last woman I was with was one of many who succeeded in fooling me."

Oh. She bobbed her head. "The gold diggers." It was kind of what she'd expected, given the things his mother and Candy had said.

"Yes." His blue eyes focused off in the distance, but when Taylor looked, she saw only the black of night. What was he looking at?

"I'm glad," she said. "I'm glad they were all stupid, shallow, materialistic bitches."

He turned his body and tilted his head a bit.

"You wouldn't be here with me right now if they hadn't been," she explained.

He smiled softly. "Right you are, Ms. Reed."

She made a quiet little huff. "I'm Ms. Reed again, am I?"

"Taylor." His voice was so deep and husky, it made her toes curl. She loved it when he said her name.

He stared at her for a moment before his jaw clenched and his dark brows furrowed together. "I don't think I can do this tonight."

"You mean, tell me whatever it was you wanted to say?"

He gave her a small nod.

"You know," she said, thinking aloud, "I came here because I thought I wanted something from you—sex, intimacy, I don't know. But I realized in the bathroom, before we . . . did that," she could feel herself blushing, "that's not actually what I wanted."

"No?"

She shook her head. "No. I mean, don't get me wrong, the sex was great."

He shot her a look.

"Okay, phenomenal," she corrected. "But I decided I just want to be here and give you whatever you need—someone who won't judge or ask for anything more than to get to know you. That's all *I* need. So if you want to talk, talk. If you want to sit here and stare into the abyss, stare. If you just want someone to break condoms with, I'm okay with that, too. I don't want you to feel like you owe me anything or have to give me anything you're not ready for."

"You are a very odd woman."

She reached and took the glass of wine from his hand. "I know. And meeting you has raised the bar to a whole new level."

He laughed. "Has it now?"

She sipped his wine and handed it back. He sipped too and then locked eyes with her, the dim lighting from the living room tingeing his blue gaze with an orange glow.

"I think meeting you," she said, "the fact that you saw right through me from the first moment, let me finally start to see myself. I was pretending to be this person who thought she was better than people, judged them, made assumptions, tried to be more . . ." she shook her head, "I mean, really, Bennett. The fact that I started a company to try to coach successful CEOs to be better is ludicrous."

"I don't think it's ludicrous. Wildly ambitious, perhaps."

She nodded and laughed a little bit. "No. Ludicrous is definitely the right word. Thinking I could change the world by teaching a handful of billionaires not to be dicks is a joke. If I really wanted to make a difference, I'd be focusing on the people who really do the work. I mean," she looked at him, "let's face it. You guys don't do squat. It's all those middle managers who do the heavy lifting."

He laughed. "Well, I do more than just squat, but your point is taken."

"I have you to thank for setting me straight." She looked into his eyes, and he handed her back the glass of wine. She took it and sipped. The simple act of sharing the glass was going on her list of most erotic things to do with Bennett Wade, right after sex and showering together. "I've literally lost everything, but I've found myself."

"And how does it feel?" he asked.

She nodded, her eyes tearing up. "Damned good, Mr. Wade. Damned fucking good."

She handed him back the glass, giving him the last sip. He swallowed it and set the glass down at his side on the porch. "I'm glad to be of help, Ms. Reed."

She took a breath and wiped the dampness from underneath her eyes while they both took a moment to stare into the night together.

It was a quiet, beautiful moment.

"I'm falling in love with you," she said, unsure of why or how the words had escaped her mouth.

She glanced his way and noticed that air of calm intimacy

had disappeared. In its place the rigid, reserved Bennett Wade sat with his trademark frown—the one he used when he felt uncomfortable.

"You don't know me," he replied.

"I may not know whatever it is you feel you need to hide from the world, but I've seen your heart, Bennett. I've seen how you sneak around and help people, how you take care of them—Candy, your mother, that Mr. Oko-sushi-restaurant owner."

"Okomoto."

Dammit! I knew that.

"And," he said, "that doesn't mean you know me."

"Okay. I'm here, ready when you are then. But I guarantee unless you're a serial killer, a rapist, or hate puppies, there is really nothing you can say that would change my mind."

He turned his body back toward the ocean, looking away. "Did you like the way I fucked you?"

Her spit caught in her throat as she blinked at him. She hadn't been expecting that question. "Well . . . yeah. It was different, but it was . . . *really* good. I liked it a lot." Of course, that was code for "do it the hell again because you blew my mind."

She added, "Not that I wouldn't welcome some other positions that might not involve having to see myself in a mirror. But if it makes you happy, I'm good with it."

"The mirror was for you."

"Sorry?"

"That is the only way I can be intimate with a woman."

Her mind munched on that for a few moments. Then she got up, went inside, and poured a very, very, very full glass of white wine from the opened bottle inside the mini fridge just below the wet bar.

She drank down half and then walked outside, handing Bennett the glass. "So you're trying to tell me you can't . . . umm . . ."

"Fuck," he said, filling in the blank.

"Okay. You can't fuck any other way?"

"No," he replied sharply.

"May I ask why?" she said.

"I find the intimacy too . . ."

"Intimate?" she said.

"Painful. Getting too attached always ends badly for me."

Hearing that made her heart ache, but she hoped his wounds would heal with time. Maybe even with her. "Feel free to avoid intimacy with me whenever you like, then."

He blew out a small little laugh. "Only you, Ms. Reed. Only you."

"I have my charms, Mr. Wade. Why hide them?" She flashed a coy smile. Honestly, she knew he was trying to say something important, something that troubled him, but it was more important that he knew she wasn't rattled.

"Never hide who you really are, Taylor. You're lovely. So damned lovely it hurts."

She unconsciously tipped her head to one side and gave her neck a sobering crack. *God, I fucking love him.* "Anything for you, Mr. Wade."

"If the weather holds, I'd like to take you to see the rest tomorrow morning."

"Rest of the island?" she asked.

"Rest of me."

She drew a deep breath. "I'd like that, Bennett. I really, really would."

He stood from the chair. "Very good. Then I'll say good

night." He leaned over and planted a sinfully hot kiss on her lips, but it ended much too soon. When he withdrew his mouth, it felt like a hard slap.

He turned and walked inside. "See you in the morning," he said, strutting in that Bennett Wade sort of way that made her well aware of what he carried between his legs.

A weapon of my womanly destruction?

She leaned forward in her chair and watched him disappear down a small hallway behind the kitchenette she hadn't even noticed. The place was pretty damned big and being in it with Bennett felt like a dream. A wet, wet dream.

Taylor flopped back into her wicker chair and let her arms hang down, feeling delicious aches all over her body and a warm buzzing in her heart. *Oh my God. That man so rocks my world.*

A few hours later, Taylor found herself unable to sleep in the big bed upstairs alone. She knew that it had been a trying night for Bennett, and he had issues with intimacy, but she longed for his strong arms wrapped around her waist and the sound of his gentle breath in her ear.

The man was such a heavy sleeper that she wondered if she couldn't curl up with him for a few hours without him noticing and then sneak away before he woke.

She tiptoed downstairs and used her hands to feel her way down the hall past the kitchen.

After turning the corner, she came to an open doorway, but from the sound of absolutely nothing, she guessed he wasn't in there. When Bennett wasn't having nightmares, he had a soft, masculine hum to his breath, the kind she might want to record and listen to every night like white noise meant for lulling a restless girl to sleep.

She found the second door closed and quietly pushed it open, placing her ear to the crack. Yep. There was Bennett, his rhythmic breath strumming peacefully away.

She slipped inside, closed the door, and carefully climbed into bed with him. He jerked and mumbled something unintelligible, but when she lifted the covers, she realized he was on top of them. Not a surprise given it was still pretty warm in the house.

She lay down next to him, and her eyes adjusted to the blackness allowing her to see the contours of his handsome face. He wore no clothes, and his long, lean, muscular body looked like the statue of a god, carved from sleek marble.

Oh, god. Is it me, or is it getting hotter in here? Knowing that Bennett lay nude right next to her might be the reason. *You are not going to molest him in his sleep.* She lay there, restless, feeling the gentle breeze through the window. *So hot. So hot.* She got up from the bed and went back out to the living room, searching for a thermostat. There had to be an A/C here somewhere.

Every corner and wall came up empty, so she made her way back to Bennett. She stared down at his naked form and decided he had the right idea. She slipped her dress over her head. *You can handle it. Just a girl and guy, sleeping naked together.*

Now cooler, and feeling more tired than she cared to admit, she closed her eyes, lulled by the sound of Bennett's breathing. She felt like she'd landed on a strange planet where simply being near him felt like home.

Something warm and hot woke Taylor from her sleep, sending sharp pleasurable tingles through her groin, deep into her belly.

"Mmmm . . ." came a low, wholly masculine groan, rousing

her from her drowsy state completely. She felt the heat of a man's chest pressing against her. "Mmmm . . . Taylor."

Her eyes fluttered open, and she realized that Bennett was tightly fitted to her back, his hard cock nestled in the apex of her legs, pushing right against her deliciously sore entrance.

Ohmygod. He's sleep humping me again. This man is so damned sexy.

She gently reached around and placed her hand on his shoulder, giving him a little shake. "Bennett?" she whispered. "Wake up."

He gripped her hip and began moving against her, sliding back and forth, right over her little c-spot.

Her eyes rolled in her head as she felt every hard inch of his thick velvety cock creating friction and pushing her toward the edge. He hadn't even entered her, but dammit if she didn't want him to.

"Oh, God. Bennett, wake the fuck up. That feels so good. So, so incredible, but . . ." Well, for starters, he wasn't wearing a condom, and second, the man was asleep.

She sighed. "Bennett, as much as I want this, it's probably not the best idea, so please wake up?"

His body jerked a little, and she felt that strong hand dig into her hip. He stopped thrusting and then pulled his hips back. She winced as the motion left her panting, needy, and sadly all alone down there.

She felt the bed shift, followed by a small rustle.

She smiled. *Wicked man. You're awake now . . . and you're—*

"Oh fuck!" she cried out as he returned to her and thrust deeply with one sharp motion. He hadn't even needed to grope or fumble. He knew exactly where to go.

"You're amazing, Bennett. I—" He thrust again from be-hind. "Ohmygod. So amazi—" And again. "Zing." And again.

She felt his lips on the back of her neck and those little sinful flutters in her belly. He may not have been awake before, but he was going hard now.

"You feel so damned good, Taylor. I can't imagine ever need-ing to be inside a woman like I need to be inside you."

He withdrew and pushed the corner of her hip, forcing her to her stomach. His knees worked their way between her legs, and he pushed them widely apart, before blanketing his body over her.

He positioned his cock at her wet entrance and thrust again. Only a man with his size equipment could make this position, lying on her stomach, feel so, so good that she couldn't speak when she wanted to say so many things, like . . .

Her thoughts drifted away with each sensual thrust of his hard flesh. Again and again she felt the coarse hair around his shaft tickle her ass as his cock pushed and slid and massaged her until she wanted to scream.

"I love being inside you, Taylor," he whispered. Slowly he withdrew, and she felt the entire force of his body hitting her, harder and faster, desperately chasing the moment of release.

He reached one hand between her hip and the bed, searching lower and lower, until he found the spot. With three strokes of his finger and cock, she was screaming into her orgasm, push-ing back into him to increase the pain and pressure and plea-sure.

He planted his arms on either side of her body and worked himself in and out with a few more powerful strokes before he collapsed, giving in to a shuddering climax as his hot cum jet-ted deep inside her.

After a few minutes of lying there, he rolled to his side, pulling her body with him, staying inside her, still hard as a rock.

She closed her eyes, savoring the heat of him deep inside, the wetness of his release at her entrance . . .

"Dammit," Bennett swore, pulling out of her. "I can't believe this. It broke again."

Taylor didn't know whether to laugh or cry. Wherever these Balinese condoms came from, they had not been constructed with Bennett Wade's cock in mind.

He grabbed some tissue from a box on the nightstand, stripped off whatever remained of the latex, and threw it into the trash. She stared at his back for several moments as he sat there panting.

Shit. This *was* scary. But what could they do now? What could she say? The river was in charge? She'd just sound corny and then have to explain.

"Come back. I'm getting cold." She wasn't feeling close to chilled, but that was the only thing that came to mind.

He nodded and lay back down at her side. He then pulled her close, twisting her body to spoon her.

"I can't imagine anything better in this world than sleeping with you, Taylor. Even your snoring is sexy."

She laughed and then snuggled her body tightly against him, enjoying the intimate sensation of him falling asleep. For a man with intimacy issues, he was one hell of a snuggler.

"Nite, Benny." She smiled.

When Taylor woke the next morning, it was to the sound of rain pattering just outside the open window. She stretched her body, immediately feeling a little sad to see the empty spot next to her, the indentation in Bennett's pillow right next to the indentation in her own, a reminder of how closely they'd slept together last night.

Then she remembered the condom fails. She was on week three of her cycle, she knew that much. *Don't worry until you have something to worry about, Tay.* Besides, she didn't want it to ruin the memory of how hot he'd been in bed.

She sat up and smelled something coffee-licious wafting in the air. She scooted from the bed and slipped on the little flowy dress she'd worn last night, then made her way to the living room. The patio doors were open to the empty beach and the rolling ocean. Rain drizzled from gray clouds, casting a somber shadow over the waves. *It's gloomy, but beautiful.*

A gentle breeze floated into the room, pushing the scent of fresh coffee and food her way. A tray had been set out on the counter with a beautiful red trumpet-shaped flower. Next to it there was a note:

Driver will pick you up at ten. Wear something that you don't mind getting wet. –BW

Wet, huh? What kind of wet? She smiled devilishly. He'd gone ahead without her, and she couldn't help but wonder where and why. On the other hand, he'd said that today he'd show her the rest of himself. Something he didn't feel comfortable showing to just anyone.

She drew a deep breath, feeling nervous about whatever he was going to lay on her. But she loved Bennett. Whatever demons he wrestled with couldn't be that bad, could they?

Taylor glanced at the clock and realized it was a quarter to ten. She took a few bites of the still warm pancakes that had been hiding underneath the metal plate cover, and then swallowed down a cup of coffee before rushing upstairs to shower and change. She didn't have any undergarments, but the hotel had delivered a few swimsuits—black, red, and white bikinis. She grabbed the red one and slipped it on. Hey, maybe they'd go for a swim in the rain later when the weather got hotter than hell.

She slipped on a light blue sundress and brown leather flip-flops. Nothing fit quite right, but it wasn't a total disaster either.

Just as she opened the front door, a man approached, wearing khaki shorts and a golf shirt with "Wade" stitched onto the pocket. He was an older gentleman with kind brown eyes, dark brown skin, and deep smile lines.

"Ah, Ms. Reed. You are ready. I am Wayan. I will be taking you to Mr. Wade. He has gone ahead to deal with some urgent business."

That was odd. Wasn't Wayan the name Bennett had mentioned in his sleep?

"Nothing bad, I hope?" she asked.

"No. Nothing our Mr. Wade cannot handle."

Taylor grinned. "Yes, he is pretty good at overcoming obstacles."

They made their way to the front of the hotel and got into a honking, army-green Land Rover with thick tires and a steel roof rack piled high with gear—gas can, shovel, winches, and rope.

"So where is Bennett's estate?" Taylor asked. *The moon?*

"It is two hours north of here. But he is at a hamlet about a half hour up the road."

"What's he doing there?"

"Negotiating with a man who's gotten cold feet," Wayan replied.

"Is it to do with his special project?" she asked.

"Yes, ma'am. His special project."

After about ten minutes of playing dodge the mopeds, which swarmed the road like angry bees (some transporting a family of four including the baby), they hit the main "highway." It was a two-lane road lined with impenetrable lush leafy vegetation and the occasional rusted-out car or small gas station (or petrol-in-a-bottle-for-all-of-the-scooters stand) dotting the way.

Eventually Wayan pulled off onto a long, muddy road that cut through thick jungle, just wide enough for one vehicle.

"I hope no one comes the other way," Taylor said. They'd have to back up and drive in reverse.

"Not to worry, ma'am. We are almost there."

Indeed they were. Just as he spoke, they came into a large open space where another Land Rover was parked in a ditch. Several shacks surrounded the perimeter of the clearing along with piles of garbage.

"What is this place?" she asked. A stray dog scampered across the muddy clearing, a few equally muddy children chasing after it.

"This, ma'am, is Bali."

CHAPTER 17

Taylor could hardly believe her eyes. Wayan explained that much of the local population lived like this. "But the resorts and tourists? Don't they bring in money and jobs?" she asked.

"Only to the wealthy hotel owners who are mostly foreign."

"I see." She'd counted ten shacks sprinkled around the periphery of the clearing, but Wayan told her over one hundred people lived in this hamlet. Where? In what? These shacks weren't big enough for ten dogs let alone one hundred human beings.

Bennett emerged from one of the larger homes—about ten by ten—and waved her in. He wore a white linen shirt, muddy khaki shorts, and hiking boots. He looked like a wilderness explorer, not some tailored billionaire.

She approached him, dodging the large drops of rain that pelted her forehead as they dripped off of the trees above.

"I trust you slept well?" he said as she approached, a shallow smile on his face.

Why did he look so . . . worried? It made her feel uneasy.

"I did. Thanks." Her flip-flops made a squishing sound with each step.

"Come inside," Bennett said. "You can meet Wayan."

She pointed to the driver still sitting in the Land Rover. "Isn't he Wayan?"

Bennett laughed. "Names are recycled heavily in this country—it's a tradition."

She smiled. "Sure. Okay." She ducked inside and saw a woman sitting in the corner with a large metal bowl in her lap, peeling some sort of fruit. Several children, dressed in what were basically rags, played with a few rusty-looking toy cars on the dirt floor. To the other side, a man with scraggly gray hair, wearing a threadbare shirt, sat at the table.

Bennett said something to the man in his native tongue. Taylor had no idea Bennett spoke Balinese. Then again, there was a lot she didn't know about this man. A lot. In fact, at this point, she'd come to expect nothing but surprises from this man. *He's like a really awesome onion that doesn't stink.*

Taylor made a polite nod at the man who smiled and flashed a set of incomplete teeth.

"So, what are you doing here?" she asked, trying to put everything together.

"I've just purchased this man's land."

"Okay. And what do you plan to do with it?" she asked.

Bennett smiled and held out his hand. "Come with me." He looked at the man and mumbled a few odd words. She guessed Bennett was saying goodbye or that he'd be back soon.

She followed him out to the other Land Rover and got inside. Mud was everywhere.

"Sorry about the mess," Bennett said, "but I had a flat tire earlier. It's a little wet today."

Another surprise. Bennett Wade changed his own flat tires. In the rain and mud.

"So what do you want to show me?" she asked, feeling anxious.

"You'll see." He cranked the engine and turned the vehicle around, down the road they'd come, waving at Wayan as they passed. But before they made it back to the paved road, Bennett took a right turn down something that looked like an overgrown walking trail. The branches of the trees slapped at the windows, and the rain began coming down in a heavy sheet.

"How can you see where you're driving?" she asked.

"I know these roads like the back of my hand. I grew up here," he said.

"The driver last night mentioned that. How come you never said anything?"

"It's not something I discuss," he replied.

"Are you going to tell me why?"

"Yes. In a moment," he replied, ominously.

Taylor's nerves amped up. He was about to drop a major bomb, wasn't he?

He turned the vehicle sharply and they began to climb a steep embankment. The tires slipped and spun in the mud, but Bennett knew exactly how to work the steering wheel and gears to keep them from getting stuck.

The car caught a rock or something and jumped forward. She yelped.

Bennett laughed. "I promise, there's nothing to worry about. I've got a satellite phone if we get stuck."

"What if we roll?"

He thumped his hand on the roof. "This is a real Land Rover, the kind they use to cross the Serengeti. Not a soccer mom wagon."

Oh. She hadn't known there was a difference.

The engine groaned up the last few meters of the steep, muddy road, and then they turned down what looked like another hiking trail.

Then the road just stopped and so did Bennett.

"We're here. Are you ready?" he said, and turned off the engine. His jaw pulsed with tension.

Taylor wasn't sure. This was all really strange. "Uh. Yeah. I guess?"

He got out of the vehicle, so she hopped out on her side, stepping right into a soupy brown puddle. At this point, not getting dirty was a lost cause. Her feet, ankles, and calves were completely covered in muck.

She met Bennett at the front of the car, and he took her hand, leading her down a slip of a path between two trees. Just on the other side, the trail dropped off into a steep cliff.

"Wow," she said. The view was amazing, miles and miles of green pastures and rolling lush jungle. Off in the distance, maybe three or so miles away, the dull blue of the ocean reflected the gray sky above. She imagined on a sunny day how all of this would look: Like a blanket of emerald green, surrounded by a halo of sapphire blue.

"It's gorgeous, but what is this place?" she asked.

He looked out across the land and put his hand on his waist. "It's me making things right."

"I'm not following."

"I know. And I've been trying to think of a way to tell you that won't make you think less of me, but I keep hitting the same damned wall. Over and over again."

She reached for his arm. "Whatever it is, you can tell me. I promise it won't change how I feel."

"This might."

He sounded so sure that he made her doubt herself. "O—okay. Try me then," she said.

He rubbed his scruffy jaw, mulling something over in his mind for several moments before he let out a big whoosh. "When I was eighteen, I helped my father take the land from the people who lived near here."

Taylor studied him for a moment. "What do you mean by take?"

"My father moved us here when I was about five after he and a partner bought a hotel. From there he bought another and another. He saw this island as an investment opportunity, a place to exploit. Although, that's not what he would've called it. In his mind, it was simply business."

"And?"

"I helped him." Bennett shrugged. "When he decided to get into the coffee business, I helped him acquire land, helped him grease palms, convince the various families that what we were offering was a good price. We bought their land for nothing and ran them off of it, forcing them to live in hamlets, like the ones you just saw, without access to clean water, electricity, or schools."

Was Bennett trying to say he and his father had basically swindled people out of their land?

He continued, "I helped him destroy hundreds of people's lives. The sad part was, I knew what he was doing was wrong, but I just couldn't bring myself to stand up to him or disappoint him. I kept telling myself that what we were doing wasn't illegal. Of course, that didn't make it right. Those families were too simple and too trusting to realize we were cheating them. Then, after a few years, we sold the farms off to a big company. It's how we became so wealthy."

"Oh." That was a pretty shitty thing to do.

"Yes. 'Oh.'" He nodded in agreement.

"So why are you buying more land?" she asked.

"After my father died and I took over the company, I was here on a trip, checking up on some of the hotels we still own." The look in Bennett's eyes became harder and more barren, as though he was holding on to something, something painful, and trying not to allow it to take over.

He went on, "As usual, I stayed at a house we had near the beach. My father had it built after we came into our money—quite the mansion. On that day, though, I was on my cell, getting ready to drive to the other side of the island, when the alarm—a text in those days—went off. I drove like hell to get away, and I did."

Get away? From what? Then it dawned on her. There was only one thing people on this island tried to get away from: the ocean.

"Oh God. What happened?" She was almost afraid to know the answer.

He pointed to a spot off on the horizon where there were several hills near the shoreline. "The wave hit, and I watched from up there as it carried off my son. And his mother."

Taylor's knees almost buckled. "Your—your *son*? Your wife?"

"We were never married. I'd only slept with her once, but it was enough. She and her family looked after the estate and lived there."

"You got her pregnant," she whispered.

He nodded. "Not by accident. By carelessness. I just didn't care about consequences. I was eighteen when she had Wayan."

Taylor slapped her hands over her mouth. Her heart felt like it had fallen out of a ten-story building and smashed on the cement sidewalk.

Last night when they'd been together, his reaction to their little condom fail had been so . . . strange. Endearing and tender, but strange. It had felt so atypical of what she expected from a man in that situation—calm and thoughtful, like he wanted to show her, or perhaps, show himself, he knew how to care.

Was this why? Was he trying not to repeat history?

"Bennett," she said, holding back the tears. "I'm so sorry. I can't imagine how hard that was."

"I didn't love her. Yes, I cared for her, but I was too selfish, too self-absorbed to really be anything more than just some stranger who gave them money. And I felt ashamed of my son— not good enough—not one of us—not someone my father would approve of."

"So you never told anyone about him?" she asked softly.

"No. Although my dad suspected. Wayan had my eyes. But my mother still doesn't know. I wanted to tell her, but it would break her heart to find out she had a grandson she never got to meet."

"But Bennett, why do you think I'd hate you or think less of you?" It was a tragedy, and he'd been young and stupid and . . . a real asshole. *But he's not that person anymore.*

"Because when Wayan was alive, I thought money was enough. He had his mother, a home, school—I took care of him financially, but that was all. And then he died because of me."

"You didn't make that tsunami happen, Bennett."

"No. But I'm the one who didn't lift a finger to save him. I'm the one who decided it was a waste of money to install an alert system on the property. That's the sort of cold-hearted bastard I was. I never thought about their safety. I thought . . ." He looked down at his hands. "I thought, 'What use would it be to spend thirty thousand dollars if I'm hardly ever here?'"

Taylor nodded, trying to take it all in.

"That day changed me—broke something inside me—but as much as I try, I can't erase the past. It's the one thing money can't buy me."

"So what is all this? What are you doing here?" she asked.

"Like I said, it's me, trying to make things right—at least, the things I can fix. It will never be enough though. Never. Not after what I did to my own child."

Taylor's eyes filled with tears. The torment in Bennett's expression was too much.

"I couldn't give these people back their land," he explained, "and if I could, it wouldn't help them. Things are different now and that land has been overworked. That's why I've been buying up this valley. It's perfect for growing flowers and a particular kind of tree."

"You're going to grow flowers and trees?"

"No. They are—the people we took land from. I've paid the previous landowners a very, very good price and am titling it to a co-op owned by the families we ruined."

"That's really nice to do, but flowers?" How would that help anyone?

"Lady Mary Fragrances is the largest purchaser of floral compounds and terpenes in the world. This place will become the exclusive source for all of their ingredients."

"You want to buy Lady Mary so you can control their sourcing?" It was . . . really, really smart. And now it all made so much sense. Bennett's company was the king of manufacturing and processing equipment. He could set up a world-class operation here.

"The ingredients they'll produce are for a premium market," he said. "The families will make good money, and Lady Mary Fragrances will be more profitable because they'll have an exclusive contract. We can use the profits to build water-processing plants, roads, schools. A lot of good can come out of it."

"Wow, Bennett. Just wow."

"It's costing me almost everything I have. Or it will if Mary Rutherford agrees to sell the controlling stake of her company."

"Wait. So you're giving up everything you've built to do this?" She jerked her head toward the wet green lands laid out in front of them.

"I'll own fifty-one percent of Lady Mary so I can ensure they do things my way, but that money will be tied up, and anything I make will go to this. I have money for living expenses and to build the factory here, but that's it. I'll just have enough—after I sell off Wade Enterprises."

"Oh my God." In a million years, Taylor would never, ever have imagined that this was Bennett's secret. It was sad and dark and . . . he was trying to make good.

"Kate, my ex, is the only other person who knows absolutely everything," he said. "She left me when she realized I'd be living a more . . . modest lifestyle. We were together for almost two years."

Taylor was speechless. How could anyone do that to this beautiful man? It ripped her heart out. "Two years?"

He went on, "She'd been hustling me the entire time—telling me she wanted to stay out of the limelight, refusing any expensive gifts I tried to give her—it was all just an act to make me think she was down to earth, so she could get her hands on my money. I'm glad I didn't marry her, but to me, there's nothing worse in this world than being stabbed in the back by someone you trust." His words reminded her of that incident in Tokyo.

"You mean like that Japanese lady you yelled at in the hotel?" she asked.

"Yes." Bennett looked slightly irritated. "I was trying to get a rival equipment company to sell their patented processing equipment for the flowers. It would've kept our costs down, but that backstabbing bitch I hired tipped off one of Lady Mary's competitors. The technology was up for grabs. I lost it.

"We'll still be able to function," he said, "but it will be more expensive—lower crop yields."

He looked at her with his big blue eyes. "Say something."

She couldn't. Her mind was too busy filling in all the blanks. His loathing for people who took advantage of others. His fear of being unable to reach people in an emergency or not knowing where they were. His obsession with this project that drove him to exhaustion. It was all such a huge shock, yet the signs had been there all along.

"This is why you took the money from your stupid fucking friends, isn't it?" she asked.

"Yes. And for the record, those idiots bet on things all the time—football, golf games, if Chip can keep a girlfriend for more than a week—to them, it means nothing."

"But you take part?"

"Sometimes. More when I was younger." He shrugged. "But with you, they just assumed I was in." He glanced at her. "And I never corrected their assumption, and I never tried to stop them. It was wrong, which is why I've promised to rectify the situation." He then pointed west. "If it makes you feel any better, their stupidity purchased everything from there to that ridge—they finally did something good for once."

"That's a lot of stupidity," she said and then turned to him. "But why keep this all a secret? Why not tell anyone what you're doing?"

He tilted his head. "Don't you think they'd ask why? Don't you think people would connect the dots if I went around telling them I grew up here or about my project? The land we purchased and sold is public record. Anyone who looks hard enough will realize what we did to these people."

She bobbed her head. It was one more piece of the puzzle—the reason he never mentioned where he was really from. "I get what you're saying, but your father was in charge then. You were only trying to be a good son."

"No one will care. It's my last name on the company's letterhead. I'm in charge now. But the bad PR could hurt Wade Enterprise's value, and I want top dollar when I sell the company to fund the factory and infrastructure."

He had it all figured out.

"How long have you been planning this?" she asked.

"Six years. It took me a while to figure things out after Wayan died."

"I think, Bennett," she whispered, "that it's the nicest thing anyone has ever done in the name of saying sorry."

He shrugged again, the sadness and regret saturating his eyes. "I can say I'm sorry until my last breath but there is no excuse for being the person that I was. None at all. I deserve a shit life for letting my little boy and his mother die like that."

Tears flowed freely from Taylor's eyes, and though Bennett's voice was cold, she knew it wasn't because he didn't care—it was because he'd probably mourned enough for a lifetime. There wasn't anything left. At least, that was her guess.

"You think you don't deserve anyone's affection or love." She looked at him, realizing why he felt uncomfortable being too intimate. "But you're wrong, Bennett. You just need to forgive yourself."

"I can't ever see that happening."

She placed herself in front of him and smiled, putting her hand on his cheek. She felt so humbled that he'd trusted her with all of this. Especially after what happened the last time he'd told a woman. Her heart swelled with so many mixed emotions now, but wanting to leave him wasn't one of them. "You just say 'I'm sorry.' You tell your son you loved him, and in a perfect world, you would've done more, but you were imperfect and fucked up and human. And then you let go, Bennett. But if you continue punishing yourself, a man as strong and smart and determined and caring as you, what good will that do? You'll die like your father of a heart attack or from exhaustion, and then what? Who's going to help these people? But if you could just let go of the past, Bennett, if you could just find a way to forgive yourself, you could use your energy to do so much more."

The line of his strong, unshaven jaw pulsed with tension, and the hard look in his pale blue eyes could easily be mistaken for anger. But that was Bennett just trying to sort something out, something painful he wasn't comfortable with. She knew that now. It was the same look he'd given her the first time they'd met and the second and the third and every single time he'd been trying in his way to . . .

Get me here. The epiphany struck her down. He'd wanted to bring her here to Bali all along. She blinked at him. *Has he been into me this entire time?* Or, at least, since she'd showed up at his office and agreed to work with him.

She suddenly felt confounded and so very special. But she also wondered—what did he hope to get from her? It felt bigger than him simply wanting her to know his secret.

Maybe he's trying to move on, but doesn't know how? She honestly wasn't sure.

"You told me," she said, "that you were in your car, already driving off the property when you got the alert on your phone. How much time did that give you before the wave hit?"

He frowned. "The earthquake was close. It gave me a minute or two. Not much time."

"So if you'd gone back for them, could you have saved them?" she asked.

He looked down at his muddy boots. "No. Not likely."

"Would two minutes warning have been enough for them to run to safety?"

"No. But you're missing the point. Back then, the alert was new; you didn't know how much time you had—it could've been ten hours—yet, I didn't try."

She understood the guilt, she really did. But had he believed he had hours and gone back for them, he wouldn't be standing with her right now. And then where would the Bali project be?

She looked up at him and brushed the messy damp hair from his forehead. "I believe that everything happens for a reason, Bennett. The only shame is not allowing that reason to exist. But you've let it flourish. You've done the right things, and made something good come from your mistakes because you are a good man." She didn't know if that's what he needed to hear, but the words were from the heart.

He looked down at her, and his angry, harsh expression was

the last thing she expected to see. "Then you're delusional, Ms. Reed. And you understand nothing."

She dropped her hand and stepped back, mentally catching herself from falling. He didn't mean it. She knew he didn't mean it. *He's pushing me away*. It was the way he dealt with things. "When he pushes you away—and believe me, he will—like a drowning man fighting for air—you push back. You hang on. He'll come around."

That's what his mother had said.

But arguing with him wasn't the right tactic either. She could feel it in her gut.

"Yes. You might be right," she said calmly with the utmost sincerity. "I wasn't there, and I didn't lose a child and I'll never really understand. But I'm here for you anyway. If it's what you want."

"What I want is for you not to try to make me feel better or say ridiculous things like I'm a 'good' man. Because I'm not."

Oh. Now she got it.

He wanted to hear he was right. He wanted someone to say he was a horrible human being and deserved to suffer. He wanted someone to validate his pain and give him an excuse to continue the self-flagellation. And perhaps be his sidekick and keep him company while he killed himself paying his penance.

Well, she wouldn't do it. Because it was bullshit. But if she argued with him, told him he was good, he'd only view it as her lack of true understanding. Because in his mind, the only logical response was to hate himself. Of course, he was wrong, and she would never agree with him, so she'd give him the next best thing: She would accept him. Just as he was. Maybe with time he'd learn to accept things, too, and see himself in a new light, through her eyes. Just as he'd done for her.

"Sorry. But you just showed me your colors, you trusted me with your secret, and I don't feel at all different about you, Mr. Wade."

"Only you, Ms. Reed. Only you." He shook his head disapprovingly at his feet.

"I think you should take me back to the hotel now," she said, wanting to give him time to let the volatile emotions settle. This had clearly been a difficult leap for him to take. But she wasn't a mound of dirt, and he wasn't going to bulldoze her to serve his messed-up needs.

Because he deserved better than that.

He looked at her, still stewing. "Yes, that's probably best."

She took a breath and walked back toward the muddy Land Rover. Despite her conviction, she was holding on by a thread. *Don't get sucked in to his emotional whirlpool, Tay. Stay strong for him, let him see that nothing changed.*

But everything *had* changed. She realized now that she loved him more than she'd ever thought possible. There was no going back for her, no other man she'd ever want more.

CHAPTER 18

Bennett was icy the entire drive back to the resort. She resisted the urge to push him to talk about his feelings (such a chick move) and simply allowed him space. She just had to have faith that he'd come around.

When he pulled up to the front of the hotel, she turned and gazed into his stormy blue eyes, wanting to say so many things, but knowing this moment wasn't about her or what she wanted. It was about him trying to dig himself out of the deep dark hole he'd been living in for the last decade. If she loved him, really loved him, she'd reach out her hand and wait patiently for him to take it. Metaphorically speaking, of course. Physically, she wasn't feeling at all patient. She wanted him so badly she ached. Ached with the need to feel his body against her and inside her. Ached with the need to feel his strong arms around her and his powerful hands gripping her hips. She didn't mind if he was emotionally distant or not ready to "face" her. She'd take anything she could get, any way she could get it. Even if it meant sitting in the car with him in silence.

"Can I come stay with you at your place tonight? I'd love to see it." It was the only thing she could think of to say that signaled she wasn't running for the hills and still wanted to be a part of his life.

He let out a deep, anger-laced sigh, and dropped his head against his arms as they rested on the steering wheel. "I don't think that would be a smart idea."

She nodded calmly, ignoring the sting of his rejection. "I understand." She reached for the door handle and got out. "Bennett, thank you for today. Thank you for letting me in and trusting me. I know it's not something you take lightly."

He looked away. "I'll call you."

She bobbed her head and closed the door. He sped away, and the moment he was gone, the emotions gushed out of her. Tears flowed from her eyes in a steady stream as she thought about that horrific story. Bennett had stood high on a hilltop and watched the ocean carry away his child and his child's mother. She couldn't imagine a more horrifying experience. But damn, that Bennett had a will of iron. He may not have forgiven himself, but he turned his pain into an undertaking she could have never imagined—trying to change the lives of an entire community. But more than that, he'd come back to face the people he'd hurt. And not just to say, "I'm sorry," but to make things right.

That took a man of unspeakable strength and character. That took some damned backbone.

A few hours later, there was a break in the rain and the sun came out. Taylor didn't want to sit around, waiting for Bennett to call—it could be a long, long wait—so she took a walk along the white sandy shore and finally got to see the hypnotic greens and blues of the Indian Ocean. It was just as spectacular as she imagined.

When the rain returned, she retreated back to the private resort beach house and decided to check emails and send everyone a quick note, letting them know she was still in Bali. That was when she noticed the Google Alert she'd set up to stalk Bennett. Apparently, they hadn't been coming through on her phone until now.

"What the fuck?" Sitting on the porch, she leaned in closer, unable to believe the words on the screen. It was a press release from Lady Mary Fragrances.

Merger offer rejected by Lady Mary Fragrances? Taylor's eyes quickly skimmed the article. Words like "clash of cultures" and "different values" were sprinkled throughout as speculation for the failed deal, but the final line, a quote from Lady Mary nearly stopped Taylor's heart. "*I would never take the company in a direction that compromises Lady Mary's integrity or the foundation of equality I've built.*"

Oh shit. Oh shit. Mary had to be referring to something Bennett had done or said. *He used my fucking training.* Or some part of it. But everything seemed to have been going well at the dinner. *Yeah, but you never really told Bennett flat out that your training was a bunch of B.S.*

Fuck. It must've happened after I left. This is all my fault.

"No. No. Goddammit no!" She ran inside and went for the phone, about to dial Bennett and beg for mercy and explain that she would fix this and that she hadn't meant to hurt him or ruin him or . . .

Shit. Everything he'd said to her in the morning about his fiancée stabbing him in the back came rushing into her head. *He'll never forgive me.* And as her finger was about to hit the last number to complete the call, she realized that she'd never be able face him again. What she'd done was simply unforgivable.

I burned his bridge to redemption. She'd burned it to the ground and ruined the man she loved.

No. You haven't. You've lost the man you love, but you can still fix this.

She hung up and dialed the concierge. "Can you help me? I need to get a taxi to the airport and the first flight to Paris."

Eighteen hours later

Once again, Taylor had had a lot of time to kill on the plane. She'd thought about every word she would say to Mary Rutherford. She thought about how she would explain to Bennett why she'd left without a word. He would think the worst. And when he learned the truth, he'd hate her guts.

Fine. But you can't not try to fix this mess. And she couldn't be the reason Bennett's project went down the tubes. Obviously, Mary's decision not to do the merger was because Bennett had used the fake coaching. *Oh, God. He must've kept telling her how nice she looked. Page eight, section three.*

Still wearing nothing but a red bikini and her beach tank dress, she entered the pink marble lobby of the *Dame Marie*. It was just after seven in the evening so she knew most everyone had gone home, but she prayed she could convince someone there to get a message to Mary. Chip was not answering her calls. So if needed, she planned to camp out all night and mow Mary down first thing in the morning.

"No. Not you again," she said to the smarmy looking security guard at the reception desk, who gave her a vinegary look.

"Okay, I know you think I'm some crazy woman, but I know Mary Rutherford. I have to talk to her. Is she here?"

He puckered his little lips and made a noncommittal shrug. "Maybe *oui*. Maybe no."

Gah! She was going to pull that stringy hair right from his little head! "Okay. Is her assistant still here? Can you get a message to her?" The French were notorious for keeping late hours.

"Oh . . . So sorry, I cannot," he said in a snide, sassy little man voice.

"I am *just* asking you to get a message to her or her assistant. Tell her Taylor Reed needs to see Mary. Please? I'm begging you."

He barked at her in French, something obviously very rude, probably like . . . "Get your pale hippy ass out of my lobby."

Okay. I totally don't have time for this.

She leaned over the desk, a look of death and destruction radiating from her eyes like Mothra on a bad day. Or was it Godzilla who'd had laser beam eyes? *Oh, who cares? Give him hell, Tay!* Because she would not let Bennett's project go down without a fight.

"You listen to me, you piece of judgmental frog crap. I will find out where you live, and when you least expect it, I will be waiting in your closet. I will put a bag over your head, chloroform you, shove your bony ass body into a duffle bag, and then drop you over a bridge where you will scream in horror as you drown in your own sick. So do *not* fuck with me!" She pointed her finger in his face as his jaw flapped. "Pick. Up. The fucking phone. And call Mary's assistant."

He reached a shaking hand out and dialed.

"Ms. Reed?" said a woman's voice from behind.

She swiveled in her sandals and found herself facing Mary, who was dressed to the nines in a pink Chanel suit. Chip was standing at her side, smirking with evil joy.

"Mrs. Rutherford, thank God you're here!" Taylor slapped her hand over her heart. "I need to talk to you."

"I just stopped by to pick up a few files from my office." Mary's critical eyes swept over Taylor's unladylike outfit—a lightly translucent sundress spattered with mud and a red bikini underneath—as if questioning her sanity.

"I know what you're thinking, but I was in Bali on the beach when I read the press release. I hopped on the first plane here."

"She's crazy." Chip, who wore some weird lime green and orange plaid outfit, tugged on his mother's elbow. "We should go upstairs and let Jean Claude handle her."

Ah. So Jean Claude was the smarmy guard, who, at that moment was shaking his buggy-eyed head no. He didn't want to deal with her.

"You be quiet, Chip Rutherford," Taylor said, "or I'll tell your mother how you helped ruin my spotless reputation and career because you and your friends took turns trying to get me into bed. All just a friendly bet with a million-dollar ante of course."

Chip's beady eyes bulged from his head.

Taylor continued, "Or I'll tell her that you blackmailed me into being your dinner date that night just to make Bennett jealous."

Mary turned to Chip, looking outraged. "Well, Chip, I can't say it's the worst thing you've ever done, but I did think I taught you better."

"But Mom," he whined weakly.

"You and I will speak later," Mary snapped and then looked back at Taylor as Chip slunk away toward the elevators. "Ms. Reed, I do apologize for my son's behavior," she said calmly. "Sometimes he has the maturity and wisdom of a turnip. But what is it you wish to discuss with me?"

"The merger with Bennett—I mean, Mr. Wade."

"Ah, I see. And you flew all the way here to try and persuade me to change my mind?" Taylor could see the indignation building behind Mary's calm façade. She didn't like anyone questioning her.

"Yes," she replied, ready to tread carefully. "But only because I don't think you understand—"

"Dear girl," Mary interrupted curtly, "I began running this company when you were in diapers. So don't patronize me. My decision is final. I'm not selling to anyone, and least of all to a shark like Bennett who will likely just chop the company into bits and sell it off. Now, I'm very sorry you cut your beach vacation short, but I must go now." She turned and began walking toward the elevators.

"Wait! Please. That's *not* why he wants the company. In fact, buying your company will cost him everything he has."

Mary turned and looked at her. "Why would that fool do such a thing?"

"He's trying to help a lot of people who were left with nothing. And I know you understand what that's like. Please, just give me five minutes." Taylor held up her hand. "Five. And then I promise I'll never bother you again."

Mary grumbled something under her breath as the elevator doors slid open. "Fine. Five minutes, Ms. Reed."

Once up on the top floor, in the glamorous conference room adjacent to Mary's office overlooking Paris, it took much longer than five minutes to tell the story about Bennett and why he wanted to give up so much for his project. But Mary listened with a dry expression to the entire sordid, heartbreaking story.

When Taylor was done, she folded her hands neatly in her lap and waited nervously for Mary to say something.

The silence likely lasted only seconds, ten at most, but it felt like an eternity.

Mary leaned back in the armchair at the head of the long glass conference table and gazed out the window. Finally, coming to some conclusion, she turned her head of white hair back to Taylor. "You've given me a lot to think about, Taylor."

Taylor's insides did little flips. "So you'll reconsider?"

"Yes, I will."

Taylor jumped out of her chair and hugged Mary. "Thank you. Thank you. You have no idea how much this means."

Mary peeled Taylor off. The hug might've been a tad overstepping, but she just couldn't contain her happiness. "Sorry. I just can't tell you how relieved I am."

Mary smiled stiffly. "Well, I haven't decided anything, so don't count your chickens yet."

"It's all I could ever ask for."

"Well, Taylor, I'm late for my dinner meeting so—"

"Yes. Of course." Taylor moved away from the table. "I've taken up too much of your time."

Mary rose. "I'll let you know of my decision tomorrow."

Taylor couldn't help herself and hugged Mary again.

Mary patted her arm awkwardly. "Okay, thank you."

Taylor wanted to bow or curtsy or do something to express how grateful she felt as she walked away, *but that would be weird, right?*

"Oh, and Taylor? I have a question: May I ask why you came all this way and not Mr. Wade?"

With all the excitement, she had sort of left that part out.

Perhaps, subconsciously she'd hoped never to have to tell anyone.

"Remember how I told you about Chip's bet?"

Mary nodded. "Money put to good use, I say, though it doesn't excuse his behavior."

"Before I knew the truth about Bennett's project, I wasn't so happy about the bet. I'm sure you can understand why. And then there was the fact that Bennett hired me because he hoped that I'd be able to help him get through to you—like I'm some magic woman-CEO whisperer."

"You did do a fairly decent job getting through to me."

"Thanks. But uh . . . I created a training course just to sabotage him. I added things I thought you would hate, like telling him to show he was in charge and to pay you lots of personal compliments."

To her surprise, Mary laughed. "I guess that explains why Mr. Wade kept talking about my outfit and hair. I thought the man was hitting on me."

Oh no. Taylor covered her face and groaned. "I'm so sorry, Mrs. Rutherford. So, so sorry."

"Well, dear, it wasn't the reason I didn't want to sell to him."

It wasn't? "But I read that quote in the press release."

Mary waved her hand at Taylor. "Oh you can't believe a word those vultures say. That quote was pulled from something unrelated I said last year."

"So-so-so why then?" Taylor asked.

Mary shrugged. "I simply love my company. I'm not ready to retire. But hearing Bennett's story—I can't imagine losing my son like that, as foolish and shallow as he is sometimes."

"Taylor?" Bennett's deep voice came from the doorway that led out to the small private lobby.

Taylor swiveled and saw a look of utter anger, tinged with hurt, in his eyes.

"Bennett?" she gasped his name. "What are you doing here?"

"I took my plane. And there was no one at the front desk. Just a dribble of what looked like urine across the floor. You told her about Bali?" He sounded somewhere between wounded and shocked.

"Yes. But I was only trying to—"

"And you tried to sabotage my deal." It wasn't a question.

Taylor's heart filled with a thousand little stabbing pains made of guilt and sadness. This was it. The moment she feared. "Yes. And I know there's nothing I can say to—"

"Anything else you wish to tell me, Ms. Reed," Bennett said, "since we seem to be getting everything out in the open?" Meaning he was pissed. Beyond pissed. For the deceit and for telling Mary something so private.

Taylor looked at her feet. "Yes, but this really isn't the time."

He laughed acerbically. "Oh, no. Don't be shy, Ms. Reed. Please. I insist. What other secrets have you been keeping?"

"Bennett, please?" Taylor pleaded.

He didn't say a word, but the look in his eyes was sheer hatred.

Taylor knew he'd never forgive her. Not in a million years. But she couldn't bear the thought of him discovering there was more. "Your mother is sick. She told me she doesn't have much time."

He didn't blink, didn't breathe, didn't change the furious expression on his face. "Get the fuck out of my sight," he said so coldly that it felt like a nail going into her coffin.

She didn't want to fight or say anything that might undermine his deal with Mary, so she merely nodded. "I'll be on my way." She looked at Mary, who gave her a consoling smile. "Thank you, Mrs. Rutherford. I appreciate your time."

"Anytime, Ms. Reed. You take care." Then she looked at Bennett. "Mr. Wade, will you please step into my office? I think we should talk."

CHAPTER 19

"I seriously can't believe it," Sarah said, curling up on Jack's pink floral couch, holding a cup of untouched tea. "Holly is going to be pissed with you." Holly was away in London, looking at a new art collection.

"Why?" Taylor asked, sitting in her pink flannel pajamas, sipping from her mug.

"You totally blew it with our dream man."

Taylor rolled her eyes. "Thanks."

"I'm just kidding. You never had a chance, anyway."

"What?" Taylor scoffed.

Sarah laughed. "Sorry. Sorry. Just trying to make you laugh."

"Don't. You're making me feel way worse." It had been two weeks since she'd returned home, feeling like she might actually die from a broken heart. Jack had taken one look at her, thought the worst, and had gone ballistic, saying that he was going to kick the crap out of Bennett, break his nose, fix it, and then break it again. Finally, after she'd gotten him to calm down and told him the entire sad story, he'd downgraded his desire to kill Bennett to some mere finger breakage.

From then on she'd stayed in her room, telling everyone she

was all right but needed space. Normally, she'd go straight to Holly and Sarah or her family, but something inside her felt broken, and she honestly felt so ashamed for everything: Having misjudged Bennett, her plan to hurt him, *actually* hurting him, and . . . ever agreeing to keep his mother's illness a secret. Somehow, out of all this, she'd ended up becoming an ugly, horrible person while Bennett was like this damaged angel who had reached out to her, looking for a path back into the land of the living. All she'd managed to do was break his wings. She'd failed the one man in the world she was meant to help. *Nice, Taylor. Real nice.*

"So? You ready?" Sarah said, standing up from the couch.

Taylor set her tea on the coffee table and nodded solemnly. She wished Holly could be here, too, but Sarah was strong as hell. She'd keep Taylor from falling apart.

Taylor rose from the couch, went into the bathroom, and came out holding the little white stick, the tip of it wrapped in clean toilet paper. "Here." She shoved it at Sarah. "You look and tell me."

Sarah took a breath, grabbed the thing, and flipped it over. She whooshed out a breath and gave Taylor a shallow nod. "What do you want to do next?"

Fuck. "I don't know." She'd honestly been in denial this entire time. She'd told herself things like, "*Not everyone gets pregnant every time the condom breaks*"; "*You don't even feel sick*"; and "*You're always late.*" But somewhere deep down inside, she knew the truth. She just hadn't been ready to face it: *I'm pregnant. With Bennett's child. And he hates me. Shit. What am I going to do?*

"You're keeping it, right?" Sarah asked.

Trying to sort out her feelings, Taylor nodded slowly. "It's not the way I imagined becoming a mother—I thought I'd have a husband and own a house. A job might be good, too."

Sarah squeezed her arm. "You'll be okay, Taylor. You have us. And I'm sure Bennett will help you."

That was the one thing she didn't want. Seeing Bennett, having to face him on a regular basis, possibly for the rest of her life wasn't something she could stomach. He hated her with everything he had, while she loved him. It would be like having her heart broken over and over again. Forever.

And, if for some reason, Bennett decided he didn't want anything to do with her and the baby, that would be a different sort of tragedy. Either way, though, having this baby would result in a prolonged, emotionally painful situation, and probably not the best for a child. *Thank you, river. This is so awesome.*

"You *are* going to tell him, aren't you, Taylor?" Sarah asked.

Taylor shook her head. "I don't know, Sarah. I just don't know."

"But why do you think he won't forgive you?"

"You don't know him like I do. He's . . . intense. And I broke his trust with something important." In some ways, what she'd done to him was worse than what his Kate had done.

"You tried to fix a mistake."

"It won't matter to him."

"Taylor, I know this is hard for you. I really, really do. And this probably isn't the time for a little tough love, so I'll dial it down a notch because you're like a sister."

"But?"

"But every time you've assumed something about this man, you've been wrong. Really, really wrong. I'll also point out that keeping the truth from him didn't work out so well for you last time."

"You're right. I know you are. But this is different." She grazed her hand over her stomach.

"Taylor," Sarah gripped her shoulders, "you need to grow the hell up. You're going to have a baby. His baby. You don't get to decide if he gets to be a father. He does. And it doesn't matter if you don't like it. It doesn't matter if your heart is broken. You have to tell him. It's his right. I'd say the same thing to you even if I wasn't a judge."

Taylor's hand trembled the moment she switched back on her phone—okay, Bennett's phone. She knew she could call him from her personal cell, but doing this felt symbolic of letting him back into her life. Or, at least, telling him in some weird way that it was what she wanted. But when she called Bennett, the number was disconnected.

She thought it was odd, but then . . . *of course. Why would he keep his number? He doesn't want to speak with me.* And anyone who wanted to reach him would go through Robin anyway, which is what she would have to do.

The next morning she called his office, and it was exactly as she'd feared.

"I'm sorry, Ms. Reed," Robin said, "but Mr. Wade is out of the country. I'll let him know you called."

"Do you know when he'll be back? It's kind of important."

"I'm sorry, Ms. Reed. I'm not allowed to share Mr. Wade's itinerary. But I promise I'll tell him you called."

She knew Robin would keep her word, but would Bennett call?

Taylor could only hope for the best.

She spent the next week dusting off her resume, researching companies, and applying for jobs. Her heart might not be ready to move on, but her bank account and credit cards were itching for some attention. She figured she would work as a consultant in the HR field, because they paid the best, and she'd have more flexible hours for the baby. It would also allow her to pay back Jack every dime.

Yes, she'd swallowed her pride and asked him to let her return that money he'd loaned her a little later so she'd be able to send Bennett a check for the full fifty K right away—the only right choice given everything.

Strangely, when she'd asked Jack for help this time, it wasn't so hard. Somehow, out of all this, she'd learned that being independent didn't mean doing everything alone.

Which was why she'd also decided to tell Jack her big news almost immediately. She'd never seen her brother so shocked. And happy. And so convinced it would be a boy. But when she told him she'd planned to get a place of her own once she'd paid him back and had a little money saved, he immediately protested. "Hell no. I'm not letting my little sister go live in some studio apartment with my nephew. You're staying here with me until he's born and you're back on your feet. Or forever. I've got this big house and no plans to ever date again. And forget about marriage."

It was a sweet, sweet gesture, but Jack would eventually get over his broken heart and change his mind. As least she hoped so. But her being there for any length of time would only discourage him from getting back on the horse. It's pretty easy to ignore the holes in your life when you have very noisy, time-consuming distractions like a baby.

"Thank you, Jack. But I need to stand on my own two feet again. I won't move far, though, so you can always help with *her*."

"It's going to be a boy. Another Reed man. I'll teach him everything a guy needs to know about scalpels and fishing and celebrity gossip."

She loved that Jack was so into this and better yet, hadn't pushed her to talk about Bennett or what role he would play. Maybe he just knew it wouldn't help the situation.

An entire week passed before Taylor attempted to call Bennett once more, but she got the same answer from Robin. Only this time, Taylor felt a thousand times more pathetic. She imagined she wasn't the first woman Robin had had to shoo off.

"Okay. Thanks, Robin. Tell him . . . never mind. I know you've already passed along my first message."

"I'm sorry, Ms. Reed," she said remorsefully. "I will tell him you called again."

Taylor hung up and stared at that phone with the tracking device. She'd been keeping it charged since she'd turned it back on, unable to bring herself to sever the connection. What would happen if she turned it off? Would he even care at this point? Would he come running to see if she was all right? As she stared at the thing she remembered there was one other option: Bennett's mother.

Oh God. She probably hates me, too. Taylor had broken the promise not to tell Bennett. But what other choice did she have? She dialed the stored number, and it rang twice.

"Hello?"

"Mrs. Wade? This is Taylor Reed. Please don't hang up."

"Taylor, why the hell would I hang up, child?"

"I figured you must be mad at me."

"No, dear. Not at all. In fact, I've been meaning to call and thank you."

"Wh—what for?" Taylor asked, a little stunned by the warm reception.

"Dear, people assume I'm the sort of woman who speaks her mind, but the truth is, I'm not that ballsy. I should've told Bennett months ago about my cancer, but I didn't have it in me. And now that the cat's out of the bag, it's brought us closer. He's . . . well, he's a changed man, Taylor. I think I have you to thank for that."

She'd broken his trust in the worst kind of way, so she wasn't sure she deserved any thanks.

Mrs. Wade continued, "It's like a huge weight has been lifted from his shoulders and now he's opened up. I had no idea what he'd been carrying around all these years, and while it breaks my heart to learn I never met my grandchild, I thank God my boy was spared that day. It was a miracle. A damned miracle. And I think he was saved so he could do good in this world."

Taylor agreed. Wholeheartedly.

"And what about you? How are you feeling?" Taylor asked.

"Oh. You know. My son has me seeing all of these crazy doctors—he thinks I'm an old fool for simply accepting my diagnosis."

"He loves you."

"I know. But when my time is up, it will be up. There's nothing Bennett can do to stop that. But who knows, maybe I'll live long enough to meet my second grandchild. Now that would be something, wouldn't it?"

Taylor began to cry as it sank in that she was carrying that second grandchild. And she wanted so badly to say something, but telling Mrs. Wade before telling Bennett didn't feel right. On the other hand, if Bennett refused to talk to her, she had an obligation to the woman.

Fine. I'll try one more time to get ahold of him, then that's it. She had to start getting on with things no matter how devastated she felt. And being sad couldn't be healthy for the baby.

Wow. It was crazy how quickly she'd mentally shifted gears to thinking like a mother. When the hell did that happen?

Uh. When you got knocked up?

Oh yeah.

"That would be something wonderful, Mrs. Wade," she sniffled. "By the way, I really need to talk to Bennett. It's important. Do you know how I can reach him?"

"Oh, Taylor. I am so sorry, but he is a stubborn mule like his father. I tried talking some sense into him, told him to at least hear what you have to say, but he won't have it. He insists it will be a cold day in hell when he ever speaks to you again."

It was as Taylor feared. "I never meant to hurt him—I mean, I did at first. I was really, really mad at him, but then I got to know him and . . ." What was she doing? Commiserating with his mother?

"I'm sure that whatever happened, dear, that you're not a backstabbing shyster."

What? He'd called her that? Taylor's temper began to sizzle. "I did *not* stab him in the back. I tried to help him and maybe I broke his trust, but . . . Ugh. Never mind. It's pointless. Please, when you speak to him, tell him that . . ." She almost spilled the beans. Almost.

"You are going to Ms. Luci's party, aren't you?"

Taylor had gotten another invitation in the mail, which had been odd because she'd never given Luci her address. Maybe Robin had provided it? In any case, she hadn't really thought about going. She'd had too much on her mind.

Mrs. Wade continued, "Because Bennett will be there. He

apparently promised Ms. Luci he'd help her bartend, if you can imagine that. My Bennett is skilled at many things; however, waiting on others is not one of them."

"Now that you mention it . . . I guess I'll be going to the party. Thank you, Mrs. Wade."

"Call me Mom, dear."

Taylor smiled. "Okay, Mom." This time, it didn't feel so strange. No, not anymore.

CHAPTER 20

The warm, mid-summer Napa Valley evening air heated Bennett's sweaty face as he moved through the crowded party tent in his tux, wanting to beat the crap out of every guest who asked him for a goddamned refill. For the record, he did not mind pouring champagne as much as he minded what happened next. How much more of this "good will" could one man take? Case in point . . .

"Ohmygod!" a redheaded woman in a shiny mess of a blue evening gown screamed at the top of her lungs, pointing in his face. "You're Bennett Wade!"

Bennett bit back a growl and forced a polite smile to his mouth just as his mother had taught him. "Always be gracious," she'd say. "Remember that not everyone in this world has it so lucky."

He cleared his throat. "Yes. I am Bennett Wade. And yes, you may take a damned picture with me."

The woman squealed and clapped. "Ohmygodohmygod!" She dug out a phone from her little purse and handed it to the man who stood by her side, looking like he wanted to take a swing at Bennett.

Bennett put his arm around the woman and gave the man a

look. *Try it. I fucking dare you. Because I'll have you in the fetal position so fast that your girlfriend here will never look at you like you're a real man ever again.*

The man, average height with blond hair, suddenly looked like he might wet himself.

Good choice, my friend. Just snap your picture.

He did and handed the phone back to his girlfriend. "Th-thank you, Mr. Wade."

Bennett gave a nod and headed through the crowd in the other direction. That man wasn't the first—more like the twentieth this evening—and he wouldn't be the last to instantly assume that men like Bennett were pussies in suits who wanted nothing more than to hide behind their money and take their girlfriends. But not all rich bastards were alike, and he hadn't grown his multibillion dollar empire by backing down from a fight. That, and hard work. Lots of it. His company was his life and the only thing he did with his time aside from exercising—which had become his primary form of stress relief these days, given he hadn't been able to get it up for over a year, except for Taylor. It seemed his dick was smarter than he was and had gotten tired of the shallow women like Kate who had only been after his money. But the minute the real deal showed herself, his dick knew.

Oh yes. It knew.

Taylor had entered that conference room in Phoenix in her tight little suit, her face flustered and flushed, and it wanted her. Not because his "friends" were lined up around the block pining for the woman, betting to see who could get her in the sack first, but because she had this fire in her sultry brown eyes—the same fire he'd seen in a picture when one of his "buddies" told him about the bet after a game of golf (a necessary evil for doing deals in his world). The moment he heard she'd turned them all down, it piqued his interest. Because she was single, beautiful, a hard worker from what the guys said, and couldn't be won over with a few cheap pickup lines and a big bank account.

They'd all tried. Repeatedly.

They'd all crashed and burned. Repeatedly.

He had to meet her.

And as luck so happened, he was headed to Phoenix to golf with an executive from Japan who was there on business and interested in selling the patent he needed.

So he made a few calls and set up the meeting.

Yes, just to meet her.

Silly, a guy like him, who could have any woman he wanted, going out of his way just to get in a room with Taylor Reed, a woman he'd never met.

But he'd been right about her. She couldn't be fooled or charmed. She could see through ten feet of bullshit from a mile away, and that, *that* was why everyone failed to seduce her.

The moment she chewed his ass out in Phoenix, he knew he wanted her because she might just be the only woman on the planet capable of seeing him for what he truly was: fucked up. *The tailored suit is a deceptive tool, indeed*. However, each time he thought of calling her, he'd pathetically lost his nerve. She had to hate him after the way he behaved, after *losing her job*, so he convinced himself to let it go, that he had no interest in her, that she wasn't his type because a woman like that couldn't be happy with what he had to offer: a mess inside a suit. And then one day, her name came up again in a round of golf, his "buddies" making fun of her efforts to start her own company, and it set him off. He might not be interested in her, but he'd be

damned if he was going to let those assholes put her down simply because they all failed to get in her pants. So he'd decided to
hire her. Yes, to snub those bastards. He also figured it couldn't
hurt to get her help with Lady Mary. Of course, the moment he
saw Taylor again in Seattle, that same fiery look in her big
brown eyes, well . . . he began to get the feeling that he might
actually need her. Really need her.

As he looked up, Bennett spotted Ms. Luci's approach
through the crowd. She had a scowl on her face. Not a good
sign. *That woman frightens me.*

"Mr. Wade!" she barked out, turning a few heads, despite
the loud mariachi music pouring from one of the other six tents
they'd set up to accommodate the thousand-plus guests. Many
were here to attend the group wedding being held for Ms. Luci's
successful matches. Apparently, they did this every year. *A goddamned nooky cookie cult.*

"Ms. Luci." He dipped his head, getting the distinct feeling
she was about to . . .

She grabbed his arm—*Ow! She has a grip*—and dragged
him to the edge of the tent. Her manservant or lover or whoever
that Sebastian fellow was stood behind her, his one large eye
poking out like it might bite someone. "Bennett, this is your
last warning," she said, "or I will send you to the kitchen. Stop
terrorizing my guests."

Bennett had a very, very deep respect for his mother—a
strong woman and the only person he'd ever known to love him
unconditionally besides Taylor—and Luci reminded him exactly of her.

Your mother or Taylor?

Both.

"My apologies, Ms. Luci. It will not happen again. However," he glanced at his watch. "I'm afraid I'll need to depart in a moment. I'll be out of the country for a few weeks, traveling on business, and must stop to see my mother before I go." Ms. Luci would understand why. His mother confessed that the two had been corresponding for months now, growing quite a friendship, so she'd be aware of his mother's cancer.

Luci's face lit up with panic. "Leave? You can't leave."

He raised a brow. "You're saying I should not go and visit my sick mother?"

"Uh-uh," she stammered. "Can you at least wait a few more minutes? Until the ceremonies begin? They are . . ." she searched for words. "Touching!"

Why did he feel like she was up to something?

Because she probably is.

"Ms. Luci, I know you are hailed as some great matchmaking expert, which I'm sure is the reason my mother contacted you initially, but I'm sorry. I'm not interested in dating." *Ever again.*

She had a guilty look on her face, which she hid rather poorly. "Dating? Now, who said anything about dating, *mijo*? I'm simply asking you to stay for a few . . ." Her dark eyes flashed to the other end of the tent, and then a look of relief washed over her face. "*Ay dios.* Thank goodness." She smiled up at Bennett. "I think someone is looking for you."

He turned and spotted Taylor in a sexy little white strapless dress that hugged her soft curves and accentuated her breasts, making them look plumper and so . . .

In need of my hands.

He gulped. *Goddammit. She looks fucking amazing.* Her dark, silky brown hair cascaded down her bare shoulders, her pouty lips—the ones he dreamed of kissing almost every single goddamned night—looked downright sinful. His dick instantly began hardening. *You are not a goddamned compass. And Taylor isn't your goddamned polar north, you sonofabitch.*

Taylor's pleading eyes locked onto his from across the crowded tent of happy, formally dressed guests. He knew she felt sorry. But what was the goddamned point when he couldn't forgive her? He'd shared his darkest secrets, he'd opened up to her when the act of doing so felt like taking a knife to his own goddamned chest. But, he'd done it. For her. Taking a risk that she'd love him anyway. Did she have any idea how difficult that had been after Kate?

He'd put his faith in Taylor. His goddamned faith. And then she ran. No note. No message. She just . . . ran. Straight to Mary, a stranger, in order to share his dark past. Yes, Taylor probably thought she was helping, but it wasn't her story to share. And why had she done it? To hide the final nail in her coffin: that she'd only come with him on that trip to ruin him. Taylor. The one woman he'd hoped, with his entire soul, he could trust. *I can't be wrong about this one. Not her. Not this time,* he'd thought over and over again. But he had been.

With their eyes still locked across the crowded tent, he slowly shook his head at her, warning her not to come closer. It was over. He didn't want to see her again.

Taylor's face then flushed with determination, and she began making her way toward him.

Stubborn woman. Why couldn't she simply leave him be? She'd already done enough damage. He made his way across the grass toward the parking lot and was almost to the security check point when he heard his name over the loudspeakers.

"Bennett. Bennett Wade. Don't you dare walk away from me!"

He stopped and looked toward the tent in the middle of the field, about fifty yards away. It was where Luci said they'd be holding the one hundred weddings later tonight.

When his eyes focused, he spotted Taylor in her white dress, holding a microphone and standing on a podium decorated in a crap load of white flowers and ribbons and wedding bullshit.

"Bennett, I know you can hear me," she said. Even though she was half a football field away, he felt her eyes on him. "Before you leave, I want you to know that I am . . ." There was a catch in her voice, and Bennett realized she was crying. A brunette woman he'd never seen before ran up on the podium to comfort her. "Go on, Tay," the woman whispered, the mic picking up her words. "Say what you came here for."

Bennett felt his body tense up with anger and so many other emotions he wasn't used to feeling. Did she honestly believe some speech would change his mind or undo the damage?

Taylor cleared her throat. "Bennett, I am sorry. And I know there's no excuse for what I did, but I love you."

The crowd, who'd gathered in front of the wedding tent, began to cheer.

Taylor dipped her head graciously. "Thank you. Thank you." She held out her hand, pleading for them to let her finish. "But it's now or never, Bennett. You can forgive the woman who accepts you exactly as you are, or you will lose her forever." She wiped away the tears from her eyes, and her friend gave her a little squeeze of encouragement. Taylor squared her shoulders and looked out across the field in his direction. "Bennett, you once told me that we were the same, that we saw people and situations for what they truly were. Then can't you see how truly sorry I am? Can't you see that I never meant to hurt you?" She sighed. "Please, I'm begging you, please forgive me. Because . . ."

Bennett stared across the field, the crowd dissolving into the night. He wanted to go to her. He wanted to say he could forgive and trust and be a fucking man . . . but he simply didn't know. So much pain weighed him down and until he made right with his demons, he couldn't truly let go, or be there for anyone, or forgive or sleep or fuck or eat or love.

And *that* was about all he knew.

She let out a little hiccup before she went on, "Because if you don't forgive me now, I'll never be able to forgive you, Bennett. Never."

What the hell did she mean by that? Forgive me or I won't forgive you? He looked down at his polished black shoes and then turned toward the parking lot, fuming at her ultimatum. Could she see him? He didn't know. He only knew that Taylor was the woman he'd thought was for him and the woman he needed to let go of if he hoped to keep breathing.

"Fine, you fucker!" a woman's voice rang out. It wasn't Taylor, but her friend who'd grabbed the microphone. "She's pregnant, and you just lost the chance to be with the one woman who could ever love a rich, famous, totally hot asshole like you! Oops. I mean . . . asshole! Just asshole."

Bennett turned his entire body just in time to see a thousand people scowling in his direction, probably willing him to die.

Taylor stood frozen on the podium while Sarah remained at her side, screaming to the world that Taylor had been knocked up by Bennett Wade.

Oh, the shame. Wasn't it bad enough she'd gotten up on the stage in front of a thousand people and declared her love like a fool?

Don't forget the begging. That was pretty pathetic, too.

But the shame was nothing compared to the heartbreak of seeing Bennett walk away like she'd meant nothing to him or wasn't good enough to deserve his forgiveness.

And, of course, that heartbreak and shame only felt exacerbated by watching Jack, a big guy with a mean right hook, who was anything but a pacifist despite his Hippocratic Oath, tearing through the crowd after Bennett.

Taylor cupped her hands over her mouth. "Oh no." *Jack's going to kill him.* "Jack!"

She looked at Sarah who grinned from ear to ear. "Go kick his ass, Jack!" she screamed into the microphone. "I'll make sure all charges are dropped!"

"I can't believe this," Taylor whispered, shaking her head as the entire party rushed off to watch the fight.

Wasn't this supposed to be a giant love fest?

Taylor made her way down from the podium and charged off to where the mob had gathered near the edge of the dirt field being used as a parking lot. They started cheering. *Oh, shit.* That meant Jack was winning.

Wait. Shouldn't she be happy about that?

No. Of course not. She didn't want anyone fighting. Period. She pushed her way through the crowd. "Excuse me! Excuuuuuse me!" She broke through just in time to see Jack straddling Bennett's stomach, cocking his fist for a blow.

Oh God! "No! Jack do—" That fist came down, and she looked away, wincing. *Oh, damn that had to hurt.* The crowd went wild, and when she looked back, Bennett was in the process of throwing Jack off. It was like watching two big lions trying to chew each other up.

As everyone seemed to be basking in a bit of pre-matrimony bloodlust, not lifting a finger to break the two boneheads apart, she decided it was all up to her. She stormed toward Bennett right as he lunged for Jack, who was on his back, his mop of brown hair in his eyes.

Everything happened so fast.

She grabbed Bennett's large arm, telling him to stop, at the precise moment his arm pulled back. His elbow hit her square in the breastbone, knocking her straight back. She landed with a thump in the dirt, choking for air.

The crowd fell silent, gasping, and maybe that's what got Bennett's attention, because he was suddenly over her. "Taylor! Fuck, are you all right. Please tell me you're all right."

Jack shoved him aside. "Get away from my sister, asshole!"

Bennett gave him a quick look. "You're Taylor's brother?"

Jack bent over her, ignoring Bennett. "Tiger, can you breathe?"

Her air returned in a gasp, and she nodded. "Yeah, I'm fine I just—"

"Did he hit your stomach?" Jack asked, calm but frantic—if that was possible.

"No," she groaned. "Just my chest."

"We should get her to the hospital," Bennett said, now hovering to the other side.

"Hey. Back off!" Jack barked, his big green eyes projecting a death ray. "I'm a doctor. And you can just stay the hell away from her."

"Like hell I will," Bennett growled. "She's carrying my baby."

Jack sprang up, completely forgetting all about Taylor. "I don't care if she's carrying your goddamned litter. You will stay away from her."

Litter? What was she, a dog now? *Oh, no. I'm a tiger.* "Guys!" She wheezed, trying to get to her feet. "Enough."

Jack regained his composure and turned his attention to helping her up. "Slowly. Get up slowly."

"I'm fine," she said, now standing and covered in dirt.

"Taylor," Bennett said, "I'm sorry. I didn't mean to—"

She held out her hand. "Just leave, Bennett. I'll call you in nine months."

He stepped toward her. "Please, let's just go somewhere and talk."

She pierced him with her gaze. "Don't you get it, Bennett?" she whispered. "You weren't the only one who put their heart on the line. It's over. Just go back to your demons and leave me the hell alone."

Jack stepped between them, facing Bennett. "She said leave."

"This is between her and me," Bennett snarled, the tip of his nose almost touching Jack's since both men were about the same height.

"Not anymore," Jack retorted, not backing down.

Oh God. They were going to fight again. She was just grateful her two other brothers, Marcus and Rob, and her father hadn't shown up. Not that they hadn't tried. The moment they'd heard Bennett Wade would be at the party, they began ironing slacks and getting out the hair gel. As a compromise, she agreed to bring Jack because he was the most level-headed of the men in her family. Racecar drivers, not so much. Surprisingly, Rob, the vintner, was a notorious hothead.

Ms. Luci suddenly appeared out of nowhere and wedged herself between the two men, facing Bennett. "It is time for you to go, young man. And don't think I am not calling your mother. Just wait until she hears about this!" She shook her finger in his face and then turned toward Jack. "And you!" She pointed at him, hissing what sounded to be like some very lewd words in

Spanish before finally saying, "I'll not have fighting at my fiesta. You take your sister home, this minute."

Jack nodded like a shamed little boy. "I'm sorry. I don't know what got into me."

Luci gave him a strange look. "You wouldn't happen to be single, would you?" She shook her head. "Oh. Never mind. Off with you."

Luci's eyes then moved to Sarah, who'd now worked her way through the crowd and stood next to Jack. "Y tú! Un juez? Qué boca tan sucia! Y por supuesto eres soltera también."

Sarah blinked at Luci, having no clue what she'd said. "Uh . . . sorry?"

"Come on, Tay," Jack said. "Time to go."

She hesitated for a moment, her eyes gravitating toward Bennett's remorseful face, his eyes—one of them swollen and red—pleading with her. His hair was all mussed, and his bow-tie had come undone, making him look like the sexy, bad boy billionaire, in need of a good spanking, that he was.

She sighed. God he was beautiful. And even now, she could feel her heart reaching out with its little arms toward him.

No, Tay. He only pities you. He'd be kind to her because of the baby. A relief, she supposed. But she'd need to save herself a lifetime of heartbreak, and allow him to only be a part of the child's life—if that's what he wanted—not a part of hers. Not any more than he had to be, anyway.

She straightened her spine. "My lawyer will send you papers so you can decide on visitation. But please don't try to contact me until after the baby's born. Goodbye, Bennett."

She walked away with Jack and Sarah, feeling grateful as hell she had them to lean on.

CHAPTER 21

Taylor had had the most exciting, phenomenal, monumental month of her entire existence, and things were about to get even better. She could just feel it. It was as if the world had shifted on its axis and decided it was her turn for a little happiness. Not that she'd felt unhappy before, but wandering through life trying to find your way wasn't the same as feeling like you were alive and loving it.

Maybe her decision to stop rowing and just go with the flow might've had something to do with it. She didn't know, but life was beginning to look damned good, something she didn't think possible after Ms. Luci's party.

It started the week following the shame fest, when she'd had her first OB-GYN appointment and listened to the baby's sweet little heartbeat—kind of like a galloping monster, but still sweet. She couldn't believe how big the little thing had already grown. To think, one night and two defective condoms could result in a tiny person living inside her. Yes, yes. She knew that was how babies were made, but it was an infinitely different experience to witness the event occurring inside her own body. She couldn't wait to meet him or her in seven and a half months. She could, however, do without the whole morning sickness thing. Awful. Just awful. She constantly felt like she'd eaten a giant can of nacho cheese food-product and then topped it off with a great big vat of jalapeños. Nausea and heartburn, big time. But all worth it.

Then, out of nowhere, she'd been contacted by a headhunter from a great HR consulting firm who offered her a fantastic opportunity as a VP, heading up a project to train and re-energize the entire management staff of a big Fortune 500. They'd heard about her CEO attitude makeover course from someone at HRTech and didn't think it was crazy at all. In fact, they'd been developing a similar concept that expanded across all levels of management. So, her idea wasn't all that insane after all! They were so excited about getting her, they offered her a signing bonus and said she could set her own hours. Of course, she'd planned to take some time off, as much as she could afford, after the baby came, but she would figure out a way to make it work.

The third thing to happen was that Holly's Aunt Glady had decided to retire and move to Arizona. But she wasn't ready to sell her house until she knew for sure she'd get used to the hot weather, so Aunt Glady offered to rent the house to Taylor. It was small, but it sure beat an apartment and had a little yard. Even better, she'd only be ten minutes from Jack's house, and would get a really nice break on the rent for keeping the place up until Aunt Glady knew what she wanted to do.

Of course, not everything was perfect. She still thought about Bennett every day, more times than she cared to admit. And every time she did, her heart made these sad little whimpers, reaching its little arms for him.

"Oh stop," she said, folding a T-shirt from the clean pile on Jack's dining room table. "You're being ridiculous." *Hearts don't have arms.* She then reached into the pile and pulled out a red bikini top. It was the top she'd worn in Bali and Paris.

She sighed, staring at the thing. Why had it all gone so damned wrong?

The doorbell rang, and she checked to make sure her pale pink "lounging around the house" sundress wasn't too see-through—*Check!*—and made her way through the everything-pink-and-floral, decorating-monstrosity living room. *Damn. He so needs to get over Doris. Maybe Ms. Luci can help.* She shook her head at the silly thought as she pulled open the front door.

"You Taylor Reed?" asked the husky man in the gray uniform.

"Yes."

He stepped aside and began maneuvering a large suitcase her way.

"It's my bag!" She'd put in a claim, but had considered it a goner.

He made her sign, and she lugged it inside, immediately opening the thing to check the contents. Everything was there, including her notes from her bogus training course.

She threw them back into the suitcase and zipped everything up. She'd have to burn those later. What the hell had she been thinking?

The doorbell rang again and she opened it, thinking the delivery guy had forgotten something. But this time it was the FedEx guy.

"Taylor Reed?"

"Yes?"

He handed her an envelope. "Sign here."

She gave his electronic pad a scribble and closed the door,

staring at the envelope for several sad moments. It had to be the paternity papers back from Bennett's lawyers. Against her own lawyer's advice, she'd offered him shared custody as long as the child always lived with her and he didn't interfere with Taylor's life. Or buy the baby extravagant gifts. Not that she knew what Bennett's financial situation would be going forward, but it was important that the baby grew up well-grounded and knowing how to work for the important things in life. Considering everything, she thought that was a fair offer. After all, she didn't want to deprive her baby of a father.

She tore open the envelope and found a set of keys and a little card with an address on it. She blinked several times, her brain trying to make sense of it. The address was . . .

Across the street?

She pulled open Jack's front door and stared right at the white and yellow, two-story house with French windows and white shutters. Maybe the neighbors had gone on vacation and asked Jack to look after their pet but had forgotten to leave a set of keys?

She looked at her watch. It was 8:00 in the evening and Jack said he wouldn't be home until late due to an emergency facial reconstruction.

She went outside, crossed the empty street, and made her way up the brick walkway that ran straight through a manicured lawn, right up to the front door with its large brass knocker. A flower bed filled with daisies and little wildflowers ran along the front of the home.

She was about to knock when her eye caught a glimpse of a *San Francisco Tribune* laid out flat on the doormat. The headline read, "A Public Apology to Taylor Reed."

What the hell? She picked it up and held the paper to the porch light. It was written by a reporter named Harper Branton and referred to a letter the paper had received, signed anonymously thirty-five times, which offered an apology to Taylor for behaving unprofessionally and with complete disregard for her reputation.

> **B.W. has assured us that unless you forgive us, our names will be made public. Therefore, we hope, Ms. Reed, that you accept our sincerest apologies for any suffering we have caused.**

"I can't fucking believe this," she murmured to herself. Then a strange feeling hit. *Wait a second.*

"You're standing on the other side of that door, aren't you, Bennett?"

Slowly, the front door opened, and there he was, wearing low-slung jeans and a faded light-blue T-shirt that matched his eyes. His dark hair was mussed and sexy and he still had a thick coating of black man-scruff on his jaw. He looked like a very, very bad boy in need of a spanking.

Op! Tay, no. Don't even think about going there.

"What are you doing in there?" she asked.

"I purchased it."

Her jaw fell open. Leave it to Bennett to be a mule head and buy the house across the street from her brother so he could be near the baby. It was nice that he wanted to be a part of its life, but he'd lost his chance to be a part of hers. It was a complete violation of her space and such a Bennett Wade sort of thing to do. *So damned like the man to only think about himself.*

She shook her head, and turned to head back to Jack's

house, deciding she'd call his mother and try to get her to reason with him. Yes. That had been the fourth wonderful thing to happen this past month; she and Linda, Bennett's mother, had made a pact. Linda would attempt a new cancer treatment that had just come on the market and focus on getting better. And who knew? Miracles happened every day. Maybe Linda might live long enough to see the baby graduate. Maybe even longer. Whatever the case, Taylor was determined to make the most out of whatever time she had left and promised to bring the baby over as often as possible. She genuinely enjoyed spending time with Linda anyway. It was amazing how they were able to separate out the stuff with Bennett, but she supposed babies did that to people, made them reprioritize.

"Taylor!" she heard Bennett's voice echo from behind.

Damned stubborn man. Does he really think he can do this? Well, ha! I'm moving next week so he can stay there and fist-fight Jack every morning. Almost to the edge of the walkway, she heard him again.

"Ms. Reed. Don't you walk away from me," he snapped.

What? Had he just spoken to her like some . . . some child?

Furious, she turned to face him. "Who do you think you are, Mr. Wade? Some god? Some supernatural being who can command me like a mindless puppet?"

His lips twisted with the hint of a cocky smile. "Oh," he crossed his arms over his well-defined chest, "I see I've been promoted. I'm Mr. Wade again."

She charged forward. "What are you doing, Bennett?" she hissed. "This isn't funny. I meant what I said at the party, and I meant what I said in that note to your lawyer. I don't want you in my life—at least, any more than you have to be for the sake of the baby."

"Oh now," he unfolded his arms, "there you go again, think-ing so little of me."

"I don't think *little* of you. I think you're a *big* giant ass. The biggest."

"I always said you had a knack for figuring people out. Ex-cept you've misjudged me again. A bad habit of yours, per-haps?" he said with an arrogant-Bennett-esque tone.

"I said I was sorry, Bennett. And I meant it. What more do you want? You want me to beg? Because I tried that. It didn't work."

"The house isn't mine; it's yours."

She looked at him, trying to process. "What do you mean?"

"Yours. All yours."

"But that's . . ." These were the Berkeley Hills—views of San Francisco, the Bay Bridge, and the Golden Gate. The sorts of people who lived there were the sort of folks who wanted to be close to the city, but also wanted privacy and wonderful views. "That's a five-million-dollar house."

Bennett made a little pucker with his lips. "Give or take a million."

Taylor looked at him, unsure if she wanted to slap him or slap him hard. "I. Don't. Want your money, Bennett."

"It's not my money. It's his. Or hers. When eighteen rolls around."

"You can't gift my baby a house."

"*Our* baby. It's our baby. And I can, and I did. Care to see inside?" He gestured toward the front door.

Did he think he was cute? Or smart or charming or . . . "Why are you doing this to me?" She began to cry.

Bennett's cocky, mule-headed, controlling disposition in-stantly turned off. He held out his hands. "Oh. No. Please don't cry, Taylor. I didn't mean to upset you." He approached her, but she took a step back.

"Don't."

"Okay." He held up his palms as if being arrested. "I won't. But please, just come inside, and let me explain. Then I promise, I'll do whatever you want."

"You'll sell this house?" she asked.

He nodded. "Anything you want."

"Okay." She folded her arms. "I'll give you ten minutes, but then I have an important dinner meeting."

Taylor followed Bennett inside the home, through the beautifully decorated living room—overstuffed furniture with neutral-toned upholstery, no coffee table, but a large navy blue ottoman with a tray in the middle. She spent all of two seconds in the room, passing through, but she noticed how every inch, right down to the plush light khaki carpeting had been baby-proofed. She'd bet her favorite pink jammies that the pale yellow walls with white trim had washable paint, just perfect for reckless toddlers armed with crayons.

And, of course, knowing the kind of workaholic that Bennett was, he'd probably overseen every detail himself. *Whatever. So the guy's been reading a few baby books? Like that matters.*

She silently followed him through the brightly lit, cheery, modern eat-in kitchen with its cute rustic table made of chunky wood. It was big enough to seat Holly, Sarah, her brothers and father, plus a few extras.

Okay. So the house is awesome.

Bennett made his way to a set of double French doors that led to a patio, with a beautiful outdoor kitchen and enough seating for at least twenty, looking out toward the shimmering lights of the San Francisco Bay. Beyond that, the city herself and all her gorgeous, awe-inspiring buildings stood like a living architectural sculpture.

"Eh-hem." Bennett had pulled out a chair at the large wooden table, facing the five-million-dollar view.

"Oh. Sorry." She knew she'd been caught gawking, and the look on his face was pure smugness and victory. "Okay, Bennett. It's a wonderful view. What do you want me to say?"

She sat and he sat down next to her, resting his large hands on the table, his fingers laced. His arms looked larger than usual, like he'd been seriously working out lately. "I'd like you to say yes to giving me—giving us—another chance."

She looked down at the table, knowing this was going to get painful. But she needed to make him see reason. He didn't really want her. She wasn't the one for him. If she had been, he would've forgiven her without knowing about the baby. "I *said* yes. Yes to a lot of things that weren't the right things for you." She looked at him holding her ground. "You're not ready for a relationship or me. I'm not even sure you're ready for her." She looked down at her belly.

He jolted forward. "It's a girl?"

"No. I mean, I don't know. I think it's a girl, though."

"I'd love a girl. But I'd be happy with either. As long as it's healthy."

"Agreed." She nodded pensively.

"But I *am* ready."

She shook her head, wishing she could believe him. "It doesn't matter. Because *I* am ready. And that's all she'll need."

"Taylor," he said, his voice shifting into that dominating "Mr. Wade" tone, "she—or he—needs me, too. So do you."

"No, I don't, Bennett. I wanted you. I loved you. Those are very different things from need."

"I can't figure you out, Taylor." He leaned back and folded his arms. "You say you loved me, but the moment I let you in, you were gone faster than a bolt of lightning."

Her jaw dropped. "I did not run—okay, I did. But I ran, as fast as I fucking could, to save your deal and to save you."

He looked at her, apparently perplexed. "Save me from what?"

"From the load of crap you'd decided to commandeer from my laptop, crap that was there because I'd been too busy falling in love with you to remember to erase it."

"But why, Taylor? Why do that in the first place?"

She shrugged. "I don't know. I guess . . . I liked you, and when I found out I was nothing more than a bet, it hurt."

He reached out and cupped his hand to her cheek. "Yes, you *were* a bet, Taylor. I went all in, hoping you'd help me finish this Bali project and put the past behind me, that you wouldn't turn out to be just another gold digger after my money, and that you'd still want me even after you knew what I'd done. And I've bet it all again, everything I have on you."

Uhhh. . . . What did he mean by that? Had he purchased a racehorse and named it after her? "I don't understand."

He reached for her hand. "Lady Mary didn't sell to me."

"She didn't?" After all that, she still said no?

Bennett shook his head. "No. She bought my company instead."

Taylor took a moment to digest. "So, she—"

"She will absorb Wade Enterprises."

"And those people in Bali?" Taylor asked.

"She will hire someone to build the factory and run the operation. She'll buy all of her ingredients from them. Nothing changes, except those people's lives."

Taylor was stunned. "But why? Why work so hard just to sell and hand over the project?"

"So I could be with you. No more baggage. No more living in my father's shadow or in the past. No more running myself into the ground. Just you." He looked down at her stomach. "And that *thing* growing inside you." He grinned.

She sat there staring out at the lights, unable to believe it. He'd given up his company and his project in Bali, just to make a fresh start with her? It was insanity. His company and work were his life, part of his identity. Yet, he'd washed his hands of it all simply to make room for her.

"You really gave it all up?"

"Yes. However, I'm hoping to get something much better in return."

"I don't know, Bennett." She scrubbed her face with her hands.

He pulled back. "What else could you want, Ms. Reed? My undying soul? My blood? My manhood?"

She didn't know what would be enough. Her heart still felt so wounded.

"If you don't forgive me now," Bennett said, "I won't ever be able to forgive you."

She looked up at him. "That's my line."

"Did it work?" he asked. "Because I don't really understand what it means."

She took a deep, bracing breath and stared back out at that ocean. She'd only managed to climb halfway up that cliff. Did she have it in her to turn and jump back in?

"I love you, Taylor. I'll beg if I have to, but I'd much rather spend my energy fucking you on this table."

She shot him a look.

"Sorry. Just being honest," he said unapologetically.

Reformed man or not, he was still cocky Mr. Wade. And always would be. *Damned fucking hot, too.*

Her eyes darted down to his groin.

"Are you staring at my cock, Ms. Reed?"

She began nibbling her fingernails nervously. "No . . . ?"

He gave her a skeptical look. "Yes, I think you were."

She shook her head, her eyes now locked on his bulge.

She twisted in her chair and stood up slowly, her gaze running up the length of his muscular torso.

He reached for her hands and guided her to her feet, looking her body over. "I don't know what it is about you, Taylor. But you being pregnant makes me want to put you on your back and keep you that way."

With his foot, he pushed her chair out of the way and backed her against the table.

He slid between her thighs and grabbed both sides of her face. His lips made contact, and there it was. Heaven. His warmth, his tongue, the sinful rhythm of his movements—it was like getting a full body slash jellybean massage through her mouth.

As she leaned in, running her hands around his tight waist, he pulled back, still cupping her cheeks. "Say yes, Taylor."

She blinked and looked up at him. *Whatever you want. Just keep kissing me like that. Maybe a bit lower.*

"Yes to what? To the house?" she asked.

He slowly shook his head, pinning his pale blue gaze on her. "No, Taylor," he said, his voice low and husky and seductive as hell. "Yes, to marrying me."

She jerked back her head in shock. "Your wife?"

"How else will this work?"

"I don't know, Bennett. Marriage is a big step."

"Oh, come, come now, Ms. Reed. Nothing is bigger than love. Or a baby. Marriage is just a legal arrangement. Nothing more."

She looked at him and laughed. "You're serious."

He nodded. "Did I leave out the part about putting everything in your and the baby's name?"

"What?"

"I figured I'd never be happy unless I had you, anyway."

"You're crazy." As in certifiable. On the other hand, it was a pretty ballsy gesture. It also showed he'd put all of his trust into her. *He said he'd bet everything on you. He really fucking meant it.*

"Yes. Crazy for you. Is that a yes?"

"It's a maybe." Honestly, it was a yes. A big yes. But she really wanted to see how far he'd go to get the word out of her. *He so loves a challenge.*

His head tipped back toward the night sky. "God, help me. I think she wants to drive me mad." He looked at her again with a devilish smile. "Let's see if I can turn that maybe to a firm yes." He kissed her hard, his sultry lips moving over hers, his tongue sliding into the intimate domain of her mouth. This time, his kiss didn't feel like domination, but like a gift.

He reached underneath her little pink dress and slid down her panties. Her entire core was on pins and needles immediately, already anticipating the delicious pleasure of his long thick cock.

Their kiss turned rougher, more frenzied, and she felt him reach between them and free his massive erection from his jeans.

When he broke the kiss, she expected him to turn her around, but instead, he took his cock in his hand and pushed it to her entrance, teasingly dipping the soft velvety head in and out to prepare her.

Oh, God. What's he trying to do to me? A little bit of teasing wasn't at all what she needed.

Deciding to take matters into her own hands, she began twisting her body for him.

He stopped her. "Uh-uh. Not like that."

"No?"

With a wolfish grin, he replied, "No." And then leaned her back slowly.

She planted her arms behind her to keep from falling, while her heart lit up with a million little sparks of joy.

Never leaving her gaze, he moved into her with an almost excruciating slowness, pushing his cock to the brink of her ecstasy and then pulling back again, allowing her to feel every inch of him riding in and out.

She flung back her head, her chest heaving toward the night sky as he drove into her with the most sensual rhythm. She fought the need to come by focusing on his breath, on the view of his thick biceps flexing as he pushed his body into her. But the moment his pace quickened, the table dancing inch by inch across the patio with each hard thrust, she couldn't hold on.

Her orgasm hit her with crippling waves of erotic convulsions, deeper, harder, more intense than she'd ever experienced. Was it the heightened levels of hormones or the fact that she was with the man she loved? She didn't know, and it didn't matter.

He bowed over her body with his large, muscular frame and pumped hard. Then he froze as he thrust himself into her one final time, triggering yet another mind-blowing orgasm. Shivers erupted over her skin, and his cock twitched inside her, spilling his hot cum.

After a moment of their hearts and lungs moving together as though they were Olympic athletes who had just finished the decathlon, Bennett let out a little "Fuck" under his breath.

She froze. "What. What's wrong?" she asked as he continued to hold her tightly, his erection deep inside her throbbing walls.

"I think I got you pregnant."

"Oh." She let out a little laugh and smacked his brawny shoulder. "Funny boy."

He laughed and looked into her eyes. "Hit me again, *Ms. Wade*, and I might need to spank you."

Her eyes went wide. *Heck no. Me first.* "You can spank me if you like, but I'm not taking your name."

"Why the hell not?"

She smiled. "I never want to stop being Ms. Reed."

"Why?"

"It's just too fucking hot when you say my name."

He raised a dark brow. "I can still call you Ms. Reed anytime you like, Ms. Wade."

She grinned, enjoying the feel of their bodies joined together. "I'll think about it."

If she was lucky, he'd give her another round of persuasion-sex.

CHAPTER 22

"So *this* was your important dinner tonight?" Bennett asked from behind the wheel of his brand-new black Land Rover with all-terrain tires and state-of-the-art traction control. All right, it was really one of those soccer mom SUVs, but to him, anything that didn't go fast or climb a muddy mountain was not respectable. He felt better pretending it was an off-road vehicle.

What does it matter? You bought it for Taylor anyway. He hadn't told her yet, but he would. He wanted to give her time to adjust to her new lifestyle, to let her settle into the notion that she now had more money than she could spend in a lifetime. No, he hadn't been joking about signing his wealth over to her and the baby. He really hadn't seen the point of having all that money if they weren't there to share it with him.

"Yep," Taylor said, staring out the window at the three-story Victorian with the big garden and white picket fence, overlooking the San Francisco Bay, "dinner at your mother's house. I hear she's making meatloaf." Taylor smiled, her flushed face a vision of sexy, feminine beauty. Everything he loved about her— that fire in her eyes, the way she looked at him and made his soul tingle—only seemed amplified by her pregnancy. Or perhaps it was because she was happy.

Or maybe it's because you just gave her five of the most incredible orgasms known to mankind.

He mentally patted himself on the back. Making love to her and getting over his little mental block had been quite the victory, but it paled in comparison to receiving her forgiveness. He still found it difficult to believe what an asshole he'd been, but everything around him had been tainted by pain. However, the moment he had heard Taylor was pregnant, he had seen everything with such clarity. Happiness was right at his fingertips, being offered on a silver platter. Yet he'd pushed it away. He'd wanted to suffer. He'd wanted to live in the past.

And then, just like that, he didn't.

He wanted her.

The day following Ms. Luci's party, he went to work, clearing the dark pain from his old life off the shelves to make room for Taylor and the baby. His proposal to Mary Rutherford took all of two minutes to make over the phone and thirty seconds for her to accept. It was meant to be. The next part, trying to find the perfect home near her brother Jack—something Taylor had told his mother was important—proved a bit more difficult, but Robin and Candy both pitched in. They said he shouldn't be allowed to pick the house because poor Taylor would end up with some sterile, modernist palace unfit for a child. Anyway, it had all worked out beautifully. There was one piece left unsettled.

He looked at Taylor in the sexy blue dress she'd thrown on before they'd left. Her long brown hair hung loose over her shoulders, prompting him to lean over and kiss her. Her lips were like luscious little pillows meant for kissing and touching and . . .

"Can we go in?" she said. "I'm really hungry after that workout." She grinned.

He smiled back. "Absolutely."

They exited the car and strolled up the walkway. Music and voices poured out from an open window.

Taylor stopped on the porch and gave Bennett a suspicious look. "Wait. Your mother didn't say anything about guests," she said.

Oh, now that was what he loved about her. She could see right through him. He'd never be able to BS her. *Or surprise her. She figures everything out.*

He flashed her a guilty little smile. "I guess she changed her mind?"

Taylor huffed and rang the doorbell. "You're up to something, Mr. Wade. I can feel it. You and your mother are sneaky folk."

She was right. In a moment, that door would open, and Taylor would find her father—a very large man with a scowl to equal Bennett's; her three very large brothers—who had made him promise to never hurt their sister again or risk losing his legs; Taylor's two best friends—he was pretty sure they were undressing him with their eyes every time they spoke; his mother, and the handful of people in his life he truly trusted, including Robin and Candy.

Taylor would also find a very big ring and a reverend waiting by the fireplace.

Bennett looked down at Taylor's beautiful face. *I hope she says yes. Because she's got all my money. And my baby. And my heart . . .*

The door opened, and Ms. Luci stood there in a pale yellow

dress next to her bug-eyed manservant, Sebastian. His mother had insisted they come because she actually believed that Bennett's relationship with Taylor was entirely attributable to the cookies.

But that was crazy. *Cookies,* he mentally *hmphed.*

"Taylor, my dear, you're late," said Luci with a warm smile.

Taylor flashed a little glance at Bennett and then looked back at Luci. "Late for what? What are you doing here?"

Ms. Luci shrugged. "You owe me a wedding. With that young man." Her eyes went to Bennett.

"Is she serious?" Taylor asked Bennett.

He nodded, waiting anxiously to see what she'd do. This entire event had been a huge gamble. She could've refused to give him another chance.

Taylor laughed sweetly and looked back at Luci. "Yeah, I think I'd like that."

See. *You'll never lose if you bet on Taylor.* Bennett let out a sigh of relief.

"Excellent," Luci stepped aside to let them pass, "I baked your wedding cake myself."

Taylor turned and threw her arms around Bennett's neck, planting a lingering kiss on his lips. She pulled back and looked in his eyes. "I love you, Bennett."

"I love you, too." More than she could ever possibly understand.

She moved to go inside, but paused for a moment, a devilish smirk on her face. "Hey," she whispered, "let's make sure all our friends and family get one of those cookies. Those things are awesome."

Ms. Luci must've overheard. "Why do you think I baked the cake, child? Now get in here and let's get you dressed."

Taylor laughed. "Coming, Ms. Luci." She gave Bennett a happy wink. "See you at the altar, Mr. Wade."

He gave her a quick nod. "Take all the time you need, Ms. Reed. I'm not going anywhere."

THE END

(No. Really! It's the end. No cliffhanger! See? I'm not evil . . . much.)

Author's Note

Hi, All!

First, I wanted to be sure everyone who has read *Happy Pants Café* (the prequel to this series) knows that "Skinny Pants," which will now be called *Sleepless in Scrubs,* will come later on! Why did I switch up the order?

Because THIS book ... Oh my God ... this naughty, naughty dang book, *Tailored for Trouble,* which was intended to come later, demanded to be written next. It seriously wouldn't take no for an answer. I'll blame it on that Mr. Wade ...

If you're looking for more, keep an eye out for the next book in the Happy Pants series! Sarah, our judge in need of some serious fun—because she's all work and no play—is about to meet the world's biggest bad boy rock star. I smell disaster and steamy sex already. Hehe.

And, as always, if you'd like a signed bookmark, you know what to do! Send me an email with your info (mimi@mimijean.net). Be SURE to mention if you posted a REVIEW so I can send you a little extra "thank you" swag! (While supplies last, of course. But hurry, hurry because I always run out fast.)

Anyway, as always, I want to thank you, my readers for continuing to read my stories and inspire me with your awesome tweets, FB posts, emails, and very, very unusual gifts. (My unicorn collection is rockin'!) Please don't ever stop.

I hope you enjoyed this installment of the Happy Pants Series. Maybe someday we'll find out what's really in those cookies!

With Love,
Mimi

P.S. "C-spot" was not a typo. LOL.
P.P.S. HERE'S MY PLAYLIST! (Don't judge me.)

"Headphones featuring LOLO" by Matt Nathanson
"The Blower's Daughter" by Damien Rice
"9 Crimes" by Damien Rice
"Tonight You're Perfect" by New Politics
"Harlem" by New Politics
"Do It Your Own Way" by The Voodoo Trombone Quartet

Acknowledgments

A huuuuge thank you to Team TAILORED! Can I get a woo hoo? Woo hoo!!

I know that no one believes me when I say this, but you guys always rescue me at the point when I think the book might need to be murdered. You then read with open minds, offer equal portions of love and slaps and help me see the light at the end of the tunnel. So thank you Author Kylie Gilmore, Dalitza Morales, Ally Kraai, Bridget Clark, Kassie Baker, and Naughty Nana!

A big warm thank you to Laura Bradford, Priyanka Krishnan, and Gina Wachtel for seeing the potential in this book and series. And thanks to Lynn Andreozzi, Jess Bonet, Alex Coumbis, Caroline Teagle, and the rest of the team at Ballantine. Because of you, I get to make a lot more people's pants happy!

Also, a big thanks to the folks at Ballantine Books for their support in making this book shine brighter!

ABOUT THE AUTHOR

MIMI JEAN PAMFILOFF is a *USA Today* and *New York Times* bestselling romance author. Although she obtained her MBA and worked for more than fifteen years in the corporate world, she believes that it's never too late to come out of the romance closet and follow your dream. She lives with her Latin Lover hubby, two pirates-in-training (their boys), and the rat terrier duo, Snowflake and Mini Me, in the San Francisco Bay Area. She hopes to make you laugh when you need it most and continues to pray daily that leather pants will make a big comeback for men.

mimijean.net
Facebook.com/MimiJeanPamfiloff
@MimiJeanRomance

ABOUT THE TYPE

This book was set in Sabon, a typeface designed by the well-known German typographer Jan Tschichold (1902–74). Sabon's design is based upon the original letter forms of sixteenth-century French type designer Claude Garamond and was created specifically to be used for three sources: foundry type for hand composition, Linotype, and Monotype. Tschichold named his typeface for the famous Frankfurt typefounder Jacques Sabon (c. 1520–80).